TENDER TEACHING

"Today, as all acolytes must, you will learn to fly," said my teacher, Nish't Ahote.

He caressed my bare breasts lightly until the peaks stood tight and small. I felt a small quiver deep inside me. Then he said, "Remove your sandals," and I hastily obeyed, throwing my yucca sandals into the corner of my room. He placed my large feather pillow, on which I often sat, in the center of the room, and told me to kneel with my head to the floor. His huge hands were feather light as he moved them down my sides and parted my skirt. His fingers fluttered lightly over my body with a knowing touch. Soon I was crying with delight. Was I beginning to fly? As he turned me over, my eyes locked with his, and I thought I would faint. Instead I exploded and all the stars of the sky burst in my brain. Yes, I was flying!

Nish't Ahote had done his duty as high priest of the Anasazi. But now he had to resist his desire as a man for this girl-woman who held the key to her people's salvation in her divinely gifted hands. . . .

COYOTE WOMAN

▼

Judith Redman Robbins

AN ONYX BOOK

ONYX
Published by the Penguin Group
Penguin Books USA Inc., 375 Hudson Street,
New York, New York 10014, U.S.A.
Penguin Books Ltd, 27 Wrights Lane,
London W8 5TZ, England
Penguin Books Australia Ltd, Ringwood,
Victoria, Australia
Penguin Books Canada Ltd, 10 Alcorn Avenue,
Toronto, Ontario, Canada M4V 3B2
Penguin Books (N.Z.) Ltd, 182–190 Wairau Road,
Auckland 10, New Zealand

Penguin Books Ltd, Registered Offices:
Harmondsworth, Middlesex, England

First published by Onyx, an imprint of Dutton Signet,
a division of Penguin Books USA Inc.

First Printing, September, 1996
10 9 8 7 6 5 4 3 2 1

REGISTERED TRADEMARK—MARCA REGISTRADA

Printed in the United States of America

To my two beloved sons,
David and Jonathan

ACKNOWLEDGMENTS

Coyote Woman would not have been possible if it were not for the support of my family and friends, and of course, my loving mother, Sarah Breme. I would also thank my other half, Paul Spano, for his loving faith in me. Then there is Richard Curtis who believes in my work. My editors, Hilary Ross and John Paine must be mentioned for their patience and endurance in advising me on many occasions. I must also thank Steve Long for rescuing me and instructing me on the computer so I could meet given deadlines, and Steven Brill, who found a way to change an obsolete language to one that could print out. Aileen Elgie, who assisted me in my research with the Inter-Library Loan System in our small local library, was also a great help. I also do not want to forget to mention my Native American friends, who provided me with inspiration and encouragement.

Principal characters from *Coyote Woman* and translation of names

1. Shawanadese ... The young female acolyte, later priestess, also known as "Coyote Woman."
2. Nish't Ahote ... Sun Priest and Master Teacher.
3. Hototo ... "Warrior Spirit Who Sings": Nish't Ahote's nephew and a young priest.
4. Taweyah ... "Magic Shield": Uncle to Nish't Ahote, ailing old priest.
5. Wisoko ... "Vulture": A young acolyte who becomes a raider
6. Mokni ... "Talking Bird": A mentor and aunt to Shawanadese.
7. Pochti ... "Sounding Board": Shawanadese's father.
8. Talasiva ... "Pollen Water": Shawanadese's mother.
9. Choviohoya ... "Young Deer": Shawanadese's brother and revered warrior.
10. Kunya ... "Water Plant": Choviohoya's wife.
11. Yamka ... "Corn Tassel": Child of Kunya and Choviohoya.
12. Eeetspapoka ... "Obsidian Shield": Mayan warrior.
13. Al Balam ... "Jaguar": A Mayan lord and Shawanadese's real father.
14. Ix Can ... A Mayan lady and Shawanadese's real mother.
15. Salavi ... "Spruce Tree": An elder who befriends Shawanadese.
16. Machakwi ... "Horned Toad": An unfriendly, gruff elder.
17. Honani ... "Badger": Another elder.
18. Pavait ... "Clear Water": Another elder.
19. Noona ... "Wild Grain": Manager of trade.
20. Pangwu ... "Big Horned Sheep": Building supervisor.
21. Wikwavi ... "Sagebrush": An architect.

Prologue

He stood on the butte observing the vast arid, un-tamed land, which was the center of his universe. He and his people, the Anasazi, considered themselves an integral part of nature. Viewing the six building complexes from the top of this sacred butte, he felt a surge of pride and more than that, a love for his people.

His name was Taweyah. He had been the founder of the holy school, which housed and educated any young people who desired more than an agricultural life. He had been the sun priest for the center of his culture for many season cycles, and was revered by his people.

On the evening of his birth, a star had appeared in the sky, a star half the size of the moon. Some of his people had been awed, and many had been frightened at the appearance of such a spectacular phenomena. It was then that his mother had noticed his birthmark. On his inner thigh was a white star that offered a startling contrast to his light brown skin. The people knew then that he was destined for greatness.

During the time since the appearance of the "Great Star," many of his people had left their subterranean pit houses and replaced the old style homes with houses made of stone. It was a period of enlighten-ment. The six complexes of the cultural center were connected with roads that gradually connected many outlier stone dwellings. Ritual and ceremony provided meaning and solidarity to all.

Remembering these great changes, Taweyah prostrated himself on the living breathing stone. To Awonawilona, the creator and giver of life he prayed.

"My words are as one
With the mountains, rocks, and trees,
One with my body
One with my heart.

All the Gods assist me
With supernatural power,
Day! Night! The Universe
All see me,
As one with this world."

Chapter 1

Becoming a Woman

I am Anasazi. I am called Shawanadese. When I was eight years old, my parents sent me to the ceremonial center as a pupil. There were many others studying at the center. My primary teacher was a large barrel-chested man with a pouting lower lip who was rigid and demanding—or so it seemed to me at that time. I learned to read and write and to calculate, and to study the heavens, but most of the emphasis in my schooling was placed on searching inside myself through meditation and prayer. Life was simply learning to know yourself, as my teacher continuously reminded me. He was as old as my father but generally he treated me kindly, perhaps more so than the other children. This may have been due to my short-cropped dark hair and my amber eyes—Anasazi in general have brown eyes. Sometimes my teacher frightened me, but I was an apt student and most often this brought its rewards.

When I was thirteen I was directed to a woman. She came from far away and had light hair and green eyes. She was to teach me the ways of a woman, for this was the Anasazi way. She first went to the river and washed, and then came to me in the small white-wash stone room that was my bedroom and my study. She told me to move my studies from my stone ledge, and sat in front of me on the ledge. She spread her legs and showed me all the parts of the female. She said it was important that a woman know these things in order to please their man. She spread her labia and pointed out the moisture. She demanded that I touch and taste. I found the taste strange but not repulsive. She explained that above the moisture, which is the normal place for a man to insert his organ, is a pleasure knob. I touched hers. She moaned. She demanded that I touch myself. I found the pleasure exquisite, for you see, I had been doing this since I was four and knew not why. She explained that the touch can be with the tongue or lips and demonstrated to me, demanding that I return the pleasure.

She said I could pleasure a man by doing the same to his organ. I should be aware, however, that the penetration of his organ and the pleasure could result in a child, and unless I was ready for that I should take a certain medicine, but that would be a lesson for another day. I found I was not shy, and I received wondrous vibrations from giving pleasure to this woman. I truly felt that a whole new world had opened up to me. I was becoming a woman.

Soon thereafter a message arrived. I was to be married. The arrangements had been made by my father, as was customary in the Anasazi way. This meant that I had to leave me little world of learning to make the long journey home. As much as I loved my parents and brother, I found my feelings mixed. Naturally I was curious about my betrothed. Did I know him? Had we played together as children? Many questions appeared in my mind, but the one prevailing thought was that I did not want to go. I was not ready for motherhood. There were too many more things to learn. Apparently I was not alone in my thoughts, for it was not long before my teacher softly opened the curtain above my study and descended the ladder saying, "How do you feel about these arrangements?"

I responded, "If it is what I must do, I will, but there is much more to learn, and I shall miss you and all I have now."

"If you have the desire to continue learning, I will make new arrangements. You have shown great promise in your studies, and your mind and heart are open."

"My mind and heart tell me I am not ready for motherhood. If you can do this, I would be grateful," I said.

He smiled and went from my room, leaving me with jumbled thoughts. I was at the age when our women married. My body was ready, but my mind was not. Why did I not feel like the other young women who were eager to fulfill the role and expectations of marriage? While my thoughts were racing, the curtain lifted and my teacher entered again.

"I have dispatched a message to your father that you have been chosen to be an acolyte. This is most uncustomary, but you are right. There is much much more to learn." He left my room with a twinkle in his eye.

"Today you will learn to fly," said my teacher as he lifted the cotton curtain and ducked through my doorway and down the ladder. "An acolyte must know this to use in meditation as a vehicle for solving problems."

I readily agreed and faced him squarely with a smile. This rigid, demanding man had been my teacher for six season cycles, and I loved and trusted him. I was fond of my light-haired green-eyed teacher for the things she had taught me, but somehow I knew that there was still much to learn and I was not yet a complete woman. As an acolyte, I had made the decision not to marry. I wondered if I would be sorry for this.

Nish't Ahote wrapped his huge arms around me in a firm bear hug. I was surprised, since this was the first time he had shown any outward affection toward me.

"I will not hurt you, little one, nor will I deflower you, but you must understand the way it is with a man and a woman."

He touched my bare breasts lightly until they stood tight and small. I felt a small quiver deep inside me, such as I had felt with my green-eyed teacher. His huge hands were featherlight as he moved them down my sides and parted my skirt. Then, as if having second thoughts, he looked into my eyes and said, "We must remove your sandals." I hastily obeyed, tossing my yucca sandals into the corner. He placed my large feather pillow, on which I often sat, in the center of the room and told me to kneel with my head to the floor. In doing so, my skirt parted, leaving me totally exposed to him. His fingers fluttered lightly over my buttocks, and he placed his hand against my womanhood with a knowing touch. I moaned and felt faint. Was I beginning to fly? My heart pounded, and I grew moist as I had when my woman teacher had touched me and when I touched myself. Nish't Ahote reached around and cupped one of my breasts as I moaned again. Then quietly he inserted a finger into my opening, and I cried with delight. It remained there as he turned me over with his free hand and caressed my pleasure knob. I saw his excitement pushing his robe at an odd angle. My eyes locked with his and then rolled back in my head, and I thought I would faint. Instead I exploded and all the stars of the sky burst inside my head. Yes, I was flying!

He withdrew his finger and rubbed my womanhood

while I gently landed on earth again. I noticed a stain on his robe that made me ask, "Did you fly, too?"

"We will talk of that another time," he said, and lifted me up with another huge bear hug. Before he left, he told me that that evening he was to do a religious sacrament to the Rain Gods, and I must assist him.

Rain! The people had not had rain for several weeks. The terraces, dams, and irrigation canals were dry and parched. The squash vines were shriveled. The corn was stunted, and the bean pods were not filling. The people from the outside pueblos were complaining. Even the amaranths, sunflowers, and tansy mustard seed that grows wild and tastes so delicious were wilted. Everyone was saying that the time of snow and cold could mean famine unless something was done.

I was very excited at Nish't Ahote's announcement of the sacrament. There were numerous kivas in our large complex, but children were not normally permitted in them. The stories of the kiva activities that were told among the children ranged from the mystical to the bloodcurdling. I felt especially privileged since women were only allowed in the kivas during certain festivals.

The remainder of the day dragged slowly due to my anticipation. Finally it was time for the sacrament. Nish't Ahote led me into the antechamber, where he donned his massive, colorful cape. We washed our hands, and I put on a robe of dark red cotton. Nish't Ahote told me I must wear a long turquoise necklace anytime I assisted in a religious sacrament.

We moved up the steps from the antechamber and into the center of the kiva. A drum was pulsing, and a flute played a hypnotic, eerie song that seemed never to stop. The fire in the firebox burned brightly, heating the kiva to almost a sweat bath temperature. A dagger inlaid with jet and Gilsonite rested on a rectangular stone box. A large fat corn-fed turkey in a cage stood next to the stone box. There were five elders of our large towns, who sat on the long bench on feather pillows. What was their purpose I was soon to find out.

Nish't Ahote lifted his arms toward the sky and began chanting. His voice soared high up toward the heavens and wove itself artfully around the drums and flute. He then knelt down in a fetal position, and his voice dropped very low and became muffled, almost as part of the earth. My skin prickled. I did not notice a large jug and drinking cups until I saw one of the elders pour some strong-smelling mead into cups. One of them went to Nish't Ahote, who partook and seemingly finished it in one swallow. He swayed and continued his chanting as the five elders did the same. After what seemed like forever, but in reality was only a short time, Nish't Ahote moved toward the cage. He removed the screeching bird and laid it down on the stone box. After telling me to hold the bird on its back, he picked up the dagger, slit the breast wide open, and lifted the heart of the turkey out. He held it skyward, still chanting, then handed the pulsing, throbbing, bloody heart to me. How long I held it, I cannot remember. More cups of mead were imbibed and more. Finally my teacher collapsed, the musicians stopped playing, and the elders made their exit through the antechamber.

For a few minutes I waited. Was Nish't Ahote asleep? Should I touch him? I had to do something with the bloody thing in my hands. I laid the heart, which had long since ceased its throbbing, on the stone box, rinsed my hands and returned to my room. It was my turn to collapse on my pillows in exhaustion.

At dawn, as my senses awakened, I heard thunder.

Rain! Did our sacrament cause it to rain? Or would it have happened anyway. Only the Gods could have answered.

My thoughts were broken with the entrance of Nish't Ahote. He sat cross-legged beside me saying, "I was proud to have you at my side last night during the sacrament. You never hesitated to do what was necessary. I was confident that your budding woman-hood had given you the power and maturity to handle the procedures of the occasion."

Our eyes locked. I sat up on my mat crossing my hands over my breasts to cover them. Nish't Ahote took both of my hands and uncrossed my arms while glancing quickly at my breasts. "Little one," he said, "you have made it clear to all that though you are of marriageable age, your way will be different from other girls."

The sentinel stood on the cliff's edge high above our complex and gave a warning, "Traders arriving from the southwest!" he yelled as he shaded his eyes from the hot sun. Everyone stopped what they were doing. I also stopped grinding corn on the metate, which I had been doing for the past hour. It was not necessary that I do this, for our food was brought to us from the storage bins, and each surrounding complex contributed a certain amount on a regular basis. Yet grinding was mindless work and gave me a break from my studies and time to think on what I should be learning.

I watched the traders approaching and saw that there were five figures. Three of them appeared to be traders and two were warriors, probably to offer protection to the traders from the looters and marauders. They were from the south, a city called Tula, and had come a very long way. They unloaded their wares, displaying them on a large mat. They spread out brightly colored feathers, jade of many shades, bright multicolored patterned cotton cloth, polished shells of many types, cocoa beans, and many other things. My teacher walked over to me and pointed at a group of clear, colorless stones with six smooth sides and single- or double-faceted ends.

"These are crystals, my child. They have a way of teaching you much if you but let them. Choose one for yourself as a gift from me."

My eyes danced. "How will I know which one to choose?"

"You will know the one that feels right in your hand."

I spent a good period of time feeling and holding each one until I seemed to be drawn to one that fit perfectly in my hand and had less flaws than the others.

"I would like this one," I said to Nish't Ahote.

"You will learn on your own from this crystal, but remember to ask me questions if you feel the need."

It was then that I took notice of one of the warriors who stood quietly nearby. His hair was long and braided in a single shiny black plait, so very different from my short, bobbed hair. His skin was light brown like my own, in contrast to the dark brown skin of the other warrior. His face showed great dignity. He wore only a loincloth and sandals made from maguey fibers. He also wore a spear and a knife strapped on his shoulder and carried an atlatl, or spear thrower. He seemed made of stone until I moved in line of his sight and he gazed into my amber eyes. His fierce demeanor melted, and he looked surprised. Had he never seen a young girl before? His eyes were very black and almond-shaped and made me feel I might melt into a puddle of water at his feet. What was happening to me? Why had I never felt like this in looking into any of the male acolytes' eyes?

Shaken, I turned away, clutching my new crystal, and returned to the grinding of the maize.

That night, though, I tossed and turned. I was hot, then cold. My body ached and throbbed. Most of the ache was in my loins and lower back. I felt the need of something and I knew not what. Was I possessed? Were the "sickness gods" taking over my body? Thoughts of the young warrior continued to run through my mind, and I questioned again my response to his gaze. I had never felt that way before. Perhaps it did have something to do with that warrior. Why did I continue to think of him when my chances of seeing him again were so slight? Had he possessed my body and brain? I finally fell asleep, after what seemed like hours, from sheer exhaustion.

A bird was singing. My room was on an outside wall of the complex, and I was privileged to enjoy Earth Mother's sounds at daybreak. I crawled from my sleeping mat to relieve myself and noticed there was blood when I passed water. I thought I was dying, but then I remembered in a lesson with my light-skinned teacher that she told me women bled and that was their sacrifice to the Gods. That meant I was no longer becoming a woman. I had become one!

I had to find something to absorb the flow of my blood. Folded on a wooden shelf in my room was a large square of cotton that I had worn tied at my shoulders or around my waist long ago, for such was the fashion with the Anasazi. Its colors were faded and the fabric had thinned, but I had to use something. I folded it into a long, thick pad and held it in place with a cord tied around my waist. I knotted another cotton cloth to cover my body at my shoulders and left my room in search of Nish't Ahote.

He looked up from his morning prayers as the curtain fluttered, and I entered the room. "Little one, you look pale. Your eyes tell me things are not right!"

I told him of not sleeping well and of my aches, and finally of my bleeding. He looked at me, his eyes twinkling, and said, "My child, you are at last a woman. For the next three days you must take your crystal and find your own space. Take it and only water and a weapon and take time for consideration of what you know. Stay in your space for three sun cycles. Each morning you must cleanse yourself and your cotton pads in the river, then return to us. At the end of that time we will see that you truly become a woman and learn the ways between a woman and a man."

I threw my arms around his neck and said, "I knew you'd know what I should do! Teacher, what would life be without you?" Having said that, I went back to my room to gather the necessary supplies for my retreat.

Once I had strapped my sleeping mat, a blanket, my cotton pads, my crystal, and a large jug for water on my back, I began my search. As I picked my way through the hard rocks and prickly cactus, I was looking for a shelter close to the river. I walked along it but not terribly close for several miles. I stopped only for frequent drinks of water to counter the effects of the blistering sun, and continued to explore the canyon area. Finding nothing, I waded across the wash, replenishing my water supply. My intention was to return from the direction I came and to explore the canyon on the other side of the river. I had to find a place before dark or I might become prey for a cougar. Then I saw a ledge among the clay red cliff rocks, and I picked my way through a rocky trail toward what looked like an opening. I was hopeful that it would not be occupied by other animals, and to my delight I found it was vacant. The ledge opened into a small room with three walls sprinkled with lichen and many different-size rocks piled on the dirt floor. It faced east at one side of the space. "A perfect place for my sleeping mat," I chuckled. I noticed as I looked down from my ledge that within walking distance were many juniper and pinyon pines. A perfect retreat! The Gods were with me.

I had hardly set up my belongings before the howls of the coyote told me it was night, a clear, star-studded night. Until this time I had felt no hunger, but only the beauty of solitude. The night was warm, and my blanket was too much. Another wash of water and I picked up my crystal. What was I to do with it? It was so different from other rocks. It was beautiful and clear. I wondered if I could see myself in it. I sat on my slab facing east and held the crystal in my right hand. I studied it. It was warm, but why had Nish't Ahote said I would grow with it? After a short time I switched it to my left hand and soon I felt a pulsing. What was happening? I put the crystal down. My hand ceased its pulsing. I picked it up again and again, and my hand pulsated. Curious, I clutched my crystal to my chest and my whole body felt an energy. What did this mean? I put down my crystal and lay back down, thinking on what Nish't Ahote' had said—"Consider what I already know." What did that mean? How was I to use it? Or should I use it at all? I fell asleep pondering.

I woke to hunger pangs on the second day of my womanly cycle. My body had ceased its cramping, and the discomfort had shifted to my stomach. Outside my entrance a family of quail were scurrying about in the cool of the morning. I watched them with amusement as my eyes adjusted to the morning sunshine. I raised my arms to the sky and said, "Awonawilona, the creator, will I feel different now as a woman than as a girl? Perhaps the only difference will be when I gaze into the eyes of a handsome warrior!"

I moved toward the wash and cleansed myself. Then I returned to the cave and noticed some soft red stones in a small pile on one side of it. They nearly crumbled in my hand and left a red stain. There were also very hard, sharp stones scattered in the back of my cave. The side wall of the cave was rather smooth. To pass the time I picked up a sharp stone and began to chip at the wall. It was not as hard as the sharp stones and not as soft as the red stone, and after much chipping away, I had made a line. I curved the line, and in what seemed like a short time—but was really half a sun journey—I had fashioned a cloaked figure and had completely forgotten my hunger.

After quenching my thirst, I took a walk, and for the first time in my young years, I began to take note of the plants struggling to survive in the desert. I took my knife and cut a tree branch called *pechit.* There were long pods on it. I thought I would take it back to Nish't Ahote. He would tell me about it. I saw no more like it anywhere in sight.

Returning to my cave, I stretched out on my mat. My head was getting lighter from lack of food, and I slept.

It was dawn of the third day. My head was very light, but the water was cooling and fresh to my empty stomach. There were no more aches, only an occasional dizziness. Again I floated down to cleanse myself, and upon returning with my water supply, a sense of total peace enveloped me. Who was I? Why was I an acolyte, and why were my desires so different from other Anasazi girls my age? Why didn't I wish to have a husband and family? Why was it I would rather be learning?

My crystal glistened in the sunlight. I reached for it and found it warm. I held it in my left hand and sat on my mat facing east. Once again it pulsed in my hand and sent its energy through me. My other hand began to shake. Being as light-headed as I was, I stretched out with my toes pointing east toward the direction of rebirth and the tip of my crystal pointing in the same direction. My body began to quiver. What was happening to me? Was my body responding this way because of my hunger?

A deep sense of inner peace descended over me, a sense of wholeness, of being something more than just a part of Earth Mother. Quite suddenly my body and hands and feet began pulsing again. The pulsating felt very good, almost as good as when Nish't Ahote had taught me to fly. Was I flying now? My eyelids began to quiver. Somehow I wanted to focus through them, and to concentrate hard. A shadow began to form behind my eyelids, dark and mysterious. I tried hard to focus on it, and it began to clarify. There was no identification, but a shadow began to emerge, and I saw someone with a feathered cloak hovering nearby. Then the vision faded, and I was left in pulsating vibrations made me feel ecstatic. I wondered, what did it mean? Would Nish't Ahote tell me? My eyes fluttered again and I tried to focus, but to no avail. I slept, for tomorrow I would return to the school and truly become a woman.

*   *   *

As the time passed before my puberty rites, I became aware that I was being watched. One of the boys my age, perhaps a year younger, was following my every movement. Seven sun cycles had passed since I had learned I was to become a woman. When I was in his presence, his eyes felt like coals burning onto my skin. He did not like me, I felt certain. I could not understand why this should be so.

Few girls attended school. Almost all, unlike myself, did not go to school beyond age ten. They learned basic skills at home. Consequently there was usually no association between the male and female students except a nod and a quick greeting.

There was nothing different about him. I only knew he must have other interests than I did, since he did not appear at any of the acolyte functions that we all were required to attend. He was probably becoming a sentinel or a warrior. We had trained warriors for defense purposes only, for we were a peace-loving nation. Why did he look like he had fire in his eyes?

I shrugged and put him from my mind. Certainly I would not choose him for my puberty rites, which I knew were to be four sun cycles in length. Just then, though, Nish't Ahote appeared before me, saying, "My child, you must choose one of our acolytes. This young man will be the other half of the ceremony on the fourth day. To bleed is to purify oneself. Who would be your choice?"

"My teacher, there is one who watches. Him I do not want! I know no others. I am too busy with my chores and my studies. May I have a bit of time to consider?"

"Of course, little one, but not very long. I shall return in a short time." So saying, he departed.

I watched him go with great love in my heart. Should I ask him to be the man? Or was he too old?

Why did I not ask him? For six years he had been as a father to me. If he had been but twenty years younger, I would not have hesitated to choose him. He was warm, tender, loving, understanding, and had he not been a priest, he would have made a wonderful husband and father. I could not decide what I should do.

My mind turned to the young warrior. Where was he? Was he at one of the outliers? Perhaps even the outlier of my parents? Of course not! I recalled that my warrior's face showed great pride and dignity. I remembered his muscular stature clad only in a loin-cloth with his weapons at his side. His look had suddenly changed when he saw me, and I knew not why. I had quivered and shook as his eyes locked with mine.

I was not able to sleep that night. I wondered if it was only my oncoming change of life, or if there was more to my feelings than I was ready to handle.

I was pondering all of these things when Nish't Ahote appeared in my door the next morning. "Shawanadese, have you an answer? We must begin preparations immediately!"

I looked at him intently and asked, "O revered one, must it be an acolyte I choose? There is no one I know in our complex, save for you. Can you be my chosen one?"

His dark eyes became brooding, and he looked at me with tenderness. After a short pause he responded, "No, I have other priestly duties. Of course, there can always be exceptions, but is there no one else among your acquaintances?"

After I paused and thought, "Should I tell him?" I said why not? I had never kept any secrets from him before. "Yes, Nish't Ahote, there is someone who made me feel strange inside." I waited, afraid to say more.

"Do you wish to tell me who this may be?" he inquired.

"Do you remember the traders who came a few weeks ago? One of the warriors, the lighter-skinned one, left me with strange feelings that night. I have thought much about him since then."

"But this warrior is Mayan and not of our people. I must consult the Gods, for this is not an ordinary request. Then, too, of course, can our runners locate him? My heart, you give me grievous problems, but I shall consult the Gods and see what I can do. Ah! Why must you be so difficult?"

As he mumbled to himself and climbed out of my room, I said to myself, "Am I so difficult? What does he mean, or is he just talking to himself? I am a woman now! Why should my desires create problems?"

Later, Nish't Ahote informed me that runners had left, hopefully to find my Mayan warrior. If they ran in shifts, it would be less than a day before we would have some report of their whereabouts.

Meanwhile my ceremony began. I awoke on the morning of the first day and faced the east with my crystal. It would not be long before the women would be with me. The sun was causing magnificent colors on the edge of earth and sky. But this day was to be different. How, I was not certain, but it would be different.

The women arrived and talked among themselves, obviously as if there was a secret they were refusing to share with me. They laughed and tittered and told me I must cleanse myself with soaproot every morning of the four days and that one of them was to show me how to use it. I had heard of soaproot, but I generally did not use it, for it was easier to cleanse myself with clear water. One of the women accompanied me to the wash and showed me how to take the strange clump and, working with it and the water, to make a lather for my hair and my body. After I did this and dried off, we returned to the complex. The women then proceeded to rub me down with sunflower oil, used only for ceremonial purposes, and combed my hair and rubbed oil into it. Afterward they rubbed me with sage. I then spent some time alone meditating with my crystal.

Before sundown, the women again approached my door and came to rub me down with oil once more. Their instructions were that they would leave soaproot with me for morning, and I was to follow the same schedule of cleansing the next morning. I heard many acolytes and other people gathering in the large kiva nearby. A pulsing drum was beginning. In the largest kiva was a fire, and many were gathering. Young acolytes began to sing and some began to dance. The first night of my rites seemed to be festivities for everyone.

An acolyte approached me saying, "I am to tell you this is the celebration of your becoming a woman, and you must dance until the sun rises." He took my hand and led me into a small circle where a few couples were moving in short, jerky steps. We danced a short time, and another young man took my hand. A flute began to play, and the singing stopped. Everyone moved to the edge of the kiva, obviously anticipating something. The drum and flute sounded in an urgent pulsing, and slowly a feathered figure descended the steps from the antechamber. The person beneath the costume was broad of shoulders and wide in the chest with a slight paunch and small hips. This had to be Nish't Ahote. He wore painted designs on his arms, chest, and legs, and his only real clothing was a loincloth. He had donned a feathered grotesque mask and held a gourd in his right hand. As if becoming sud-

denly aware of the urgency of the music, he leaped
into the air and danced. Sometimes his steps were
quick and small, and other times he twisted and
leaped. There were men and women from some of the
outliers gathered around the kiva. Nish't Ahote leaped
over to one attractive woman and danced in motions
reminiscent of two dogs in the mating process. His
frantic dance continued with the same sexual motion
at various intervals in the performance. His body paint
was becoming mixed with perspiration, and finally his
body shook and then folded into a kneeling position
as the flute discontinued its playing. The drum slowed,
and Nish't Ahote backed away from the center of the
kiva and ascended the steps back into the antechamber.

I was asked to dance again and again. It was in
this way that I spent the rest of the night. Everyone
disbanded at daybreak and returned to their outliers.

I did not feel tired, only exhilarated. Picking up my
soaproot and cotton cloth, I made my way to the wash.
It took some time and lathering to cleanse the oil from
my hair and body, but once I was done, my muscles
began to relax. I felt weary as I made my way back
to the complex and to my room.

The women were there waiting for me. I was rubbed
with a light coat of oil and sage, and fell into a deep
sleep on my mat.

I awoke wondering if the runners had found my
warrior. It was exciting to imagine. What if they did
not find him? I was in a turmoil. I considered whether
it was proper to ask Nish't Ahote any questions. He
had not visited me, and this might have been his way
of telling me not to ask any questions. He, of all in
our complex, knew of my insatiable curiosity. I knew
if I asked the women, they would only laugh in that

strange, secretive way. These were my thoughts as I awaited my meal and the coming night's festivities.

It was not long before the women were with me again. After the oil and sage, they dressed me in a beautifully designed cotton cloth, and one of them gave me some turkey feather earbobs to wear. An acolyte informed me that my family had arrived and awaited the night's festivities. I was most anxious, since I had not seen them since the cold season rites.

At last it was time, and I made my way to the great kiva accompanied by one of the women. My mother, father, and brother awaited me in the kiva. While tearfully embracing me, my mother said, "My sweet daughter! At last you are woman! Now you can grow your hair long and experience the joys of adulthood. May your heart be as wise as the owl and your mind as brilliant as the sun."

"My mother, there are so many questions I have. Can you answer them?"

"Of course, but not now! The festivities are beginning. We must pay attention so the Gods will be with us."

Once again I was drawn into a circle dance. The fire blazed and drums beat while many singers sung what were becoming familiar chants. One partner danced with me, then another took over. Sometimes my partners were other acolytes and at times young men of the outliers. Nish't Ahote danced his wild, turbulent dance again. Everyone seemed joyous.

A feeling that someone was behind me made me turn abruptly. It was the brooding acolyte of before. His gaze was burning with resentment and then took on a questioning look. He took my hand from my present dance partner and led me around the circle with the other dance partners. I felt down deep that

he did not like me. He was named Wisoko. I wanted
to yank my hand from his, but if I caused a scene, I
was certain Nish't Ahote would be angry. With all the
strength I could gather, I asked, "Why do you always
watch me?"

His hand tightened around mine as we continued
our dance. "My heart will not permit me to tell you,"
he said. He offered no more response, and I was
forced to dance with him in uneasy silence until another young man took my hand from his. Relief swept
over me, but I noticed he backed off and continued
to watch me. I wondered why I had not noticed him
the night before. Why did I feel this overwhelming
tension when he was around me?

The attention of all the others soon made me forget
him, and I was swept clean of my anxiety. The night
raced by quickly. Then Sotugnangu, God of Sky,
raised the light from the dark, and again the people
and my family disappeared into the early light. I
picked up my soaproot and cotton cloth and went to
the wash. I washed my wearing apparel to rid it of
smoke and oil residue.

Suddenly I had the overwhelming feeling that once
again I was not alone. Someone was watching! I
turned to look around and saw no one, but my skin
crawled, and hastily I picked up my belongings to
make my way back to my room. The women awaited
me, and after their attentions I once again fell into an
uneasy sleep.

The third night was much like the second, and still
no one told me if my warrior had been found. Nish't
Ahote was nowhere to be seen, so another night went
by quickly. On the morning of the fourth and final
day, I could not sleep. I wanted to, but I tossed and
turned. Finally, when the sun was high over the horizon, I slept for a short time. When I awoke, the

women were there, but no food was brought to me. On the final day of my rites I was to fast. The women escorted me again to the wash and cleansed my body and hair. They crushed sage again and rubbed my skin and hair, this time using no oil. I was dressed in a colorful cotton skirt, yucca sandals, and a feathered vest with feather earbobs and a leather thong with a large piece of turquoise threaded through it. The women lightly lined my eyes with kohl and rubbed red ocher powder on my cheeks. I was given a pyrite mirror. "Can this be me?", I asked as I gazed at my reflection. "What will I look like when my hair grows long?"

The drum began again, and I was brought to the large kiva for my fourth and final night. I looked around with concern, for my warrior was nowhere to be seen. The elders were there, my family was there, but no proud warrior.

Wisoko grabbed my hand and led me to dance. His face was hard and hateful. Hear me, Gods, I thought. Must my special night begin this way? He squeezed my fingers until I grimaced with pain. But this was my night! I could not let him know he was hurting me. It was clearly not my imagination. He did not like me! Why did he dance with me, then? I wished the Gods would hurry the dance to its finish.

Another acolyte took me away. At last the Gods had heard me. The flute began to play and the chanting faded, while descending from the antechamber was Nish't Ahote, who was dressed as Sotugnangu, God of Sky, accompanied by another dancer dressed as Tawa, Father Sun and Giver of Life. He was costumed much like Nish't Ahote, but his headdress or mask was different. It was red, yellow, and orange with huge, bulging eyes and a wide mouth with many teeth. Yellow and orange feathers fanned out around the headdress as the rays of the sun.

They began moving slowly, but the drum gradually quickened, and once again their movements were twisting and leaping. All in the kiva were silent, their attention fixed on the dancers. Then, at the end of the dance, they prostrated themselves in front of the fire. The flames of the fire leaped and danced as if an extension to their dance.

Nish't Ahote took my hand and led me to the entrance of the antechamber. The door opened, and my warrior emerged. My heart beat furiously. He was dressed in only a loincloth. Several chunks of turquoise were hung on yucca fiber around his neck. His long jet-black hair was in a single braid down his back, just as I had remembered. He was slightly taller than most of the spectators and carried himself proudly. His golden skin seemed to glow in the dark, and he walked as though the sun, moon, and stars were his. His eyes pierced mine in a meridian connected to my heart. I wondered if he could hear its loud beat.

We danced a dance alone accompanied by only music of the flute. His fingers burned on mine, and he held my hand tightly. I marveled that there could be such a difference between my feelings for "the one who watches," Wisoko, and my warrior. Who was he? Had he a name? Had it been difficult for Nish't Ahote to convince him to participate in my puberty rites?

Nish't Ahote then led us to the fire, where we were told to face each other. I could hardly keep from trembling when he untied my feather vest, leaving my breasts exposed and my nipples hardened. He circled each breast with his long, dark golden fingers, then took my hand. As the flute continued to play, he led me out of the kiva and to my room. The drumming, chanting, and dancing resumed, but the flute ceased.

One of the women had prepared a fire in my room. Another mat had been laid next to mine. I also noticed extra cotton blankets. I turned to look at him. He did not speak the language of the Anasazi, but his large almond eyes were clouded and he seemed rather nervous. His skin had also been washed and rubbed with herbs. He led me to the fire, and pushing my vest aside, he cupped my breasts in his hands. I was trembling. He turned me around until my back was to him. He gasped, then turned me back and looked long and hard at me. Was there something wrong? I wondered.

After a short pause he removed my turquoise and took one of my breasts into his mouth. This was a new sensation and I shivered and shook, for something was happening inside me. I was flying again! Then he circled the nipple of my other breast with his tongue, and I moaned. His tongue moved to my navel, and this loosed feelings I had never known. My insides were churning, and I was once again melting. He loosened my skirt, and it dropped to the floor. He removed my sandals and then I was completely naked. He stood back to look, and his eyes were misty. Then he removed his loincloth.

I was startled by his erection, though Nish't Ahote had had the same erection when he taught me to fly. He clasped me to him, murmuring I knew not what, and I felt that I might explode. He pushed me onto the mats, and I looked up at him, very excited but apprehensive. Would he do what Nish't Ahote had done? Would there be more? As if reading my thoughts, he again mumbled something and began to run his tongue over my body. The sensations were such that I had never experienced, and I noticed a feeling of fullness between my legs. When he had covered every inch of my body, he came back to my womanhood and found with his tongue the same spot my fair-skinned teacher had taught me about in her instruction.

It was not long before I was flying again—higher than with Nish't Ahote. My body did not shiver. It quaked. It churned! His golden body bent over me, and in one quick motion he spread my legs farther apart. He entered me instantly, and I felt a sharp momentary pain. It subsided as we began to move together. I was flying higher, higher, and higher, and then I fell over the cliff of the canyon and continued to vibrate—like my crystal! He moved again within me, and I began to fly again. He trembled and shook and then spasmed as we both soared toward Earth Mother. He held me in his long arms as we drifted into a light sleep.

Chapter 2

Blossoming

Once more in the night he took me, but the second time there was no pain, only pleasure. We then both fell into a deep sleep.

At dawn I was awakened as he quietly donned his loincloth. I sat up to watch. He seemed unaware at first of my observation, then suddenly turned with a big smile that melted my heart. He pulled me from the mat and folded me into his arms. One of his hands smoothed my hair while he softly whispered in Anasazi, "Till we meet again, little one." A final squeeze, and he was gone.

I was left to sort out the meaning of all that had happened. He would return to his homeland, but what of me? Would I see him again? Only the Gods and the passing of time would tell. In our hours together we had spoken no words. I knew not that he spoke any of our language. I would ask Nish't Ahote to teach me his language. Then if the Gods willed it to be so, I would speak to him at our next meeting. From this I had learned an important lesson. It was that there are times when words are not necessary. There are many ways one can communicate. It might take a lifetime, but I would learn all of those ways.

Later in the sun cycle I said farewell to my parents. My father, who was called Pochti and was always aloof, took my hand and looked into my amber eyes.

My mother, who was called Talasiva, hugged me to her and murmured, "You are as much a woman now as I am. You must shoulder your responsibilities seriously. Take much thought in what you do and think well before you take action. Your duties differ from mine, but have a care! They may affect more people than my decisions do. And remember we are your people. We love you." So saying, they both departed to begin their long journey back to their outlier.

My eyes grew moist as I thought of my mother's words. I wondered if there would be a day when I could visit her and talk to her. She had become something of a stranger to me over the past six season cycles of attending the school here in Chaco.

I arrived back in my room, and my thoughts again turned to the blissful happiness of last night. I picked up my cotton cloth and soaproot and headed for the wash that was beginning to show signs of drying up again. I was becoming addicted to cleanliness.

I felt so fresh and alive after my cleansing. If the wash dried, as it often did, what would I do? Cleanliness made me feel fresh and new, for I never really knew this feeling before or perhaps I just never thought about it.

The remaining part of the day seemed mundane compared to the last four days. My corn and squash stew tasted delicious that evening. Perhaps it tasted particularly good because nothing out of the ordinary had happened. I washed my meal down with water we collect in cisterns when it rains. We did not get a lot of rain, but when it did, it poured heavily and we had to gather the water and carefully ration it out. When the wash dried up and I could no longer cleanse myself in it, the women told me to wash my most intimate parts with a rag and rub sage on the rest of my body and in my hair. They said I was woman now and must be extra clean.

I climbed my ladder and walked out into the evening air. I continued up the stone stairs behind the complex until I reached a high point with a wonderful view of Fahatta Butte. This giant rock was our sundial. The sun priest could calculate the seasons, the solstices, and the equinoxes using the sun and shadows on several huge jutting pieces of rock. Parts of some of our festivals and ceremonies were done on the top of the rugged butte with the sun priest dancing and sacrificing a turkey or a dog while the people from most of the outliers watched from below. This was followed by another night of dancing usually in the open square of our complex.

I felt the presence of someone close by. It was Nish't Ahote who touched my shoulder and turned me around. "The land is beautiful with all its glorious rocks, plants, and creatures. Don't you agree?" he said.

"Yes, Nish't Ahote, this is one of my favorite spots to view the wonders of Earth Mother and Sky Father."

After a time of sharing the magnificent view, Nish't Ahote said, "Dese, one or more of those plants, rocks, or creatures will become important in your life. The people refer to this as your spirit guide."

"I understand what you are saying, for already my crystal is important in my life. It especially helps me in my meditation. How will I find out who my other spirit guides are to be?"

"Our young men at puberty go on a vision quest. They fast and pray for as long as it takes to learn of their spirit guide. Our women, however, at puberty do a vision quest every moon cycle. They isolate themselves, as you do, for three sun cycles during their bleeding time. This is most likely the time when sooner or later your spirit guide will be shown to you. When that happens, you will know."

"Can this happen at any other time?" I asked. I knew of this because of hearing some of the older acolytes as they discussed their quests.

"It may," he continued, "but more frequently it happens during isolation, prayer, and fasting. Just remember, you will know. Each of Earth Mother's animals and birds has special gifts and special ways to share with the people. These gifts and ways give us additional powers. We must only remember to use them wisely."

As I listened to him and gazed at the wondrous view, I felt an exciting anticipation of things to come. I became so engrossed in thought that I did not realize that Nish't Ahote had disappeared.

The sun was sinking along the horizon. It painted the sky with streaks of orange, red, and blue. The sun priest has always said that this means another day without rain. A lizard ran from under the crack of another rock. I walked off the road and picked my way through the cactus. After a short time I sat quietly under a small rock overhang and breathed deeply again and again thinking of my warrior. My mind seemed light as a feather, almost as though I could will it to go wherever I wanted it to go. I continued to drift and suddenly realized it was late. I had to get back to the complex before dark.

As I mentally prodded myself into moving, I spied, out of the corner of my eye, a moving object. A single golden-coated coyote walked stealthily by me, a pregnant female almost ready to have pups, but whose ribs stood out. She paused as though she was catching my scent, then moved carefully on for a few more steps.

She paused again, and my heart was wrenched in pity for her. I wanted to reach out to her, but I could only do that mentally. She looked straight at me and silently moved on. If she had had a mate, perhaps she would not have been so skinny. I wondered about her pups. Would she die in birthing them? Would she have sufficient milk to nurse? I wanted to help her, but she was a wild thing and probably would not have accepted me. Such were my thoughts as I made my way back to the road that lead to my complex.

The sun had all but disappeared, and the sky was a darkened red and purple against the sienna rock .nonoliths. The air was cooling down, and I returned to my room and my straw mat, which less than a sun cycle ago was the scene of more happiness than I had ever known. Surely I would remember that event all the seasons of my life. As I lay my weary body down, my heart knew it had somehow been changed. Perhaps it had been changed because I was now truly a woman.

Nish't Ahote descended the ladder through my door. His look of concern told me something important was on his mind. He sat on my mat next to me and took my hand. "You must realize that you are moving into a new realm of learning. This leaves us with a vacancy in our school. The outlier house of the 'prairie dog' is next on our list of those desiring education and enlightenment." He paused and patted his robe.

"Why do you tell me of these things?" I inquired, feeling the strength of this loving but brusque man emanating from his hand to mine.

"We, that is myself and the elders, have been in lengthy discussion and have decided that you shall go to the 'prairie dog' outlier and inform the family of the vacancy. You will then escort the new student back here to our holy education center, where he can begin his studies as you did at the tender age of eight season cycles."

"I am honored, my teacher. How shall I find this outlier? Is it far from here?"

"No, only a sunrise and a sunset away. I shall give you instructions to get there, and you must pack extra water and supplies. I am pleased you do not hesitate to do as we ask."

I tightened my hand in his and said, "My beloved teacher, have you not taught me over and over that each new experience expands one's mind? When do I leave?"

"At sunrise tomorrow. You have the remainder of the day to make your preparations." So saying, he hugged me and, adjusting his robes, departed the way he came.

I gathered together my mat to sleep on, a heavy poncho wrap for the chill of the night, my mirror, comb, soaproot, and cotton cloths. I filled two large skins with water and put it all in a heavy cotton sack to be strapped on my back. I threw in my blowgun, a knife, a firestone, and, of course, my crystal. I was ready and waiting for the sun to set and rise again.

At daybreak I set off. Nish't Ahote had given me instructions as to how to get there. My back was loaded with my belongings, and I began my walk along our smooth road. Although the sun was low on the horizon, it was promising its usual seasonal heat. I scanned the horizon, viewing clouds that were fluffy against the blue sky. All was parched and dry, as was typical of the warm moon cycles. What little green I saw was struggling in the intense rays of the sun. I moved at a steady pace, stopping in the first few hours of travel only to drink. One must drink often in the intense desert heat. I threw a small cotton cloth over my head and tied it with a cotton cord.

Just before the high point of the sun, I stopped to eat some parched corn and desert rabbit. As I sat in the shade of a huge rock and enjoyed my break, I heard a skirmish not far away. I moved ever so slightly to see a coyote (could it be?) chasing a desert rabbit from some cactus. Her ribs were showing, and she was pregnant. She had to be the same one. She chased the rabbit and soon tired. Her strength was ebbing. Discouraged, she sat on her haunches and panted. The heat and her condition were exhausting her.

I picked up my rabbit, which was only half gone, and finished my corn. Then I picked up the remainder of my rabbit and left it in my shady spot. While doing so, she heard me and shied away, watching me all the while. I packed up my belongings and began my walk again, feeling that at least I had tried to help. She would have some nourishment, perhaps enough to sustain her through another day.

The heat of the day was searing! Nish't Ahote had suggested I break for a time, then go on. I walked to the shade of another rock overhang and sat upon another rock. I removed my sandals and flexed my tired toes. I removed my cotton top and my skirt to lay them in the sun to dry. I put down my mat and reclined nude on it for a time. I lay thinking of Nish't Ahote, and then my thoughts wandered to my warrior. His proud virility was etched as a rock painting in my mind. Was he on his way back to his people or was he at one of our outliers still? Had he a mate at home or was he still unattached. Would that I could have understood his language and known more about him. I vowed to remember when I returned to ask Nish't Ahote to teach me the Mayan language.

I finished my mental wandering by picking up my mat, packing it, and getting on the road again. Nish't Ahote said I should be able to reach the outlier of

the "prairie dog" by sundown. I plodded on, stopping
only for water. Suddenly I saw on my left a path that
Nish't Ahote said I should take. After a short time on
this path, I saw a very small complex, in comparison
to ours, and a dog bounded to greet me. On the left
was a rather large field of corn. There were some
squash and beans beside it. There were ears of corn
on the bush corn hiding low on the plant away from
the sun. As I approached, I got a closer view of activity. There were two women grinding corn on the metate with a mano. Another woman was cooking thin
bread, dipping her hand in batter, spreading the batter
thinly and evenly over the heated stones. In the patio
of the small complex were two men who were making
a boomerang, used to kill small game. One of them
looked up and came forth to greet me. The dog was
by now barking at my heels.

The man took my elbow, saying, "Welcome to the
house of the 'prairie dog'. From where do you come?"

"I am Shawanadese of the holy school. I am here
to speak to you of your youngest son. He is of the
age of enlightenment, is he not?"

"Of course! Please come into our humble complex
and be our honored guest!"

I entered the small complex by the ladder. The
room was small, containing corn stored in stacks, and
opened to another in which the family lived. A suspended pole served as a place to store clothes and
blankets. I saw a small shelf built into the wall that
served as the pantry. There were several water jars in
the room and three flat stones for grinding corn, one
coarse, one medium, and one fine. By the fire were
several smooth stones that could be heated for cooking. The man who greeted me spread out a mat and
invited me to sit upon it.

I began the conversation. "I am Shawanadese of the

holy school," I repeated. "I am sent to bring you the gods' protection and love. I am also sent to inform you that your youngest son has been chosen for our holy school."

His broad face lit in an enormous smile. "I am honored to have you as our guest. I am sure you are tired from your travel. I shall have some refreshment brought to you. Please make yourself comfortable, then we shall talk."

I nodded and watched him as he climbed the ladder and out.

Not long afterward, one of the women who had been grinding corn came down the ladder with a large jug of water strapped on her back and warm cakes that smelled enticingly sweet. These were amaranth cakes, a common grain but small in comparison to maize and obviously for special guests. This was followed with a sage tea and was altogether delicious at the end of a hot dry day of journeying. I used the water in the jug for cleansing myself, using my soaproot.

A small foot descended the ladder. A child climbed down with short black hair wearing only a loincloth. He looked at me somewhat timidly, and it seemed he wanted to speak. I rose from the mat and said, "My name is Shawanadese. I am an acolyte from the holy school. Who are you?"

"I am Kotoki. I am eight warm seasons of age. I want to learn more than I can learn here at home. My father says I am to travel with you to the holy school and begin my studies. When do we leave? May I take my dog?"

"No, there are no dogs living in the rooms in the school. I must speak to your father tonight, and we will decide when you and I are to leave. Are you anxious to go?"

"No—er, yes! I did want to take my dog, and I shall miss my parents, but Father says I must be brave." He shuffled his feet and scratched his head and said, "I must go now!" Then he hurriedly scuffled up the ladder, leaving me staring after him.

My heart went out to him. I so well remembered—it seemed like yesterday when I too was eight season cycles old.

I slept very soundly that night. I remembered no dreams but one, that of a coyote dying on the side of a rock formation and her unborn cubs dying with her. I woke sobbing, and hoped nobody had noticed or heard me. Rousing myself, I sat on my mat for a few minutes and picked up my crystal. As I sat quietly holding it in my left hand, it vibrated, and gradually I gathered an inner peace to give me strength to begin a new day.

Soon the family was up, and the boy's father came to me, saying, "I have instructed my son to be ready to leave within the hour. May the Gods guide you on your journey. Take care of him, for he is my pride."

We left the small house as the sun began to rise and bring warmth to the horizon. The breeze was slight, and the day promised to be hot and blistering. We set out on the road and stopped every so often for water. We had corn cakes and some dried venison in our knapsacks.

The boy said, "I have never traveled this far from my home." His anxiousness combined with excitement was apparent. His eyes twinkled with enthusiasm. Although my experience as a traveler was limited, I was older and felt more assurance. Yet I had a gnawing feeling that I could not describe. I knew only that I felt uneasy. I didn't want the boy to know, but I felt an evil presence that I couldn't explain. I hoped my feelings were not due to the fact that there could have been raiders nearby. I immediately thrust such negative thoughts aside.

We moved on through the barren desert with occasional orange rocks jutting here and there. A desert dust devil danced across the road in front of us. The air was hot and dry, and we sat down in the shade of a rock to drink and rest and partake of a little food. I had been told it was not wise to eat too much when you travel or you will grow tired and want to sleep.

Not wanting to stay too long lest we not reach the complex by night, we moved on. The road was hot under his yucca sandals and my cotton ones. We covered our heads with a light cloth and continued on our way. An uneasiness pervaded the air. Suddenly an arrow penetrated my poncho and grazed my arm. My immediate response was to roll the boy and myself to safety. We ran for a rock formation I saw not very far away. My heart was pounding. Beads of perspiration lined my brow. Suddenly even the rocks seemed to come alive and speak in their own vibrations. I knew we could not possibly be safe very long, and I was at a loss as to what to do next.

I drew my knife. A shadow was creeping slowly around the rock. It loomed threateningly over us. My heart sank. I covered the boy with my head cloth and stood ready to defend us both. My education at the complex included some instruction in defense. Now it was coming back to me. The shadow, however, never showed itself, for not far away appeared a pregnant female coyote, who slunk around as though looking for me. Though she was gaunt and undernourished, my adversary seemed intimidated by her presence and backed off. I stood for a while waiting, and when nothing happened, I said that we could move on. My heart again was torn for this starving female, and I left our dried venison for her. Nothing unusual seemed to happen as we reached the complex, and all I felt was a thankfulness that we were there—alive!

Upon reaching the complex, I noticed the boy looked overwhelmed. His home was so small in comparison to our enormous complex, which could house five hundred Anasazi if we were under attack. Nish't Ahote and one of the elders was there to greet us, and after an affectionate look from the boy, I realized I must let him go. I took my belongings to my room and unfolded my mat. I had not been in my room long when Nish't Ahote and an elder entered my room. The two of them sat upon my mat and arranged their robes around them. Nish't Ahote looked anxiously at me and took my hand. Again I felt a strange warmth emanating from his hand. The elder looked nervously about, his eyes resting on my crystal. "Our young man tells me of your travails on the way from his home to our complex. I am concerned for you. Are you all right?"

"I am fine now, but I would like more instruction on defense. I did not feel properly prepared, and I do not understand, in our peaceful community, who would threaten my life. I would also, since I am asking for more instruction on defense, ask that I have additional instruction in the language of the Mayans."

Nish't Ahote seemed to brush my second request aside. He seemed much more concerned with my first request. He nervously picked at his robe and asked me, "Did you see anyone at all during the attack? The boy says he did not, but tell us what you saw!"

"I am sorry to disappoint you, but I truly saw no one. I wish I could say more!"

The elder's gaze left my crystal, and he said, "Have you any intuitive feelings about what has happened?"

My gaze shifted anxiously to Nish't Ahote, who gave me a reassuring nod. I ran my hands through my short-cropped hair and paused to think how to voice my concern. I carefully gathered my thoughts and replied, "I know not if the boy or his parents have enemies. Have you asked him this?"

The elder said that the boy seemed to know nothing and that was the purpose of asking me. His eyes were not unfriendly but were riveted on me.

I had little to say until Nish't Ahote revealed, "The smaller outliers all around us have spoken of some minor attacks and thefts. There has been no bloodshed, but the security and peace we enjoyed for many years has been breeched."

I felt a deeper tension developing as the elder added, "A report has come in that there are raiders who steal our reserves and in one instance even captured one of our children. True, no one has been killed, but we must tighten our security in order to alleviate this new development. Let us strengthen the communications between the outliers and this, our cultural center, so we can be more on the defensive."

After a moment of silence, the tension was broken by Nish't Ahote, who said, "So it shall be. I hear no other responses. Let us do as suggested."

I slipped back into my study habits. Truly I was blessed, I thought, for I was a chosen female amid this male world. I spent time grinding corn, and gathering wild seed and pinyon nuts, for this was woman's work which I needed to understand, even though I did it infrequently.

Several sun cycles passed before Nish't Ahote again visited and said, "You were interested in the language of the Mayan." He stood looking at me as though he thought I might have forgotten.

"Oh, I thought you had not heard me. You changed the subject and ignored me when I spoke of it, but— yes! I want to learn the language of my warrior!"

He rearranged his robes and said, "I have a tutor arranged for you. You will meet with him once every three sun cycles for instruction time. You start at sunrise. Do you have any objections to that?"

Did I have any objections? He had never asked that before! Was this because I was grown up now? "Oh, Nish't Ahote!" I threw my arms around him. He hugged me, then pushed me back, looking at me. "My child, I am glad you are happy, but do not hug me too long! Let us begin your lessons at sunrise tomorrow. Report to me in the kiva. I will guide you and introduce you to your new teacher."

With that he picked up his robes and climbed out of my room rather swiftly as I clutched my bosom in excitement. Perhaps the next time I saw my warrior I could talk to him. There was no doubt at all in my mind that I would see him again.

My Mayan language lessons would be taught to me by one of the older instructors. He was a fairly tall, misshaped old man who limped and had poor eyesight. He had a crystal flat sphere he saw through when he wanted to point to something I had written and this was rather curious to me. Where had he gotten this crystal sphere? I was certain that time with my Mayan teacher would tell.

Chapter 3

Coyote

When the time came for my womanly cycle, I thought of the pregnant female coyote. After praying that she was alive, I gathered my belongings for three days in my retreat and headed across the hot parched desert toward my secret place. I found the familiar ledge that opened into a small room and threw my supplies down on the stone slab. It would be a problem staying clean this time. The wash had dried up entirely, forcing me to bring a supply of yucca pads to use instead of soft cotton.

During the heat of the afternoon, I picked up the hard stone and reviewed my work from my first visit. On the side wall was the cloaked figure I had carved so painstakingly. I picked up the soft red ocher and colored a red headband and red trim on the bottom edge of the cloak. I stood back to gaze at my work for a while, and an idea image began to enter my head. I began to chisel some curved lines, then four legs and two ears. I added a tail. I wanted to put in some brushy hair, but perhaps later. The lonesome female coyote had emerged on the wall looking up at the cloaked figure. Much time had passed, and the air, I noticed, was suddenly much cooler. Then I heard it . . . the rumble of thunder. The wind was getting stronger, and a dust devil raced across the mesa top to the other side of the canyon. The wind increased dramatically and whipped the pinyon pines. A desert rabbit raced for cover. I stepped out of my cotton cloth and ran for my soaproot. Standing outside my door, I raised my face skyward as the cold raindrops pelted and stung my face. The chill of the raindrops were a shock at first, but my body began to tingle with delight. I could remember wanting to play in the rain as a little girl, but my mother had always said to come in. She said the Gods' fire that flashes in the sky might strike me dead. In terror I would run inside for shelter.

But today I felt no fear, only a blissful sensuousness. Heedless of the wind and fire of the Gods dancing across the sky, I used my soaproot and marveled at the intensity and heaviness of the rainfall. Then after feeling cleaner than ever before in my life, I stepped inside the entrance to dry off. The water felt so good on my body, I allowed the air to dry me as I continued to watch the rain. Then as quickly as it began, the winds died and the rain stopped, and the only sound was that of water as it rushed over canyon walls and raced down the wash. I felt purified and exhilarated, yet wished for something more, and I knew not what. I knew only I had a need inside that I could not explain. I picked up my crystal and went outside.

As I walked through and around the mud that oozed through my toes, I hummed a little tune that popped into my head. The sun was sinking in the west, and the brilliance of the blue sky was striking against the rust, red, yellow colors of the canyon. Surely this was the Gods' country. I was so fortunate to have a home as magnificently beautiful as this.

The next day was uneventful, but on the third day the Gods would smile on me. I arose at the break of dawn and gathered my belongings to go to the wash.

There were a couple of prairie dogs here and there, and a desert rabbit that scurried between rocks in the dry morning air. As I stumbled toward the wash feeling dizzy on the third day of fasting, I noticed again the tree with the unfriendly thorns and pods. There were pods on the ground and only a few on the tree. I plucked only the few that I could reach and that were left on the tree, and put them in with my belongings. I remembered that I had intended to ask Nish't Ahote about this strange pod, but I had forgotten to do so.

I washed myself thoroughly and rubbed my body again with sage. As I was doing that, I heard a whimper not far from me. It was not a bird, a desert rabbit, a prairie dog, or even a quail. My mind cleared. I listened intently. I moved toward the soft whimper. In a crevice in the rocks covered with lichen I found a tiny frail coyote pup. Not far away I found five other dead coyote pups clustered together in a little heap. There was no sign of the mother. Then my foggy mind cleared enough to remember.

This poor tiny, skinny golden bundle of fur must be—yes—it must be one of the pups of that starving pregnant female coyote I had seen. The pup that was not dead was very weak and having difficulty in moving. Instead of a playful plump pup, he was scrawny and weak and looked at me with pleading eyes. My whole body ached for him. What could I do? If I took him to my hideaway, what could I do to keep him alive? My thinking was muddled, and then, because I knew he would surely die out there, I gently lifted the small bundle and carried him carefully, as if he were a fragile piece of pottery. I laid down one of my cotton pieces, and as he rested he looked up at me with such sadness in his eyes. It occurred to me that he probably would not remember his mother, and so was totally dependent on me. I was his mother now! But how could I keep him alive? I had no milk as his mother would have had.

I gazed around my retreat and then an idea came to my mind. I picked up my boomerang and headed out for territory I knew would have small game. I walked for a while, then sat down to wait. In the heat of the day it was not likely that any game would be available, but I sat quietly by a rock that jutted out. As time passed, I became more hot and discouraged, until suddenly a desert rabbit scurried into view. I stood and readied my boomerang. I prayed that the Gods would grant me a straight and true aim! I tensed as I uttered my small prayer. The weapon flew from my hand and hit its mark, bringing the rabbit down. I raced toward the rabbit, and found it still breathing. My knife found its mark, and the rabbit was mine. I said another prayer of thanks to both the rabbit and the Gods.

I took it home and skinned and gutted it. I prepared a fire and cooked it. All that time I was constantly checking my pup. He seemed so weak and frail. I felt I was racing time for his life. Finally the meat was cooked, but I knew the pup could not eat it. When it cooled enough, I pulled it off the bone, and then an idea hit me. I found two stones, one flat and one rounded. I took a small piece of meat and pounded and ground it. It became almost mush. I put some on my finger and put my finger into the pup's mouth. No response. Then as though the pup had been sleeping, it grabbed onto my finger and suckled. I returned to the warm rabbit and pounded some more, and once again the pup responded.

I ran back and forth teasing the pounded rabbit into him, when a cricket appeared in the corner where I had laid my belongings. Crickets ate our precious fabric, so I raced after it and finally killed it in front of the pup. I picked it up and noticed his nose quivering as the cricket passed him by. I stopped. I put the cricket down in front of him, and he devoured it! I was amazed!

This then, was something that he liked to eat. For the remainder of the third day, I looked for crickets. By sitting by cracks and crevices, I found several crickets and a couple of grasshoppers. I took them back to my pup, and he devoured them. Perhaps the Gods had assisted me. The pups eyes were open, and though he was very skinny, he seemed no worse than when I found him.

Late that afternoon, I packed my bags again, and wrapping Puppy in a cotton sack on my back, I walked back to the complex. Nobody noticed my entrance to the complex, but the few dogs that usually were outside jumped all over me as I trudged toward my room. One of the dogs had just had pups, and my mind began to work. Perhaps she would accept my pup into her brood.

I threw my things down in my room and ran to her carrying my pup in my arms. She was back with her own pups, and they were gathering around her. I gently lay my pup down with her and her brood. He seemed so timid and shy, and did not seem to understand what I was suggesting. His little ears lay back on his head, and his nose sniffed as if saying, "This is not right! This is not my mother!" His frail little body hung back, and he made no advances, much to my chagrin.

My supper arrived—corn gruel and peppers with herbs. My pup wriggled his nose at the smell. So I dipped my finger in the corn gruel and put it under his nose. He licked it off. Ah! Now I dipped again in my corn gruel. He seemed to enjoy it. Perhaps I had discovered something. The corn gruel was slightly sweetened with honey, and my pup seemed delighted. And so we shared.

The next several sun cycles was a time for gaining strength for Puppy, and so he seemed to thrive. I had him in my room when I resumed my Mayan language lessons, and we lived together compatibly. He suckled the gruel off my finger, and I brought him crickets and grasshoppers. He seemed content and, of course, I was very happy with my newfound friend. As I looked back on this in future years, I realized that my motherhood instinct had been satisfied.

There were visitors again—traders. These were from the southwest of us, and brought us many articles that were very different to us. In return we gave them turquoise and our cylindrical vases.

Hearing they had come, I left my studies and rushed out to look at what our visitors had. There were clay figures of different animals and people that had been fashioned into useful containers. There were flat palettes in the form of animals. There were incense burners carved from stone, and shell jewelry with etched figures and designs in them. Truly beautiful! There were also some beans like the ones I had found in my four days of my womanly cycle.

My love for beauty drew me to the etched shells, and I picked out a shell medallion that I thought would be beautiful as a necklace. I was examining it when Nish't Ahote came up behind me. His familiar touch on my shoulder made me come alive. He smiled and watched me as I gazed longingly at the medallion.

"That pleases you, little one?" he asked.

"Yes, it is different from anything I have ever seen. How do they do the design?"

"It is done with the fermented juice of the saguaro

cactus. I'm not sure, but you are right! How can anyone do this to such a delicate thing as a shell? But look! There are etched shell hair pieces to match. Do you like them also?"

"Oh, yes, but," and I stammered.

He said, "If you want them, take them. I have a large piece of turquoise," and he stared off in another direction.

I threw my arms around his neck and hugged him. He grunted and I backed away, suddenly caught by the sight of the beans. I pointed out to him that I had found a few during my womanly cycle. He told me that they could be ground up, like maize, and served as a very rich flour. He said he had also heard that there were medicinal properties within the bean and the plant.

At this our conversation stopped, and I was left thinking. Did the Hohokam have an abundance of this bean product? If so, then they did not have to worry about the drought and maize crops as we did. Perhaps I would be wise to look further into this. The significance of the beans would become apparent only later. Yet my other discovery at the wash proved momentous only a few sun cycles later.

That afternoon while I was with my Mayan teacher, Puppy left my room and began exploring. He found my door to the next room and then the door to the next and so on and disappeared. I returned from my language lesson and—no Puppy! I heard in the courtyard many dogs yipping. I rushed out and found Puppy backed into a corner of the courtyard but holding his own. The dogs in the complex seemed to know he was wild. I walked through the dogs, shooed them away, and when I broke through their ranks, Puppy lunged into my arms and hid his head in my armpit.

His little body was trembling, and I tried to soothe him.

At that moment Nish't Ahote and one of the elders came upon the commotion. Seeing the coyote in my arms, they both stopped and stared. There was a long pause in which they exchanged glances. Then Nish't Ahote came forth and looked at me with strangeness in his eyes. "How did you find this pup? You are surely full of surprises!"

I went over the story of seeing the mother coyote and how I knew she was starving and twice left her food. I explained how I thought she had deterred the attack on the boy and I in the desert. I explained how I had taken Puppy in and kept him alive, and my eyes glowed when I spoke of it. Nish't Ahote could see my happiness.

He looked long and hard at me. He shook his head and said, "You have found your ceremonial symbol. The coyote is an animal of stealth, cunning, and wisdom. May you learn these things and how to use them wisely. As you know the Anasazi view the coyote with much reverence. May you do the same, little one, and you and pup learn from each other."

Preparations were being made for the festival of the corn harvest. The cooks were preparing great quantities of food and there was much excitement in the air. People from the surrounding outliers joined us, bringing their own quantities of food. Costumes were being checked and repaired if necessary. There would be a dance for the women in which I would take part. The elders had called the people together for a corn festival because the Gods had not given us the usual amount of rain to harvest our squash, beans, and corn. By doing this perhaps the Gods would be merciful now and the next harvest season also.

Crowds of people began arriving at the plaza. Once again I hoped to share some time with my family, but as I searched among the faces of the people, I did not see them. I had thought that if there was not enough space, they could stay in my room. It seemed, however, that it was not intended.

I went to the wash and cleansed myself, and rubbed myself down with sage. Returning to my room, I colored my cheeks with red ocher powder and lined my eyes with kohl. My hair was still too short to style very well, but I combed it and twisted the top section into a small knot at the crown of my head. I then inserted two macaw feathers into the knot and put on my macaw feather earbobs. I wrapped a piece of cotton around my waist. It had a design with symbols of clouds and rain. I donned my feather vest, which caused me to remember the lightning-charged fingers of my warrior, who was the last person to unlace it, and I felt a deep need that I could not describe. To top off my attire, I added the necklace made of shell and inlaid with turquoise strung on a leather thong that Nish't Ahote had given to me after the Hohokam traders visit. I tied some turkey feathers on a leather thong and wound them around Puppy's neck. He would be enjoying the company of the other pups and dogs in the complex.

Puppy bounded away from me to join his canine company as soon as his little feet hit the plaza. My joyous anticipation quickly changed to an ominous one, however, as I turned to find Wisoko keeping stride with me. How I wished I could make myself invisible as an accomplished shaman could do. My skin crawled as he walked entirely too close to me and said, "Your loveliness is a gift. Why you chose to give such a gift to an outsider, a Mayan, I cannot imagine. You will live to rue that day."

Saying no more, he stepped aside and disappeared among the people leaving me in shock and fear, for in a manner of speaking, he had threatened me. I shivered and closed my eyes as I clenched my fists. Since the success of the corn crop would depend on only positive thoughts, I struggled with my fears to change them. Puppy came to my rescue as he returned to leap and nip at my feet wanting to play. A few moments of play soon put my mind at ease again.

The ceremony that would take place was a combination of song, drama, dance, and party that formed a prayer for rain, bountiful harvests, and propagation of animals and plants, and the well-being of our complex and all the contributing outliers of those who attended. Each outlier or kiva had their own group of dancers. Some dancers were painted in black and white stripes, some in black and yellow stripes, and some of the dancers had divided their bodies vertically so that they were half yellow and half black with white spots or stripes. Deer hoof rattles were worn at the waist. There was also a group of people who performed practical services for the dancers, such as making needed adjustments or repairs to the dancers' costumes during the performances.

When all was ready, I was aware of a tap on my shoulder. I turned to find my father next to me with my mother standing slightly behind me. My father was dressed as a dancer representing our kiva, and Mother looked lovely in her black manta tied at the waist with a red belt. Her breasts were bare in imitation of the long wisps of summer rain that swept the land. Her headband had a sun and stars design worked into it. She was one of the female dancers. We embraced, and the festivities began.

The chorus was the first to appear in the plaza accompanied by a drummer. Each carried a sprig of green, a symbol of growing things and everlasting life. The main procession of the dancers was led by a figure who bore the sun symbol, a long pole that had a painted gourd and a dazzling cluster of macaw feathers. The bearer of the sun symbol was Nish't Ahote and under this symbol the dancers would perform. Nish't Ahote was now the sun priest, for Taweyah was too old and too ailing to fulfill most of the required duties. Who could have been more fitting than Taweyah's nephew, Nish't Ahote, to carry our standard. The symbol constituted a blessing and a purification as well as a request to the rain cloud people.

Then came the five elders. They were dressed in white skirts to the knees worked with symbols of clouds and rain tied with a sash. Tied to their right knee was a turtle shell rattle with deer hoof tinklers. In their right hands were gourd rattles imitating the sound of falling rain.

First the outlier dancers took turns dancing, then the elders followed. After a long period of this dancing, there came the time for the women's games.

Women and men who were not dancers entered the large kiva. The women sat in a semicircle, and a few singers sat behind the women. They sang and the women danced. At the end of the song the women threw gifts to the men, and the game became a free-for-all. Feathers, baskets, trinkets, and even pottery were thrown. Needless to say, at the end of several rounds of this, many of the gifts, especially baskets and pottery, were in shambles. The man who had collected the most usable gifts was the winner. Everyone in the kiva was enjoying themselves when suddenly my nose picked up the smell of smoke. It was much stronger than the smell of the huge bonfire in the plaza. The noise and commotion and chanting had so absorbed everyone's attention that no one else seemed to have smelled anything. It was obvious that I had to do something. Walking toward the musicians was so out of the ordinary that everyone stopped to stare at me. The musicians ceased their singing, and I raised my hands to all in the kiva:

"Are our senses so dull that we do not smell? There is fire, a grease fire, very close by! Look! The roof of our kiva is smoldering!"

Everyone looked up, and I went on. "Do not panic. We can get out if we must through the antechamber." Having said that, I ran to the antechamber door, but in opening the door I was rushed with a very strong grease fire smell. Apparently the antechamber door was also afire. My heart skipped a beat, and I looked desperately around me. Then gathering my senses and overcoming the urge to panic, I said to everyone, "My people, have faith! The Gods will hear us!" If I could have only convinced myself that this were so.

The smoke was becoming more intense. There was no air! The faces of the men and women were pinched, wide-eyed, and nervous. The fright displayed by everyone as the smoke thickened could have led people to do foolish dangerous things. Everyone knew how quickly we could all be suffocated.

Then I heard a long, lonely yowl. It had to be Puppy! The baby coyote had been left in the plaza along with the other dogs in the complex. He must have smelled the smoke and knew that I was down there! I waited and prayed to the Gods and hoped. Just as we were all coughing, hacking, and gasping for breath, water began to seep through the roof and the antechamber door opened, wet, dank, humid, and muggy, and much of the smoke thinned and escaped through the antechamber door.

My people clambered for fresh air, and I stepped out into the marvelous sweet-smelling night air. Puppy leaped into my arms, licking my face and rubbing me and whimpering as though he had not seen me for several moon cycles.

People's eyes were reddened from the nightmare, and it took several more moments of panting and wheezing for them to return to normal. I finally focused on my parents, who were holding me by the shoulder with an intent look of concern, and then saw Nish't Ahote, who stood behind them to see if all was well. I nodded and sat down, and after a short time the dancing in the plaza resumed.

Nish't Ahote pulled me aside, and we walked to his room. His room was much like mine but contained a stone slab shelf with a few carved figurines on it. One was a carved replica of a macaw that he must have gotten from the Mayan traders. Another was of a walnut black on white bird, and another was a pipe made of stone. There was also a chunk of turquoise. I was deeply flattered to be taken into his quarters, for this was the first time.

Nish't Ahote pulled me down on his mat. "I have been concerned for your welfare, little one, and have had time to do much thinking. I find your spiritual abilities most intriguing."

"What do you mean, honored one?"

"You told me of your dream, the one of the figure at your mat and of the fire. It *was* an omen. I know that now. You, little one, have more spiritual ability than you realize. Do not hesitate to share with me any other dreams or visions you may have. Some of them may be warnings or premonitions, and some of them may offer ways of solving problems."

"But I do not want to waste your time with those that may be insignificant. How shall I know which ones need to be told?"

"Spend time with your crystal and the answers will

come. Do not let Puppy distract you as he is doing now."

Puppy had one of Nish't Ahote's sandals and was thrashing it around his head. I moved to retrieve the sandal before Puppy ruined it. Puppy sat on his hind legs and looked at me inquisitively. I realized that Nish't Ahote was correct when he said Puppy took up much of my time. I needed to make some better accommodations for him. He needed to have his own mat for sleeping, and to learn some discipline.

"Nish't Ahote, there was a dream I had, perhaps a moon cycle ago that has turned out to be meaningful. I dreamed of a mother coyote and her pups dying. I woke up crying. It was a vision of what I saw when I found Puppy."

"Do you understand what I have said, little one?" he asked.

"Oh, yes," I replied, "but why would anyone do such a horrible deed?"

He looked away from me and put his hand to his mouth gazing at I knew not what. Then slowly turning back to me, he said, "There is much we don't know and much we can suppose. The Gods will show us in due time."

The next day the people of the outliers dispersed to pack and return home.

There was to be a council held when the sun departed the horizon. Nish't Ahote asked that I attend. He said that representatives from the largest outliers would be in attendance and all insisted on my being present.

I was startled by this request, for I had never attended a council. A council was only for men. Perhaps I had done something wrong and was to be rebuked. My eyes were wide with turmoil and questioning. At that moment Nish't Ahote arrived in my room. As though he read my thoughts, he pulled me to him and lay my head on his shoulder. He stroked my hair and said, "Nay, little one, do not be concerned. The elders and representatives mean you no harm. They only desire your side of the story." Having said that, he turned and climbed the ladder out of my room.

At nightfall, the council began in the next largest kiva. I had rested during the day and made myself ready. I was nervous and apprehensive in spite of the reassurance Nish't Ahote had tried to give me. My heart was pounding so loud I was sure all could hear as I entered the kiva. The elders and representatives were all seated on benches around the perimeter. A fire burned in the firebox, and Nish't Ahote sat alone. He was obviously the council chief.

When I was seated uneasily, Nish't Ahote declared, "The issues are several tonight, but first we must tell Shawanadese what was happening in the plaza while 'my people' were below in the great kiva."

I jerked my head and looked closely at him. "My people!" I thought. "He has mimicked me in saying— my people. Yes, I did say 'my people' when I spoke to them. Was that so wrong or too arrogant?"

He moved on. "Who among you would tell Shawanadese of the happenings in the plaza while 'my people' were below?"

The representative from the "house of the prairie dog" stood and spoke. "The noise and commotion was great in the plaza. Dances were being performed. Suddenly a great howl rose up, first from the coyote, and then he was assisted by the yelps and howls of the other dogs. Many nipped at our heels. Some rushed from us to the great kiva and back again. The baby coyote seized the kilt, then the sandal of Nish't Ahote and pulled him toward the kiva. It was only then that we knew something was very wrong." The representative sat down again having done his duty.

Nish't Ahote resumed, "We would like to hear from your mouth, Shawanadese, what happened below. We are getting somewhat different stories from those who were with you. Please tell us!"

I narrated the story, what I said and did, and my feelings during the time of horror and no air. Then everyone became silent. I squirmed and fidgeted on my mat. The quiet was lengthy and nerve-racking.

At last the representative from the "house of the white-tailed deer" rose and extended his hand. "The coyote is powerful in spirit. He is cunning and clever and has shown his strength and God power in the deed he has done. Shawanadese has shown wisdom, leadership, and strength in what she has done. Indeed the people were *hers* at that time and perhaps now also. None of 'her people' speak in any but hushed and respectful tones toward her. Many feel that she and the coyote are the God's spirit and offer reverence."

One of the elders rose and addressed the rest saying, "Nish't Ahote tells us that Shawanadese has the power to see the future. If this is so, her status should be changed. She is no longer just an acolyte, but an assistant to Nish't Ahote, and as such will learn more of his priestly ways."

Hearing this, I was overcome with thoughts of my own shortcomings, and I wondered if I could continue to meet the expectations of the elders and representatives. Most of all, would I be able to retain the image that Nish't Ahote seemed to have of me? My thoughts were short-lived because one of the elders stood, saying, "The problem remains, who could be responsible for this attempt to kill our people?"

Another rose, stating, "There has been much unrest

in our society recently. We have had many seasons of
peace before now. We have not had any problems
with the migrational people in the past seasons, and I
cannot understand the sudden attacks we are experiencing. Perhaps there is someone who is responsible
and if so, we must look out for that person."

Nish't Ahote through that declaration said nothing
and allowed the concern to die of its own accord.
Then, quietly, he dismissed all in the kiva and turning
to me, he said, "So, little one, you have not only rescued your people, but you have them very aware of
your powers. I wish to congratulate you."

The memory of Wisoko's harassment prior to the
fire and the council meeting had been haunting me. I
was unsure if I should say anything and so I waited.

Chapter 4

Sun Priest Assistant

Although it was only the next day, I intuitively knew that somehow my life would change. It was exciting to know that the opportunity to learn so much more had been presented to me. Moreover, being an assistant would permit me, a woman, to assist in and understand many of the "men's" ceremonies. Whatever else I might have learned, only the Gods in their own time and ways would teach me, with the help of Nish't Ahote, who was our shaman. As the day would prove, he had decided to begin teaching me in my new role immediately.

Then a young acolyte descended my ladder interrupting my pondering and said that I was to report to the kiva closest to my room. I tied on a skirt, combed my hair, and pinched at my cheeks to awaken myself. After rubbing my body with sage and directing Puppy to the plaza to play, I descended the ladder into the small kiva. One of our youngest students had apparently been hurt and had developed a high temperature before reporting his illness and requesting any help. A nasty gash in the boy's knee had festered, and now his condition was not good. His breathing was labored, and his face, though turned away from the fire in the kiva, was red and flushed. Another young man, Nish't Ahote's nephew, Hototo, whom I later learned had recently become a priest, was standing anxiously to one side of the sickened boy.

Nish't Ahote was chanting and seemed not to notice me. His body swayed and glistened in the heat of the small kiva. He sang

"O ye Gods of the four corners, Gods of above and below, and Awonawilona, our supreme being, hear our plea.

Let your infinite powers soothe the one who is sick. Accept this, his offering! Pacify his soul!

O Great Ones, give your powers to this medicine. Strengthen his body and renew his life!"

This was repeated many more times before Nish't Ahote moved toward the boy and gave him a button to chew. The boy, almost immediately, spat it out and vomited into a large bowl by his mat. Nish't Ahote insisted that he take it again into his mouth and just suck on it. Then he resumed his chant, but this time with a deep sounding drum played by the young priest. The sound was so deep, it penetrated through the center of all our bodies. His chant was so low, it seemed to come from the bowels of the Gods of the lower world.

I felt as though in a dream. I was certain the young priest felt the same, for his body also glistened in the heat and his eyes were glazed. After much chanting, Nish't Ahote whispered to me to hold the boy's hands above his head, and he instructed the young priest to hold his feet. The boy's eyes were dilated, and he did not resist us. Nish't Ahote moved toward him with a sharp obsidian knife and cut open the festered flesh, not just in one long slice but in several cross slices also. The boy writhed violently at this and, for this crucial time, was difficult for the young priest and I to control. An ugly greenish fluid oozed around the red blood. Nish't Ahote continued to chant, and the boy became still. Nish't Ahote packed herbs in a poultice and laid it on the drained knee. Then he wrapped the knee and the poultice with clean cotton and continued his chanting. By now we were all sweating profusely, and Nish't Ahote inserted some willow bark into the boy's mouth and removed the button. Then laying his barrel-chested body across the boy's small form, he extended his arms: one toward his head, and one toward his feet. Dead silence filled the kiva. Perspiration sparkled on Nish't Ahote's broad, curved back, and his body seemed to vibrate, merging all his power into the body of the boy.

Suddenly his muscles went slack, and he sagged. His arms hung wearily, and he motioned us to move away and up the ladder. We quietly ascended the ladder, and I stood on a lower rung, unsure of what to do next. The young priest assured me all was finished, and I returned to my room.

Once again I was in awe of the abilities of our shaman. My thoughts tumbled over each other as I stroked Puppy, who sat in my lap while I reviewed my newest experience. My thoughts turned to the boy. Would his fever break? Why, when he cut his leg, did he not keep it clean and covered? I thought it must be because I was a woman that I did not understand this thing. Of course, boys always played rough games. That I could remember when I was younger and living at home. My male cousins and neighbors were forever climbing or falling, or racing and crashing into each other. When they fell, their mothers were always there to wash and wrap their wounds. Perhaps this young boy with his ugly laceration had been afraid. He had not been at the school very long and was very young. He may have feared the hurt of cleansing and dressing, so of course he suffered more. Such a foolish boy! My mother always said, "A little hurt now spares agony later!"

I was summoned later that day and found Nish't Ahote putting together a kind of salt and dried whites of turkey eggs together in a potion. My curiosity was piqued, and I asked him the purpose of this concoction. He explained that it was an emetic and would be used for a ceremony to begin that evening. I was curious, but said nothing. He looked at me from the corner of his eye, and continued his work. I watched him and noticed his languorous, dance-like movements, and I rose to go to his side to watch what he did, so that I might understand more clearly. He described in great detail what he was doing, then looked down at me saying, "Little one, you have much to learn!" His eyes devoured me and made me think of the warm doe eyes of the female deer. He turned toward me and took my hand, then turned away from me, gazing at the ladder of the kiva. I was aware of a piercing energy from his hand to mine, but not of the kind from which I wanted to escape. The energy caused my nipples to harden and pucker. It was the same excitement that my warrior had stirred deep in my soul. I wore only a kilt around my waist, and Nish't Ahote could readily observe my excitement. He knew and showed in his expression that I was a woman now. I was only too aware of his experienced manliness.

He took my face in his hands and looked into my somewhat dilated eyes. Then his lips touched mine, very tenderly, and he said, "You are very special. You must know that, do you not?"

I was so taken by surprise, I knew not what to say. However, my nipples hardened even more, and I felt a dampness between my legs. The kiva was cool. There was no fire as in the ceremonials, but I was

sweating. Nish't Ahote's hands touched my breasts
and circled them. The fabric bound around his waist
and between his thighs, which was all he wore, bulged
with his excitement. He asked me, "How much do
you want to learn, Coyote Woman?"

With my body quivering and a need rising deep
within me, I answered, "I wish to know everything, O
Gracious One!"

He pulled me to him and crushed my body against
his. Then his mouth possessed mine and left me gasping for breath. As though sensing that he had been too
rough, he again claimed my lips and mouth tenderly,
exploring my mouth with his tongue. A wave of shock
surged through my lower area and the world began
to spin.

Then, as though he was confused, he pushed me
away from him saying, "Not now, woman, not now!"

I also felt confused and rejected. Rejected by the
man I had admired for more than eight season cycles.
Rejected for what reasons I could not explain or even
begin to understand. He seemed very anxious and told
me, "Do not think it is you or anything you have
done. It is my problem, and I must deal with it accordingly. Now, get you up the ladder and be gone until
tonight's induction ceremony."

For dinner, I ate corn dumplings in brine sauce,
then followed my routine of cleansing and rubbing
with sage. Telling Puppy to stay, I left my room and
stood on my roof adjusting my eyes to the brilliance
of outside light and the magnificence of the colors of
the setting sun. I breathed deeply of the fresh air.
Surely there could be nowhere more beautiful than
this canyon land in which I lived.

Crawling down the ladder to the large open plaza,
I walked slowly to the small kiva for inductions. Nish't

Ahote was busily lining up the emetic he had con-
cocted, seven prayer sticks, sweet grass in an incense
burner, and a large pitcher of *balch* with eight cups.
One of our young acolytes wished to become a member of the southern society "Ember People." The
young priest whom I had worked with in the healing
ceremony led in the young man for induction. The
young acolyte had angry red spots all over him. I
learned later that his spots were a result of sitting for
several hours in a nest of fire ants. By doing this he
showed his strength, for he was not allowed to speak
out unless to answer a question by one of his guards.
Following this ordeal, he was brought into the kiva to
await further initiation procedures. His eyes were wide
in anticipation, but his chin was courageously stiff.

The elders entered wearing kilts and turquoise and
shell beads. Four of them stood around the fire, one
on the north side, one on the south, east, and west.
The fifth stood next to Nish't Ahote. The young man
stood alone next to the *sipapu,* the hole in the center
of the kiva from which the Anasazi believed they
came on the earth's surface. I, too, stood next to Nish't
Ahote, who remained near the shelf where his preparations awaited their use in the ceremony. The
younger priest remained next to the anxious young
man.

The elders took turns with lengthy prayer chants,
followed by Nish't Ahote, who passed out *balch* to
the elders, himself, the young priest, and finally to me.
To the young man he gave some of the emetic and
set a bowl down at his feet. The young man had not
eaten for a sun cycle, for the purpose of the fasting
and the emetic was to cleanse the body, which in turn
would cleanse the mind. More prayers were said, but
this time all of us used prayer sticks as we all knelt
down with our heads touching Earth Mother. During

this time the young man retched and vomited into the bowl at his feet. He was very brave, for he did not scratch his bites, though he was surely miserable, nor did he complain of his discomfort. After the second cycle of prayers, again we each received a cup of *balch,* and the young man once again was given the emetic. Seven cycles of prayers, seven cups of *balch,* and seven emetics later, the induction was over. The young priest led the young man, followed by the rest of us out into the plaza.

Many people had gathered, and feasting and dancing began. There were dogs, turkeys, and even mule deer roasting on spits, along with boiled breads, dumplings in brine, thick lime-yeast cakes, wild berries, and pinyon nuts. It all made me very hungry and being quite tipsy from seven cups of *balch,* I was glad I'd had sense enough to eat my dinner or I might have passed out. The entire badger clan of the young man was there to help support him and celebrate in his honor, and thus the honor of their own clan. The feasting and dancing went on all night, and at dawn everyone returned home. I returned to my room and to Puppy and lay down on my mat to rest my weary bones.

Under Nish't Ahote's instruction, I spent the next few days with my crystal. There was a new addition in the process of construction not far from my room, and the masons were busy trying to finish before the snows and cold weather arrived. Timber and logs had been brought in from the mountains. The masonry was done by day so the men could work on whatever side was shady. Then the women followed along behind to chink the leaks and solidify the walls. There was much noise, laughing, and joking that I could hear from my room, and this broke up the solitude I needed for meditating. Nish't Ahote had told me why my crystal was special. It had six sides, one for north, for south, for east, and for west, one for above the earth, one for below the earth; the center of the crystal was for the inside of the earth. It represented the universe. All things were the same. All had four sides, a top, bottom, and a center of sensitivity. But this was not so obvious in the rocks as it was in the crystal. He said when I meditated, I should look within the crystal and try to become part of it.

At this time also I found a woman who became a mentor of another sort. Our granaries and storage bins were gradually being filled in preparation for cold and snow. This was the time when the sun was lowest on the horizon. Our complex faced south and remained somewhat warmer than those that did not. The cliff behind us blocked off the cold north winds, and the snow melted more quickly around those of us who faced south. The bitter cold in our canyon often killed off many of our young and very old. There would be many more healings to attend soon. Since there was little to do in this harsh time, we spent much time in ceremonies and festivals. Many of the people from the not too distant outliers came not just for the festivities, but to stay several days to enjoy the warmth of our complex. This had been a good year so far for our crops, and much time would be spent to thank the Gods for our blessings. The check dams and irrigation canals had been successful in giving us the water we needed. The cisterns were full, and the ground had yielded. I watched many people carrying huge loads of dried corn, squash, beans, acorns, pinyon nuts, juniper berries, yucca, wild roots, and dried fruits. All this would feed us during the winter. Of course, the people also brought in huge quantities of deer, bighorn sheep, desert rabbit, jackrabbit, prairie dog, and other kinds of meat. Our cooks would lack for very little this winter.

Our cooks were older women whose children were grown and who volunteered to come to cook during the "time of many festivals." In return for their labor they knew they would eat well and stay warmer than in their own outlier, so there was never a shortage of volunteers. As I watched a few people approach our complex with food, a short, wrinkled-skinned, crinkly eyed figure moved at a slow steady pace toward me. She carried a huge water jar wrapped in cloth on her back. A strap on her forehead connected to water jar for added support. There were two large fat cloth bags hanging on each of her ample hips, which were secured by another strap around her waist. Her head was covered for protection from the burning sun, like the rest of her body. As she got closer, I saw a peep of gray hair at the edge of her scarf. She turned to look around, and suddenly I ran toward her.

"Mokni! Mokni! Is that you?" I asked.

She looked hard at me, then broke into a warm, toothless smile. Her gnarled hands reached out, and her arms encircled me in a fierce hug. "Of course its me!" she cackled. "And how is my pretty one doing in her world of men?"

"Oh, Mokni, I am doing well, but much better now that you are here. Is everyone well at home?"

"All was well when I left. Your mother and father send their good wishes and love. They told me to look after you," she said with twinkling eyes.

"Are you here to stay?"

"Yes, my child. I shall remain for the snow season. You may come and watch me cook and talk to me when you find the time."

"And I have much to tell you. There are many things you might help me to understand," I said, and wistfully thought of Nish't Ahote's rejection of me and of my confusion.

"Yes, Shawanadese! I see from your expression a love light in your eyes. I cannot promise to help, but I can promise to be an able listener. I must move on for now! My load is heavy, and I will lighten it when I find my new living quarters."

So saying, she hugged me again and shuffled toward the old part of the east wing, where grinding and cooking was done.

That evening Nish't Ahote summoned me to a council with both the man who directed the building of kivas and the one who designed them. Also present was the man who directed our trading and the five elders. One of them, Honani, was speaking as I quietly took a seat on the perimeter of the gathering. "We need a kiva large enough to contain the outlying communities who wish to use it, one that is not a part of our larger town complexes. One kiva of this type would serve many during our solstice ceremony and offer more unity for our culture. I suggest the construction of a large kiva at the sandy point protruding from the north wall of the canyon. It is far enough away from our main town complexes but close enough to unify our people with us."

Another elder, called Machakwi, added, "This kiva would then serve not just one community but several. More outliers would feel comfort during our many sun cycle ceremonies and be drawn here to the heart of our culture."

The building engineer, who has been listening intently, said, "And what of the design of this structure?"

Nish't Ahote responded deliberately as he spoke, "It must be simple yet beautiful. It must have an antechamber, bench, vaults, firebox, and seating pits to hold vertical roof supports. This construction cannot begin until the cold season is behind us. Wood must be brought in during the sun's climb on the horizon, when green begins to show itself."

"Of course, but my men might begin the cutting of the trees now," said the man in charge of building.

Noona, the man who oversaw our traders, who had been quiet all this time, firmly interjected, "Our trade center grows too small as well. More storage rooms are needed. Turquoise from the mountains arrives daily, and our space for storage is sorely limited. May I request an addition on the complex for these?"

"When the sun rises, we shall inspect your northern complex and see that your needs will be met. Again, the wood should be cut now," said Machakwi.

"After this evaluation we may ascertain the size and number of rooms to build and where to add them," said Pangwu, the man in charge of building.

The members of the meeting thus dispersed and went their own way except for Nish't Ahote. His mood was contemplative, and as I started to climb the ladder, he said to me, "Stay, little one! Tell me your thoughts."

"They are too many to speak of my teacher. Why do you ask?"

"A fresh view is often valuable," he said, and he laid his big hand on my shoulder. A shock rippled through my body. His touch was magnetic. My nipples hardened, and he was also visibly shaken. Thanks be to the Gods, this only happened when we were alone. As though reading my mind, he said, "Have you any thoughts you wish to share with me?"

"Yes, but only if these thoughts are not shared with others," I replied, after thinking out my answer.

"You have my word as the sun priest that your thoughts will not leave the walls of this kiva."

"Then, Nish't Ahote, it would seem to me that our most important need is water. Why are we not building cisterns? Why is it we build a new kiva, new storage rooms, when it might be better to protect against times of no rain?"

There was a pause before Nish't Ahote took my chin and turned my head to look into his eyes. "My child, without unity for our nation, we would be as the wanderers and raiders north of us. Do you understand what I am saying?" He gazed into my eyes, and I quite forgot what my thoughts were before. Then his hand lightly brushed my bare breast. His eyes were smoldering. I quite forgot the context of our conversation and melted at his touch. His mouth covered mine in a sweet, slow caress. He then stopped and, looking into my eyes intently, he professed, "There is much you do not comprehend about my role as the sun priest."

"Then, teach me, honored one!"

"The role of the sun priest is not an easy one. I must serve all the people. If I err, the people will reject me."

"I do not understand why you tell me what I already know," I said as I looked at him inquisitively.

"Listen well, my child! A priest must work for the good of the people, not for personal gain. We are not supposed to have any involvement in mundane affairs, or have quarrels or other indicators of dissension. We are not to be distracted from our prayers or other ritual behavior on behalf of our complex, or in any case on behalf of the Anasazi culture."

"What is it you are trying to say?" I asked as I moved toward the seating pit of the kiva.

He seemed terribly uneasy and shifted his weight

from one foot to another. Then he looked at me and beckoned me to him. He folded his warm arms around me and said, "The elders have seen to it that we will be together much of the time. You will learn from me, they say. And so you are my assistant."

After a pause in which I patently waited, I inquired," What are you trying to tell me?"

"Little one," he said, "the light in your eyes tells me of your love. Can you not see the same light in my eyes? I want to touch you, to hold you, to stroke you when I am alone with you. Your eyes say much and reach out to me. But I cannot reach back. I am trying to explain why."

"Are you saying the elders would not approve of any intimacy?"

"Ah! Such an intelligent young woman. Your young body belies your maturity. Yes, that is precisely what I am rather clumsily trying to explain."

"But, Nish't Ahote, they need not know. If it is as you say, than I am mature enough not to tell anyone— not even old Aunt Mokni. Oh, Nish't Ahote, teach me to fly again, but this time in the ways between men and women. I have loved you for many sun cycles."

"Little flower, your nipples harden against my chest. You have said you want to know everything. And so you shall, but for now you must help me to be strong. Help me by climbing the ladder and returning to Puppy, who waits for you in your room."

"I go, but I am not happy. I shall meditate on your words." So saying, I climbed from the kiva and stumbled toward my room to nurse my rejection.

Chapter 5

Harvest Parade and Vision

In the time of snow our population increased due to the sun solstice ceremonial celebration. At that time our celebrations were numerous because there was no farming or building to be done. Our visitors were many, and our large houses were like ant colonies. We also had a few storage towers scattered along our road system for outliers who were too far away to travel to us in the snow time to obtain food supplies. The year had been a good one. Old Aunt Mokni would not lack for cooking ingredients.

On a beautiful crisp cool morning, when the complex was still shaded from the sun, I strolled toward the cooking room looking for Aunt Mokni. In doing so I bypassed the rooms where toolmakers were busy at their craft, and then Puppy and I passed the jewelry crafting rooms. The craftsmen in both areas were working hard to make ready for the ceremony. The smells of food got stronger as I neared the kitchens. There were many older women in the cooking rooms, each involved in different activities. Several were simply grinding corn and singing and joking. One woman was working a fermented mush yeast made from lime and salt, which she mixed with a moderately fine corn-meal and warm water. She placed the mixture in narrow-necked pots near the hearth until fermentation took place. That was what made our bread rise. An-

other woman was cooking venison stew in an enormous cooking pot with prong-like irregular legs. An
immense pile of greasewood and pinyon wood was in
one corner of the room to provide fuel for the hearths.
Hanging on the walls were sieves, meal trays, bread
plaques, huge cooking pots, carved pudding sticks,
and more.

Aunt Mokni was busy making a sweet pudding of
yellow corn meal sweetened by a mixture of dried
flowers, which she wrapped in green corn leaves for
the purpose of drying. She would revive it by immer-
sion in hot water at the time of the ceremony. She
threw her arms around me, then held me at arm's
length. Smiling her warm toothless smile, she said,
"Ha, my sweet little one! Come sample my sweet
cakes!" She took one she was preparing and dropped
it in a pot of boiling water.

"Oh, Aunt, you are too good to me." I could hear
Puppy whining, for the smell of stew had awakened
his hunger. Aunt Mokni walked to the pot and ex-
tracted a chunk of meat, which she expertly deboned.
Putting the meat back into the stew, she said, "Here!
Feed your poor friend."

After giving the bone to Puppy and leaving him
outside the cooking area happily gnawing this splendid
gift, I returned to Aunt Mokni. She had withdrawn
the sweet cake from the water and handed it to me
in a small bowl.

"Now, my sweet, what is on your mind? Tell me!
Old Mokni's lips are sealed."

As I picked up my delicious sweet cake, my mind
flitted from thought to thought. It flew from my warrior to Nish't Ahote and then to my recent experiences as the assistant to Nish't Ahote. As assistant to
the sun priest, I knew I must be careful what knowledge I shared. I wanted to believe Aunt Mokni's lips

were sealed, but could I be sure? With these thoughts I timidly said, "All is well, Aunt, but it is not easy to live in a world of men. It seems they do not think as I do."

A hearty chuckle escaped her, and she said, "Awonawilona, our creator, caused these differences assisted by Alosaka, God of Fertility, and Tawa, Giver of Life. Without these blessed differences, all would always be in accordance and very dull."

"But will I grow to understand?"

"Ho, child! One never fully understands, but with maturity and experience you will expand your patience, thus your comprehension."

"Then, you say I must be patient and wait?"

"Everyone must wait and listen. Listen to all around you, but most of all listen to your own heart. However, do not let your heart rule logic and reasoning. The father of my children was not an easy man to understand. His moods were many, but he was a good man. Occasional mood changes do not make a man a bad person. More than likely he has something on his mind. You must listen and wait."

"But listen and wait for what, and for how long?" I asked in exasperation.

She threw her hands into the air and turned to face me, saying, "This I can not tell you, for the time to wait may be short or long. With each man it is different. You must meditate on this, and the Gods will help you." So stating, she turned back to the cooking and quietly asked, "Do you want to tell me more?"

In my heart I wished I could have told her all, but my mind flickered caution. "No, Aunt, you have given me a wonderful meal and much to think on. I thank the Gods that they sent you to me to offer a woman's advice in a man's world. I must go!"

"Come back if you are troubled, my sweet one. May the Gods guide your steps."

The day of the ceremonial parade was upon us. There was a hushed excitement in the air. Many outsiders had been arriving, bringing their customary ceremonial dance costumes to be housed in our many extra rooms. Many were staying in the three smaller complexes on either side of us. Many extra cooks had come in temporarily. Pieces of costumes could be seen here and there in the plaza in the state of being repaired. The dogs barked, the turkeys gobbled, as though they too felt the high tension of the people. The air was cooler this late in the harvest sun cycle, and the parade event was scheduled for just before sun peak time. The parade was to begin at one of our larger complexes to the east, and the participants would dance their way to the largest complex where I lived.

I had been informed that I was to be a part of the parade. My robe and long turquoise necklace had been brought to me. I washed and cleansed my hair in the chill air of sunrise and ate nothing for breakfast. The priests also fasted, for we would not partake of food until the feasting after the parade. I donned my red robe and turquoise and earbobs. My hair had grown and was long enough at that time to put in two tiny knots over either ear. With a bit of kohl and ocher I darkened my eyes and blushed my cheeks. Puppy watched me, and I tied deer hoof tinklers around his neck, for I knew he did not want to be left behind. My crystal was in a small cotton pouch I had made worn on a yucca string under my robe. I slipped into my sandals. Then checking myself as much as possible in my pyrite mirror, I was ready. Puppy and I moved along the plaza, which by that time was thronged with people in various stages of preparation. We walked the long road to the eastern complex to await further instructions.

Soon we began lining up. Nish't Ahote, the young priest, and myself were to be with the dignitaries at the head of the parade. The priest from the eastern complex was behind us. Then came the elders, and the heads of building and trade and our aged war chief. Thus the parade started.

The sides of the roads were thronged with people. On the rooftops of our easternmost complex, people stood to get a better view of the pageantry. Never had I been in front of so many people, and I felt an exhilarated nervousness more intense than ever before. Nish't Ahote looked calm, for he had done this many times before, but I saw the same tension I felt in Hototo, Nish't Ahote's nephew. We moved slowly along the circuitous route, and I occasionally waved as we moved along. I was concerned that I might not get to see the rest of the parade, but as it happened, when we had come into the complexes in which I was most familiar, there was a reserved section for the dignitaries on a platform. That overlooked the whole spectacular parade.

The first group of dancers were the olla maidens, who balanced large jars of grain and water on their heads. Each Anasazi maiden was dressed in white cotton skirts and blouses trimmed with colorful sashes and turquoise jewelry. They were quiet and dainty in their movements and moved carefully and precisely, depending on the musicians of the antelope dancers behind them. The olla was the sun and moon, which made possible the plentiful harvest we had.

Following the olla maidens, the antelope dancers wore golden-brown skins with the head of an antelope perched snugly on their heads. Copper bells were tied around their knees, and their legs were painted in white dots with stripes of golden brown. Their dance step was a reflection of the graceful steps of the animal they were representing.

From the mound builders to the far east of our culture came a group called the spear and shield dancers. They carried strong shields made of buffalo hide painted with symbols. Their spears were feathered and their dance was performed to show off their ability in handling their war implements.

After a slight pause between groups came the chant and drums of the four buffalo dancers. The power of the buffalo was often used to cure the sick, and a buffalo headdress touched to a patient after a dance was believed to have curative powers. Thus there were many elderly and sick on the sides of our roads who anxiously awaited the touch of one of the headdresses. Because the dancers stopped to offer curative powers along the way, there were frequent pauses in the parade.

At a light touch on my arm, I turned to see Hototo looking at me warmly and pointing. "Did you see that old woman?" he asked.

"What old woman?" I asked.

"The one who is bent and gnarled with the cane to your right."

"No, I had not noticed. I guess I was too busy watching the dancers."

"But the dancers are who cured her. Look! She walks straight now! Do you see her?"

I lifted the wisps of black hair away from my eyes, and yes, I could see. Clutching Hototo's arm, I excitedly explained, "She has thrown her cane into the road and is doing a slow dance with the buffalo dancers. May the Gods protect her old soul." My eyes misted with tears, and I hugged Hototo's arm.

"Surely the Gods protect us this year," said Hototo as he looked down at me, his eyes also misted with emotion.

Music from the Hohokam hoop dancers brought me back to reality. Their feathers were vivid and colorful, for they came from the south and were much closer to Mayan country, where the trade of parrot and macaw feathers was more prominent. There were three dancers. Two of them carried four hoops, and the third dancer carried five hoops. Each dancer showed how skillfully he could maneuver his head, body, and limbs in, out, over, and under several hoops at a time all the while dancing to the rhythm of the drums. Since our stand marked the end of the parade, for a grand finale the dancers put on a daring display with their flaming hoops. Because this was the first time I had such a spectacular view, I tensed and spontaneously grabbed Nish't Ahote's arm, and he looked down at me with an amused fatherly expression. As the dance ended, there was a wild hooting, yelling, stamping, and clapping in response and appreciation for the death-defying performance.

The next group were our own corn dancers. Whenever it was deemed necessary, our sun priest called for a corn dance to perform a ritualistic prayer for rain, bountiful crops, and good fortune. The women wore *tablitas* depicting the sun, stars, and lightning— the life-giving forces for our crops.

Following the corn dancers were the rain dancers. They wore tunics with long colorfully decorated sashes and belts and ankle strap sandals. They wore painted armbands and strands of turquoise nuggets around their necks. As a reminder of man's relationship with animals, they wore fox pelts hanging from the back of their belts. In their right hand were evergreen sprigs, and in their left were gourd rattles to shake and awaken the Gods so they would send down the much-needed rain.

Behind them were the Mogollan eagle dancers. The eagle was a sacred symbol. Its feathers carried back prayers to earthly beings, for its flight reached the sun. If a brave captured an eagle, he was especially rewarded and a dance followed. The dances told the story of the eagle's capture and death. They portrayed the dying eagle with downward fluttering motions and at the end of the dance lay motionless. They did such a graceful imitation of the eagle that there were tears in many eyes.

Next came the home dancers, celebrating the return of the Gods at the end of the snow season to their homes in the nearby mountain, followed by a group of clowns, who soon had everyone laughing. The body of the main home dancer was painted with sun, moon, and stars. He wore a kilt of red, green, black, and white with a belt of the same colors. His headdress was topped with a three-story *tablita* painted with blue-green and red with black and white symbols. The bodies of the clowns were reddish-brown with blue-green spots. Their breechcloths were the same colors as of the main home dancer. Most eyes were on the clowns and their antics. Their gestures were very coarse. One clown tumbled down with his feet in the air while another grabbed him by the feet and dragged him through the dust. Another imitated a woman grinding corn. The spectators laughed and threw ears of corn at the feet of the clowns and were again rewarded with more entertainment. One clown ripped away the husks and ate it raw while another snatched the ear of corn from him resulting in an all-out brawl with both clowns eating as much dust and dirt as corn. The clowns were always a lesson to our children since they were a perfect example of how not to behave.

A group of children of all ages were seated and standing at the edge of the road, laughing hysterically at the clowns. At that moment a very fat middle-aged couple waddled across the road and stood directly in front of the children, blocking their view. The young ones struggled to see, but the wide bottoms of the couple, who stood side by side, made the viewing impossible. The children's delight turned to outrage, and yet respect for their elders prevented any verbal complaint.

A gentle nudge proved to be Nish't Ahote, who was aware of the situation and pointed to the clowns. Two of the clowns had seen what was happening and ripped off the sashes of two of the spectators nearby. They lumbered clumsily over to the wide-bottomed couple and blindfolded the couple, then pushed them to the ground into the dust. The children's laughter was rewarding to everyone, but the humiliation of the couple was complete. They picked up their cumbersome bodies out of the dust and faded into the crowd. Nish't Ahote's chiseled angular features softened in a wide smile, a smile I rarely saw, for we were too often in serious council with one another.

The end of the parade was nearing, and a lump formed in my throat as I saw who was next. Approaching were the Mayan dancers. Their access to colorful tropical bird plumage made their costumes the most spectacular in the parade. Their headdresses were so immense, I wondered how the small human head could bear such a burden. The feathers were extremely long and iridescent in their many colors, and fanned out from the headdress in a wide high rainbow. I immediately recalled my puberty rites, for my Mayan warrior was also built like these muscular dancers. His lean, trim body, I remembered so well, caused me fluttering feelings in my female anatomy, and suddenly I felt empty. There seemed to be something missing. I realized that what I longed for was for what happens between a man and a woman. I gazed at Nish't Ahote and as though knowing exactly what I was thinking, he turned. An unexplained energy flowed between us, and he smiled again, but this time for me. I knew he cared for me. The magical moment was broken, for one of the Mayan dancers had begun climbing a very tall pole, as tall as the five stories in our complex. He carried a small drum on a string around his neck, and all five of the dancers had removed their elaborate headdresses. The first dancer slowly made his way to the top of the pole, where upon reaching the top, he played the drum and did a dance. At the end of the dance he sat at the top and continued his chanting while four other dancers began slowly climbing up the pole to meet him. At the top they worked carefully with ropes and each tied a rope around his right ankle. When all was secure and all four were ready, they threw themselves upside down, circling the pole, gradually getting lower until they reached the ground. Cheering, stamping, and screaming could be heard from the spectators. The four resumed the music as the fifth dancer made his way back to the ground from his high perch. Again there was more screaming, cheering, clapping, and stamping.

The grand finale to the parade were our own snake dancers. There were three dancers who each carried a cottonwood shelter. Then there were six snake dancers. Each dancer wore a huge spray of red feathers attached to the top of the black ugly face masks. They wore leather kilts and strips of brown leather decorated with shells crossed diagonally on their chest. Their ankles, knees, and upper arms were banded in fringed leather trimmed with yellow shells. An additional fringed belt and sash trimmed with shells was wrapped at their waists. Huge turquoise necklaces adorned the costumes. The six dancers paired off, and one dancer reached into the cottonwood shelter to bring forth a snake. His partner danced close behind and distracted the reptile with his eagle feather snake whip. A circuit was made with each snake until a dance had been done with each snake. The snakes were then returned to their shelters while all the spectators cheered.

That marked the end of the parade, and the spectators dispersed to go to the four large complexes for social dancing and feasting. As Nish't Ahote took me by the elbow to escort me off the platform, I suddenly felt as though I was wrapped in a dark cloud. The cloud seemed to envelop my body, making me weak and shaky. I struggled for control. There was no reason for my feeling this way! My knees buckled, and my body began to quiver. Nish't Ahote stopped to ask, "Are you all right, little one? Has the excitement of the day been too much for you?"

At this point I realized I needed to sit down, and as my quivering increased I clutched Nish't Ahote's arm, saying, "Just let me rest! Please stop and let me rest!" I noticed Puppy's ears were laid back, and he sat looking at me with his tail between his hind feet, for he knew something was not right.

We stopped along the side of the road. I closed my eyes and held tightly to Nish't Ahote's arm. An explosion of fire leaped at me through the dark cloud. I jerked out of my escort's arms. "Something is amiss! Something evil was happened or is going to happen. There are evil forces among us. I see fire! Someone must help! Oh, Nish't Ahote, do not think badly of me please! Just listen to me and do something!" I realized that to him I must sound as though I was babbling, but if anyone could understand, then he could.

Nish't Ahote looked at me with a deep concern. Sitting beside me, he pulled me to him and held me close, cradling me in his lap and soothing me. My shaking began to subside, and the dark cloud gradually dimmed. "Is there anything else you can tell me, my little Coyote Woman? Do you want to be taken to your room to rest?"

His body warmth and soothing manner pervaded me, and I calmed and lay my head against his chest. How I wished I could remain wrapped in his blanket of love and peace forever. I reveled at his touch as I felt his warm breath on my neck and ear. I murmured, "No, I do not need rest. All is well now! It's just that something is wrong. I've had these feelings before. I hope I do not embarrass you!"

"No, Shawanadese, the Gods have spoken to you. It is only a matter of time before we will know what they have said to you. I am overjoyed that you do not have a sickness."

For a few more minutes he held me. People passed by and looked at us curiously. Some probably thought I was sick, but some may have thought we were lovers. I wondered if I was creating problems for Nish't Ahote. I scrambled out of his grasp and stood up, brushing the dust off my robe. "It is time to go to the gathering in the plaza!" I exclaimed as Puppy leaped into my arms. "I am sorry to have caused you any concern!"

And so we walked together toward the feasting and dancing. As I crossed the threshold to the plaza, my parents waited at the side of the entrance. They beamed with pride and hugged me to them. Nish't Ahote used this opportunity to disappear into the crowd. My mother's beautiful hair was wound into

thick shiny black coils at each ear, and she looked
lovely in her tunic tied at one shoulder. She sported
a lovely turquoise necklace and earbobs, a shell ring
and bracelet. My father wore a kilt woven with bright
colors and a large turquoise pendant. An eagle feather
was stuck through his hair, which was pulled back at
the nape of the neck with a soft piece of leather. Since
my father was the quiet one in my family, my mother
was first to speak for both of them. "We are proud
to see that our daughter does well. You look wonderful, my child! A bit tired, perhaps, but you are truly
growing into a beautiful woman." She held me away
from her to look at me.

"No, Mother, I can not begin to compare to your
beauty. How I would like to come home to spend
some time with you and Father. It has been so long."

"Yes, my child, you must do that. You are our only
girl, and I have missed your companionship. My house
is empty since your brother has gone to live with his
wife's family. Please do come home for a visit. But
your brother is here! Let us find him!" With these
words, she took my hand and led Puppy and me with
Father trailing along behind into the plaza.

The courtyard was ablaze with activity. Many people had not seen each other for a full season cycle,
and many were catching up on all that had happened
since the last parade. We worked our way through the
crowd and finally spotted my brother. He was tall and
sinewy with long black hair caught at the nape of his
neck with yellow cotton. Like my father, he wore an
eagle feather inserted in the cotton at his neck. His
muscular body was clad only in a kilt and yucca sandals. I really did not know my brother well, for he
was four season cycles older than I. He had left home
as I did to go to school. Choviohoya was a warrior
and was called to duty only in time of emergency. He

lived in a very small house on the south road and farmed most of the time. He took my hand and looking me over, said, "The Gods are good. They have turned my baby sister into a beautiful woman. This is my wife."

Standing behind him was a sweet young woman not much older than I. She was small and delicate with large almond black eyes and a smile that displayed small pearly white teeth. Her hair was caught at her neck and coiled into a huge bun, while on her back she carried a papoose. I could hardly believe I had become an aunt. The baby was very tiny with black hair and eyes fringed with long black lashes. "Little sister, this is my wife, Kunya. She is of the deer clan. This child is the new addition to our family. Her name is Yamka. She is only two moons, but you see, she sleeps through anything." My brother chuckled and hugged me. "You must come to visit us someday to get to know your niece. As for me, I am hungry! Let us join in the feasting."

So saying, we worked our way toward the feasting table. Surely Aunt Mokni and the older women who cook had outdone themselves. The long table was covered with many kinds of food. There was antelope and mule deer roasting on a spit. They were being basted with water and herbs. There were huge flat serving dishes with roast turkey and rabbit. Pots of stew sent out their tempting aroma. As in all our feasts there were boiled breads, corn mush, dumplings in brine, thick lime-yeast cakes—no doubt made by Aunt Mokni—ash bread, corn pudding, squash, beans, bean cakes, wild berries, and pinyon nuts.

In a far corner of the plaza were the daredevil Mayan dancers. As I gazed at their lean, muscular bodies, my thoughts turned to my warrior. Would I ever see him again? Had he married some lucky woman? It was a pity that he had not come to this, our largest celebration. My thoughts were fleeting, however, for the musicians were beginning to play the large drum and were singing one of our favorite songs. Thus, the social dancing began.

For the first period of dancing, it was the men who asked the women to dance. They held their partner by the hand and danced beside each other with quick heel-toe steps. Altogether the couples formed a huge circle. My brother and his wife joined the circle and were followed by my mother and father. They danced, they said, to make room for more food. I stood to watch them thinking how long it had been since I had seen my mother, father, and brother together. My heart was warm with love when I felt a touch on my right arm. I turned to find Hototo standing next to me asking me to dance. We joined in the circle, his hand firmly holding mine. His firm touch caused thoughts of Nish't Ahote to run through my mind. Where was he? What was he doing? Of course his duties as the high sun priest demanded that he meet with everyone.

After some searching about, I saw Nish't Ahote, and graciously leaving Hototo, I made my way to ask Nish't Ahote to dance with me. As he took my hand, a heated energy went through me. I floated in happiness as we moved to the chanting and drum beat. Suddenly an exhausted, wretched figure came stumbling into the plaza. The dancing ceased, and Nish't Ahote pulled me violently toward the figure, whose breathing was raspy and whose body was bathed in sweat. He collapsed in a heap at Nish't Ahote's feet and babbled incoherently, "Burning! Storage bins!"

Nish't Ahote bent down and cradled him in his arms, telling someone to bring water.

"Take one breath at a time and calm down," Nish't Ahote said as the poor runner gasped for breath.

Water was brought with a cup and a cloth. After a drink and cool compresses on his head, he said, "Two granaries burned. Sentries dead—one still alive—north road—send help!" His eyes rolled in his head, and he fainted away.

Nish't Ahote instantly requested warrior volunteers. "Take a litter for the one still alive and be prepared for anything!"

My brother stepped forward, saying, "Let me have any warrior willing to go. We all leave immediately!" Many wanted to go, but my brother took only a handful of warriors. Thus our feasting and dancing came to a halt as we waited in anxious anticipation.

The runner was taken to the kiva for the healing of the sick, and Nish't Ahote grabbed my hand as we headed for the kiva. The fire keepers stoked the fire. The unconscious runner was laid on a rectangular stone bed covered with willow mats and cotton. I applied more cool compresses to his head as Nish't Ahote examined him. At length he reassured us that he was only exhausted and not sick. It was only a short while that he awakened and asked for a room in which to rest. The complex was full, but I offered my room saying I would find quarters with my parents or brother. So our fatigued runner was put to rest in my quarters. I packed what little I felt I would need to stay with my parents.

There was a superficiality now in the feasting, and no dancing was taking place. Everyone seemed to be waiting, concerned and anxious. There was a heaviness in the feelings of everyone. Some talked and ate, but it was only to bide time. The sun set, and I looked anxiously at Nish't Ahote. His chiseled features showed no emotion as we waited. This was a terrible way to end what should be a joyous occasion.

No one retired for the night. A pervading gloom

settled over the place. Our storage bins were very large. Everyone knew there would be a shortage of food during the snow season. The moon was rising high in the sky, and the stars shone brilliantly when at last we heard the approach of my brother, Choviohoya, and the warriors nearing the plaza. Everyone was still in anticipation. The warriors bore two litters. One was an old woman who babbled incoherently, and the other was of a sentinel. The old woman was taken into the healing kiva and placed near the fire on a mat laid on a pedestal. The sentinel had an ugly head laceration and a bleeding shoulder. He too was taken into the healing kiva and lowered onto the other stone pedestal covered with a mat. A huge fire roared between the two pedestals, giving intense warmth to the large sunken kiva.

An enormous jug sat on the floor close to the fire containing water that had been boiled. A smaller container sat next to it, and it was from this jug that Nish't Ahote bade me wash. When our hands were clean, he reached for his shaman supplies, selecting two very large crystals, which he placed at the head and feet of the babbling old woman with the faceted ends facing toward her worn-out body. He placed two smaller crystals in each of her hands, the facet of the crystal in the left hand toward her head, the other toward her feet. This would reestablish the balance of the woman's energy and cleanse her of negative and destructive thought patterns. Holding a large milky crystal over her head, he chanted, "All energy passes through you. You are all the energy. It all resides lovingly in your heart. Look within your heart, and you will know you are whole again." He repeated this over and over and moved the crystal to hold it over her heart. She gradually ceased her gibbering and sank into a deep sleep.

Meanwhile I was not idle. I bathed the sentinel's head wound and his bleeding shoulder to reveal an obsidian arrowhead embedded deeply in his shoulder. I also gave the man a straw from which he sipped a red liquid in a small bowl that was an infusion of willow bark. He waited patiently while chewing on a dried button containing an opiate.

When Nish't Ahote was sure the old woman was sleeping, he walked to the pedestal of the patient. Together Nish't Ahote and I chanted our healing song; the same one he had used to heal the young student with the diseased knee.

We repeated this several more times while the willow bark and opiate took effect and eased his pain. When enough time had passed, Nish't Ahote began. He again cleansed the head wound and packed it with an herb poultice. Then he bandaged it with cotton cloth tied around the patient's head. Nish't Ahote's brow glistened with perspiration as mine did, and I felt the sweat begin to roll under my breasts and arms to tickle by sides.

Nish't Ahote prodded the area around the embedded flint arrowhead. The patient winced. He mapped out with his fingers the incision he would make to remove it. He took a sharp obsidian knife in his hand and slashed straight across at the top of the foreign object and again at the bottom of it. As quickly as possible he inserted his fingers to grasp the flint. I mopped blood with one hand while my other rested on the forehead of our agonized patient. Nish't Ahote's fingers probed, then with one swift move he plucked the flint out of the shoulder. Instantly I moved to staunch the fresh flow of blood. I knew that the bleeding was good, for it cleansed and helped keep infection from setting in. The incisions were held open and washed out. I vigorously blew some of the red willow liquid into it and removed the button from the patient's mouth. I dipped a gourd of the red liquid and filled his mouth several times. Our patient's face was drawn and ashen in color while great beads of perspiration stood on his forehead. His breathing came in short, quick gasps. His grim expression never changed, for he was seeking to emulate the animal spirit guide of his ancestry.

Finally Nish't Ahote filled the openings with pinyon gum softened by the warmth of his breath. More of this gum was spread on narrow strips of cloth, and the wound was neatly closed as with a plaster. Then he sprinkled a yellow pollen and root powder over the wound and neatly bandaged the shoulder with clean cotton rags.

At this point the patient slept, the old woman slept, and the kiva was quiet. Once again, as I had often seen him do, he lay his heavy body across the patient as in a cross, extending his arms toward the patient's head and feet as he concentrated. His robe was soaked as was mine, but he vibrated and mumbled unintelligibly. Then looking at me almost as a stranger, he sat on the floor beside the young sentinel. He was exhausted as was I, and I sat quietly on the floor beside him. His eyes were closed. He opened his robe and allowed it to slip down to cover the lower half of his body. Seeing this, I moved to do the same. I closed my eyes and suddenly realized how very tired I also felt.

After a time, I could see that Nish't Ahote was in a trance and did not move. I quietly picked up my robes and descended the ladder to the outside world. The night was clear and chilled. Puppy waited for me at the bottom of the ladder. He bounded into my weary arms and licked my chin. I moved despondently under the milky sheet of stars and the full moon. Puppy whimpered, for he was getting older, and the natural urge to yelp and howl at the moon would get stronger as he matured. Then whatever could I do? He was wild and yearned to be free. Perhaps I would be forced to set him free.

There were still a few people in the plaza, but the celebration that ordinarily went on all night had died bleakly due to the unpleasant events. One couple stopped and asked, "Is all well?" I nodded and moved on toward my parents' rooms. Everyone was asleep. As I reclined on my mat in the center of the small room, my handsome brother sat up beside his wife and child. He was not sleeping. As exhausted as we both were, we could neither one sleep. As he realized that I too, was unable to sleep, he came quietly to sit on my mat.

"Shawanadese, you are not sleeping. Come sit on my other mat so as not to disturb everyone in this small room."

He moved back to his mat, and I picked up my cotton cover. I threw my cotton blanket over my shoulders and joined him on his mat. In whispered tones we talked.

"I am proud that my little sister has come a long way to become assistant to the sun priest. But tell me! How are the old woman and the sentinel? I have been much concerned."

"They are fine at the moment. The old woman's babbling is probably due to shock, but only the Gods can tell. Our sentinel's wound should have been cared for right away. Let us hope the evil spirits did not find the time to enter his head or shoulder."

There was a thoughtful pause in our conversation. "Choviohoya, what did you find when you saw the storage bins?"

"A small burned pueblo nearby was where I found the old woman. The sentinel must be her grandson, for no one was at home to protect her, and she had been so badly frightened as she hid in the room of refuse that she has babbled since. Who can tell how many the raiders? Fortunately there was little additional to burn around the small pueblo and storage bins, so although the destruction was complete, it died out and did not spread. There was only the charred, smoldering remains when we arrived."

"And the sentinel? How did he escape death?" I asked.

"I can only guess! Perhaps the raiders took him for dead due to his head wound. It may have been this blessing that gave him the chance to escape. We found him quite a distance from the granaries under a canyon ledge looking as though dead."

"So you saw none of the raiders?" I asked inquisitively.

"No, but our sentinel said at a more coherent moment that there were many. Perhaps when he is better, the Gods willing, he can tell us more."

"Yes," I quietly answered.

He did not talk anymore, and a silence ensued. Then quietly my brother said, "Shall we try once more for sleep?"

"Yes, for it is late and who knows what the sunrise may bring." I picked up my tired body wrapped in my blanket and retired once again to my mat.

The sunrise was too soon for everyone. A small table in comparison to the feasting of the night before was set up with corn cakes and honey for breakfast. Huge, flat straw plates were filled with pemmican. This was made of venison, venison fat, cornmeal, and herbs, and was taken by all the travelers since it was an easy, quick energizing meal. The runner had long since vacated my room, and seemed to have gone on his way. My parents were packing as were my brother and his sweet wife. They were ready to depart. We embraced and bid our good-byes.

Returning to my room, I decided to meditate with my crystal. I plucked it from the hanging shelf in my room and sat cross-legged on my mat. The tragic events had left me with a strange feeling of responsibility—one I could not define through fact, but one that intuitively I knew was so. How, I pondered, could we supplement the shortage that would result in the cold months. These granaries would have fed many of our people. Something had to be done!

I clutched my crystal possessively and received a warm glow through my body. I was enjoying this warm glow when a messenger dropped down my ladder saying, "I am sent to inform you of a council meeting at sundown in the usual kiva." He efficiently made his statement and ascended the ladder from which he had come. Instantaneously awakened from my trance, I remembered that several moons ago when I was in my womanly cycle, I had found a long bean pod.

Chapter 6

Coyote Woman

Three elders were assembled on the perimeter bench of the kiva. Two of them were carrying in the old priest, Taweyah, who had been very sickly and therefore unable to attend any former meetings. They seated him carefully on the floor of the kiva. A great fire roared in the fire pit. The kiva was very warm and dry, and the burning pinyon and juniper emitted a clean but musky fragrance. Nish't Ahote was standing by the fire, and Hototo was not far from him. All of them seemed to be in deep contemplation. It was as though they waited for me. Strange!

"The seriousness of the events today should not be underestimated. For this reason we are assembled in an emergency meeting to reconsider old decisions and make some new decisions," solemnly stated Honani.

Salavi, another elder, said, "With the destruction of our two granaries, feeding the people through the snow months shall be a problem. Of course we must rebuild them immediately. Perhaps some old plans should be changed or postponed. We must also take measures to see that it cannot happen again."

There was a short period of silence that was broken by Noona, head of our trading, who said, "We should consider delaying the construction of our additional storage rooms and also on the new large kiva. The wood being cut now cannot wait till spring for usage but must be used at once for the new granaries."

In his slow deliberating manner, Nish't Ahote's deep voice commanded everyone's attention. "The kiva must be built later, but the additional storage rooms must be erected sooner, for they provide storage for additional turquoise, which can be traded for grain."

There was a murmur of agreement among all. The designer of buildings, whose name was Wikwavi, stated, "I shall draw up plans for two new granaries and plan the storage rooms. Construction shall begin immediately."

Salavi rose from the bench. "We must send out traders laden with extra turquoise southwest to the Hohokam, south and southeast to the Mogollan and to the large Mayan trading center still farther south. Extra warriors must be sent with the traders to guard them. Additional men must be sent to bear the burden of transporting the grain for which we trade. All must be done with much haste before the snow season makes travel impossible. We must pray that the Gods postpone the bitter cold and the snow."

During the next thoughtful silence, I struggled with the thought of speaking. I had never asked Nish't Ahote my rights in the council meetings. Being in doubt, I quietly moved closer to him, placing the bean pod in his hand. His eyes looked at the object I had placed in his hand, then looked at me with a smile and a twinkle. To the chief of trade he addressed himself. "My able assistant has placed a bean pod in my hand to remind me that those beans are a staple in the diet of the Hohokam. Inform your traders that we will accept these beans in trade as well as grain."

Thus, with heavy hearts, the council meeting ad-

journed. There was much to be done and little time
in which to do it.

I could not sleep! I tossed and turned. Puppy was
also restless. There was a chill in the air, and my
feather blanket and cotton throws were tossed in
many directions as I churned on my mat. Puppy
whined sensing my distress. After what seemed like
forever, but in actuality was only a short time, Nish't
Ahote descended my ladder. He sat at the end of my
mat. "It looks as though you are not sleeping! I also
cannot sleep. There is much to discuss," he said
quietly.

I sat up. My body was naked and bathed in sweat.
"Yes, revered one, there is much to say." I drew a
cotton blanket up to cover my nakedness and to ward
off the chill in the air.

"Do not cover your body on my account!" said
Nish't Ahote, though he plucked at his robe and
seemed very nervous.

"I cover my body because of the chill. I would have
no reason to hide it from you," I said as I looked at
him inquisitively.

"You are lovely to behold even in your disarray,
but we must speak of another issue. I know that you,
Shawanadese, our 'Coyote Woman', had a vision after
the parade. There was nothing I could do about it at
the time, but Hototo and I were concerned for your
welfare. Are you well tonight?"

"I cannot say, Nish't Ahote. My mind tumbles and
turns as does my body, and I cannot sleep!"

He took my hand in his, which had an immediate
calming affect. Then he took his other hand and
placed it on my forehead. I felt an overwhelming
peace taking hold of my body. My breasts hardened,
and I looked at him adoringly. He bent down to my
mouth and tenderly took it into his own, tasting and

probing searchingly. His hand traced my breasts again and wandered around my waist and to my most private parts—the parts my warrior had awakened. He touched my female spot—"my spot of power." He traced light circles around it while his mouth probed mine. I trembled, I shivered, and a strange full feeling overtook me. I felt as though I might burst, or as though I might have even passed on to the next world. I was flying again, but could not tell where I was going. He placed my hand on his excited member, and I caressed him. He seemed about to burst and was perhaps even more enlarged than my warrior had been. I wondered why he did not insert himself as my warrior had done.

Then he removed my hand and stopped to look at me. His eyes kissed mine with a burning passion. "Little one, I adore you. You are a natural shaman. Your sensitivity, for your age, overwhelms me, and I feel in you the path of power."

My mind was in another world at that moment, and I said to him, "Why do we stop? What do you mean the 'path of power'? Is this like my 'spot of power'?"

"Your 'spot of power' is as another world. Your mind moves into another world as does mine when you touch me. You will learn the 'path of power', for it is already in you."

With that he gently pushed me from him and held me at arm's length to look at me with a warm and loving expression.

It was as though nothing had happened between us. I stared at him and wondered at the power of this man. A kind of terrible frustration—one I could not begin to describe—overwhelmed me. Once again he kissed me on the forehead and ascended the ladder, leaving me with my disheveled bed. I tossed and turned the remainder of the night.

I found it was time for my womanly cycle once again. I packed my basket with additional covers and even a feather blanket to take to my retreat. The day was warm, but the nights were getting quite cold, and I needed a fire to warm Puppy and me through the night. With the heavy weight of extra provisions it took longer to reach my secluded spot, as it required more frequent stops along the way to ease the stress on my forehead and neck from the straps. Puppy and I followed the flat valley bisected by a deep-sided arroyo as the sun began its gradual descent toward the western horizon. The strong red tones of the rocks were contrasted with the soft tones of valley sand, sage, and grass. Within the arroyo were striking patches of green, and giant cottonwoods that would soon turn the color of the canyon walls to usher in the dry cold of the snow season. The occasional pinyon pines would be the only green to struggle through the snow season to offer hope of the coming warmth of the planting season.

Just before dark we arrived at my little cave, which was becoming very special to me. It was my meditation place and offered peace and solitude. Puppy was old enough now to fend for himself. He scampered playfully over the rocky terrain, pushing his nose between and under the rocks to find crickets and grasshoppers to eat while I gathered firewood. By dark I had built a fire and settled my belongings in the protection of the cave. Darkness arrived much earlier now, for the angle of the sun was not as direct. I stayed awake to stoke the fire to keep it from becoming ashès by the chill of the morning.

Puppy jumped into my lap as I sat down in front of the fire. He licked me and squirmed for quite a while, then finally settled down for a short nap. I reached for my medicine bag and withdrew my crystal. It was milky at the bottom where it had been joined to Earth Mother and very clear at the facet. I held it in my left hand, noticing the prisms of color that seemed to be dancing in the firelight. I closed my hand over it and stared into the fire for a time. It sent vibrations through my hand and into my body, giving me a calm sense of well-being. All was well at that moment, but I wondered if all would be well toward the end of the snow season? Would my people be hungry and sick, or would the traders arrive back safely and with some success in acquiring additional grain? The Rain Gods were so fickle! I hoped the Mogollan or Hohokam or Mayans would have enough to feed their people and some of ours, too. I could only pray. After doing so, I stoked the fire and reclined for the night. Puppy snuggled close to my side under my warm feather blanket.

I remained under my covers until the sun offered warmth outside the cave. Puppy had long been gone, probably routing his breakfast out of the rocks. I waited awhile longer, then went outside to relieve myself. The air was brisk but the sun was hot, so I wandered down to the wash. There was not a lot of water in it, but I cleansed the best I could. Then feeling refreshed, I returned leisurely to the cave. As the day progressed, I chiseled at my picture mural and walked the land with Puppy at my side. At one point I climbed down into an arroyo and glimpsed a pile of tufts sunken toward the earth after the rainy season. My sandals were engulfed with the fluffy compact stuff when I saw a white stalk sticking up in the upturned down. I picked it out of the fluff to find it was a magnificent eagle feather—obviously one for my medicine pouch. It glimmered in the sunlight, and I praised the Gods for leading me to it.

Then suddenly through a mist, an eagle soared. He

loomed into my vision and perched on what, I did not
know, and stared at me. I did not feel intimidated. He
moved to the left of my vision, then to the right, then
took off as he looked back at me. I slowly got up and
returned to my cave, feeling a strength I could not
begin to describe. So my day, which began as very
routine, ended with my vision. I did not know what it
meant. I only knew I felt strong, and I thanked the
Gods for an unpredictable and fascinating day. It was
with this kind of feeling that I retired for the night.

When my three days were over and Puppy and I
returned to the complex, my thoughts returned to my
vision. When I was alone in my room, I picked up my
eagle feather and stared at it, as I had for the past
few days. Intuitively I knew it was powerful. The eagle
was a most revered bird. It soared in flight higher than
any other and so was able to converse and transmit
messages to the Gods above. When I held the feather
and meditated, I felt a power and a peacefulness I
could not explain—a feeling of well-being. When I
combined this with the crystal, I was complete, whole,
and lacking nothing.

Aunt Mokni, I thought suddenly. She was wise! I
had talked with her before. I rushed across the complex to the cooking area. Mokni was at the metate,
mindlessly grinding corn. There were two older
women on either side of her, and they were singing
together as they ground the corn. I thought perhaps I
should not bother her. I began to move away, but she
saw me and said, "Ho, sweet one, where do you go
and what can I do for you?"

"Mokni, I don't wish to bother you!"

"If you do not wish to bother me, child, then why
are you here?" She stopped her grinding, wiped her
hands on her cotton skirt, and proclaimed, "My

friends, please give my niece and me some time together. She comes to talk, and I would have some time with her."

The women, who seemed grateful for the break, backed out the door into another cooking room. Mokni took my hand and led me to a corner where we sat on a mat. "So, my sweet, what is on your mind?" Her eyes twinkled as she peered at me through hooded, wrinkled lids.

Her radiant warmth enveloped me, and I quietly asked, "Aunt Mokni, is it wise to speak of visions?"

"I have never heard otherwise," she stated in a very matter-of-fact manner.

"Then, I must ask you! Is it possible to have more than one spirit guide?"

"My child, everything is possible in this, our fourth world. We emerged to discover wondrous delights in this world we live in. Do you wish to tell me more?"

"No, only that I am restless. Nish't Ahote says that coyote is my spirit guide, but I have seen an eagle who beckoned to me, and I am confused."

"My child, I have only one spirit guide, that of the owl. But I am told shamans sometimes have several spirit guides. They must, according to their role and as need requires, give much energy to others. Thus they often have more than one spirit guide." She offered me a corn cake and gave Puppy, who waited for me outside the cooking area, a bone on which to gnaw. "Are you certain that is all that bothers you?"

"Yes, I think so!" I said hesitatingly. "Yes, that is all that troubles me, Aunt Mokni."

"I do not think you speak truthfully! I sense something more amiss. Is it possible that you are not happy in your world of men? Perhaps you should be married as any other young girl your age would be. It is a lonely life, is it not?"

"Yes, but I am surrounded by warm caring. It's just that—"

"My sweet, at your age the newly awakened sexual energy flows in your blood. Wait and you will see. Good things come to those who wait."

"Oh, Aunt Mokni, it is so good to have someone to talk to. There is nowhere else I can get a woman's point of view. I am so glad you are here, and I hope I am not a bother."

"The gossip flies around here all the time, but much of it is just that. Owl has told me to listen but to keep my mouth shut. Please feel free to come to me anytime!" She looked at me as a wise old owl looks at the world.

I hugged her and taking my corn cake with me, I departed for my quarters again with Puppy bouncing and leaping at my heels.

My Mayan language studies were going well. My teacher told me there were written signs of the Mayan that were very complicated and not necessary for me to know. He said I would do well enough just learning to speak the language. He told me something of their ways, and I learned that they do not regard human life the same way as the Anasazi. We sacrifice birds and dogs, but they sacrifice human lives in their ceremonials and view human blood as sacred, something that the Gods crave as appeasement. He spoke of the men piercing their ears, nose, and penis to draw blood to appease the Gods. My stomach turned as I heard this, and my thoughts turned to my warrior. How could such a tender, loving, seemingly caring person not be revolted by such actions? Were the Mayans really that bloodthirsty? I knew when I saw him again—why was I assuming that I would see him again? Did I really want to see him, having learned these things? Perhaps I would be wise to put him from my mind, for I could never condone, or even understand, the beliefs of the Mayans.

That night my dreams were filled with things that were happening to Nish't Ahote. I awoke to a feeling of unrest. I felt totally apprehensive. I seized my crystal to help me to calm and center myself.

My crystal exuded its warmth and left me with the feeling that somehow things were different than they had been during my puberty rites, for my respect and love for Nish't Ahote had grown. I knew that whatever came I must be the master of my fate.

An acolyte announced the arrival of my guest. I had washed and dressed, but I wore no jewelry or any other adornment. Soft footsteps descended my ladder. I kept my eyes closed, for I was so unsure of my feelings.

There was a long pause of silence. Then the person said, "Daughter of the stars. I bring you greetings once more. You are truly a beautiful daughter of the Anasazi."

I closed my eyes again, realizing I knew very little of the Mayan language. I was fully aware, however, that I could not just ignore my visitor. I opened my eyes to a vision I would never have expected.

His hair was done in two plaits that coiled at the nape of his neck. On his forehead his hair was cut in fringe. His high cheekbones and dark obsidian eyes— yes, Nish't Ahote's eyes—penetrated my being to the core. His mouth was the same sensuous mouth I remembered. His body was painted red and black, which my Mayan language instructor had told me were a warrior's body colors. That this man was of humble origin was obvious, since he did not display the crossed eyes and flattened skull of the elite in Mayan society. He wore a breechcloth in a striking pattern, and his body exuded a muscular strength that could only have come from vigorous physical activity. He wore massive silver earrings and a bone necklace. His entire demeanor was such that I was overwhelmed. It was then that I noticed that his left nostril had been pierced with a hole in which a lovely yellow stone had been inserted. I found myself staring. Never would I have thought my warrior might return. All emotion was suddenly drained from my being as I took in what seemed an apparition.

My use of the Mayan language was very limited, and so he signed. With his hands and body language he used the language of all the people—even the raiders.

"Are you surprised? I could not forget our night together." he said.

"Yes, I am very much surprised," I signed, as I stared rather rudely at his handsome maleness. I seemed unable to control my lust.

"I realized when we made love that you are a child of the stars. I have not been able to keep peace of mind. You have haunted my dreams. That is why I am here," he signed.

I shifted uneasily not quite knowing what to say next. My devotion and role as Nish't Ahote's assistant weighed heavily on my mind. I wondered why Awonawilona was burdening me with such difficult choices. I knew I was in love with Nish't Ahote, but it was a difficult decision to make. Then suddenly I laughed aloud, for I did not even know his name.

"Why do you laugh?" he asked with a surprised look on his face.

"I laugh because I do not even know your name."

Giving a deep-throated chuckle, he signed and said, "My name is Eeetspapoka. In our language it means

'Obsidian Shield.' " He withdrew a small leather bag
from his breechcloth. Turning to me he whispered
softly, "I hope you will accept these as a symbol of
my caring and sincerity." He took from the bag orna-
ments for the ears made from a yellow metal that was
shaped to resemble an eagle. There was a green stone
in the lower part of each one that was the jade of
which my Mayan teacher had spoken. They were a
truly beautiful power symbol. Then my mind turned
around, and I knew I could not accept them, however
beautiful they may have been.

I fingered them thoughtfully, then looking up at him
with misty eyes, I said, "I cannot accept these." I
turned my head so that I did not have to look at him.
I did not see his expression as he placed the lovely
strange earbobs back in their leather pouch, but I felt
he was disturbed by my rejection.

"Little one," he signed. It seemed strange that he
would call me the same pet name as Nish't Ahote. "I
will not leave until you know that I have not been
able to get you out of my mind's eye. I was with the
traders in the land of the Hohokam people when your
Anasazi traders arrived to bargain for grain. Perhaps
there are two reasons why I returned. One was the
thought that you and your people need help, and the
other is, of course, because of you. I would have you
as my first wife if you would so desire. I have loved
you from the first time I looked into those amber eyes.
Your eyes speak to me. They told me of your love
once before, and now they do not. There must be
someone else, and I can completely understand that
this would be, for you are lovely to look upon. I want
you to know I care. Again there is no other reason
for me to be here." He moved uneasily, as though he
was not certain of his next move.

I watched his compelling and yet nervous movements. He was truly beautiful to look upon, but surely he had to know it, for the Maya had many mirrors. A long period of time passed between us. I then said I was in need of attending other duties at that moment and I hoped he did not object if I excused myself. In reality, nothing was pressing at that time. I felt I needed to gather my thoughts.

He graciously took his leave of me, saying he desired to see me again at the same time on Sun Father's next journey. I watched his muscular body move up my ladder. When he was out of hearing distance, I let out a cry. "Awonawilona, why do you do this to me?" Without another thought I flew to Nish't Ahote.

I found him counseling a student, and I waited. When at last the student took his leave, I stood quietly waiting for Nish't Ahote to acknowledge my presence. He proceeded about his business in his usual way, as though he was unaware that I was there. I waited patiently and when at last he seemed ready, he said, "Yes, little one."

I was unsure what to say or even how to say anything, but at last it all came out in a waterfall of words. "Nish't Ahote, my visitor is one I could never have imagined. He is Mayan, and he comes in peace. He brought me a lovely gift, which I refused, and . . ."

"And he is your warrior," he said quietly.

I stopped as a short silence followed. I should have realized he would know, and I said so. I knew I had been babbling. Regaining my composure, I asked, "Nish't Ahote, is there anything you do not foresee? Does a shaman learn to know everything?"

"Little Coyote Woman, I only know that which I wish to know. I understand much about those who are near and meaningful in my life and little of those who are not."

Without hesitation I sat on his mat next to him placing my hand over his hand on his knee. He looked away as I took in his strongly chiseled handsome features. Even in profile I could read a melancholy expression in his eyes. The muscles on his face sagged a bit as he bit his full lower lip. Making an effort to feel brave, I said, "Nish't Ahote, I come to speak of my warrior who is called Eeetspapoka. He asks that I return with him to his homeland as his first wife. I do not want to leave either you or my people."

He turned to hold my eyes with his. I was acutely aware of his ability to read my innermost thoughts. The love in his eyes reflected pain. Could that pain have been due to the thought of losing me? I wanted him to take me in his arms to soothe my confusion, yet I was sure he would not, and I dared not ask. Then in answer to my thoughts, he stated, "Whether or not our own Coyote Woman wishes to remain Anasazi or to go with Eeetspapoka is a decision only she can make." He seemed to be withdrawing from me. Then he continued, "There is little I can say, for this is a decision that must be made by you alone. You know that I care, but I wish to remove myself from your company until you have made your decision." So saying, he dropped his sad heavy-lidded eyes from mine. I read in the tension of his muscles that he had nothing more to say.

After a short time of silence I knew I had been dismissed. My anxiousness was compounded by a strange depression, and I pressed my hand tightly around his and rose to take my leave.

The burden of my indecision weighed heavily on my shoulders. My thoughts were so intense that I almost blundered into two figures lost in the shadows in a corner of the complex. Even then, because they were both signing, I did not immediately recognize who the figures were. One was Eeetspapoka, and then my heart filled with dread as I realized the other was Wisoko, "the one who watches." Though the light was poor and I needed to make certain I remained hidden, I still was able to piece together what was happening.

Wisoko strutted like a proud bird waiting to attack. "Why don't you return to your own country! We don't need your kind of warmonger scum around the chosen people of peace!"

Eeetspapoka backed away only to find himself against one of our solidly built stone walls. He shifted uneasily and glared at Wisoko. His hands were clenched at his sides, and it was obvious he was using all his strength to contain himself. At last he signed: "If I were in Tula, I would challenge you to pay for your insults, but I am a visitor among you, the Anasazi, the people of peace. It would seem to me that you are the one who does not belong here."

Wisoko continued to strut like an angry turkey. He closed in on Eeetspapoka jabbing his index finger into his opponent's chest. "What does it take to get you to leave us? You show yourself off in all your ridiculous finery, putting stars in Coyote Woman's eyes. Not only are you a warmonger, but a whoremonger. You are too pretty to fight!"

With that Wisoko withdrew a knife from his robe and would have mortally wounded Eeetspapoka were it not for the warrior's quick reflexes. He moved aside quickly enough that the knife only grazed his arm.

Shocked at seeing his own blood, Eeetspapoka lost the control he had worked so hard to contain. Having no other choice but to defend himself, he seized Wisoko's wrist that held the knife. Bringing his knee upward, he struck Wisoko in the groin. Wisoko bent double and gave Eeetspapoka time to land a hard fist

in Wisoko's right cheek, narrowly missing his temple.
Wisoko landed on the hard earth and did not move.
Eeetspapoka calmly walked away.

I shivered with fear of being discovered should Wisoko regain consciousness. I knew I could not return to Nish't Ahote after having been dismissed. My only choice was to back up and circle around Wisoko.

Upon reaching my room my mind was obsessed with thought of Eeetspapoka and Nish't Ahote. Focusing on the songs to be learned for the Solstice Ceremony was nearly impossible. I did not sleep well. I tossed and turned until at last a very light sleep overtook me, but for only a short time.

I awoke to accompany Nish't Ahote as he tracked the rise of Tawa, Sun Father, at the onset of his journey. Few words passed between us, for there was little we had not already said. I took my leave of him very slowly, waiting to see if he might show any sign of affection. When it was apparent that he had no such intention, I climbed out of the sun kiva and headed toward the kiva for healing. One of our acolytes had an acute respiratory ailment, and had requested my attendance. I spent a generous amount of time applying herbal packs to his chest and using touch healing. I then returned to my quarters once again.

En route to my time of solitude in my room, I ran across the path of my beloved Puppy. He begged to be held, and I picked him up and took him down my ladder to keep me company. At that time of indecision his warm company was welcome. He was, after all, my first spirit guide. Perhaps he might help me in my plight.

We settled on my mat. He nudged my shoulder, my neck, and my chin. Then he settled in front of me on my mat with his head in my lap. He looked up at me with dark brown liquid eyes of adoration, then closed his eyes. I placed my hands lightly on his head, and he appeared soothed. In that manner I meditated. My eyes also closed to shut out the light of the fourth world. A feeling of confidence gradually overtook me, followed by a brilliant white light that enveloped me. Suddenly the way was clear. It became obvious that I never really had any doubts, for I had always known the path I would take.

Feeling at long last a comforting peace, I was interrupted in my serenity by Puppy, who had become restless. Opening my eyes, I saw that Puppy was upset because there was someone else present. Eeetspapoka's tall muscular form stood quietly close by while Puppy fidgeted and pranced. He did not growl or snarl, which I took as a sign that Puppy detected no negative vibrations from my warrior. Puppy made it obvious that he wanted to be free and out of the confines of my room. Once again I tucked his little body under my arm and climbed the ladder, holding the ladder with my free hand.

After giving Puppy his freedom, I returned to Eeetspapoka, who was as strikingly handsome as ever. Once again I took sharp notice of the golden yellow stone in his left nostril. I recalled my Mayan teacher's lesson that explained, to the Mayans that type of ornament was used to control the flow of strength in and out of the natural breathing orifices.

He greeted me warmly. "Coyote Woman, you are as beautiful as ever. You create beauty wherever you go. Have you had enough time to sort out your feelings? I am in no hurry. I can wait as long as is necessary."

"Eeetspapoka, my decision cannot wait, for my people are already in the sixteen sun cycles of our Solstice Ceremony. My responsibilities are many." I paused to sit upon my mat and motioned him to sit next to me.

When we were settled, I continued. "If I leave my people, I shall create an emptiness in our community and, in fact, within the very structure of our people. In that empty space, the evil spirits would find a point of entry into many lives in our society. For this I have great concern."

He waited a short period of time to give me time to say more. Then noticing my silence, he asked, "But what of the inner desires of Coyote Woman? Do you not consider your own personal welfare? What do you really feel?" He placed his warm ringed fingers on my cheek. I jolted at his touch. Softly he said, "Yes, the fire is still there. Can we ignore it?"

"I must ignore it!" I realized my voice was louder than usual, and so once again I paused to regain my reserve. When at last I felt in control, I began again. "Eeetspapoka, my blood is Anasazi. I cannot desert my people. I have spent much sleepless time thinking this through."

He fingered the shell ring on his first finger. Then he softly replied, "You would not be deserting your people. Our union would only insure better trade relations between your people and mine. I can assure you, I would see to that."

"My loving warrior, the ways of my people are very different from yours. Though there are many similarities, there are also many differences—in fact, one very important basic difference. My people are a people of peace. We do not make war for any reason. Yours are a people whose culture is based on war. I could not be happy in that kind of life. I was brought up a child of peace. I could not live each day knowing that you may or may not return to me."

He quickly interceded. "We do not war to kill— only to capture."

"It is all the same. You still might not return to me,

and the entire idea of capturing for sacrificial purposes is repulsive to me."

A short period of silence followed as he seemed to be gathering his thoughts. Then very sadly he said, "I am very sorry you feel as you do. Your eyes tell me much of your inner feelings, sweet one, but why do your eyes shine when you speak of Nish't Ahote? Do you love him?"

"Yes, Eeetspapoka, I do. I cannot say more." And so the truth was out. I wondered how I could be drawn into the spell of two men.

As though reading my thoughts, my Mayan warrior touched my chin and brought my eyes up so that they met his. Our glances met, and he said, "I also love you. I have since the first time I saw you. I knew you had a special destiny. I hoped it might be with me, but perhaps this is not so. I envy Nish't Ahote." His face moved closer to mine as he spoke. I was enchanted. His lips touched mine as lightly as a feather. I felt lightning flow between us.

A very brief time of magic followed as he held my chin. Then his arms encircled me, and his lips seared mine with a heat that would not stop. His arms encircled me pinning me to the ground beneath the heat of his body. I responded eagerly as his lips moved onto my nipples. The flames were rising within me, and threatened to become unbearable. Then the vision of Nish't Ahote flashed in my mind's eye. I tensed and said, "No, my warrior, not now!" Gasping and trying to regain control, I pushed him away.

He followed my lead, sitting back on the mat looking at me with disappointment in his eyes. Once again I gained control, then stared at him with torment reflected in my eyes. His showed intense frustration. Once again, a quiet period followed as we both gathered our thoughts.

He broke the silence as he said almost in a whisper, "I want to love you, Coyote Woman."

"It cannot be," I answered. "I am sorry."

He rose to leave, then turned back with a thoughtful expression. "Perhaps you will visit me one day and feel less threatened. If you are ever in Tula, please do not forget me. I would be delighted to accommodate you—show you our magnificent country." Then as though suddenly struck by the words of a spirit guide, he added, "We will meet again—in Mayan country. I will wait."

Turning, he hastily climbed the ladder out into the enormous world that beckons all souls with a lust for travel.

Chapter 7

New Fire Ceremony and Races

Nish't Ahote had calculated that it was time for the New Fire Ceremony, the sacred races, and the closing of the roads. This was an eight-day ceremony with an additional eight days of preparation. We celebrated this ceremony when the harvest was over and the work of our plating year was done. It was celebrated one moon before the solstice. Once again many of our people came to join us in this—the center of our culture. Each clan made prayer sticks over which they prayed and smoked for three days. Then the eight days of preparation began. I accompanied Nish't Ahote as he smoked and prayed with his prayer sticks. Then messengers from each complex all over our culture, whose vastness spanned many running days, announced from the rooftops that the sacred days were beginning.

We erected our altar. All in it was representative of the north, east, south, and west, or fire, earth, water, and air, the elements of our sacred fourth world. In front of the altar was a sacred statue of a man who held his bow and arrow. The carving was of Awonawilona, the creator. The priests prepared special sacred pieces of round wood painted white to represent the purity of creation. One end was painted green, representing vegetation, with two additional blue lines to denote water. Tied in the center was a perfect ear of corn representing man, and hung from the center was a ball of soil wrapped in cotton representing the earth. There were four of these. Nish't Ahote, our revered sun priest, carried the second largest, but the really large one—almost the length of a man, was laid at the door of our kiva to identify it as the holy kiva.

Thus the fire ceremony began. With fire life began. So now on this first cold dawn of creation, a fire was lit kindled by flint and native cotton. Wood had been stacked, for it was necessary that it burn for eight full days. The fire represented the sun, who projected its germinating warmth to earth and mankind. This took place before the sun rose, and brands from the new fire were carried to each of the other kivas in all our large complexes.

Meanwhile, above our kiva, preparations were being made for the sacred races. Shrines were prepared on the east, west, and north roads. Three large round stones with a prayer stick denoted the three worlds from which we came, and marked the boundaries for the races. After these races would be the conclusion to our ceremony, which was the closing of the roads. Then for three sun cycles all roads would be closed to travelers or trespassers, or they would die immediately. So began our celebrations.

The first four sun cycles were spent in fasting, prayer, meditation, and ritual songs. On the evening of the ninth sun cycle, Nish't Ahote rose and said, "If I am right, during my duties tomorrow, there will be many clouds to gather around me." He then retreated into prayer and meditation once again. The next day in the evening the clouds were piling up in a rosy sunset on the horizon. The prayers continued until it was the day of the races.

My mind was so full of preparations for the coming events that I had all but forgotten the return of my warrior and his clash with Wisoko. I had prepared the three prayer sticks that would mark the boundaries for the races in my room while Puppy played with an old sandal. Leaving Puppy busily frisking his play toy, I ran from the ladder of my room across the plaza to the altar. As I turned a corner, I ran headlong into Wisoko.

I clutched the prayer sticks to my bosom as my heart skipped a beat. His eyes were only slits as he grabbed my shoulders.

"Ho, Sun Priest's Assistant, what's your hurry?" His fingers dug into my shoulders. I took a deep breath and tried not to let him know he was hurting me.

"I go to prepare for the races!" I answered.

"And what is that you hold so tightly?" he asked as he at last released my shoulders.

"Why the prayer sticks to mark the boundaries for the race."

"Why do you clutch them so tightly when you must know they are worthless."

I stared at him unbelievingly. "You blaspheme to speak as you do!"

"Believe as you will. The Gods really do not care! Such is my belief, and I must be on my way."

He left me speechless with feelings of sorrow that he could be so out of balance.

The three roads were open, and there was to be a priest at the halfway point with holy water in a container. The sacred shrines marked the end of the run, and the runners were ready. They were supposed to be the fastest runners in all the complexes.

The day of the races was hot, but the air was cool—perfect for running—and there was anticipation in the air. The starting point was seven laps out on each road. Nish't Ahote marked the north road with cornmeal at the starting point with a line running east to west. He blessed all the runners and trotted toward the finish line at our holy kiva. About halfway in he was met by an elder who handed him prayer sticks and a small jar of sacred water. When the lead runner arrived, Nish't Ahote would hand him the prayer sticks and water jar. He would say "Bless you, my son. Carry these to our blessed home!" If another runner caught up to the lead runner, he must turn the jar and sticks over and say the same to the new leading runner. Hototo had made the same preparations from the west road, and the aged priest had been carried on a litter to do the same on the east road. The south road was left open, for it was from the south road that we received most of our traders.

Each road had a starter who swung an eagle feather to begin the races. The beginning of the race was not very exciting, for most of the crowd patiently waited in groups fairly close to the finish line. Gradually, one at a time or in small groups, the runners appeared over the curve of the roads. Tremors of excitement rippled through the crowd. Men along the sides of the road urged the runners on while waving cornstalks and squash vines. Near the finish line were elders who whirled sticks on strings that simulated the roaring sound of low thunder. When the winner reached the kiva and disappeared into it, the men in the crowd above threw their cornstalks and squash vines into a pile. The women and children scrambled to grab a stalk, vine, leaf, or tendril to carry home. The winner awaited the arrival of Nish't Ahote or the aged priest or Hototo to be blessed, then quietly slipped to his home, if it was close by, to plant his prayer sticks and jar of water in his family's fields.

There was much joking, ribald calls, and laughter. Not to be outdone, the young girls prepared for their race, which came much later after the boys race. Again the procedure was the same. A young girl was able to enter this race only until she began to flower, for most were too shy to run naked at the onset of womanhood. These two races took up most of the shortened sun cycle and were symbolic in two ways. First they were a salute to rainmaker and cornmother, but more important each road designated the energy source of man. Each road represented the backbone or spine of man through which all sacred energy flows. There is masculine and feminine energy in each of us, which was symbolized by the boys and girls races. Thus ended the sun cycle of the sacred races. Everyone retired to eat and enjoy much needed rest for the remaining three ceremony sun cycles.

While all this had been going on, preparations had been made for the closing of the roads. This was done symbolically to denote the fact that we, the people, were hibernating, as were the animals, and that we protected what is ours from invaders and raiders. At sundown on the fifteenth sun cycle, an elder emerged from the kiva to close each road by drawing four lines with sacred cornmeal to seal the roads from any evil power during the last part of our celebration. If a man crossed these sacred lines, he was to be torn asunder, for he did not respect our cultural festivities and deserved to die. Any friendly travelers or traders knew to use the south road if they needed to reach us at that time.

At sundown on the fourteenth sun cycle, Nish't Ahote emerged from the kiva. He made a long symbolic journey to the shrines, and in this circle he made a journey to the world beyond. At this point all spirits gave their blessings to not just our people, but all people and living creatures on earth. At dawn he stood at the top of the most sacred kiva and said to the people, "Sing praises and prepare the food. Sing praises with your voice, body, and feet and make ready. That being done, bring eagle feathers you may have, and think in doing so that your actions shall be in harmony throughout this world of ours. Then emerge from your kivas when the sun is overhead to bring your blessings to all."

Very soon, after the time when the sun was overhead, the elders and the priests and, of course, myself appeared from the ladder of the sacred kiva. Each elder was dressed as the animal that was his clan totem. I was "Coyote Woman," dressed in a coyote tail attached to my black mantra. Nish't Ahote had given me a necklace and earbobs of coyote teeth, and had made a mask of clay that resembled the head of the coyote.

Nish't Ahote was dressed in an antelope skin and horned headdress, which was his totem—or one of them. Hototo was dressed as a hawk. His headdress was as a bird, his arms were feathered. Together with the elders, each dressed according to their totem, we began our journey. A drummer dressed in a black mantra walked in the center of us to maintain a pulsating heartbeat rhythm. The song we sang was low and deep, accompanied by the power of the drum. The elders made four successive circuits around the complex from right to left, each smaller than the other, for this represented the cycles of the earth and its four directions. While they did this, we walked in four circuits from left to right, each smaller than the other, for this was the path of our Sun Father. Having accomplished this, we descended into the kiva again to carry on our ceremonial prayers until sundown.

Finally we began our star watch. As I descended the ladder, my knees felt weak and my hands and forehead felt cold and became beaded with perspiration. The night air was cold and crisp. There was no reason for me to be so warm and weak. I barely reached the top of the kiva, when my legs would no longer support me, and I collapsed in a swoon. Hototo was closest and caught me to break my fall. "Shawanadese, can you hear me?" he said desperately. Nish't Ahote and the elders gathered close by, and Nish't Ahote took my hand as he stooped over me.

"Shawanadese, what are you seeing, child? What is it this time?" pleaded Nish't Ahote.

I gathered my strength, and sitting up, I weakly rearranged my disarrayed mantra and struggled to rise. After a very short time I was again on my feet. "All I saw was evil on the roads and a dark form. What does this mean?" I asked of Nish't Ahote.

"Let us hope it means nothing, little one," Nish't Ahote said with a concerned and anxious look in his eyes.

Yet as the sun rose in the morning, an elder from one of our outliers approached us. He looked shaken. He stretched his hands toward Nish't Ahote and said, "Hear me, revered one. We saw an intruder—one who dared to travel on the north road."

"Was he one of us?" inquired Nish't Ahote.

"No, great one, if he had been one of us, he would have answered, 'I am I,' as we the people all know to do!"

So ended our fifteenth sun cycle of the New Fire Ceremony. I wondered if this unfortunate event was an omen. Everyone retired with uneasy thoughts, for we all awaited the evening. If we saw no double rainbow, then a curse was upon the people for the next year.

Even as I thought of the curse and its evil possibilities, I saw a figure wrapped in a dark cloak moving swiftly into the shadows of night. The figure was the same height as Wisoko. After my confrontation earlier with him, I felt somehow that he had had something to do with the intruder. I knew it was not he who was the intruder, for the intruder had been dismembered and his parts scattered as custom dictated. I was certain that Wisoko had somehow been connected with the event.

The sun began to set, and we anxiously awaited the appearance of a rainbow. From the southwest had blown clouds that sat heavily in the later time of the sun. There was a heavy gray area that looked like rain but was not close enough to give us moisture. Then in a short time it appeared. The colors in the sky began to share their brilliance, and colors gradually formed. All the people assembled on the rooftops to watch. A rainbow, its colors in the usual correct order, formed slowly and then, yes, slowly, another began to form. It never totally formed, but it was enough. Now we knew that all our rituals had been of positive thoughts, and somehow we would survive the winter and reap a successful harvest in the next season cycle. Nish't Ahote and Hototo took me by my elbows, and we moved back once more to the sacred kiva. It was then that from the corner of my eye, I saw a figure leaning against the wall not far away. Although no one else seemed to notice him, I was certain that the sour unhappy expression on Wisoko's face probably reflected the fact that he had been unsuccessful in his blasphemous efforts.

I felt a vibrant hand on my shoulder. I turned to

gaze into Nish't Ahote's warm, loving eyes, and I was held for what seemed like an eternity in that magnetic search that his eyes betrayed.

"Little one, the Gods have gifted you," he stated as he held my shoulders. "You knew of this foul deed on our sacred roads. Will you not share with me your feelings more frequently?"

"I have been meditating with my crystals, and a vision appeared saying I am foolish—that I should share another vision I had with you—that it is of great importance. I do not want to be rude and break up your observations. I am sorry!"

"Come, child, tell me of your vision. My hands will not leave your lovely shoulders until you speak of it to me." He grasped me holding me firmly.

"On the third day of my last womanly cycle Puppy and I took a walk. We stopped by a beautiful arroyo, and I shut my eyes to enjoy the peaceful silence. The sun was brilliant and reflected in the water of the arroyo. I descended a tunnel beneath the earth that opened into mountains surrounding a small lake. I felt as one with Awonawilona. Then an eagle loomed into my vision in flight. It perched right in front of me to stare at me. Then it turned to the left, then right, then flew away looking back at me. I think much about it trying to decipher its meaning. Now perhaps you will understand my preoccupation."

Nish't Ahote's eyes bore into my very soul. Then, breaking into a smile, he hugged me to him, running his hand soothingly over my hair. "Yay, little one! Now I understand. But why do you think on it so frequently? Do you not understand how to interpret this wonderful vision?"

Enjoying the warmth of his embrace, I made no attempt to withdraw from it. "But I am Coyote

Woman. The coyote is my spirit power animal. Can it be possible to have more than one?" I murmured.

"Let us sit down and speak of this," he said as we relaxed on his mat. "The coyote is a clever quick-witted animal. It is an animal of much stamina. These are also qualities you possess. But the eagle flies higher than all other birds and brings messages to the Gods. Yes, you may have more than one spirit power animal. A shaman has many of them, and through them, he finds his healing energy and understanding of his people. You should feel as a chosen one, for as the eagle rises in flight, so shall your star rise into the heavens. May your mind be at ease, my sweet one, for truly you are blessed—more than you know at this moment. But as your star rises in flight, you will grow to understand the wisdom of the Gods. Your inner growth will blossom as it flies like the eagle!" His big hand rested on my leg with his fingers pressuring my inner thigh.

A sense of joy and awe rushed through me. Then suddenly my good feelings became foreboding ones. It seemed very important that Nish't Ahote be aware of other dark feelings I had been experiencing for some time.

"O revered one, I am aware of my many blessings, but at times I think wisdom can be a curse."

"Little one, you surprise me at times. What is it that bothers you?"

Plucking up my courage, I answered, "There are some things you should know and that I have hesitated to speak of." My heart beat loudly perhaps because I did not want to speak falsely.

Softly he responded, "And those things are?"

Hesitatingly I answered, "As I brought the three prayer sticks to the altar for our races, I chanced upon Wisoko." It seemed impossible to continue.

Sensing my nervousness, Nish't Ahote said, "Continue, please, little one."

"It was during the time of the preparation of the altar for the New Fire Ceremony and races." I then related to Nish't Ahote how Wisoko had ridiculed the importance of the prayer sticks and also the fact that he believed the Gods really do not care. I also spoke of the dark-cloaked figure I had seen after the announcement of the intruder. I mentioned seeing Wisoko's sour unhappy face after the appearance of the intruder. Continuing on, I said, "I feel very strongly that Wisoko's bitter expression was due to his failure to blaspheme our ceremonies."

"Those are very strong accusations," he said. "It would be unwise to repeat this to anyone else."

"You may be certain I will not, but I still feel that though Wisoko was not the intruder, he somehow was responsible."

"Is there anything else you wish to tell me?" he asked as his piercing obsidian eyes looked into my soul.

I only hoped he would not see that there was more, for I felt that the fight between Eeetspapoka and Wisoko was not relative to the issue.

"No, Nish't Ahote, I think not. I must go. Puppy will be anxious."

Chapter 8

Witchcraft and Solstice Celebration

Soon we would celebrate the solstice, and like the New Fire Ceremony, it would require eight days of preparation. I was meditating in my room when a figure slowly worked her way down my ladder. It was Aunt Mokni, who picked at her deerskin shawl and shuffled when she looked me in the eye.

"Aunt Mokni! What an honor to have you visit me!" I exclaimed.

She embraced me and sat on my mat, continuing to pluck at her shawl as she began. "Shawanadese, I have heard some hearsay—it is only hearsay, but well!"

"What Aunt Mokni?" I asked anxiously.

"It seems that an elder from one of our outliers is visiting, and he has accused Hototo of sorcery. He claims many reasons, one of which is that Hototo was called to heal his son and his son died anyway! I don't know any more! I just thought that you being who you are, that maybe—" There was a pause. "You ought to know, I thought."

I sat cross-legged and stared at my hands on my knees as I flexed my fingers and thought. This was a tragedy, for Hototo was Nish't Ahote's nephew, and aside from the fact that I worked often with Hototo and had grown very fond of him, this made my heart ache for Nish't Ahote, for I knew it would not be easy for him. I longed to rush to him to find out if it was true.

"Aunt Mokni, I love you very much, and I am grateful to the Great Spirit that you have chosen to come to tell me of this rumor. I hope it is not true—I cannot imagine it to be true!" I said as I embraced her.

"My sweet, be careful, for everyone talks, and may it never be about you! I must not stay! I must go now!" she said. She tucked her skirts under her arm and ascended my ladder, leaving me with my tumultuous thoughts. I wasted no time finding Nish't Ahote in his observation kiva. I descended and sat down beside him on his stone bench. I placed my hand on his knee and quietly said, "Nish't Ahote, is it true that Hototo has been accused of witchcraft?" I inquired.

"Yes, little one, it is so. His case will be heard this evening, for it is time to begin the eight days of preparation for the solstice celebration. My heart is heavy for my nephew. The elder from the outlier of the rattlesnake claims that Hototo killed his young grandson. He says that Hototo has caused demons to enter his dreams and accuses Hototo of possessing owl feathers."

"This cannot be true! Have you spoken to Hototo?" I asked.

"Yes, and Hototo denies all of it. However, I do not believe he understands the seriousness of it all. Inwardly he may be in a turmoil, but outwardly he maintains his usual quiet reserve. I had not the heart to tell him that I cannot speak on his behalf, for he is my nephew. Now can you see how precarious are our positions, and how difficult it is to be a servant to the people?"

"Yes, I do understand. Is it right for me to speak to Hototo? Perhaps I could gather more details and gain better insight." I said as a new plan evolved in my mind.

Without waiting for an answer, I quietly ascended the ladder and walked resolutely to Hototo's quarters in the complex. I had decided not to tell Hototo that his uncle would not be able to speak on his behalf. I just offered myself as a friend who cared enough to want to know his side of the story.

Hototo's quarters were clean and sparse. An eagle feather and a crystal rested on a suspended shelf in the corner of his room. I found him sitting on a mat in what seemed to be deep meditation, but his face lit into a huge, surprised smile.

"What an unearthly vision I now perceive! Can it be that the Great Spirit, Awonawilona, sends a spirit to me?" he asked. He looked genuinely surprised.

I suddenly began to wonder if I should be here. The awful thought ran through my mind that he might be guilty. So I nervously picked at my clothing and waited.

"Can it be true?" he said as he looked at me inquisitively. "Are you really here?"

"Yes, Hototo, it is I. We have spent much time together, and I wish to hear your side of the story. You are my friend, and I feel sure you tell the truth."

"I have often wished you would come to my quarters to talk to me. I cannot believe it is really truly happening. But since the Great Spirit has sent an apparition, I most certainly will take the time to talk to you," he said.

"Hototo, I hope you realize the seriousness of your situation," I quietly remarked.

"I am not so terribly worried. I went to the outlier of the rattlesnake clan to heal a small child who had not been well all his life, and I did my best. He could not have been more than six season cycles of age, and his symptoms were of shortness of breath and fainting on occasion. He was as in a trance when I attended him, and I stayed several days in the house of the rattlesnake clan to do further treatments. After seven sun cycles I left, and very soon after that the child died. His grandfather doted on him and claimed to have had demonic dreams since his death. He wants to make me responsible to assuage his anger over the death of his grandson. The owl feathers are all hearsay. They may search my quarters and my body if they wish. I want no part of being involved in sorcery!" He looked at me with a sincerity in his eyes I could not deny.

I began to understand. Here was a man who was young and inexperienced, like myself. He saw the earth as basically pure and good, and had had no real confrontations until now. He knew he was right and felt that right always wins, but even I, at my young age, knew better. So I prodded him again.

"What more do you know of this child?" I asked.

"The child was born slowly. He did not cry out the life energy that most babies do, but had to be severely stimulated to grasp on to Earth Mother's energy. All during childhood he exhausted himself quickly after any physical activity and was forced to rest frequently. He was smaller and more delicate than most children and very quiet in everyday life. When his spirit left us, I felt sorry, but somewhat relieved, for he had always struggled to survive. I truly did the best I could." He looked at me despairingly.

My heart was wrenched, for truly he was a good person. He really did not comprehend the severity of the problem.

"Is it not probable that the child had a disorder

since birth and would have died anyway?" I asked him.

"It is not just probable! It was obvious that the child had a disorder with the life energy center and would not have lived a long life. This I cannot prove."

"And what of the owl feathers?" I asked.

"I know not why I am accused of having owl feathers. I am an educated person. I know of their evil. Perhaps the owl feathers are an extension of the old man's imagination due to his disturbance over the death of his grandson. I am sure the Gods will continue to watch over me as they have done before. Nish't Ahote will speak on my behalf."

I had not the heart to tell him that because Nish't Ahote was blood relation, he could not defend him. Instead I took both of his hands in mine and said, "I believe all that you say. When you speak on your own behalf, do not leave out any of the details you have told me. My heart is with you!"

It began snowing, and a thin blanket of white covered the plaza, lending its unearthly beauty to our world. Ordinarily the silence that only snow can bring was beautiful, but today it seemed almost ominous. Puppy rolled in the snow in a frolicking mood. This was the first snow he had seen in his short life, and if I was not so concerned with Hototo's problem, I might have played with him. There seemed to be a hushed silence over the entire complex. I spent the time until the sun returned to the horizon to rest in meditation. The sun rested very early in this season, and it was not long before I knew the elders, priests, and leaders were assembling in the main kiva for what should have been a routine meeting to discuss the solstice ceremony and the preparations necessary to bring the receding sun back to earth to warm the soil and ready it for planting. I entered the kiva with an anxious heart, for the elders were there, including the elder from the outlier of the clan of the rattlesnake, who was deep in conversation with the other elders in attendance. The old sun priest was brought in on his litter. Nish't Ahote was seated and waiting with Hototo at his side.

Nish't Ahote stood to announce the Solstice Ceremony that began the eight sun cycles of preparation. It was scheduled to begin when the sun next awakened. There was murmuring and nodding and a long silence. Then the elder from the rattlesnake clan stood saying, "My people, we have one among us who employs the power of the evil spirits. I wish permission to speak to that issue." Again there was silence and Nish't Ahote said, "Proceed."

The elder puffed out his chest and continued, "My grandson, who was seriously ill, was attended by our young shaman priest. For seven sun cycles our young priest was a guest in my home, and each day he administered his medicine to my grandson. On the seventh day, in spite of all of the shaman's power, the Great Spirit took my grandson to the next world. That should have been enough for my old heart to take, but no. My dreams each night were riddled with demons—demons who attempted to possess me. I cannot rid my sleep of these creatures. They always return. I cannot rest in peace. Never have I been visited by such demons before. I would submit the fact that our young shaman priest killed my grandson, and now attempts to kill me by these visiting demons." There was a horrified silence in the kiva. I glanced quickly at Nish't Ahote, who sat silently listening, and then to Hototo, who did not show much concern at all. He waited for Nish't Ahote to respond, but then the elder continued. "Furthermore, I am told by my other granddaughter that the young priest was in possession of owl feathers during the time that he was our guest. I believe he is a sorcerer, and we should deal with him accordingly!" With these dire words, he sat on the bench waiting for a response from anyone in the kiva.

No one moved. A hideous cloud hung over us all. When Nish't Ahote offered no response, Hototo started to become nervous. Machakwi rose saying, "This is a serious accusation, and one not to be taken lightly. Our priest's responsibilities are the most sacred of all. Their duties must be for the good of the people, not for their own gain. The management of that power must rise above all self-indulgence. Let us hear from our young priest. Let him speak for himself."

Slowly Hototo rose. All eyes were fastened on him. The fire reflected dancing shadows on the walls of the kiva. It was so quiet that each person's breathing could be heard. Hototo stated his side of the story as he had explained it to me. He did not discuss any possibilities, just hard facts. In conclusion, he gave permission for his quarters to be searched to prove that he possessed no owl feathers. Then he looked at Nish't Ahote anxiously once again to see if there would be any response. When there was none, he again resumed his sitting position on the bench.

I had been clutching my crystal during all those proceedings and after jamming it back into its leather pouch beneath my skirt, I rose to speak. All eyes turned my way, and I broke out in perspiration on my brow, beneath my breasts, and under my arms. Gathering my energy forces, I cleared my throat and began. "Witchcraft is a serious accusation! Oftentimes, things are not really as they would seem. Before anyone is condemned of witchcraft or sorcery, the entire picture should be examined. And who are we to allow ourselves to get caught up in a case such as this, when there are more critical problems to be discussed, such as the security and well-being of all our people? We are in the midst of a crisis where all could starve if we do not deal carefully.''

Nish't Ahote looked up suddenly at me and stared as did all others in the kiva. The accusing elder stood and pointed his finger at me. "Coyote Woman, you are impertinent and young. If this young priest is a sorcerer, then he can affect the well-being of us all. What say you to that?"

"Again I say things are not always as they seem! I may be impertinent and young, as you say, but I cannot stand by and watch this young man, whom we all love and respect, be condemned as a sorcerer without someone speaking on his behalf. So please! May I proceed?"

Again there was a period of silence. Then Machakwi stood and said very quietly, "Coyote Woman, this meeting is yours. Please continue."

I gathered my thoughts quickly. "Before you sits a quiet, loving, reserved young man. He has studied many years to be the shaman priest that he is. He came to the house of the rattlesnake at the request of the elder of that clan to do his best with the ailing grandson in that home. After seven sun cycles, that grandson, only twenty-four seasons old, was taken by the great spirit, Awanowilona, to discover the next world. For this child, death is a time of discovery. It is not a sad occasion, but should be a joyous occasion, according to the laws of our land. Has anyone thought to ask what the child's health problems may have been before he became critically sick? Perhaps the elder can answer these questions!"

Slowly the elder rose and said, "My grandson was not able to run and tumble with the other boys, it is true." Then seemingly he had no more to say and sat down again.

Leading on from this statement, I said, "I am told that when the child was born, he did not cry out the life energy as most babies do, but had to be especially treated in order to grasp on to the energies of Earth Mother. He rested frequently and became exhausted quickly in his childhood years. He was small and delicate and not of a robust nature. So I suggest that he was not intended long for this world, but was taken by Awanowilona to begin anew in a better, more comforting life than what he experienced here. I would also suggest that the demons are of the elder's making, for he was very fond of his grandson. If he wishes that the demons leave him alone, he must only think of the new and better world into which his grandson was born. Like the wounded eagle who falls from the nest down the cliff, he had to crawl while others jumped, but still he climbed the ancestral path of stone footsteps leading to our ancient village. And so he offers the gift of life."

No one spoke. There was much mumbling. After a short time Machakwi stood and said, "Let his quarters be searched!" Then Honani rose and stated, "This meeting should be adjourned, for unless we find owl feathers, there is no case!"

My heart beat madly. Where had I come up with those words and confidence? The elders began to leave the kiva, and in a short time, only Nish't Ahote and Hototo and myself were left along with our thoughts. Mine were tumultuous! I began to shake, for I had done something I never thought I could.

Hototo came slowly over to me and took both my hands in his. He looked lovingly at me, then at Nish't Ahote and said, "Always will I love the goodness in your heart. You were sent by the Gods, and I will never forget it." He hugged me to him and hurriedly climbed the ladder.

Nish't Ahote remained silent. I wrapped my skirt around me to ascend the ladder and with my foot on the first rung of the ladder, I heard, "Ho, Coyote Woman, why do you hasten?"

My heart leaped into my throat as I waited for him to say more. He said nothing, but gathered me in his arms and held me as though I would not be there the next moment. At last he spoke:

"Coyote Woman, you are a woman now!" Then he placed his hands on my shoulders, and pushing me away from him, his eyes gripped mine in a feast of love.

I was so relieved that a tear escaped the corner of my eye, and my insides turned to corn mush. I knew I was hopelessly in love with Nish't Ahote and had been for a long time. He returned the love, but I could not allow myself to think of my desire. I now understood what he meant when he said he was a servant of the people. To be such, I must be guarded at all times. For the people were loving and dangerous at the same time. I wondered if Hototo understood this.

Chapter 9

Solstice Celebration and Banishment

Most of our celebrations and ceremonials were during the time of cold and snow. Because the sun cycles were short and the dark times were long, we filled our time with feasting, dancing, and worship. Often I imagined how lonely it would be to be a reaide during this time.

Our Solstice Celebration was beginning. This was the part of the cycle when the sun spent the least amount of time in the sky and when we called it back to give us warmth and to give its strength to budding life. This great celebration symbolized the second phase of creation at the dawn of life, and was dedicated to giving aid and direction to those of Awonawilona's creation. Nish't Ahote and I had spent many sunrises calculating solar observations to determine the exact number of days until the solstice. The preliminary four days were for the making of our prayer sticks, *pahos* as we called them, and for smoking over the *pahos* and planting them at shrines. After those four days the actual celebration began. Now the great ceremony began, which would last twenty sun cycles and conclude with a rabbit hunt, feast, and more blessing rites.

At midnight on the sixteenth day of our ceremonial preparations, in the main solstice kiva, all members of the other kivas gathered to purify themselves with water that had been boiled with fresh sprigs of cedar. Everyone also drank of the medicine water that had been waiting for this occasion. Another spirit dancer representing Alosaka, our God of Fertility, appeared. He had a star on his head to indicate his journey from other worlds. The star was made of very large corn leaves, with a blue center to represent the sky. He was given two *pahos* when he arrived, one with a small ear of corn and eagle feather, the other with a small ear of white corn. His arrival was heralded by loud drum beating, and he danced a furious tumultuous dance honoring each of the sacred four directions, north, east, south, and west. He then handed his *pahos* to Nish't Ahote, the solstice priest, who guided all of us up the ladder and out into the fresh air, where a young girl waited. We all then walked in a slow procession to the butte on which occasionally sun readings were made.

The earth was very cold and still. Our ceremonial robes made of feathers and skins of various animals felt warm and comforting. Our feet were covered with soft skin socks, and our yucca and cotton-cord sandals were tied around the socks. We climbed very slowly up to the top of the butte, using toe-and-hand holds. A deep, sensuous drumbeat accompanied us as we made our laborious climb. A very large crowd of worshipers followed our ascent and sang praises as we climbed. They raised their voices and hands as they gathered at the foot of the butte to watch one of the most sacred of our rituals.

Upon reaching the top, Nish't Ahote escorted the young girl toward a fire pit that flamed intensely into a leaping fury. She gathered her ceremonial robes and sat next to the fire pit waiting. The place where she sat was filled with seeds and *pahos*. Her hair hung loosely around her shoulders, freshly washed and gleaming in the firelight. Here she would remain through the rest of the ceremony. She was symbolically hatching the seeds on which she sat. She was also surrounded with male and female *pahos* who represented people yet to be born. Upon her leave, the seeds and *pahos* would be distributed to each clan to carry home for planting. Others would be sprinkled over our corn in storage bins that it might fill abundantly.

There was an air of mystery and secrecy around the young girl, for every four season cycles she was chosen for spiritual sacrifice. She was usually the daughter of a clan chief and was not quite of marriageable age. Her name was whispered to a special *paho,* and she would die within four years. She represented the rebirth of life, for life must be paid for with life. It was our belief that a seed that germinates gives up its identity as a seed and a new form rises from it. So she would die to insure rebirth just as the seed periodically dies to be born fresh again. All was a great cycle.

An elder handed a large buckskin shield to Nish't Ahote. It was painted red, yellow, and blue, and had the face of the sun painted black in it's center. Long human hair died red edged the face and the circumference radiated eagle feathers. While the sun was a most important God to us, his was but a face through which our creator looked upon us.

The drums accelerated and became louder, whereupon Nish't Ahote began to dance and to spin the shield. He danced rapidly toward each of the four directions and whirled the sun shield at each directional point as the song mounted in excitement. The dance became more frenzied, the shield spun faster, and the song grew louder. All minds concentrated on turning the sun back on its trail and on harmony and unity of all mankind. The dancing continued, but it would be concluded before the sun rose to begin its journey across the sky. All had to be done perfectly, and not an evil thought could be allowed in anyone's mind or all would be lost in our efforts. When the stars were in the correct position, it was done. The sixteen days were over, and we were left with our blessing rites.

There was much dancing and socializing in the next few days—a time of many dances. The air was crisp and very cold. Ice crystals sparkled each sunrise to reflect multiple colors to any observers. During the night, the stars were a vivid and yet milky gathering in the sky as each of the other six worlds were displayed. These were the worlds through which we would pass in the development of our soul. If we were pure in heart and lived as the Great Spirit wished us to live, we would move on to the fifth world with no stops along the way. The dancers were spiritual forces of life representing the physical forms of life. Their purpose was to bring rain, to assure the abundance of crops and the continuation of life. They were not Gods but representations of birds, animals, minerals, and other life-forms, both visible and invisible. So the men who danced as a "spirit dancer" lost their personal identities, becoming imbued with the spirit they impersonated. They danced in the plaza and stomped on the kiva roofs, emitting an eerie, high falsetto cry to announce their presence before they descended the ladder.

In times that the "spirit dancers" were not performing, there were social dances. There were buffalo dancers, butterfly dancers, deer dancers, and eagle dancers. The time was filled with delight and happiness while hunters were hunting rabbits by day. My dancing partners were few, and most of my time was spent watching the dancers.

It occurred to me that perhaps I was not asked to dance by the students and acolytes because I had been made Nish't Ahote's assistant. Yet even as I thought about it, someone grasped my arm forcefully, dragging me from my reverie onto the dance floor. I found myself staring at the dark half-shut eyes of Wisoko. My anger flared, and I exclaimed, "Don't you even bother to ask a girl to dance?"

Holding me even tighter, he asked, "Why do you always spurn me? Why don't you like me? You always make your feelings very obvious."

"You wonder why I feel as I do? You, who have no manners! You, who takes what you want when you want it! You must always be in control with no feelings for anyone else! You are despicable! Take your hands off me and leave me alone!"

Now it was he whose temper rose. Pulling me out of the line of dancers, he gripped me roughly by the shoulders. "So," he said, "maybe you should be the one who needs to be hit on the head to knock some sense into you!"

He took one hand from my shoulder and grasped my chin giving my neck a sharp twist. "Begone, woman, before I lose more of my temper because of you!"

He released me suddenly to disappear into the shadow of an alcove.

All seemed quiet as I approached the west wing. I climbed up to the roof of my room, and one last time I surveyed the people in the plaza. Then I descended my ladder into my wonderfully peaceful quarters. As my feet hit the floor, I nearly tripped to avoid Puppy, who laid in an unnatural, twisted heap near the bottom rung of the ladder. He made no sound, and I bent down to pet him. Still there was no response. This was not my Puppy. I lit a small fire in the corner of my room. With better lighting I could see that Puppy was not asleep. He had been hit on the head and was unconscious. I had brought him out to play with the other dogs at the beginning of the day's festivities. How, then, had he gotten down the ladder? This was very strange!

I reached to touch him with the urge to gather him into my arms. This would be wrong, however, for I knew something might be broken. I needed help! Checking the fire to assure its lasting warmth, I quickly climbed the ladder and worked my way back into the crowd. I found Nish't Ahote in the company of the elders. Not wanting to interrupt their conversation, I quietly but anxiously waited close by. At last Salavi noticed me as I nervously waited, shifting my weight from one foot to another. He nudged Nish't Ahote, who turned to me asking, "Ho, Coyote Woman, what is on your mind?"

"Nish't Ahote, you must come immediately! I need you!"

Nish't Ahote excused himself and followed me through the crowd to my quarters. Seeing Puppy at the bottom of the ladder in his pitiful, broken heap, he bent his ear to listen to his breath. Then, after checking him over, he said, "Nothing seems to be broken. He is very bruised and has a nasty gash on his head. He may have fallen down the ladder. We must apply cool compresses to his head and cleanse the gash. Other than that there is little more we can do than to make him as comfortable as possible." We then moved my baby closer to the fire, bathed and cleaned the gash in his head, and put cool compresses on at frequent intervals.

For a long time I heard nothing, not even a whimper. Nish't Ahote left me to return to the celebration, saying he would return in a while. I hugged him before he ascended the ladder, then rushed back to sit by Puppy and offer my prayers to the Great Spirit.

My mind was turbulent as I scanned what had happened. The gash on Puppy's head was not of another dog, but of a heavy object. Why would anyone want to hurt Puppy? Or perhaps it was only a way to get to me. It seemed to me that Puppy had been deliberately hit, then thrown down the ladder. How thankful I was that he still breathed. I placed both my hands on his head to offer him the addition of my own energy to hasten the healing process. I sang healing songs to him while rocking my own body back and forth. Was this what it would have been like to be a mother? Puppy whimpered, and I praised the Great Spirit—Awonawilona. So great was my trance, that I did not realize anyone else was near until there was a light tap on my shoulder. I turned to the warm loving brown eyes of Nish't Ahote—Nish't Ahote, who was always there when I needed him. Sensing my needs, he took my hands from Puppy and pulled me to my feet. Once again I was wrapped in his loving arms, and I really wanted never to be anywhere else.

He whispered just above my ear, "There are always forces of evil, little one. You have had a difficult day!" His large loving hand stroked my hair, which hung loose and had grown by this time below my shoulders.

"Why, Nish't Ahote, why? Once again I felt the forces of evil and knew something was amiss. Once again that uneasy feeling, the hovering of a dark cloud—but not in time to prevent it from happening. Why had not the power manifested itself earlier?"

"These are questions that only you and Awonawi-lona can answer together. The more important problem is who did this foul deed. Do you have any intuitive feelings to share with me?"

I was so comforted by his warm embrace that I hated to draw away, but did so reluctantly. I pulled a yucca mat next to Puppy, and sat upon it close enough that I could place a loving hand on the poor, battered creature. I extended my other hand toward Nish't Ahote, beckoning him to sit down. When he was seated, I placed my other hand on his large warm hand and began to tell him of my thoughts.

"The forces of evil come from Wisoko. This I know in my heart. But I have done nothing that I know of to deserve this. My thoughts, I try to keep pure and loving. Why would anyone be so vindictive? Why, Nish't Ahote? Do you know that I was forced to dance with Wisoko only a short time ago? He grabbed me without asking to dance and asked me why I did not like him. After I answered him he said, 'Maybe you should be the one who needs to be hit on the head to knock some sense into you.' Why would he say such a thing? He must be trying to get to me through Puppy!"

At that moment Puppy whimpered, and opened pain-crazed eyes. He was so pitiful that a tear escaped my eyes. Nish't Ahote took my chin in his hand and tenderly kissed my mouth and then the tear on my cheek. "He will live. Take good care of him for the next sun cycle, and he will be fine. He lives for your love. Give it to him and nurture him. Come to me if you have any more inner visions or thoughts you wish to share."

I nursed Puppy with compresses and affection. Nish't Ahote had said he would be fine, but my anger festered as does an unkept wound. At last I could no longer contain my feelings. Racing across the plaza I headed for Wisoko's quarters. My only thoughts were to put an end to Wisoko's evil and to make him aware that I knew what he was about. The closer I got to his quarters, the more confident I felt. This was something that had to be done. I needed to confront him for my own sanity.

His room was next to the plaza, but I still had to climb down the ladder. Stopping at the top of his ladder, I took a deep breath. Quickly I descended to find him reclined on his mat as though asleep.

Shaking out my cotton robe, I said quite loudly, "Wisoko, don't pretend you are asleep, for I know you are not!"

He rose slowly on one elbow, though still reclined, saying, "Why our little Coyote Woman has finally come to her senses. I knew you would come." Then langorously he came to a sitting position.

"Yes, I came to my senses! I know that you were the one who bruised and hit Puppy. You may have even thrown him down the ladder. Why Wisoko? Why? To get to me?"

"Why would I ever want to get to you when I knew you would come to me?" He rose to a standing position and walked toward me. "It is such a shame that we cannot be friends. I have felt all along that you desired me as I desire you."

A sharp warning echoed in my mind's eye. I had unwittingly placed myself at his disposal. Moving very slowly toward the ladder, I lashed out, "Your mind is warped. I came here only to ask why? You have not denied. You have only answered with a question."

He closed the gap between us and pressed my back against the ladder. Looking at me hungrily, he placed his hands on my cheeks and planted his lips on mine. He pressed so hard that he forced my mouth open as his tongue probed the recesses of my mouth. I felt nausea welling up within me. What sweet justice, I thought, if I vomited in his mouth. Grabbing hold of myself, I turned my head away.

"You bastard!" I yelled.

Suddenly he grabbed me and pulled me down on his mat. Turning me over and pinning me under him, he lifted my cotton tunic and placed his hand between my legs.

"So, Coyote Woman, I have you at last! You are mine. This is what I have wanted for so long. But you are much too proud." His breath was coming in rasps. I struggled and twisted and bit him on his nipple drawing blood.

His hand grabbed my breast, and he squeezed. The pain was searing, and I screamed. He put a hand over my mouth. I bit him again tasting more blood. He held me with one hand and attempted to spread my legs with the other. I screamed again. I tossed and turned and flayed wildly when I heard a voice.

"What are you trying to do to our 'Coyote Woman'?"

Wisoko jumped up on his knees to find Hototo standing over him. Salavi was also there.

"This does not seem like a friendly discussion!" exclaimed Salavi as he bent down to pull me to a standing position. "Perhaps our Coyote Woman will explain if given time to recover." Putting his arm around my shoulders he led me to Hototo. I buried my head in Hototo's strong chest and sobbed.

Without another word the three of us climbed the ladder, leaving Wisoko with whatever perverted thoughts he might have had.

I slept very poorly. Hugging Puppy was a balm to my troubled mind. He was weak and whimpered frequently during the night. I rolled from one violent dream to another. It was quite clear in my mind's eye that Wisoko was capable of anything imaginable, and I tossed and turned as I thought that this was the time when I should speak of the fight between Wisoko and Eeetspapoka.

Just before dawn I went to Nish't Ahote's quarters to watch the rising of the sun. As I sat on the bench next to Nish't Ahote, he softly spoke of a meeting that would be held in the kiva when the sun reached its zenith. Little was said between us, but I felt a tenderness between us that was different from any I had felt before.

At last, just as it was time for me to leave, he lifted the back of my hair with his fingers and pulled me to him. "Little one," he said, "today will be better than yesterday. I'm well aware of how you must have slept, but perhaps the meeting at Sun Father's zenith will solve some of our problems."

Although I ached for him to touch me, I wept as I realized that the meeting must at least in some part pertain to Wisoko and me. I decided to wait to speak of the fight that I had witnessed. And so I departed.

I was escorted to the meeting, much to my surprise by Hototo. The five elders were there as well as Nish't Ahote and Taweyah. The fire burned brightly casting eerie shadows on the whitewash walls. Its heat felt comforting in contrast to the bitter cold in the plaza. I glanced at each face and read on each one an expression of grim concern.

At last Machakwi called the meeting to order saying, "This meeting has been called in an emergency. The Anasazi are a peace-loving people. We must remain so at all cost. Let the prisoner be brought forth."

Wisoko and an acolyte climbed down the ladder.

Wisoko showed no sign of nervousness, but instead seemed very steady and sure of himself. After seating himself on the bench next to Honani, he stared blankly into the fire. Taweyah was propped in a sitting position watching Wisoko intently.

Machakwi continued, "This meeting has been called to preserve and protect the path of peace that the Anasazi revere. The violence of yesterday must stop! If anyone wishes to speak, let them speak without interruption. Let us look at the facts objectively and make no hasty decisions." With that he returned to his seat on the bench. When no one seemed willing to speak, Machakwi said, "Salavi, will you speak first?"

Salavi rose to his feet and cleared his throat. "last evening after the dancing, Hototo and I were walking in the plaza when we heard a scream. It came from the direction of Wisoko's quarters. We hastened toward that direction, and we heard a second scream. Climbing down the ladder, we found Wisoko forcing himself on Coyote Woman. She had drawn blood while defending herself. Wisoko immediately came to his knees, and I myself pulled Coyote Woman to a standing position. We escorted Coyote Woman to her quarters, and Hototo and I went our separate ways. I agreed to inform the elders, and he agreed to inform Nish't Ahote and Taweyah. It was, I believe, Taweyah who called this meeting." After a short pause he added, "That is all I have to say."

Waiting for a brief time Machakwi said, "Hototo, will you honor us with a statement?"

Hototo rose to his feet. Pulling his robes around his slender body, he began. "As the youngest and most recently ordained priest in the community, I am somewhat hesitant to speak. However, as Coyote Woman spoke on my behalf not so long ago, I must put aside my nervousness and speak in her defense. Salavi has spoken of what we found after following the screams. I must add to that by speaking of an event you may not know about. We all know that Coyote Woman adopted a coyote puppy, and he is her totem. Nish't Ahote told me earlier today that last evening after the dancing Coyote Woman returned to her quarters to find her puppy battered and beaten in the head lying at the bottom of her ladder." A gasp could be heard from the elders. Continuing he said, "Though we have not heard from Coyote Woman yet, I would suggest that she may have suspected Wisoko. That may be the reason she went to his quarters. To attack someone's animal totem is the same as attacking them. I would have done the same if someone somehow attacked my power animal." Then coughing from the dry heat of the fire he added, "Thank you for giving me the opportunity to speak."

Machakwi rose again, saying, "Coyote Woman, will you speak?"

I rose slowly keeping my eyes downcast. Very softly I said, "During the social dancing last night, Wisoko dragged me forcefully out to dance. He then asked me why I did not like him. I called him rude and unmannerly. I said he took what he wanted when he wanted it. I called him despicable and asked him to leave me alone. He said, 'Maybe you should be the one who needs to be hit on the head to knock some sense into you.' He then told me to leave before he lost his temper. Returning to my quarters, I found Puppy in his pitiful condition. Nish't Ahote examined him saying he would live but that he had been beaten on the head and may have even been thrown down the ladder. I went to Wisoko's quarters, feeling certain it was he who had done the deed after what he had said on the dance floor. When I got there, I asked him why he would do such a thing. He evaded the issue by insisting that I had really come to his quarters out of desire for him. He then grabbed me and tried to have his way with me. I fought hard. I bit him twice and drew blood. I screamed twice that I can remember. He would have had his way if Salavi and Hototo had not arrived just then. For that I give thanks to Awonawilona."

I paused only long enough to look around. Every face wore a look of deep concern except for Wisoko, of course. I knew I must go on. "Thee is one other thing I must speak of. It is a thing I have not told anyone." At that moment even Wisoko's head snapped to attention. "Not long ago when my Mayan warrior was here . . ." I spoke of Wisoko's calling Eeetspapoka "warmonger scum" and of his telling my warrior to go home. I told of Wisoko's ridiculing my warrior's mode of dress and further calling him names. I let them know it was Wisoko who drew a knife and that Eeetspapoka had been wounded in the arm and had had no choice but to defend himself. I said it was a compliment to my warrior's character that he had only disabled Wisoko and had not killed him.

Wisoko looked shocked and then I added, "One other thing you should know. As I was making my way to the altar with prayer sticks to mark the boundaries of the races, Wisoko stopped me and said that the prayer sticks meant nothing. He said that the Gods don't care, anyway. I told him he blasphemed, and I went on my way. There have been other unpleasant encounters prior to those I have mentioned but I have said enough. I thank Awonawilona for being given the chance to express what has too long been burdening my mind."

Wisoko blanched and stood up to speak. All eyes were intently on him. "I have not been asked to speak, but I feel I must. In defense of myself, I must say that never would I ridicule the spiritual significance of our prayer sticks. Never would I say that the Gods do not care. I did not drag her to the dance floor. I asked her to dance. I treated her politely, and I never threatened her in any way. As for Eeetspapoka, her warrior, I never called him names. This bruise on my cheek is simply from a fall I took in the darkness of night. In short, I must say our Coyote Woman has a wild imagination and should have been a teller of stories. It is her word against mine." He swung his head arrogantly and sat down.

Now it was Honani who stood to speak. Pulling himself together, he said, "There may be a way out of this dilemma." He paused as though thinking through what he wanted to say and also perhaps to give us all a chance to think on what he had just said. Slowly and carefully he continued. "We have a serious number of accusations here. There is no proof of any of them, but there is the bruise on Wisoko's cheek. The only other person who could in any way confirm Coyote Woman's story is Eeetspapoka. He is gone, but not so long ago that we could not send runners for him to return. We could then learn if, indeed, he has a knife wound on his arm and hear what he has to say."

Everyone exclaimed enthusiastically except Wisoko, who suddenly stood saying, "That would be a mistake for he is in love with Coyote Woman. A man in love does not speak the truth."

His statements caused a sudden hush. Silence prevailed for a brief time. I watched Wisoko as he fidgeted as a child who cannot keep still.

At last Machakwi said, "We have heard enough! We must make a decision. Does Wisoko remain with us or not?"

Salavi said, "It is strange that he does not want us to send for the warrior. I say he is guilty! He knows the warrior would be his undoing. Therefore let us make a judgment and be done with this unfortunate case. Let us think seriously of the future and decide now!"

"Let us banish him for the troublemaker he is!" shouted Honani.

"Banishment is difficult at this time of the year. He will have to weather the cold season. Let us not banish him forever but only for four season cycles. Then he may return if he wants or . . . !" said Salavi.

Machakwi interrupted, saying, "It seems that banishment is what is in our minds. Let us vote. Those who feel that it should be permanent, please stand."

Only one person stood. That was Salavi. Inspite of his kind statement, he rose, perhaps because he had been with Hototo when they rescued me from Wisoko's attempt at rape. He did not back down but stood proudly and firmly.

Machakwi continued, "Those who feel it should only be for four season cycles, please stand."

The other four elders stood, and so it was decided. I knew that Wisoko would hate me even more for this turn of events, but I also knew I would have to accept it.

Chapter 10

The Priestess

The sun was just past its high peak when I was summoned. What purpose this meeting might have, I could not imagine. Wrapping my feet in skins and throwing extra ones on to protect me from the cold, I hugged Puppy and hurried out into the bit of warmth the sun had to offer. A few chilly souls were in the plaza, but most were enjoying the warmth of their quarters. I hurried to the ladder of the kiva of meetings. After a deep breath of cold, crisp air, I descended the ladder.

The meeting was in progress—how long I could not have said. Salavi was saying, "The rank of the priest is dependent on ceremonial knowledge. One must know the chants and ceremonial procedures. As Nish't Ahote's assistant, she has spent much time under his instruction and knows all there is to know. In thinking over recent events, we know the Great Spirit has bestowed upon her additional powers."

My ears could not believe what they were hearing. The discussion was about me and the rank of the priest. I wondered why this was so. I knew the old priest was still alive. I dropped my eyes demurely and waited quietly at Nish't Ahote's side. He stood proudly, arms folded across his barrel chest, feet planted firmly on the earth. Hototo was at his left side, and the old priest lay on his litter close by. The old priest looked as usual as though he was asleep.

Machakwi stood, and after a puff from the pipe, he began speaking. "I hear all you say, but I still feel she is young and she is a woman. We have had no woman as priestess in several lifetimes. Her role is as a bearer of children, not as a priestess. She should be head of a household, as are all other Anasazi women!" He resumed his seat at the bench.

Salavi rose again to speak. Scanning the room and resting his eyes upon me, he took the floor. "Priests, elders, and officials. Listen with open hearts and open minds! We have already gone over the deeds she has done, all of which are good. If, in fact, the only objection is that she is a woman and she is young, then hear me out! She is young, valiant, and pure in heart. Is that not what being Anasazi is all about? She is intelligent, she speaks well publicly, and she knows the ceremonial procedures. She has shown an unusual rapport with the informing spirits and warned us of several events. Her spirit guide is the clever coyote, and more important than that, she has a second spirit guide—that of our sacred eagle. She also can tune in to the thoughts of others, perhaps even one of you. Is this not a prerequisite of what a priestess should be? More important than all this, she is Earth Mother reincarnate, as are all women. This one, however, is special! She can think and conceive as a woman not burdened with children and family but with the thoughts of Earth Mother. With Coyote Woman we can obtain the feminine insight, an insight we have not had for years and perhaps have sorely needed. With such an insight we may prevent many problems, for we will have a new view. I have said enough!"

There was a long silence. I was in a turmoil of shock. I was the cause of this important meeting. How could this be possible, I wondered. What had happened to bring about this event? They were discussing me! Could it be—no, never! They were only discussing my history. There was no way—

"We are a peaceful people. We must consider all seven directions when making a major decision. To do so may mean we need a fresh opinion. I am in favor of making 'Coyote Woman' a priestess. She reflects our sun priest's spirit and has many talents to offer. By electing another priest or priestess, we enable the aged priest to return to the spirit world in peace. We, in turn, know that he has had no objections to our Coyote Woman. He has even promoted her and given his approval. Who are we to disagree with our most honored and revered priest!" Honani then seated himself on the bench.

At last, the leader who seemed to object to my being a woman and to my youth commanded the attention of all by rising from his seat. Glancing around the room and clearing his throat, he announced, "It is apparent that I am the only one to raise objection to the appointment of Coyote Woman for priestess. I would not want to be the one to prevent our unified agreement. Therefore I respectfully join the rest of you to give her a vote of confidence. May she live up to our expectations remaining pure in heart. May she always see in all seven sacred directions and never succumb to the forces of evil!"

A loud murmur of agreement was finally culminated by Salavi, who affirmed loudly, "So be it! Let her confirmation be made public at our Purification Ceremony. Let us adjourn this meeting and return to our duties."

With this statement the elders and officials gradually dispersed, leaving me overwhelmed with surprise and emotion. They had placed their faith in me. I realized

I had been made their equal. I knew that I must never doubt that I could live up to their expectations. Hototo tapped my arm, whispering his congratulations. Then taking his leave, he ascended the ladder. Two acolytes arrived to lift the litter of the aged priest and took him to his quarters. I noticed, however, before they took him away through the secret opening in the east corner that there was a smile upon his venerable face.

Nish't Ahote took me in his warm, loving arms and looked into my eyes. He said, "Coyote Woman, you have entered the hearts of many. This includes my own, and I stand before you with trust, faith, and love. This is a special moment in both of our lives, and not one to be taken lightly."

Then wrapping me in his long arms, he grasped my now below-shoulder-length hair and looked at me giving a low guttural groan. I nestled into his arms to reply softly, "I am hardly able to believe what is happening. It is something—" He stopped my speaking with a kiss, a deep, probing, searching kiss that shook me to my core and, of course, my power spot. I read the naked adoration in his eyes, but then he again withdrew.

Painfully he pushed me away from him saying, "We must ready ourselves for the Purification Ceremony and your official seating as priestess. Our thoughts and actions must be without any evil thoughts, and we must set an example for all in the complex."

I gathered my skins and discarded foot wrappings, and said to him, "You smile on your people, the Anasazi, but still you warm my heart. Someday we will meet, creating a world of our own, one that will be of no effect on anyone." I then ascended the ladder into the chill of the late-day air.

We prepared for purification. Again, as in our other

ceremonies, there were eight sun cycles of preparation followed by eight sun cycles of ritual. I was kept busy making prayer sticks as was everyone else in the complex. A messenger was sent to inform my parents of my appointment and to invite them to my confirmation as well as the rest of our ceremony. Nish't Ahote instructed me in what would be expected of me. He said I must play the seven songs of blessings on my flute. All Anasazi learned to play the flute and drum as children. This meant I needed to work hard to regain the proficiency I once had. The ceremony required the use of the largest kiva, and that was where Nish't Ahote, Hototo, and myself spent time fashioning two *mongkos* (spirit sticks) and *pahos* (prayer sticks), and an altar at the west end of the kiva. The altar would be for the sprouting of the beans. Sand was brought in and put on the floor, and a great oak rod was suspended from the roof of the kiva with cornmothers hanging from it. The two *mongkos* would be carried many sun cycles later by our two most important spirit dancers.

During four of these eight sun cycles, I once again returned to my room for my womanly cycle. It did not prove to be a problem in my preparation, but was actually a help. It gave me time to meditate, and time on my flute.

On the first day of my cycle, I sat on my mat with Puppy curled up at my side. He had been playing with an old piece of leather that was his toy, and having exhausted himself, he slept quietly at my side. I took out my flute to practice. After only a few tones, he looked up at me, raised his head, and gave me a howling lamentation. I stopped playing, and he stopped howling. I chuckled aloud, saying, "Puppy, my playing must be awful. Is that what you are trying to tell me?"

He laid his head on my lap, looking up at me

through great liquid pools of pity. Yes, now I knew I really needed practice. Ignoring him, I continued to play while he howled. This went on for quite a while, and the thought occurred to me that anyone walking by would certainly wonder at the strange noises coming from my quarters. As I persisted in playing, Puppy began to quiet down, and finally after a time he stopped howling all together and shut his eyes. I knew I would be ready.

During the first four sun cycles, acolytes were sent out to gather soil. Each one carried a prayer stick to plant in the spot where they took the soil. Afterward they returned to the kiva to fill numerous pots and trays in which they planted the beans. Day and night the fire was stoked and the beans were watered, ritually smoked over, and sprinkled with sacred meal. Under this care the beans would burst forth with green shoots by the eighth sun cycle. We used beans, for their germination was faster and we could eat all of it. Corn was planted, but only a few special sprouts. These would be carried by the chief of all our spirit dancers. Each night unmasked spirit dancers wearing corn husks in their hair arrived to lend their energy through music and danced to the little beans to make them grow. Others composed songs to be sung during the ceremonies.

A messenger arrived to tell me my family had arrived and was being sheltered on the east side of our complex. Tomorrow was the day of my confirmation. I needed plenty of rest to be alert for what was expected of me. I prayed that Awonawilona and my eagle guide would lead me confidently through all that was about to happen.

Just before retiring I was visited by Nish't Ahote. He slipped his hand beneath his robes to withdraw a soft deerskin medicine pouch. It was not the one he usually carried, and it looked newly made. From the leather strings that drew it tight at the top hung a lovely large chunk of turquoise. Stooping to his knees in front of me, he set the pouch on the floor and took me by the shoulders.

"Coyote Woman! A woman you have become and a gifted one at that. I know your lifestyle here among so many men and boys has created for you a lonely existence. Please do not continue to walk within your crystal. Your visions and opinions are valuable, and should be shared for the good of the people. I would hope you would share them with me." Picking up the leather pouch, he handed it to me saying, "This will help to fill your time alone. It will enhance your powers and perhaps also be a reminder that I am reaching out for you. I care for you a great deal and want you to know it."

The pouch was heavy when I took it from him. Placing it in my lap, I pulled the strings apart and withdrew a truly huge crystal. It was very clear and too large for me to hold in one hand. My eyes misted, and with a quivering chin I gasped, "Oh, Nish't Ahote, it is truly magnificent. I shall always treasure it!" I clasped it to my breasts.

"Would that I were that crystal to be clasped to your breast!" chuckled Nish't Ahote, and reaching for me, he pulled me to a standing position. I gazed lovingly into his eyes, as if hypnotized. Slowly his head moved closer to mine until our lips gently touched. My hands dropped to my side, and he crushed my body against his in a moment of aching ecstasy. I wanted to crawl inside him as I would into the *sipapu,* to be cherished and protected. I wished I could have turned that moment into forever. Did he not know that the Gods had created us for each other?

He gently backed away from me to pull my head down to his chest and continued to hold me tightly. His excitement bulged between us to match the excited dampness between my legs. As though suspended in time, we remained so for a while. No words were necessary. Then letting go of me, he straightened his robe and walked toward the ladder. I smiled as he left, for I knew at that moment of the truly special place he had for me in his heart, and that should have been enough.

I awoke refreshed with Puppy snuggled next to me. At once I was aware that this was my special day, and my heart began to flutter. Puppy rose as though sensing my nervousness and pranced around my room, finally working his way to his corner to relieve himself. When he was done, I covered it with clean dirt. It was now time to make myself ready. After washing with yucca soap, I rubbed myself all over with sage. I coiled my hair into two knots, one over either ear, put a bit of ocher on my cheeks, and put on the dark red robe I had worn only on a few occasions. My inlaid shell necklace and feather earbobs were next. Last, but more important, I tied my medicine pouch around my waist. In it were my smaller crystal, my eagle feather, the *pechit* bean, and the large chunk of turquoise Nish't Ahote had given me. A glance in my pyrite mirror reassured me.

When a figure descended my ladder to tell me it was time, I emerged above to find the plaza swarmed with people, many more than usual. The elders formed in a group behind Nish't Ahote, Hototo, and myself, and the people arranged themselves on either side. A group of musicians—drummers, singers, and flutists— followed us, maintaining a hypnotic song as we began our march. Very slowly we made our way to the center

of the plaza, at which point I took a basket of cornmeal and walked first to the east (the direction of
birth), then to the north (direction of the Gods), west
(direction of death), and then to the south (direction
of warmth and fertility). In each direction I sprinkled
cornmeal and quietly recited a prayer. Then returning
to the kiva, I made my entrance followed by the
elders.

A small group of musicians were softly chanting in
the kiva. As usual it was dry and warm due to the
huge fire in the fire pit. The five elders were gathered
in the west side, Hototo was at the south side, and
Nish't Ahote was at the east side. He was the sun
priest, and the sun rose in the east. The altar had been
finished, and beans were beginning to sprout. The heat
was intense but tolerable. The chants were low and
sublime, and as I stood at Nish't Ahote's side, they
became gradually louder. Each elder chanted his own
prayer, then Hototo, then Nish't Ahote. A pipe was
passed around by Salavi. The smoke wafted toward
the entrance of the kiva to purify us all.

Upon completion of the smoking ceremony, a group
of women descended the ladder for the washing of my
hair. Chief among them was my own beloved mother,
Talasiva. I reclined upon a stone slab, and two women
held the bowl of yucca suds under my head as my
mother proceeded to wash it. Then two more women
brought in a huge bowl of water in which Talasiva
rinsed my hair. The chanting went on softly during
the sacred cleansing. Symbolically this also purified my
mind to ready it for its new responsibilities. Then the
women dried my hair and took out the tangles. One
of them reached inside her robes to display a very long
necklace of turquoise nuggets, which she displayed to
all, then wrapped ceremoniously around my neck. At

this point all the women involved in the ceremony, including my mother, ascended the ladder of the kiva.

The music became more intense. I was still lying on the slab when Nish't Ahote began to dance. His dance and the chanting became louder, faster. I had been told that there was nothing to be anxious about. I lay with my arms and legs somewhat spread upon the slab and waited for I knew not what. I only knew that this was the moment of my consecration. The intensity of the heat and rhythm had mounted to a crescendo when Hototo parted my dark red robes. I lay almost as naked as the day I was born, exposed to the membership in the kiva, but somehow it seemed right. Nonetheless, I could not help but remember the stories my Mayan language instructor had told me of the sacrifices. Yet Nish't Ahote was there, and I had nothing to fear, for he had told me so.

An elder presented a basket of cornmeal to Nish't Ahote, who accepted it lovingly and sang a prayer over it. Then walking reverently toward me, he stood at my side to continuously utter prayers as he looked at me. Then taking some of the sacred cornmeal, he traced a line of cornmeal from my right side to my left side and over my breasts. The musicians stopped. Then he chanted further and traced another line of cornmeal from my neck to my power spot—my most intimate spot. These lines indicated the four directions, or so I assumed. Then still chanting, he threw cornmeal into the air, then onto the ground to complete six of the seven sacred directions. The only one left was the direction within me, and as he sang, he gave me a mouthful of cornmeal to chew and swallow. Thus were completed the sacred seven directions, and at this point the singers resumed.

Another song was sung, then with a touch on my shoulder, I knew it was my turn. With my flute I played the long, chilling sounds of the song of the north, the direction of the blessings of snow and moisture without which man cannot survive. The second song, the song of the east was quick, pulsing, and brilliant, for this was the direction of the rising sun that gives birth to a new and glorious day. The song of the south was warm and loving with crystal-clear sounds that reflect its fair weather. The song of the west was sad and mournful with a wailing to suggest death and the setting of the sun that ends each day. The song of our lower world was eerie with strange, sliding low tones. This was the place of emergence, the womb of Earth Mother. The song of the upper world, the home of the Gods, had brilliant and high-pitched soaring sounds that seemed to take flight as the wings of the eagle, our messenger to the Great Spirit.

The seventh song was the center or core of my being. I composed this differently than the others. I played it as I felt it, for I was the seventh direction. The Gods had blessed me with wonderful abilities, exciting experiences, and loving people all around me. My song began with low sliding tones to suggest my birth. This was followed by quick, happy sounds of my childhood. In a short while the song took on a somber seriousness to reflect my many season cycles as a student and acolyte. My song ended with a long, loving sensuousness, for I was a woman with the desires and needs of a woman.

After the final tones of my song, everyone in the kiva was silent. I noticed a tear in the eyes of Taweyah, for he knew exactly how to interpret my songs. His eyes moved to his beloved nephew, who also seemed to be in a trance. Then an elder took my hand to lead me to a large, feathered hoop that lay on the floor of the kiva. I stepped into it, and the music began again. The other four elders stood around it, one at each of the four directions. The song of purification began, and the elders slowly raised the hoop from my toes to my head to symbolize purification. Then slowly lowering it to the ground, I remained inside the hoop awaiting the end of the song.

From a cache Nish't Ahote withdrew a headband. Its beauty was breathtaking, for it consisted of a soft piece of buckskin with tiny crystals held in a series of slits. An eagle feather hung from each end. This Nish't Ahote tied snugly around my head, leaving the eagle feathers hanging in the back. Then from behind the altar, Nish't Ahote took a cape. I gasped, for surely it was the most wondrous creation I had ever beheld. It was pure white and was made of egret feathers, for which we traded with the people to the west. With gentle, loving hands, Nish't Ahote placed it around my shoulders and tied its leather strips loosely around my neck. Then he took my hand and directed me to follow three of the elders up the ladder and out of the kiva. Then he and Hototo ascended behind me.

A large crowd had gathered. My parents stood proudly watching me. The crowd became hushed. The other two elders brought the old priest on his litter from the side entrance of the kiva. When everyone had assembled, a shell horn blasted, and I was given a flat basket of cornmeal. I walked first to the east to sprinkle a line of the sacred meal with Nish't Ahote and Hototo behind me. Nish't Ahote recited a prayer, and we moved back to the kiva and then to the southern most point of the plaza as I again left a line of sacred meal behind me. After still another prayer, we did the same procedure in the other directions. Then all was done, and the crowd dispersed to the warmth of their allocated quarters.

At long last I was able to be united with my beautiful mother and loving father. After removal of their masks, they both embraced me at the same time. No words passed between us for a time. Then, when we finally parted, Pochti said, "We always knew you were a star child. You have brought many blessings to our house, and now you bring the ultimate blessing. May the pride born within us all be tempered with humbleness and purity of thought."

"Thank you, my beloved parents." I lowered my eyes. I felt a light tap on my left shoulder and turned to the happy faces of Choviohoya and Kunya. They, too, congratulated me.

"We could not miss this occasion. My sister surely outshines me, but I feel only love and the proud feeling to be your brother. I hope someday you will visit our dwelling to get to know us better. We will be honored by your presence. Your little niece Yamka also wishes to know you better." My brother put one arm over my shoulder and one over his wife's shoulder to smile warmly at each of us.

"Yes, Choviohoya, perhaps that can be arranged when we see the first signs of green shoots and the air warms for travel. Where is my niece?"

"She is with your Puppy and Aunt Mokni. Let us all partake of the feast, for I hunger," he said.

After much feasting and more circle dancing, we all retired for the night. The Purification Ceremony had ended. As Puppy and I retired, I went over in my mind the significance of this, the third of our yearly rituals. All three ceremonies were simply a reenactment of the creation of man in the fourth world. In the New Fire Ceremony we honored the emergence of man into this new world where the first fire was lit. The Solstice Ceremony redirected the sun to give warmth to germinate life. The Purification Ceremony honored the appearance of plant life, and our entire road of life was purified. Now my people stood, fully formed and informed, ready to function harmoniously down our road of life. All three ceremonies honored the master plan of the creator, whose power supersedes any human will.

These thoughts are simply inborn within the minds of the Anasazi.

Chapter 11

Seduction

In the complex there was nothing more than a pervading silence. There was no activity in the open plaza. Truly Earth Mother had stilled the voices of all her creatures. Even the trees were still, as there was no wind. The rocks were blanketed with a beautiful white covering, and they could not speak. It seemed that this was the time that the earth truly rested. I enjoyed the calm after our many sun cycles of meditation and festive activity. I also enjoyed my solitude. I had experienced three days now of very little activity, and it was a welcome relief. My new position with all its new responsibilities weighed heavily upon me. Nish't Ahote had told me I must report to him later in the dark hours. He did not say why.

I washed myself and donned my kilt and my skin leggings. I also put on a cover over my shoulders with a hole cut for my head. Coiling my hair into two small side knots and putting a bit of ocher on my cheeks, I grabbed my turkey feather cape. Then I realized, I must stoke the fire. Puppy seemed to know I was ready to go and then I sat down—wondering. I did not know what Nish't Ahote wanted of me or how long I might be gone. With this in mind, I took Puppy across the plaza to Aunt Mokni, who was still awake and who took him without question. She hugged me, and I was on my way.

Quickly I made my way to Nish't Ahote's quarters. Climbing down the ladder, I noticed he had built a fire that made his quarters quite cozy. I removed my feather cape.

He sat on his mat, and his chiseled aquiline features were sensuously softened in the firelight. His eyes were misted from meditation. "Little one, come and join me. We have much work to do, and you have much to learn!" He was dressed in only a kilt, and his medicine pouch was tied around his neck. He smelled of sage with a slight tobacco odor. He emanated the power of a mountain lion, and it occurred to me that this animal might be another of his spirit guides. I also realized that this was as much privacy as I had ever had with this wonderful man and that I should relax.

As though reading my thoughts, he said, "Is it warm enough for you?"

"Of course, O revered one!"

"You do not need to address me as such, for now you too are revered."

I felt slightly nervous, and I could not say why. I knew that our positions were different now, and that I was at his level. It was exhilarating but frightening at the same time.

"You are here to learn more of the healing points on the meridians of the body. These are things a shaman priestess must know. I would ask you to lie down on my mat on your stomach and remove your apparel."

I stared at him in amazement, wondering if this man had the strength of a rock. Putting this from my mind, I removed my shoulder cover and then my kilt. I looked at him, and seeing no obvious emotion, I lay down on his mat. I waited.

"The human body, as you already know, has meridians. Everything is connected with something in the body from head to toe. In reality one of the best places to work on a health problem is not on the body but on the hands or feet. This is so because the life-carrying blood is closer to the skin in the hands and feet, and stimulation is easier. For instance"—he bent down on the mat at my head pressing on certain points—"we can alleviate a headache problem by pressing on these points, or we may go to the toes and press on them or even the tips of the fingers." He moved from my head to my feet, and pressed just behind my toenails with his thumb. I was traveling with the Gods by now, and wondered at the knowledge, love, and compassion of this man.

He moved from my head to my upper back, pointing out more healing points and their purpose, then down to the center and lower part of my back. His deep, hypnotic voice mesmerized me while I struggled to remain alert. He moved on down my legs and to my feet, all the while pointing out healing points along the way. My body was totally relaxed, but my mind was finally active and alert. I knew I must remember all he was saying, but my body felt as a piece of soft clay. He could mold it any way he wanted. Oh, Great Spirit, I thought, help me!

As though the Great Spirit heard my call, I felt a calm settle over me, and found I could only feel the warm flush that Nish't Ahote had caused to overtake my body. He bid me to turn over, and slowly with great lethargy I turned over on the mat to expose my breasts and the mound of my power spot to him. He seemed not to notice. His strong bronzed fingers applied pressure to various points on the sides of my head, then my forehead, and on my cheeks and eyes. If anyone else were giving me this instruction, I would in all probability have fallen asleep; but Nish't Ahote's touch was magically energizing while relaxing at the same time. He explained as before what each point was for, but there was so much to remember. I was overwhelmed and said so.

"Little one, soon you will give me a treatment and then you will remember more."

He began to talk of those who have trouble breathing. He spoke of palm with thumb pressure, and at one point in his instruction his palm covered one of my breasts as his thumb pressed on a point of healing. My nipples hardened, and I looked up at him with concern. He was as in a trance, and I could not read his thoughts. Then slowly he ceased his speech and lightly traced circles around my breast. I closed my eyes and waited.

All too quickly he resumed his instruction. He bent down on his knees and pressed nine points from my stomach to my abdomen and synchronized this with deep breathing. At the point closest to my power spot, I gasped, and a moan escaped me for I felt moisture and excitement mounting between my legs. He moved his hand over my most private parts and gently flicked his fingers over my energy source. He bent to kiss me, then as though becoming another person, he backed off, looking at me strangely.

He quietly murmured, "May the Gods help me through the most difficult temptation of my life!" Rising from the mat and turning away from me, he did not speak, but stood along, strong and silent.

I continued to wait. When there was no response, I asked, "Will you guide me through the same steps and healing points on your body?"

Then, as though grasping an inner strength, he became once more the stern teacher I had known and loved for so many years. Removing his kilt and medicine pouch, he reclined facedown on the mat to guide my hands through the same routine as before. When my fingers or palms were not just perfectly positioned, he told me to move them accordingly. Then, seemingly pleased with my skill and progress, he turned over on his back. His body was magnificent! It was a mature image of the body of my warrior. There were lines on his face. His long, coarse black hair was grayed at the temples. His mouth turned down slightly at the corners, and his eyes were a sultry warm brown. He had lost his paunch due to the ceremonial fasting and rationed food supplies, acquiring a lean, sinewy, muscular body. As he lay before me, it was my turn to ask the Gods for help, for I wished to touch where I should not.

After reiterating the healing points in his head, I moved on from his chest to his abdomen, and my first touch caused the rise of his manhood. I fervently tried to ignore and to work around it, but he moaned and, grasping my hand, guided it to encircle his swollen organ. I bent to rub it against the nipples of my breasts when he suddenly pushed me away and rolled to a sitting position.

No words were spoken, only an awkward silence followed. I wanted to say I was sorry, but I had nothing for which to be sorry. It was so obvious that we intensely desired each other and that we loved each other. We were meant to be together. Why, I thought, did he fight it so? Would there ever be a time for us? My frustration mounted within me.

He said huskily, "Coyote Woman, you must leave me now. Do not ask why! Just go!" He wrapped his kilt around himself once again and handed me my garments. His hands shook slightly when he touched my fingers. Then he turned away.

Watching him add wood to the fire ignited anger within me. When he had built up the fire, I turned on him. "No, I will not leave you now! You have built the fire within me, and you cannot just walk away and leave a raging fire!"

His eyes locked with mine in surprise. "You cannot mean what you are saying."

"Yes, I mean that you are inconsiderate, perhaps even inhuman. You want and desire me. You lead me up to an unbearable point and then turn me off. The fire has been built many times, and you have not put out the fire. You are not being fair to me and least of all, you are not being fair to yourself. Your own fire is not put out, either. Perhaps you are used to combating your sexual energy, but I have not had the years of experience that you have had. I want, desire, and love you. Why do you constantly torment me, then reject me?" I was shaking with emotion.

"Beloved, you have a place in my heart and I also love you dearly, but I am old enough to be your father. I also realize that loving you may not be for the good of the people. All that I do must be for the good of the people, and now that you are a priestess, all that you do must also be for the good of the people."

"Nish't Ahote, I have loved and revered you for many years. If it were my choice, you would have done my puberty rites. You must remember that you were my first choice. Nish't Ahote, you are my first love above all else! Do you not understand that?"

He walked nervously to gaze into the fire again. He remained there for what seemed to be forever. Then he turned, and striding toward me took me into his arms. "It does not matter!" he whispered hoarsely. Hungrily he grasped my shoulders, then claimed my lips in an urgent probing kiss. His mouth searched the recesses of my mouth while his hand gently cupped my breast. I moaned and his lips traveled down my neck and to my breast. He encircled my breasts with his tongue, then traveled in kisses back up my neck and grasping my hair, held it above my head so as to bite me gently on the neck. I could not begin to describe the intensity of my feelings. I loved my warrior for his gentleness, but this was an urgency of desire I did not know was possible. He trailed kisses down again to my breasts and teased them for a long time until I reached a point of ecstasy that I never imagined possible. As he moved down to my navel and on down to my inner thighs, I cried out. His tongue went on probing my power spot, sending me flying over the tops of mountains. I was flying higher than ever before. Then he reclaimed my lips, exploring all parts of the recesses of my mouth.

Suddenly I was possessed. I wanted to return the ecstasy. I probed his mouth with my tongue and licked his sultry, closed eyelids. Moving very slowly down his body, I kissed his manhood, and he groaned very loudly. I wondered if I hurt him, but he soon answered.

With deft manipulation, he turned me over and fingering me in my most private parts, he firmly and quickly joined us as one. Suddenly I shook and quivered. I was flying toward the stars. His rhythmic motions stopped, and he gazed with his half-closed eyes into mine as if he had never really seen me before. Then they glazed, and he resumed his motion while searching the hollows of my neck and ears with kisses and nibbles.

A quickening of energy in the deepest parts of my body gathered, and I grasped him tightly as I became truly one and exploded, then gradually began to fall as does a falling star. Only a very short time after, he groaned and quivered to let me know he had joined me in our travels. Yes, we were flying! This time I was not alone. This time he was with me. We grasped each other for quite a while. Then he moved from above me and turned on his side as he pulled me to him.

Not a word was spoken for a time, for we were still traveling. Then I began to think clearly once again. I nuzzled against him and once again nibbled on his neck. He returned this with a kiss and a sigh. Holding me closely, he enveloped me with a kind of warm security I had never experienced, and we both gave ourselves to the land of dreams.

Someone kissed my eyelids and nose saying, "Rise, my love, for we must trace the pattern of the sun as it begins its journey across the sky."

As in a mystical fog, I tried to rise to join Nish't Ahote in his sun observations. As I came into reality, I stretched like a mountain lion and rolled over. I noticed Nish't Ahote staring at me. Had I done something wrong? Shaking my covers off me, I rushed to relieve myself and put on some clothes. His sleeping room was warm, but the sunroom would be very cold. Donning my turkey feather cape and tying leather around my feet, I rushed to join him in his observation room. He sat next to me on the bench and did not speak. Perhaps, I thought, speech was not necessary.

We charted the path of the sun on the horizon and the angle on which it rose. Its brilliant blue, purple, red, and orange rays were magnificent as they swept the sky. Nish't Ahote said little, and when the sun had completed its rise over the horizon, I knew it was time for me to depart. I tried to catch his gaze, but I could not. Then after several more attempts, I realized he did not want to look at me. Feeling rejected, I silently made my way out to the plaza. He called me back saying, "Wait! I have something for you!"

He turned to his herbs and vials and handed me a potion. "Drink this, little one, lest you intercept my seed." Obediently I downed the horrible concoction and made my way to the plaza.

My mind was in turmoil as I walked toward the cooking area and to Aunt Mokni to get Puppy. To be fulfilled as a woman and yet somehow feel guilty left me in a horrendous state. He had demanded that I leave him, and I had not. He had needed help in finding strength, and I had denied him. I was the weak and inconsiderate one. I begged the Gods to help me and to understand the love I felt.

Brooding over these facts, I watched Puppy race toward me, bounding into my arms. Aunt Mokni was busy at her mano and metate, grinding corn with several other older women while a flute player sweetened the work with his song. Raising her eyes to mine, she exclaimed, "Child, you are here! Is everything in order, or do I detect concern in your eyes? Shall we talk?"

"No, dear Aunt, all is well. I would not burden you with my problems. Thank you for caring for Puppy, and I am sorry I was away so long. I shall go now."

Wiping her hands and rising to her feet, she walked quickly toward me. "No, Coyote Woman, you may not leave until you tell me what it is that is bothering you. Let us go find some privacy!" She took my elbow and guided me behind the cooking quarters to the food storage quarters. Inviting me to sit on the earthen floor of the dimly lit room, she placed her hand on mine and said, "I would hope that becoming a priestess will not cause you to forget old Aunt Mokni. I read pain and pleasure in your eyes. If you wish to share your pain with me, I can assure you of my silence. I do not chatter of others problems as most of the old women do." Seeing my eyes lowered and a tear escaping, she went on, "Can one night with our revered sun priest be as bad as that?"

Wiping the tears from my eyes, I looked up. "Oh, no, Aunt Mokni. It is only that I am confused. I have much to sort out in my mind."

"He loves you. He has loved you for a long time. Will you allow that love to grow? Or will you allow anger to destroy it?"

"Perhaps I am still a child. Perhaps all this has come too soon, for I am having trouble understanding it. My mind is utter confusion!" Then it suddenly dawned on me what she had said and I gasped, "Oh, Aunt Mokni, are you a witch? Can everyone see that he loves me as you do?"

Chuckling to herself, she pulled herself to a standing position, then reached for my hands to pull me up and into her ample warm embrace. "My child, the elders have full knowledge of it. Awonawilona has put you in the position you are in now to learn to deal with these relationships. He has placed enormous responsibilities on very young shoulders. Whatever the problems are, you must work them out with unconditional love."

Gently pushing away from her, I straightened my disheveled clothes. "Your wisdom gives me comfort. I must return to my quarters to meditate."

Walking behind me as I returned to the grinding room, she left me with one last comment. "Remember, child, we are all here in the fourth world to encourage each other to evolve spiritually."

Once alone in my room, I meditated and considered my unhappiness. I had been angry and would not leave at Nish't Ahote's request. I had lashed out at him. I had told him he was not being fair to himself—or was it myself? I demanded he make love to me to satisfy my own selfish desires. But when he made love to me, it was in a loving artful, masterful way. It was obvious he was well versed in the arts of love. I only knew it was the most intensely exciting experience of my short life. My warrior had been loving and kind, but his flame was small in comparison to Nish't Ahote's. Good feelings enveloped me momentarily as I thought on Nish't Ahote's touch.

Then I sank into a deep depression, for I had surely let him down. The thought of working things out spiritually and of unconditional love, which were Aunt Mokni's last words, began to haunt me. In my attempt to love Nish't Ahote, I had not accepted him for what he was and what he felt. I forced a change in his behavior, and my training told me that this could result in an unsatisfactory change in his relations with me. My need to be satisfied was causing me to lose him completely. I had not tried to communicate. I had been angry simply because I could not control his actions. I had been exalted as a priestess and then, due to my selfishness, perhaps ruined the most meaningful relationship in my life. I prayed, "Awonawilona, I despair! I am unworthy." The tears fell unchecked.

Chapter 12

Wisdom of the Snake God

The acolyte descended my ladder. It was just past the high point of the sun. He brought me a bifurcated basket with a skin covering. This I had requested, for inside it was a rattlesnake. Puppy was instantly uneasy. I climbed the ladder with Puppy under my arm and ran once again across the plaza to Aunt Mokni.

"Well, my child, twice in the same sun cycle. Will the Gods never cease to surprise me!"

"Aunt Mokni, please keep Puppy for just a short time. I shall not be long!"

"Of course, child! And may Awonawilona be with you!"

I turned back toward my quarters and sat despondently on my mat. I stared at the basket and my mind seemed as a blur. I attempted to clear my mind of its depression, but it refused to let go of me. I walked as in a trance to the basket and gently removed its cover. The snake clan knew just where to find hibernating groups of rattlers. The snake too was sacred. It was used in our annual snake dance in the season of the greening. As the snake slithered out of the basket, I spontaneously backed away. It coiled and glared at me rattling violently all the while. I felt hypnotized as its eyes bore into my soul and beckoned me. I stepped toward it, and it struck. The pain was excruciating in my ankle, causing me to fall backward against the stone wall. I watched it move to the opposite corner, where it quieted its rattling. Then darkness overtook me. It was over!

I lay as in a coma. I could hear much of what was being said, and Nish't Ahote told me what I did not hear after my recovery.

Nish't Ahote was summoned to Taweyah's quarters, and found him alive but with his mind in another world. He treated his ailing uncle. Returning to his quarters, he found Honani awaiting him. They sat on Nish't Ahote's mat, lit a pipe, and shared a sweet smoke.

Honani cleared his throat of the smoke and said, "I come to bring news of a possible problem. Three of our elders wish for a revote on the order of the building. They change their minds as often as does a fanciful child. They now say that the large kiva should be built first and the storage bins and additional irrigation ditches later. They are trying to convince the fourth elder and may very well be successful. The fourth elder vacillates."

Nish't Ahote asked, "and what are your feelings?"

"I believe the welfare of the people must come first." Honani further added, "A hungry, starving population has no need of expanding our buildings for the sake of power. Coyote Woman may be young, but she possesses an unspoiled wisdom, an almost childlike knowledge that is usually lost in maturity."

Nish't Ahote later told me that suddenly the air in the room thickened and seemed to choke him. He said he knew something was amiss. He also claimed that he could not help the feeling that there was something he should be doing, but he knew not what. He forced himself to pay attention to Honani as the elder continued to expound on his feelings and concerns.

A messenger arrived summoning Nish't Ahote. A

woman awaited him in the plaza with Puppy prancing and barking nervously at her side. She told him that Puppy could not be quieted and led him to my quarters. As Nish't Ahote followed her, he told of a horrible sense of foreboding.

He climbed down the three levels to my quarters. Upon descending the first few rungs of my ladder, he said he heard first the deadly rattle of the sacred snake. Then he saw me in a crumbled heap on the opposite side of the room. He said he could not tell if I was dead or alive. He only knew he needed to get me out of my room and to the healing kiva if, indeed, I was still alive. Then he said he remembered a song. As he chanted it, the snake seemed less nervous. He continued his song as he reached the bottom of the ladder. Mentally he merged with the snake's spirit, telling the snake that our people worshiped him and that he had come only for me. The snake seemed to quiet, and Nish't Ahote quickly threw me over his shoulder and climbed the ladder.

He wasted no time, but hurried to the healing kiva where he gently placed me on a mat on a stone slab. I remember none of this, but he told me he checked me over to find only one puncture in my ankle. He thanked Awonawilona that the snake had struck me only one time. He felt utterly helpless, for he knew he should have been by my side when it happened. As it was, there was nothing he could do but watch and wait.

And so he waited by my side. His mind turned over a multitude of reasons that might have caused me to do what I had done, but none of them made a lot of sense. He said he was a man tormented, and that he felt a part of him was dying with me. Then he spoke of a prayer that came to him, and he repeated it over and over as he lay his head on my breast listening to be sure I still lived. It will be always a part of me, for its beauty is immeasurable.

Like the young eaglets tied on our rooftops in the season of greening, whose talons are captive;
So you sacrifice yourself—to bring the people the gift of life. No longer captive, you soar!
Return Coyote Woman—to my love and the love of your people.

Life is fragile. We all hang on by a thread. For a full sun cycle I continued breathing, but was not conscious. I broke out in heavy perspiration and moaned in my sleep. Nish't Ahote said he did not sleep. He remained by my side frequently, using his touch healing and placing crystals around me. He blew healing smoke periodically. Hototo came in and stayed long enough for Nish't Ahote to treat his uncle. The tragedy was general knowledge within the community. Each elder paid his respects to both Taweyah and me, then quickly took their leave. Aunt Mokni frequently sent a messenger to inquire of my condition. I was told a deep depression settled over the school and that the students and acolytes spent much time in prayer.

Nish't Ahote said he talked often to me. He was unable to determine whether I heard him or not, but he continued speaking to me. He reminded me of my responsibilities on earth and in the complex, and of my healing powers and farsightedness. I remember him telling me that. I could hear, but I could not respond. I do not remember him telling me of his love and that he would not deny me again.

Hototo came to call saying, "I come to inquire on the condition of Coyote Woman and also, O revered one, to bring you news. In the setting of the next sun cycle, the elders are calling a meeting to revote on the order of importance in the new construction. Without the old priest and Coyote Woman to vote, we will be outvoted. Is her condition improving?"

Nish't Ahote answered, "Her condition is stable, but completely unpredictable. I have no doubt that the elder who fought with her in the last meeting counts on the fact that he will not have to contend with her in this one. Only one of the elders is sure to vote with us. Three are solidly against dividing the construction equally, and one elder vacillates. We need her vote and her wisdom."

Nish't Ahote's last statements I was able to hear, but again I could not respond. I heard Hototo saying, "Is there a chance?"

"Her condition is in the hands of the Gods. I cannot speak for them. We can all speak to them and pray."

Hototo reverently spoke again. "I shall come more frequently then to double the healing energy, for she is loved by many and has a special place in my heart."

I sank once more into unconsciousness.

I continued moving in and out of consciousness for a second sun cycle. Nish't Ahote said he saw no difference in my condition, but that I occasionally moaned. He sponged my brow and cleansed my ankle, repacking it with herbs to prevent the evil spirits from entering through the snakebite. There was nothing to do but wait.

A messenger arrived to inform Nish't Ahote of the meeting that was to take place when the moon rose at the end of the next sun cycle. Hototo and Nish't Ahote took turns attending me so that Nish't Ahote could also care for Taweyah.

The next rising of the sun told of no change. Time was drawing near for the meeting. The sun had completed its path, and darkness was blanketing the world.

Nish't Ahote said he knew it was only a matter of time before the moon rose and all would be decided.

He was dressed and ready to leave when a moan escaped me and I called out his name. He rushed to my side and embraced me. I tried to speak of my concerns. I told him I had not been able to say what I wanted to say, but that I had been hearing and listening at times. I struggled to stay awake, but sleep overtook me once more.

I must have slept only briefly, for Nish't Ahote was making his way up the ladder to attend the meeting when I struggled to speak. "Stop! I know I am needed. Please take me to the meeting! I know I am needed. I could not speak, but I heard. I know now I am truly needed. I have been selfish and—" My eyes dissolved in tears.

Nish't Ahote said he knew then I would survive and that the rattlesnake was now another spirit guide. My life would begin anew.

"Are you sure you are strong enough?"

"Your strength has given me what I need," I answered. "Please take me to the meeting!"

Praying that I would truly have the strength, he sent for a litter and two acolytes who gently carried me up the ladder and laid me on the litter. I lapsed into sleep once again.

The meeting was attended by our five elders, the trade manager, the building engineer, and the project supervisor. Hototo was also there. Nish't Ahote told me later that judging from the complacent expression on everyone's face, he knew everything had been preplanned.

Two robust acolytes entered the ceremonial door with the litter on which I rested. An awed hush was felt by all in attendance as my litter was quietly deposited beside Nish't Ahote. Three of the elders exchanged uneasy glances, making it obvious that they had not counted on my presence.

As was customary, Nish't Ahote lit a pipe that was ceremoniously passed around. The smoke filled the kiva with its pungent scent, while silence followed. My eyes remained closed.

Honani called the meeting to order. He then turned the meeting over to Machakwi, who gathered his robes imperiously about his girth and rose from the bench. Clearing his throat, he began:

"We gather here for a reconsideration. In a short period of time the weather will warm with the return of Sun Father and the budding of all that is green. It will be warm enough to begin construction. Some of our discussions since the last meeting have been with the feeling that the building of the new large kiva must take priority over the new granaries and the storage rooms. The construction of the new kiva must take priority, for it serves the most important beings in our lives. The Gods are all powerful. They bring rain, which in turn allows our crops to be abundant. The new kiva will appease the Gods and the Creator. Our crops will be so abundant that we will have no need for additional granaries. We will have the protection of the Gods, who will take pleasure in our new kiva dedicated to them. Upon its completion we can then decide which is more important—the granaries or the new storage rooms. I suggest a vote for reconsideration!" He returned to the bench.

There were murmurs of agreement. Then Honani, who had informed Nish't Ahote of the meeting and the strong undercurrent of disagreement among the others, rose to speak.

"Fellow elders! We have had many years of peace and abundance. The Gods have long smiled on us.

However, recent events have broken that period of tranquility. I do not feel the need to reiterate. I only feel the need to express my feelings. I agree that the Gods and the Creator are first priority. They are our protection. Our people depend on their goodness. But the Gods do not protect the raiders of the north, nor bless them with the peaceful ways that they bestow on us. Their Gods are not ours. We cannot control the raiders and their gods by sitting in our kivas and building more kivas. Awonawilona will only protect us if we try to protect ourselves. To protect the people, we must have foresight. We must be prepared for extra abundance, and this means extra storage rooms and granaries. Lack of foresight may force us into dependence on our neighbors, and what if they do not have a surplus? Or worse, what if they ask us to reciprocate the favor in their time of need? Will we be prepared to offer them aid? I urge you to take a bit of time to think on these things. Let us not hurry with our vote of reconsideration!" He proudly gathered his robes around him and sat on the bench to await further reactions.

I had no memory of what followed, for I lapsed into a trance. Later when I awoke, Nish't Ahote told me that I stirred restlessly and all eyes were upon me. Slowly I rose to a sitting position. My eyes glittered like stars as I stared into the fire as though in a trance. My damp hair lay on my shoulders like a mat while beads of perspiration appeared on my forehead. I raised my arm and pointed to the fire. The stillness was such that one could hear everyone breathing.

Then I spoke in a rasping voice, "The Guardian Snake of the West speaks through my mouth." I continued to stare into the fire and then rose to my knees, my body slowly undulating in the heat of the kiva. "There must be harmony within. The people must be adaptable and have the ability to shed the old skin of ideas. It is time for a new phase of being. Complacency will breed destruction to the people. This is a time for foresight and transformation." My body waved and swayed, and I lowered myself onto my litter to lay on my side, coiled into the fetal position, which is also our burial position.

The expressions on all faces ranged from astonished respect to terrifying wonder. Then finally Machakwi, who had called for reconsideration, firmly stated, "The Gods have truly spoken through Coyote Woman, who has now taken on the spirit guide of the snake. The snake is a messenger from other realms and has the capacity to bring life-giving rains. To heed the words will assure us abundance. I therefore withdraw my request for a vote of reconsideration."

A murmur of agreement rippled between the elders. There was discussion among them of the new ways, of my spirit guides, and the insurance of the future welfare of the people. Each elder walked to my litter, as if wanting reassurance that I still breathed. Then in a profusion of hushed conversations, they one by one took their leave.

Hototo walked to my litter and laid his hand on my head. After seven short prayers to the seven directions, he quietly took his leave. Then the acolytes who had brought me in, returned me to the healing kiva.

All was quiet. Nish't Ahote sat on his mat beside me and smoked a pipe and prayed to the seven directions. The smoke wafted its way toward the hole in the center of the kiva while silence prevailed. He placed one of his hands on my forehead and one on my heart to add his life energy to strengthen my life force. I somehow found myself hearing what he was thinking. I knew he was wondering what a young woman like me could possibly see in a man old enough to be my father. Opening my eyes, I whispered, "When I recover, I shall tell you of my reasons."

He looked at me suddenly, as though struck by a bolt of lightning. His eyes bore into my amber ones, betraying his love for me. For a time he seemed unable to speak. Then at last he softly said, "There is no need for talk. You must save your strength!"

I reached for him with my left hand, and he tenderly took it in his while planting a tender kiss on my palm. Holding it gently, he gave praise to Awonawilona and the lesser Gods for looking with favor upon us both. He seemed to be silently saying that without me, there would have been a huge void in his life, and the Gods had shown him that he was human after all. He now knew that all that had happened and all that would happen was preordained.

My next womanly cycle was spent in deep thought. Having successfully traded with the Hohokam, we had restored our supply of grain, but what if this burning of the granaries should happen again? Why did we not have surplus granaries in anticipation of such an unfortunate event? Then an attack of this sort would not be so crippling. Surely the Hohokam must have planned ahead, or they would not have had the surplus of grain and beans on hand. I knew I must speak of this to someone, or did I dare! This was an issue about which I felt strongly. I did not understand why we must build more storerooms for turquoise and other trade items when the important issue should be the feeding of the people. Why, I thought, must we have a new extra-large kiva for the unification of our people when these same people might experience unification along with starvation? But perhaps this was only the woman's view, for additional building represented power to men. The larger our complexes, the mightier the structures we erected. Power for what purpose? Power to defend ourselves against our enemies? No, the power to appear significant. There could be no significance where there was starvation of the people!

These thoughts continued to rush through my brain, and then I remembered. I had the power! Every person has power to use as they will. And woman is Earth Mother incarnate, who must protect her people. I picked up my crystals and meditated with them, for I felt a heavy responsibility. As they vibrated in my hands and throughout my body, I realized that a woman's view was a rare thing in our governing society. Few women, if any, remained in the school to become acolytes, and none to my knowledge had become assistants, much less a priestess. For by pursuing this path, I had assumed the role of a man. Yet, as a woman, I was Earth Mother incarnate. This gave me a very different power than the male possessed, and I had every intention of using it. At the worst I might be ignored and later, privately reprimanded.

So for the three days of my womanly cycle, I pursued these thoughts over and over in my mind, building up confidence—the kind it would take to make my concerns demand attention.

On the day of the meeting, there was little activity outside our complex walls, for the animal spirit in man gave him the same urge to hibernate as the animals of the Great Spirit. Occasionally an animal skin–cloaked figure moved rapidly and soundlessly across the plaza to disappear into the warmth and security of their quarters. I peeped out and decided to wait next to my fire until I was summoned to the meeting.

When the sun was at its peak, I was served corn mush, which was usually the first meal of the day.

Then I checked and cleaned up around Puppy, and settled down once again. This time I picked up my feathered cape and put the last of the turkey feathers on it. It would not only provide me additional warmth, but it also would envelop me with power. For the eagle was one of my spirit guides, and to my people, the turkey was the eagle of the south direction, the hawk was the eagle of the east, the golden eagle was of the north, and the osprey was the eagle of the west. All were sacred to the Anasazi. All gave of themselves to breathe power into man.

I was thus occupied with my thoughts when a messenger descended the ladder to inform me that the meeting was to begin. Wrapping my feet in deerskin tied on with strips of leather and throwing a heavy antelope skin over my cotton skirt and shawl, I ascended my ladder.

As I hastened down the ladder, the warmth of the huge fire in the kiva felt comforting. As I walked toward Nish't Ahote, many eyes greeted me and the murmuring continued. I glanced around the bench built into the thick wall of our sacred kiva, and my eyes came to rest on Taweyah, who was laying on a litter resting on one elbow. His color was not good. There were dark circles under his old sunken eyes, and his body looked withered and exhausted under the tests of time. I wondered vaguely if he and Aunt Mokni knew each other, and that if he were not of the priesthood, would they have gotten along. Maybe the number of season cycles were too great between them. Age could be difficult to tell. As though reading my thoughts, he turned his wise old eyes to me and offered me a weak smile. I softly returned it and lowered my own eyes. Nish't Ahote raised his right hand to signal silence and the call to order for the meeting. I took several deep breaths.

Pangwu, our building supervisor, stood imperiously to indicate his readiness to speak. "It is an opportune moment to implement our plans to build more storage rooms in the north trade complex and to pursue the construction of the large kiva to further unify the spirit of the people."

Machakwi gruffly nodded his agreement and reaffirmed in different words that which Pangwu had stated. The unification of the people and the building of storage rooms for more turquoise and other trade items seemed to be unanimously agreed upon when the old Taweyah again rose on one elbow and cleared his throat to demand attention. In his wheezing, croaking voice, he made only one statement. All eyes were reverently upon him when he said, "Has your desire for power deprived you of seeing in all seven directions?" Then he again reclined with his head on his pillow.

A hush descended over the kiva, as though all were trying to decipher the meaning of his words. Priests did not usually have much to say. It was not their role to govern. This was the responsibility of the elders. They might, however, on rare occasion, if things were not as they should be, voice their shamanic knowledge of the universe to steer deeper or more encompassing thinking.

An uneasiness pervaded the warmth of the kiva. Respect for our elder grandfather priest was one thing all Anasazi were brought up with. Finally Salavi slowly rose and, running his finger over his forehead, said, "Exalted one, are you saying we are partially blind? Can you tell us more?"

The old priest made no effort to respond. He simply closed his eyes as though sleeping. I was certain that he did not sleep but was listening intently. His body might have been tired and sickly, but his mind was very alert. His words invoked a feeling within me of respect and love. Truly he was a worthy wise uncle to Nish't Ahote, and I was surprised that Nish't Ahote did not make the statement.

Machakwi arose and said, "With all due respect to the grandfathers and to our exalted one, I cannot see where there are any directions we have not thought out. He is also a very sick person. Perhaps he hallucinates!"

Our chief of trade assumed his full height and commented, "The building of more storage rooms will enable us to trade more widely and enrich our status as people indivisible. What can be wrong with such?"

Honani hurriedly added, "The addition of the large kiva will serve the same purpose. I see no directions we have missed, nor can I understand the meaning of the old man's words. Perhaps our revered Nish't Ahote can elaborate." He looked quickly and searchingly at the sun priest.

Nish't Ahote stood proudly and silently, but offered no reply. His body was rigid and taut. Then he moved his eyes to me, as if as a signal. I took a deep breath and, gathering my courage, I stepped forward.

"The Great Spirit has directed that I must speak. May I be permitted to do so?"

A long tense pause followed. Then Salavi rose to say, "Your words have been wise in the past. Speak on!"

There was a short time while the elders exchanged glances, then one of them agreed, "So be it! Speak!"

"First I must thank you for permission to speak. I am only recently a priestess. I have listened to all of you in great respect through many meetings, but there are thoughts I would share with you—concerns that come from the center of my being. We are not wanderers as are others around us. We are a proud people. We are proud because we can sustain ourselves and grow as a unified people. Our priorities, then, should be in that order. We should not reverse the order."

Machakwi, who was at times somewhat hotheaded, jumped up, a highly irregular thing to do, seething in indignation. "Why must we listen to this? We are the elders! We are experienced"—and Salavi pulled him by the arm back to his position on the bench.

I was visibly shaken, but Honani said, "Go on!"

My courage was making a major effort to leave me, but I somehow pulled my reserve together to move on.

"With all due respect to everyone, this is what I see. We are a unified people. We are a populace different from all other people. Our culture descends from the south, but we are a society of peace, unlike the peoples of the south, who are bloody and warlike.

"To build on what we already have, we must consider many things. First, and foremost, we must consider the welfare and security of the people. They must be fed. The Hohokam have come to our rescue this past winter, but let us not forget to listen to the stories of the Hohokam. They have very complex irrigation systems, much superior to ours. They had a surplus to offer us. Will we ever have a surplus to offer them? Obviously not, unless we build extra irrigation ditches and dams, and construct extra storage houses to accommodate the extra corn we produce.

"The raiders are a given. These barbarians are bent upon besieging our surplus. It baffles me why we are not considering a way to prevent similar plundering in the future. Will we barter with the Hohokam or Mogollan or whomever else next year, in order to feed our people? It bewilders me that we have no more pride as a self-sustaining people! I beseech you! Let us build more granaries and expand our irrigation sys-

tem. Let the storage rooms and large kiva come later.
This will truly provide unity for our people!" So saying, I bowed my head and lowered my tense body to
the bench. I had spoken deliberately and tried to
choose my words carefully. I only hoped someone—
one or more—would consider.

The silence was short-lived. Suddenly Machakwi
rose saying, "She is but a child! Are we to listen to
this? How can we understand if this is what the revered one is insinuating? We have had minor problems before, and they have come to nothing. Are we
to consider these problems more seriously than others? We have managed very well in the past. Why
change now?"

Honani rose and, mopping his overheated brow, exclaimed, "Those who do not change with the times
perish. Perhaps the Gods have led us to a point where
we must change our ways. It is entirely possible that
we should reevaluate our status and use another approach—an approach to protect our people. We know
not how weak or strong these raiders are. Perhaps in
the time of greening, we should send our scouts. What
if the raiders strike with more intensity next harvest
time or even during the time of the longest sun cycles?
Then, what?" Again all looked toward the old priest
and to Nish't Ahote for clarification, but both remained silent.

I could not help but wonder why they were both
silent. If I had spoken out of turn, I would want to
know, so I had to assume that my comments were not
so out of the order of their way of thinking that they
felt the inclination to correct me. Did I dare speak
again? I did not know.

Then Salavi stood to say, "She is but a child. We
do not have to listen to anything she says, but this I
know. We saw fit to make her a priestess. Children

often see things more clearly than adults, and we laugh at them. Perhaps we should weigh what she has to say, for our sun priest is suspiciously quiet. What, I ask, can be the reason for that?" He then folded his arms after wiping his brow, and reclaimed his seat on the bench of our now very warm kiva.

"A shadow of doubt is risen within us. To me, this indicates a time for no action until we have thought many things through with much care. This may be what the aged sun prist means when he says, 'Have you seen in all seven directions?' " Having spoken his mind Machakwi lowered his bulky body to his seat at the bench, and a stony silence pervaded the kiva.

The tension was unbearable. What had I done? I felt a strength I could not describe, and yet an insurmountable anxiety. The kiva walls projected heat, and I was nervous to the extent of breaking out in a hot sweat. Then, as though the Gods had heard my plea, Honani said, "Let us adjourn and meet again with all due haste. We have much on which to think."

Gradually all the elders left the kiva while I stood quietly at Nish't Ahote's side. As the last elder disappeared from sight, I began my ascension of the ladder. "Do not hasten, Coyote Woman! My uncle would speak to you!"

My heart leaped into my throat, and I immediately sweated more profusely. What had I done? I had only spoken my mind! But yes, I must have spoken out of turn. I felt I must have been impudent. I was led to the side of the aged sun priest, feeling very numb. I wished to speak, but fear gripped me and I stared at him reverently.

He rose once again on one elbow, and, taking my hand in his feeble one, he said, "As a flower, you smile on your people. You warm my heart. With your wisdom we will all meet at the sacred point of the path of power. Maintain your unspoiled ways, and may the Great Spirit bless you in all the paths of your life. May warmth, love, and understanding continue to follow you all your life." Then as though this had taken the last thread of energy from him, he reclined and looked as though in sleep. Nish't Ahote and Hototo quietly motioned me to leave, and as I crawled up the ladder in sheer mental exhaustion, I watched them lift the litter to take the aged sun priest through the shorter secret ceremonial exit to his quarters.

The next sun cycle, I was again summoned to the kiva of the meetings. I found things much the same as before. Honani was saying, "We must reevaluate our priorities in light of recent events. The Great Spirit has warned us all that pride goes before a fall. Let us not be so proud that we refuse to consider the words of Coyote Woman." Then turning to Nish't Ahote, he added, "O revered one, what are your thoughts? Perhaps you can clarify our confusion."

Nish't Ahote stood tall, expanding his barrel chest as he spoke, "Coyote Woman reads my thoughts well."

After a long pause, it became apparent that Nish't Ahote had no more to say. The awkward feeling that permeated the kiva was interesting to observe. Each elder and official seemed to be reluctant to say anything, and either stared blankly into space or nervously picked at their clothing.

A pipe was passed from one to another, and finally to me. The smoke sent its clouds to the top of the ladder, where it ascended toward the heavens to deliver its message to the Great Spirit.

At long last Noona, our trade manager, stood to speak. Planting his feet firmly on the ground, he puffed out his chest, saying, "I see the necessity to reevaluate! There are many things to consider. First, we must think of trade and the need for more storage. Second, we must understand the need for another large kiva to keep the people unified. Third, we must build more storage for grain, and fourth, we must expand our irrigation system. This is as I see it, after having spent many hours in contemplation." He took his place at the bench and waited.

Salavi added his own thoughts. "I also agree that we must evaluate all four items as stated by Noona. I beg your consideration of the thoughts that follow." He seemed to be gathering his thoughts. Then, laying his pipe on the bench, he ventured, "We have much to consider, and a limited number of hands to work. If we wish to accomplish all four goals, we must split our forces up. Instead of dividing it into two projects, we must parcel out four projects. This means all will be completed in a longer period of time, but perhaps in doing things this way, we are truly seeing in all seven dimensions."

Machakwi, the indignant one of the earlier meeting, stood to speak. I knew he might be negative, and my heart skipped a beat. "The Great Spirit and the Sun Father have guided us all these years—years of peace and prosperity. Perhaps it will not go on forever. If we are going through bad times, evil may be stalking. To fight this evil, we must purify our minds and bodies to repel the evil walking among us. Let us all think clean, pure thoughts and repel the evil among us. However, if there are any who think unclean Anasazi thoughts, let us take the precautions as suggested by my fellow elder. Let us divide our building forces, allowing construction of additional granary bins, more irrigation ditches, and the large kiva along with additional rooms for trading purposes." So saying, he mopped his brow and returned to the bench.

Salavi said, "Let us assume that all will be organized when the first tender shoots begin to thrust through the ground. May the Great Spirit direct us in the correct path that we may continue to enjoy the repose and quiet of our former years. May we continue to enjoy the protection and guidance of Awonawilona through whatever we may encounter. He did not sit down, but remained standing, and after a pause, finished by saying, "Peace and love to all!"

A long silence filled the kiva and then, as though the elder's statements were a benediction, the meeting ended and the elders dispersed. Slowly they climbed the ladder out of the kiva. Two of them carried the litter of the old priest back to his quarters. The officials, after a brief conversation that probably involved another meeting for reorganization purposes, finally ascended the ladder.

I was left in the warmth of the kiva with Nish't Ahote and Hototo. We looked at each other, and no words were spoken. I saw concern and love in Nish't Ahote's gaze. As for me, I was elated, for they listened! They heard me, and Nish't Ahote reinforced my thoughts. Giving both of them a huge smile, I climbed the ladder and reentered the world outside.

Chapter 13

Exquisite Resolution

The winter snows were past, and the time of greening began. The cold red rock cliffs behind our complex were heated during the day by the warming Sun Father, who began his return to bless us with the warmth necessary for the revival of the sleeping plants and animals. For the people and myself, it was an exhilarating time that boosted the spirits in everyone. In my daily walks with Puppy, I enjoyed seeing the cactus that had been flattened to the ground perk up day by day. I saw an occasional prairie dog sitting quietly by his hole to bask in the delicious sunshine. A few desert rabbits bounced across my path. The ground was spongy and damp from the melted snow, and the muddy rainy season was only a moon cycle or so away. The wash flowed, and I was able to resume my bathing during the time when the warm sun was overhead. The nights, however, were still very cold and required a fire for warmth.

Puppy was acting strangely. This was the mating season for the coyote. Though he was not old enough as yet, the instinct was still there, and he left the complex by day, returning at night. He was almost six moon cycles old and becoming very independent. He had nearly lost his puppy look to gain the longer, sleek lines of coyote the clever, coyote the trickster. I knew

I would lose him when he met his soul mate, for he would want his freedom.

The activity in the plaza was increasing. Most of the young acolytes were seen now and then in small groups, racing each other from one end of the plaza to the other. Occasionally I saw a few of them gathered around in a sunny corner, playing our stick gambling game—though I'm certain they had nothing with which to make a wager. As I watched my people awaken from the long period of cold snows, I was aware that the raiders were also doing the same. It would not be long before they would rally their forces to begin their raiding, plundering, and burning. I knew we must be ready, and that I should speak of this to Nish't Ahote or perhaps to Salavi.

I had a feeling of restlessness. The world was awakening, and so was I, for I was a part of creation. I went in search of Nish't Ahote to tell him of my concerns.

Puppy and I found Nish't Ahote in the healing kiva. He was mixing herbs and elixirs for his shamanistic priestly duties. I had often watched him and marveled at his knowledge. Some of the potions I had mixed, but there was still much more I would learn. I watched him quietly. He hardly seemed aware that I was there at his side. Puppy nudged his leg, and he turned to exclaim:

"My little Coyote Woman! You surprise me! I guess I was so involved, I—" Then taking both of my hands he added, "but as always, I enjoy your presence anytime."

He continued to hold my hands in his, and as I locked my eyes with his, a ripple of desire rushed through me. His liquid deep brown eyes held mine in a caress, nearly hypnotizing me. I nearly forgot what I had come to ask. Then gathering my senses, I said,

"Nish't Ahote, I need to discuss a few of my thoughts with you if you have the time."

"Little light of love, I shall always have time for you. What is troubling your mind?"

"I would like to make a visit to my family. I see them so seldom."

"Little light of love, I understand your loneliness. I understand your confusion. Your life here as a priestess is different from all other women. Even the young men who decide to stay in what ever capacity also feel an inner loneliness. I, too, experienced similar emotions in my early years. Of course, you may visit your family. I could not say no. It is early in the season of greening, and hopefully the raiders are not out. Your trip should be a safe one, but please take all the precautions—for I—!" Then he stopped abruptly to look at me.

"For you what?" I asked as I embraced him with my eyes.

"I was going to say, us—!" He stared off into nothingness, and my curiosity was piqued. Here was a man who was never lost for words. What was it he could not say? My mind spun as does a dust storm.

"Nish't Ahote, revered one, I—!" Then grasping at pure chance, I rushed on. "I made a terrible mistake! I berated you! I acted to satisfy my own desires. I demanded from you, and I know you did not wish to respond. I did not accept you for what you are and what you want to be. I feel so very foolish."

He turned to look at me, and placed one hand on my shoulder and one under my chin. As he held me with his hands and eyes, for what seemed like forever, a tear escaped me, and I felt like crumbling into the dirt in the kiva. Then he gently touched my lips with his, brushing them as lightly as a feather. He buried his face in my neck and hair and urgently grasped me and pulled me tightly to mold against his body.

"Little light of love, you continually amaze me. Let us discuss it later. Please return at the time the Sun Father makes his descent on the horizon."

Holding me a short time longer, he loosened his huge arms to allow me to tell Puppy it was time to depart. And so we did.

I returned to my quarters to think over my visit with Nish't Ahote and to gather my belongings for my visit with my family. I was elated, for I was actually going to visit my family, but somehow I also felt an anxiety, for the sun would complete its cycle soon. I packed my few belongings. I realized that the nights were cool, so I gently folded my feather robe and tied it lightly with yucca, for it would offer warmth to Puppy and me wherever we were. I packed salt to rinse and rub my teeth. I packed yucca root for cleanliness. Of course, I also included my crystals and feathers and medicine pouch. All this I put into a bifurcated basket.

Then I began to shake as with a chill. I thought perhaps it was excitement. Perhaps it was excitement combined with anxiety. I only knew that the rhythms of my body were not what they should have been. What was it that Nish't Ahote had to say to me that needed to wait? All my fears and doubts were folding in on me. I had misconstrued the kind of love he had for me. I thought of not returning to him that evening—but no! I could not even think of it, for he was our revered sun priest. My heart was heavy. Awonawilona was playing with my emotions. I wrestled with my guilt as I lay down to rest.

When I awoke I felt somewhat rested, for I realized that I could do nothing but obey. I was a priestess. My duties were to my people, and Nish't Ahote was one of my people. The creator had placed me here among these people, and though it would be impossible to think of Nish't Ahote as just one of "my people," I knew I needed to frame my thoughts in that fashion.

Puppy leaped into my lap when I sat on my mat, and looked at me anxiously. I stroked his golden brown hair and laughed when he licked at my fingers. Then we departed to ask Aunt Mokni to watch Puppy again.

Her eyes twinkled at my request. She had the same knowing look as the women who did my puberty rites. She chuckled and took Puppy from my arms. He nuzzled her, and she offered him a bone. He snatched the bone and went to a corner to happily chew on it.

"So you have been summoned once again. Our revered sun priest seems demanding." She gave me a mischievous smile. "Do not hurry. Puppy and I get on well together. He knows the value of the food quarters and will be quite happy."

Then after hugging me in her ample arms and bosom, I took my leave. I stepped reluctantly over the dirt in the plaza. Arriving at Nish't Ahote's quarters, I took a deep breath and descended the ladder. I had arrived in ample time for Sun Father's descent, and I found my beloved teacher quietly sitting on the stone bench, observing the movement of the sun shadows. His strong, chiseled features were wrinkled at his brow, as though he was in deep thought. I quietly took my usual place on the bench beside him. His glossy hair was pulled back in a whorl at the base of his neck. I felt an unexplainable pull—perhaps energy was a better word—that I felt with no one else.

Just before the Sun Father completed his descent, Nish't Ahote rose to pile many juniper logs on the fire. I noticed his double mat and a bottle of oil and herbs beside it. A huge turkey feather robe was carelessly thrown at the foot of the mats. That was where he most often slept so that he could rise early before the Sun Father made his ascent into our world. He returned to his bench, and together we watched. Just before the Sun Father dipped below the horizon, Nish't Ahote placed a red ocher marking on the white plastered wall. There was a succession of red markings from previous observations.

Then silently he turned. To my surprise, he pulled me into his arms. "Little Snake Woman, how I adore you. You give me magical energy!" His lips kissed my throat, my neck, then traveled to my breasts. My body quivered, becoming clay to his touch. He returned to my lips with a deep kiss that sent my blood racing madly through my veins. He lifted my hair and bit at the back of my neck, a bite that proved that pain can be ecstasy. Then he hoarsely whispered, "Explore me, little one!" He sealed that command with another probing kiss.

I was on fire! My mouth and hands wanted to be everywhere. With both my hands I cupped his backsides, grinding myself against him. I helped him remove his robe with one hand while the other encircled his swollen rod. Then while continuing to hold him, I removed my robe and leather footwear. Together we moved to his mats.

I rained kisses on his neck and shoulders, moving down to his nipples. After some time I moved on down to his navel and on to his inner thighs. He moaned and rubbed and probed my power spot and on inside me as he had done so long ago. There was no outside world. There were only the two of us urged on to become one, the merging of Earth Mother and Sun Father to complete the universe.

My lips and tongue kissed his engorged penis, and then I took him into my mouth. He groaned loudly and quite suddenly to my surprise, he flipped me onto my back. His lips and tongue were now on my power spot. I flew like the eagle. I was drugged, for there were no words to describe my happiness. Just as the stars began to burst in the sky, he moved on top of me, very slowly entering me to truly make us as one. His rhythm was slow at first, then became somewhat faster. I tried to pick up speed. He made me slow down. So we continued for what seemed like forever. Suddenly, I could stand it no longer. My body shook violently, and I pulled him furiously inside me. As though sensing that I could not last much longer, he quickened his pulse and in a shudder and gasp, he groaned loudly, "Ah, my love!" My shaking subsided, and he folded me into his arms. The room was hot, so we did not need covers. He simply held me, and for a while no words were said.

He turned to look at me. Lying on his side and rising on an elbow, he stared at me through half-closed eyes. Then he traced with his finger my brows and on down to my nose and mouth. "Little love, you do not need to go to such great lengths to make me realize how empty my life would be without you. Of course you have acquired your third spirit guide, the revered snake, and a very powerful one at that. May I ask that you not put us both through so much torture to find a new spirit guide in the future?"

I noticed he was smiling, and then I chuckled in response to his humor. "I suppose you are right. May I assume you are saying that I misread you?"

"Coyote Woman, I am a man of many moods. Yes, I wrestle with myself and my emotions perhaps too often. As a priest, I must not make any hasty decisions. I have watched you grow in the past four season cycles from a child into a lovely young woman, and have berated myself over and over for desiring you.

Our ages are too far apart. I was deeply concerned about what the elders, Hototo, and Taweyah would think if I were to seduce you. You should know that I desperately wanted to do so. You have crept gradually into my heart and—I love you! You knew that! I just never said so in those words."

"You mean that you were not upset by my insisting that you make love to me?"

"No, my little love, my happiness has never been greater. I am amazed to think I had to wait so many years of my life to come to this point. May Awonawilona grant us many season cycles of happiness."

"Oh, Nish't Ahote, I cannot speak, for my heart is bursting with joy." Then I began once again to caress his body. He in response lightly stroked my nipples and hips, and then we drifted off into blissful sleep.

We rose before the sun began its journey. Nish't Ahote said, "Little love, you must begin your journey now. It will be better that no one in the complex knows of the time you set out or even that you go. Say nothing to anyone! Just gather your belongings and go. I await your return anxiously. Please use all your senses and hurry back to me."

Once again he handed me the liquid to keep his seed from finding mine. I quietly accepted it and then began to take my leave. As I ascended the first rung of the ladder, I was seized in a fierce hug, and then he grasped my chin to lift my eyes to his. No words were spoken. None were necessary. Our eyes locked, and he planted a searing kiss on my lips probing the depths of my soul.

"Now, go, love, and carry my love with you!"

I climbed the ladder—or did I float up the ladder. I could not remember crossing the plaza to get Puppy. I was lost in thoughts of love, of being the happiest young woman alive. Aunt Mokni only slightly stirred from her mat when I touched her shoulder to thank her for watching Puppy. He leaped into my arms, and I burried my face in his warm golden fur. We crossed the plaza once again to my quarters, where I began to gather my things.

I was ready to go when it occurred to me that I could not leave without a prayer to our creator, Awonawilona. Lifting my arms high above my head, I sang,

> Awonawilona, Creator on high
> Awonawilona, Creator on high
> Your life-giving force has blessed me.
> Your life-giving force has blessed me.
> I lift my eyes to your power,
> and ask your guidance in all things.

Then picking up my flute, I played a song of long flowing sensuous notes. This I followed with short vital life-giving sounds, after which I stopped to offer a silent prayer.

Puppy and I then began our journey toward my home, that is—my other home.

Chapter 14

Home

We walked quietly until we cleared the many buildings in the area. The sun was showing only a slight glow as it began its journey. Earth Mother was very still, and the cold caused me to wrap my feather cape closely around me. My belongings were in a huge basket that was strapped to my forehead. Puppy and I walked on in silence.

The sun began its journey, and I was able to see some of the beauty of the season of the greening. Though it was rocky and arid, the spring rains had caused Earth Mother to put on a show. The prickly pear cactus as well as other cacti were coming to life in the warmth of the height of our Sun Father's journey. As Puppy chased prairie dogs and other small animals, I was enchanted by the loveliness of the birthing season. The flash of red of the wild rhubarb and the paintbrush plant against the open uneventful landscape was startling. There were small white daisies with yellow centers similar to the sunflower and other less conspicuous flowers that heralded the season of rebirth and joy. The cold rocks of the landscape, contrasted by life that springs eternal, was a part of my meditations for the day.

When Puppy and I stopped, I thought on those things. I saw the arroyos cut from torrential rains. I saw the trees felled, though there were not many, and

I wondered. Could the cutting of those trees have anything to do with the deepening of the arroyos? I somehow felt it was so, and then I wondered if the roots
of the felled trees were somehow important.

We stopped several times along the way, and I
breathed in the clean, crisp air warmed by Sun Father.
Puppy was having a joyous time, and he disappeared
for short lengths of time and then mysteriously reappeared out of nowhere. The trip was peaceful and
uneventful thanks to Awonawilona, and soon the sun
began its descent. I realized we were to turn off soon.
A part of the road not far ahead marked by a huge
arrowhead was the path I would take to the house of
my people.

The land was dry and filled with small hills. The
path to my home was narrow, twisting around a hill.
A yellow-haired dog dashed toward me, yapping furiously at Puppy and me. After some low growls and
sniffing of each other's heads and tails, they gave chase
and tussled with friendly intent. It had not occurred
to me that my parents would still have a dog as when
I had lived at home; but then the dog might not be
theirs. I would soon know.

My mother's slender form appeared at the door of
our three-room home. We had one room for living,
one for storage, and one for my father's craft. He
made arrowheads and spearpoints from chert, and
knives from obsidian. She brushed her corn-dusted
hands on her skirt and then suddenly recognizing me,
she threw her hands into the air, yelling jubilantly,
"Pochti, come! We have guests!"

Running to meet me, she took me in her warm arms
and with a tear in her eye, she exclaimed, "Oh, my
beautiful revered little girl. It has been so long!"

My father appeared at the door, and seeing us, he
ran to us and we all three embraced. "Let us go in-

side!" my father finally said. He took my basket from me, and we made our way to the warmth of the house.

It was just as I remembered it. The front room, though not large, was for living, cooking, dining, and sleeping. On two suspended shelves were mats and blankets for sleeping. In the other corner were mother's metate and mano with bowls and jars stacked in the corner. In the plaster on one wall were four figures—my father, my mother, a smaller one that was my brother, and an even smaller one—me, of course. Behind the living quarters was a storage room that opened into my father's workshop. His shop was littered with tools and partially worked arrowheads and knives. In one corner was a large selection of the finished products. We did not grow our own food. My father had always traded his craft for food, for his points were some of the finest among all our people.

Puppy bounded alongside of me while Father said, "Shawanadese, we welcome you with loving arms. We are so very proud to have you find the time to visit us. We know your duties are many."

"Yes, my daughter, but I detect a glint of happiness in your eyes. Is it for us, or is it for other reasons?"

"Talasiva! Shawanadese has only just arrived. Let us at least make her comfortable and feed her before she is questioned!"

Looking at both of us, she recoiled and apologized. Hurrying to the cooking fire, she heated a stone slab to spread a thin batter for piki bread. She had already prepared a desert rabbit stew, which she warmed over the same fire.

We sat down on two large mats to enjoy our repast. The stew was filled with delectable things such as wild onions, yucca root, and greens. We dipped the delicate piki into it and finished with a mint tea. The bones were enjoyed by Puppy and our house dog.

Wiping his face with the back of his hand and giving a satisfied belch, my father shifted to his knees saying, "Now, my lovely daughter, the only person missing is Choviohoya and his little family, Kunya and Yamka. They are not far away, so I shall rise early before the sun begins its journey to take him the news of your arrival. Perhaps we can all be together for our next large meal." He looked lovingly at my mother, who smiled back flashing her large brown eyes.

In my mind's eye, I could hardly believe that my parents were now grandparents and I was an aunt. They did not seem old enough, though I knew they were. Then the thought occurred to me that I could also make grandparents of them. I flashed back to my night with Nish't Ahote, and my facial expression must have changed, for Mother said, "Little daughter, you blush and look radiantly happy. May I be so forward as to ask you what you are thinking?"

"Sweet Mother, I am thinking how young you and Father look. It does not seem possible that you can be grandparents."

"Dese," my mother used my shortened childhood name, "such a thought would not cause color to flush your face and throat, nor cause such a wistful far-away expression."

"Hold your tongue, Talasiva. Do you not remember that children will talk only when they are ready? Our priestess daughter will share when she is ready. Let us make ourselves comfortable for a good long sleep. When the sun next begins its journey, you can talk." Then rising to his feet, he opened his and mother's mats to prepare for sleep.

Mother and I quietly cleaned up after the meal and then settled down for the night.

*   *   *

I lay thinking into the darkness. My mother, father, and brother were beautiful people. They were typically Anasazi with their golden brown skin, wide cheekbones, long lustrous black hair, and short stocky bodies. My mother was slender and delicate with large pendulous bosoms, which all Anasazi women had due to the strenuous activity of corn grinding. My father was muscular with the usual warm brown eyes that everyone in my family had.

But my eyes were light brown flecked with green and gold. The water in the Chaco wash that showed my reflection had only recently shown me my image. My head was different from mother's and father's. Theirs were somewhat flattened in the back from the cradle board that all our mothers used for transporting their babies. Mine was not flattened at all. I wanted to remember to ask my parents why this was so. Perhaps in the early sun hours—

I drifted into the land of sleep and suddenly awoke again. My thoughts were of Nish't Ahote. I had wanted to come home, but now I wished I was back with him. I wondered what he was doing at that moment. He would have completed his sun observation. Perhaps he was in one of the kivas with Hototo or an elder. It did not matter, for in reality the only important thing was our love for each other. Truly Awonawilona had blessed me, or perhaps all young girls felt similarly when they fell in love with their husbands. Marriage was out of the question for me, but I really did not need it. I felt more married than any young woman in the eyes of Awonawilona. Then, feeling an unearthly happiness, I drifted off to sleep at last.

The sun began its journey, and I began my first full day at home. I awoke before Mother, but Father was already gone. Mother brought me a large bowl of water and some yucca root to cleanse myself. Feeling refreshed and ready to start the day, I joined my mother for some breakfast. She handed me a bowl of corn gruel with a dash of honey, then dipped some up for herself.

"My child, did you sleep well?"

"I cannot remember, I am afraid to say."

"My daughter, we are so very proud of you. You chose a different path, as your father and I both knew you would." She paused to enjoy the gruel.

"What do you mean when you say that you and Father knew I would choose a different path?"

She put down her bowl and said, "As a child, you were very quiet and contemplative. Other children ran and played while you enjoyed your solitude. That is one of the reasons we were sure you would do well in your schooling. Yes, you were always a different child—self-reliant, always entertaining yourself."

"Was I really that unusual a child?" I asked.

"You were a very sweet, mild-mannered, delightful child. While your brother created mischief, you were gentle and unassuming. I seldom needed to reprimand you."

I hesitated. "Mother, I have seen myself in the reflection of the wash."

"Yes, my daughter, and I am certain you have seen what a lovely woman you have become. I suspect there are many in the school who have noticed you, too."

"No, Mother, that is not what I want to speak of. I have noticed that there is a cast of red ocher color in my hair, and my eyes are not dark brown as are those of all Anasazi. I also notice that my head is round in the back while everyone else's head is slightly flattened due to the cradle board. Why am I so different?"

"My child, as I already explained, you were an unusually quiet, gentle child. I did not need the use of a cradle board for you. If I put you down in a spot, you remained in that spot. You were a joy to care for. But, tell me, who is the person who brings fulfillment to your expression?"

I was taken back by her question. Would it be so awful to confide in her? After all, she was my own mother. Would Nish't Ahote be upset with me if I were to speak of us? I wondered. No, Mother would learn in due time anyway from Aunt Mokni. Looking her square in the eye, I chose my words very deliberately. "My lovely inquisitive mother, my duties are many as a priestess. My primary duty is to my people, as are Nish't Ahote's and Hototo's duties. There are many things of which I am forbidden to speak. Suffice it to say, if I were allowed to speak of those things, I would speak of them to you above all others. I am sorry I cannot say more."

She took some time to think over what I had said. Then with a gentle smile, she concluded our conversation. "I suppose I should be happy, knowing that you are happy, for I can see clearly that you are."

Our breakfast finished, we cleaned up, and I excused myself to take Puppy for a walk.

My brother and his family arrived. I watched them from just outside the door as they came around the hill to follow the path that led to the house. I had been thinking over what Mother had to say at the early meal of the sun cycle. All those differences, she said, were due to the fact that I was such as easy child to care for. In my opinion, this did not explain my hair and my eyes. I intuitively knew that her answer was far too simple. My thoughts were soon forgotten, for my brother, his wife, and their tiny one had arrived.

"Choviohoya, it is good to see you again!" I hugged him to me, noticing his sage smell that reminded me so of Nish't Ahote. "You seem in good health."

"I am so blessed, little sister. You also look absolutely glowing. It would seem that all goes exceedingly well with you, though you seem a trifle skinny. Personally I believe women should have more meat on their bones, like my lovely wife, Kunya."

I turned to her, and we embraced. Her long black hair was coiled into a large knot at the nape of her neck, while nestled down in a pile of turkey feathers in her cradle board was Yamka. "My lovely sister-in-law, you look beautiful, as usual. How is little Yamka?" I asked.

"She has a greening season ailment, Shawanadese, but otherwise all is well," she answered.

"Then, let us go in and get settled," declared our mother.

Moving into the house, Choviohoya assisted Kunya to remove the cradle board from her back. Kunya placed Yamka on a mat near the fire, waking her from a sound sleep. The small one let out a cry of misery and would not accept any consolation. It was difficult for us to hear each other, so we stepped outside into the warmth of the sunshine to converse.

I stepped over to Choviohoya, and laying one hand on his arm, I asked, "How long has Yamka been feeling this way?"

"Perhaps seven or eight sun cycles. We have tried juniper tea sweetened with honey, but it seems to be doing no good. Yamka spits it out due to its taste, but we keep trying."

"Would you mind if I check on my little niece?"

"Of course not, we would welcome any expertise you may have to offer," he said, looking at me gratefully.

Taking my leave, I went to join Kunya and Yamka. Yamka seemed angrier and more miserable than ever, so I took the baby from Kunya, asking her to leave me with my little niece.

When Kunya had stepped outside, I realized that though I had had experience healing school-age children adults, my knowledge of babies was limited. Perhaps there was little difference between babies and adults except that their stomachs and bodies were more delicate. Seating myself next to the poor little wretch, I checked her forehead. She seemed mildly warm and full of mucus. I checked her over carefully, then singing softly, I placed my hands on the sides of her tiny head. She continued to wail for a short time, then gradually began to quiet. Soon she emitted only short little cries, which may have been pain from gas bubbles. I needed to ask Kunya about her bowel consistency. I continued my singing and placed my hands behind and under her head. She seemed somewhat more tranquil and began to relax. Finally I placed my hands lightly over her eyes and soon she slept.

In the meantime, Choviohoya, Kunya, Mother, and Father had decided to spend some time away from the baby, so not to awake her. The two men went into my father's shop to talk of weapons and tools, while Mother, Kunya and I found a sunny corner outside of the house. We spread a couple of mats, and enjoyed a rare time of leisure with the opportunity for female conversation. For me, this was an almost unheard-of occasion. My only other female conversations had been with Aunt Mokni.

I was the first to speak. In my concern for Yamka, I asked, "Dear sister, in checking over the tiny one, I noticed some elevation of temperature and much mucus. What is the consistency of her stools?"

"They are very liquid. I cannot seem to find enough soft bark lining to supply her. She also has a rash as a result of this problem. Mother says to use very finely ground corn powder on the rash, which I am doing. But her sickness has gone on for seven or eight sun cycles, and I am exhausted, as is Choviohoya. Extra grinding, extra bark lining, juniper tea, and lack of sleep, I fear, may be having an affect on the quality of my milk supply. I wish I knew what else to do!" She wrung her hands with concern.

"Perhaps, my daughter-in-law, you should consider staying for a few days to allow Dese and myself to ease your burden," offered our sweet mother.

I nodded in agreement, taking in the look of relief that overtook my sister's expression.

"I do not want my little Yamka to make our visit unpleasant, but I am very worried that the death sickness may find its way into her body. Yes, thank you for your offer, and I accept."

"Good," proclaimed our mother, "the problem is solved. We cannot nurse her, but we can see that you get some much needed rest." Then changing the subject, she said to Kunya, "My newest daughter, does Choviohoya treat you well? My son can be very trying, and at times difficult to manage. He does not always take criticism well!"

"Choviohoya treats me well. Occasionally I am lonely, for his warrior duties take him from me sometimes for days in the greening, growing, and harvesting seasons. Yamka keeps me company, but sometimes I wish she could talk to me to give me more stimulation." Then she leaned forward and, whispering, she said, "I am secretly worried now that the season of greening is here again, the raiders from the north may attack. Do you think I should speak of this to my husband, or will he be insulted? Perhaps he already has taken care of the problem and has just not spoken of it."

"While you are here, my daughter, we will broach the subject of the raiders. We may then learn what may be on his mind." Then turning to me, Mother asked, "Dese, what of Aunt Mokni? How is she doing?"

"Mother, Aunt Mokni is just wonderful. She is sagacious and wise. She is not a gossip as many of the other women seem to be. There are many things I feel I could tell her if I were able, but sometimes it is not necessary to tell her; she just knows."

"It is a blessing that she happens to be a part of the school. At least she is a tie to your family," stated my mother.

"You are so right. She is really my only female link within my chosen path of life. She watches Puppy for me when necessary and has acted as a sounding board for me during some of my moments of frustration."

"My revered daughter, we heard of your illness as a result of the snake. Gossip has it that you allowed the rattler to bite you. Is that so, or is this another subject you cannot discuss?"

"Mother, suffice it to say I am well and much wiser!" Then I remained quiet, hoping that she would not prod any further.

"And Nish't Ahote and Hototo," she said, "do they treat you well?"

At his name, my heart swelled. "Yes, I am in constant contact with our revered sun priest, and somewhat less in contact with Hototo. Hototo is quiet and unassuming. He is considerate and intelligent and a younger version of his uncle, Nish't Ahote."

"And what of our revered sun priest?" she persistently prodded.

"He frightened me in my younger school years, but

now I know him as a fair, just, brilliant, loving person. The eyes of our minds see things most frequently in much the same way. He teaches the way of all things, working in his mysterious shamanistic ways. Indeed, I am fortunate to have such a special teacher."

"But you are his equal now. Why do you still regard him as 'teacher'?" she inquired.

"Because life is always nothing more than a path of learning. It is a joy in my life to always be learning." Then to change the subject and stop her inquisition, I asked, "And what of you and Father? Is Father well? Are you well, my lovely mother?"

"I am well with the exception of some little ailments that go along with advancing years. Your father is well, except for some pain in his shoulder—probably due to the impact of chipping on his arrowheads. But in spite of the pain, which comes and goes, he is happiest when he is working on his weapons," she replied.

There was a squall of sound quite suddenly from Yamka. Our conversation ceased as Kunya excused herself and rose to attend to her baby's unhappiness. Mother and I sat for a time in silence, then rising, we returned to Kunya to see if we might be of any help.

We found Kunya with one full breast exposed for Yamka, who suckled it hungrily. Then she rocked her and sang to her until finally, once again, she fell into a restless sleep.

Mother and I began dinner preparations. We had some strips of dried deer meat out of which we made vegetables and dumplings. This necessitated much grinding, so we took turns telling Kunya to rest while Yamka slept. Mother and I sang quietly as we worked, so we did not disturb Yamka.

When Mother took over the grinding, I found the

time to walk outside. I was only out a short time
watching Puppy and my parents' dog as they romped
together when I realized I was not alone. Kunya
joined me with a timid smile saying, "May we walk
together, my sister?"

"Of course, but why do you not rest?" I inquired.

"I shall rest soon, but I needed some sunshine. I
have had too little of it lately. It has been a long, cold
snow season, and now the season of the greening is
too beautiful to miss. It is my favorite time of the
year."

"Then Kunya, let us walk slowly and enjoy the tiny
plants pushing their way through the ground, tiny
plants that will grow as Yamka grows."

"Revered sister, I—"

"Please call me Dese. You are part of my family!"

"Dese," she hesitated, "I would ask a favor of you."
Again she paused.

"Please go on."

"Dese, Yamka needs a second mother in case something happens to me. You are her closest kin. I have
no sisters—only brothers. Will you do us the honor of
being Yamka's mother-by-the-gods?"

"Kunya, it would be a great honor, but as a priestess
I am not allowed children of my own. I must speak
of this to Nish't Ahote and the elders when I return."

"Good, then you are not saying you will not," she
said thankfully.

"I shall send you word of their decision as quickly
as possible, but now let us return to our mother, for
it is my turn to grind."

We picked our way over the rough rocky ground
and found Mother softly singing over her metate.

Dinner was delicious. Mother made a separate dish
of venison and dumplings for Kunya, leaving out the

wild onions and other strong herbs so that her milk supply would remain sweet.

Before Yamka's last feeding, I boiled some willow bark tea. The small one's forehead seemed hot, so I asked Kunya to wait for her feeding that I might give her a decoction of willow bark for her fever. I sweetened it with honey and using a small bowl, I was able to get some of it into her mouth. Then we managed to feed her some mashed corn dumpling, and then she nursed. After cleaning her and putting her to bed, we all rolled out our mats to get some sleep.

My dreams were disturbed by someone lightly tapping my shoulder. It was then that I realized that everyone was awake. A look of terror glittered in Kunya's eyes. "Dese!" she cried. "Can you help? Yamka is congested, feverish, and breathing poorly. I don't know what to do!"

Her urgency awoke me immediately, and I asked, "Will she nurse?"

"No, she has no interest. She does not even cry— only whimpers."

I crawled out of my covers and over to Yamka. Touching the child's forehead and seeing her listlessness and shallow breathing, I turned, asking everyone to leave me with the child. In a short time everyone was gone to my father's shop, where they built a fire to stay warm.

I breathed a short prayer to Awonawilona. "Hear my cry, O Great One! Guide my hands, O Great One! If it is your will, help me save this child!"

Then turning to the fire, I boiled some water. In it I placed some mullein leaves to alleviate the diarrhea, and some inner bark of the mesquite tree, which aids in reducing fever and congestion. Nish't Ahote had taught me to carry a pouch with many herbs for many ailments, and for this I was grateful. I allowed this concoction to boil, then removed it from the heat to steep and cool down. While it was hot, however, I added a generous amount of honey to make it more palatable to Yamka.

Then I lay down beside Yamka to go into a power trance. Holding my crystal in my left hand, I floated into a dark, huge cave. As I proceeded farther into the cave the dampness and slime became unbearable, and I climbed through a small opening into a new cave. Suddenly a rattlesnake wrapped itself around my leg and carried me into a tiny cave, where an infant was lying on a mat. I placed my hands in front of me, reaching for the child while my power animal crawled away and coiled up in the corner of the small dark cave. Walking only a couple of steps to the child, I placed my hands on various points on the tiny body. A heated, feverish energy radiated from the center of the front of the child's torso. I chanted a tune that had no words and bent down to bare the torso of the small one. I placed my mouth over the skin of the feverish energy spot and sucked out the intrusion. I retched and spat the intrusion into a bowl. Then I sang my power song again and repeated the process. After doing this several times, and feeling no more heat radiating from the spot, I passed my hands four times over the site to provide a definition of unity for the cleansing process. I then took the bowl outside and after burying the intrusion in the ground, I filled the bowl with dirt to cleanse it.

By now I was coming out of my trance, so I sat quietly for a moment to watch Yamka, who seemed much more relaxed. Taking my herbal liquid and a bowl, I took the small one in my arms to find that Yamka readily took this decoction. After seeing a good amount ingested, I placed Yamka once again on her mat singing, "Awonawilona, stay beside her to work good spirit charms." This I repeated several times.

My treatment concluded, I hastened to call my family back, but warned all of them not to bring any anger or anxiousness back with them.

Kunya made Yamka comfortable, and we all settled down for what darkness still remained.

Sun Father began his journey once again. Yamka woke with a healthy wail. Kunya bared her breast, and much to her delight Yamka nursed lustfully. She looked at me with an expression of gratitude, but said nothing. We all knew we must wait a sun's journey and a darkness before we would know for sure of her improvement.

The early part of the sun cycle passed routinely. Shortly after the sun's zenith, Yamka resumed some fussiness, but my hands on her seemed to quiet her and she slept. Mother and I prepared dinner, which consisted of turkey cooked with greens, squash, with corn cooked to a gruel. We made piki bread to dip into the thickened gravy. We washed it down with hot mint tea. After cleaning up, we all sat down for a short time. We spoke of many things, then decided to say good night. In all our hearts was contentment, for we were all certain that the sickness had ended.

I reclined on my mat, thinking. My mind slipped away from the present to the fact that I missed the school. I did not like doing menial chores during the day. I loved learning. I loved my solitude. When I could not learn and there was no time for meditation, my mind felt wasted. I realized there would always be so much to learn, no matter what my age. Knowledge—never ending! I knew so little and yet so much more than Mother, Father, Choviohoya, and Kunya. But age had taught Mother And Father more than I could know, and I was certain their knowledge was of different things.

Chapter 15

Reunion

The beginning of the next sun cycle was upon us. Little Yamka did not awake at all. She slept until just before the beginning of Sun Father's journey, then woke to demand a feeding. Kunya awoke joyfully and gave of her milk supply.

I awoke to the sounds of everyone else as they began to rise. I was anxious to return to Nish't Ahote, of whom I had dreamed of in the night. Intuitively I knew it was time to go. I arose and washed myself in the water Mother had left. Puppy was anxious also. He paced from one wall to another, then stepped outside and in again as though to reflect my mood. After informing everyone that I would leave, I ate some corn gruel and packed up my belongings. After hugs and farewells to all, Puppy and I set out on our way.

The way was cool and crisp. The landscape was beautiful, for there were a few wildflowers determined to make a showing. The sun was yet low on the horizon, and the road was cool and well defined even far away. Puppy and I proceeded happily. I was returning to Nish't Ahote, and the world could not be more promising.

After a time we approached some rocks close by on the road. Puppy laid back his ears and scampered behind them. He hunched down to the ground, looking at me very quietly. I went to him to see if he was all right. He inched his way behind the rock, and I followed. Then he tucked his fluffy tail between his legs, and lay so quietly that I knew something was wrong. I sat next to him in the dark shadow of the rock. The shadows seemed larger than usual, as my anxiousness was inflamed.

Then I perceived a feeling. It was a presence that I could not explain, the same presence that Puppy sensed. Now I was concerned. I realized we were still quite far from the complex, and that there was a great danger here. Puppy lay flat like a rock, and I hid behind the tall rocks with Puppy at my feet. Silently we waited. I watched a figure swagger along the road.

I peeped out from behind the large rock where Puppy and I hid. I saw a brave, a raiding wanderer. He was dressed in very little but a breechcloth and strange-looking hide shoes. His hair was in two heavy braids. He was very thin. From my side view I saw that his face was gaunt and his ribs protruded nearly out of his skin. He carried a bow and arrow, and his face was turned away from me. I could not see who he was, but I knew who he was and I breathed very lightly so I would not give my position away. Puppy remained very still. He seemed to have sensed the danger even before I did. We continued watching ever so quietly.

He stood and gazed into nothing. Then he turned and—may Awonawilona protect me—it was Wisoko. He moved his hands between his legs and rubbed. His swollen member popped out from behind his breechcloth and, by the Gods, he was almost as large as Nish't Ahote. After rubbing a short time, I saw from the distance his seed as it spurted forth.

I turned my head toward Puppy. Then I could not help myself, and I turned to look again. As I watched, I realized that I had not thought that a man could satisfy himself in the same way as a woman. I realized we did not need each other all the time. But Wisoko frightened me, for I felt intense negative energy coming from him and surrounding me. Then I watched him rearrange himself and walk away finally to disappear from view.

Puppy and I picked up our belongings and proceeded on down the road toward the complex.

Upon reaching the school, I was greeted warmly by those in the plaza. Puppy scampered to greet his friends, and I let him play while I took my few belongings to my room. I was thinking how very fortunate I was to have two homes, both filled with such loving people, when a figure descended my ladder. Hototo grinned and closed the short distance between us. He held my shoulders whispering, "Welcome back, Coyote Woman." He hugged me, then took a step back. "My uncle and I both felt an empty space without you. We are glad you have returned."

"It is good to be back, Hototo. Where is Nish't Ahote?"

"He is with our uncle, who needed constant attention since you left."

"Are you suggesting I go to him?"

"Yes, Coyote Woman, for he seems to be growing more frail each day. I'm sure you would cheer him if you let him know you had returned to us safely from your visit."

"Of course, Hototo. I had planned to visit both Taweyah and Nish't Ahote soon, but I will go now."

"Nish't Ahote will also be glad to know you are safe." He smiled at me with a twinkle in his eye, then turned quickly and departed.

When I reached Taweyah's quarters, he was reclining on his mat while Nish't Ahote used touch healing on his chest. Nish't Ahote's eyes were closed as he chanted softly to himself. I walked to Taweyah and placed my hands on the sides of his head. Without opening his eyes, Nish't Ahote said in a whisper, "So our little priestess returns."

Taweyah's eyes fluttered, then opened. "We are both happy that you have returned. My nephew has been nursing an empty space in his life," he whispered.

Nish't Ahote's eyes opened wide, and he exclaimed, "And what does my uncle really know of his nephew?"

"I am old, Nish't Ahote, but not stupid. I see the glow of adoration when Shawanadese, our Coyote Woman, is by your side. I feel your despondency when she is away. Rejoice that you have found each other. I once also had a love. We were very young. Time did not work for us. I became a priest, and she wanted a family. My priesthood came first to me. She found a husband to father her children. I wonder sometimes where she is and what has become of her."

"What was she called, O revered one?" I inquired.

"Her name was Mokni, talking bird."

I wondered if this could be. Was this one of the reasons Aunt Mokni volunteered to come here? I was certain it was no coincidence. Nish't Ahote stared at me incredulously.

Taweyah continued. "Life is short, my children. Enjoy it while you may. You are so fortunate that your circumstances are different. Only beware that your love for each other does not make you foolish. Be patient with one another, for the age gap is wide. Beware of jealousy, for it ruins a beautiful relationship. Above all, do not let your love interfere with your duties to your people." Then closing his eyes, he said, "Now, let an old man sleep. Go and be blessed."

My eyes were misty. When they met the dark brown

eyes of Nish't Ahote's, great large tears escaped me. He wrapped his arms around me, then kissed away the tears. Together we quietly left Taweyah's quarters.

Puppy was waiting for me outside and leaped and licked Nish't Ahote and myself on our legs and ankles. We walked silently across the plaza together to my quarters, where at the bottom of the ladder he said almost inaudibly, "When your mind and body have had time to think, come to me, little one. Keep Puppy in your quarters."

So saying, he walked away. I watched his magnificent broad shoulders that curved softly beneath his robe to a small waist and small muscular hips. The heels of his sandals flickered from beneath his robe. My eyes moved back up and over his body to his glossy black hair, fashioned in three fat braids down his back. At the end of each braid was an eagle feather. He turned back to look at me with a quick gentle smile, then moved on to his own space in the complex.

My body quivered with desire, while my mind tumbled from one thought to another. I tucked Puppy under my arm to ascend the ladder of the main part of the building and then descended the ladder into my own private space. An acolyte brought me dinner, which consisted of beans and squash soup cooked with a small piece of venison with greens. I washed this down with tea.

My thoughts were filled with Taweyah's words and, of course, with my love and desire for Nish't Ahote. He had said to come to him but to leave Puppy in my quarters. It seemed he did not want me to see Aunt Mokni. He most likely wished to speak to me of this new development before any action would be taken. I realized I was very unsettled. Grabbing my crystals, I clutched the small one in my left hand and placed the large one between my legs. When the small one was warmed, it caused my hand and arm to vibrate. In a short time, when the large one warmed to my body, I began to pulse all over. Then a great calm engulfed me, allowing me to shed my concerns and erase everything from my mind. In my mind's eye I rose above my body and remained suspended over it as I observed my fluttering eyelids and the gentle throb in my neck, where my lifeblood rushed and surged through my body.

After remaining this way for a while, I gradually willed myself back to reality and calmly made myself ready for Nish't Ahote. Telling Puppy to stay, I ascended the ladder and quietly made my way to our revered sun priest.

He sat in his observation corner when I arrived. I stood respectfully at the bottom of the ladder. He rose and crossed to me in two swift steps. We did not touch. We simply gazed into each other's eyes, as if feasting at the sight of one another. He had unbraided his magnificent head of waist-length hair. He wore no clothes and no sandals. There was only a single necklace strung with the teeth of the antelope, of whose society he was a member and the chief in the Chaco area. A hot fire glowed with torrid embers, which was reflected in his almost black eyes. His tapered forefinger flicked gently over the nipple of my breast as a butterfly over a flower. His other hand loosened the bone pins that held my hair in whorls, allowing it to cascade over my shoulders. He ran his fingers through my hair, as a comb lifting it high over my head. Then clasping both hands together while holding my hair, he pulled me to him and rained kisses on my neck. I moaned and quivered with delight.

My hunger for him was great. I reached for him,

pulling his buttocks tightly against me, pressing and molding my breasts and body against him, searing the heat of my body as fire into his. He gently removed my clothes even as we continued to embrace. The world dissolved around us as he pulled me to his mats. He laid me on my back and spread my legs. I closed my eyes, tossing my head from side to side. His hands seemed to be everywhere. I also could not get enough of touching him. He turned me over and, as he did before my puberty rites, he lightly encircled my most sensitive spots. While he tickled and lightly prodded, his left hand reached around to cup my breast. I moaned loudly while my mind flashed back to that first time he had touched me. This was the reason I had wanted him to do my puberty rites, but now I knew there was more. He continued to prod and stroke and nibble and tickle until my excitement was so fevered, I could no longer control myself. I exploded in an ecstasy that left me so weak that my knees would no longer support me. Knowing of my weakness, he pulled me on his lap, inserting his swollen member as I sat. My back was to his chest. His hands cupped my breasts. I moaned loudly and so did he. I rode him for a short time until he pushed me back on my hands and knees continuing to thrust as he did so. Once again I no longer could contain myself and quivered all over. He held me up with his strong arms and hands. His member seemed larger than before. Then suddenly he gasped, saying, "I am here!" He shook, then exploded within me, pulsing violently, then gradually less so. Remaining in that position for a while longer, he finally withdrew, pulling me into his arms as we reclined on the mat.

Neither of us spoke for a while. Then with gentle kisses on my forehead, nose, and eyelids, he spoke. "My little love, how was your stay at home?"

"It was pleasant. I had the opportunity to become better acquainted with my brother, his wife, and my niece."

"And what of your parents?" he asked.

"They are well. It was pleasant to converse with my mother, for there has been no chance to do so since before I entered the school. She is, however, held in check by my father due to her nosy prodding. Truly they were made for one another."

"And your brother and his family are well?"

"Choviohoya and Kunya are well. Little Yamka was not well. She had been troubled by digestion problems and elimination problems for eight sun cycles. I made some mesquite tea for her. Afterward, the Gods and I spent some time with her during the later part of the sun cycle. She slept through the night and drank greedily of Kunya's milk just before the sun began its next journey. It was then that I decided to return to the complex and my people and, of course, to you."

He propped himself on one elbow to look at me. "Little one, how was your return trip?" He eyed me fondly, but inquisitively.

"It was uneventful at first, but then I saw a raider. Puppy and I hid behind a large rock to watch."

"Was there only one raider?"

"Yes, there was only one," I paused, hesitating to go on. But his mind's eye penetrated mine.

"Little love, tell me all. I have asked you before not to live within your crystal."

Then plucking up my courage, I spoke to him of who I had seen and then rushing on, I told him what I saw. Finally at the close of my story, I added, "Nish't Ahote, I did not know that men relieve themselves this way! Do you do it?"

He chuckled heartily. "Yes, little one, I did do just that. Sometimes my dancing brings the same kind of feelings. Now that you have come into my life, I have no need to stroke myself. I save myself for you. Have you not ever relieved yourself in a similar manner?"

"Yes, of course!" Then after a short silence while I touched his manhood, I murmured, "I have much to learn, don't I?"

"Little one, we all have much to learn. If we are wise, we never stop learning. Never forget that!"

I circled his breasts with my fingertips and very softly asked, "Taweyah is wise. Did you have a blank space in your heart for me in my absence?"

He moaned at my touch. "Yes, little love, Taweyah is right. He reads me well."

Then I sat up next to him saying, "Do you think it is possible that Aunt Mokni—well, you know."

"Yes, they are approximately the same age. Does this come as a surprise to you?"

"Yes, it is hard for me to imagine Aunt Mokni at such a young age—or Taweyah at a young age. Perhaps he is one of the reasons Aunt Mokni volunteered her services in this complex."

"It may be so, little one, but I doubt that Taweyah knows of Aunt Mokni's presence at all."

After a short silence in which my mind worked furiously, I timidly inquired, "Nish't Ahote, do you think I might speak to her? If indeed she was Taweyah's first love, perhaps she would make his last bit of time on earth much easier to bear."

"That may be so, my love. I have tried all else and still his strength and spirit slips away." Then pulling me on top of him, he continued, "But enough talk! Love me once more!" He gave me a deep, probing kiss that immediately lit the flame once more. As we sank into oblivion together, my only thought was that of being the happiest woman alive.

*　　*　　*

I awoke to Puppy licking and nudging me to take him outside. My body still glowed from Nish't Ahote's touch. Tucking Puppy under my arm, I climbed the ladder to a sunny, bright, cheery, beautiful world. Rather than report to Taweyah's quarters, where I felt certain Nish't Ahote and Hototo should be, I crossed the plaza toward the cooking quarters.

A flute player spun a lovely rhythmic melody to make the grinding and food preparation more pleasant. Seven metates were lined in a row with troughs that ran straight through, so that the ground corn would push through with the mano into a long, slender container that ran the length of the seven metates. Some of the women were singing with the flute spinning their melodies around it. Thus I found Aunt Mokni.

She ceased her grinding, wiped her hands, and removed the cloth that covered her knotted gray hair. "Ho, child!" she said, "to which gods do I owe this pleasure?" Puppy jumped up and down, waiting to be noticed, while Aunt Mokni went to a crock nearby. Removing the lid, she pulled out a juicy bone.

"I come to tell you of my visit home, dear aunt. Mother, Father, Choviohoya, Kunya, and Yamka send their warmest thoughts to you. I hope you have time to talk a bit."

"My dear child, I am surprised that you have the time to talk, but of course, I'd be delighted. Let us go to the warm sunshine in the plaza. I could do with some fresh air."

Moving into the brisk early air, we searched for a sunny spot. Finally settling down in the warmth of a northwest corner and sensing the fact that Aunt Mokni would not rest until she knew what was really on my mind, I asked, "Aunt Mokni, you are a member of my family, warm, caring, dignified, and loving. You are not in spirit like the rest of the women who surround you. I wonder what you might tell me if I asked you about yourself. You must know that you are different."

A long pause followed. Then looking at me strangely and wondrously, she said, "I am an old woman. I have raised my children, and my husband is dead. There is little else for me to do but volunteer my services to this, our center of education." Then she seemed to be satisfied with what she had said.

"But Aunt Mokni, you are different. You are not a gossip. You speak eternally of patience. You share a dignity with others I know. Did you once attend this center for education? Or is there a reason you keep this a secret in your heart?"

"My dearest child, I once was your age. I, well, you must have guessed that I did attend this school until the age of fourteen season cycles. I was very much in love with a young man in this school. Ah, but it does not matter! I found happiness with my husband and my children, and that is as it was."

"Why did you not marry this young man?"

She paused, as though thinking through her answer. "Sometimes circumstances will not permit even that which you want to happen." She plucked at her skirt and sighed.

"Is that why you always tell me that I must learn patience?"

"Perhaps that is so. I have never forgotten that young man, who by now must be an old man."

"What was the young man's occupation?" I was aware that she was probably wondering why I was showering her with so many questions.

"You certainly are a curious young woman today. He was an acolyte destined to become a priest, but I moved away, and only in later years realized that he had attained his most precious goal. He became the sun priest of this complex and helped the school to grow very large compared to what it was."

"Aunt Mokni, if that priest's name was Taweyah, he needs you now very desperately." I riveted my eyes upon her, for I did not wish to miss any reaction.

Her eyes opened into huge liquid pools. A tear escaped from one corner of her right eye. "Oh, I could not" she said becoming very nervous. "I am only a volunteer cook. I am . . ." She sniffed, and larger tears escaped like great pools of water over a waterfall.

I stifled an urge to cry with her. The sheer wonder of her patience and grace could not help but to have its impact on anyone with a heart as soft as mine. "Aunt Mokni, Taweyah is not well. He has been ailing for three season cycles and grows ever weaker in spirit. He made mention of a lost love and gave the name of Mokni. Will you see him?" I asked with concern in my voice.

"What of Hototo? What of Nish't Ahote?"

"Aunt Mokni, Nish't Ahote and I have spoken at great length of you and Taweyah. Hototo does not know, but if you would like, I shall speak to him."

"I would not want to step into this situation without the approval of all three of you." Then almost fearfully, she grabbed both of my arms. "Yes, Shawanadese, I must be honest. I have known of his sickness for at least two season cycles. I . . . " She quietly stopped and sat heavily on a large rock nearby. She looked very despondent and very spent.

Pulling her up again, I hugged her to me. "Aunt Mokni, too long have you been patient. Let me see what I can do." Her wistful face haunted me, driving me on to say, "You are a unique woman with an inner beauty that radiates like that of our Sun Father. You are not an ordinary person. I love you very much!"

After another hug I excused myself from her presence to make my way to Hototo.

Puppy and I found Hototo, after much questioning around the complex, working with one of our students who was experiencing breathing difficulties. Not wishing to interrupt, I sent an acolyte to check his progress. Puppy and I waited patiently for Hototo to emerge. Puppy, although beginning to reach maturity, still retained many of his playful ways. He nipped at my legs and ankles rolling in the dust begging me to play. Such was not my desire at this time, for I was lost in speculation as to what Hototo's response might be. The acolyte emerged to say that if I would wait, Hototo would not be much longer.

Then suddenly a handsome figure emerged from the ladder and down another to the plaza. His sleek, shiny black hair was caught at the center of his back in one long shiny fat braid with a piece of rock turquoise tied to the end with a leather thong. His robes covered his sinewy muscular torso, while once again I noticed how he was simply a younger version of Nish't Ahote. He lit up in a huge loving smile. His eyes twinkled in their deep brown depths while he quickly strode to my side hugging me, then took my hand. "Hototo, I am here to speak of Taweyah."

"Let us hope your news of Taweyah is good news!" he said.

"As you know, Hototo ..." and I went on to explain the recent turn of events.

He listened with rapt attention, his big eyes softening as the story developed.

"So," I concluded, "I feel, and Nish't Ahote does not object, that his last bit of time on earth might be made easier with the addition of Aunt Mokni into his life. Aunt Mokni refuses without your approval."

There was no immediate response. Hototo sat on the ground, and I sat beside him. He seemed deep in concentration. At last he responded ever so quietly, "All this time! All this time they waited. Let them not waste any more precious time." He looked up. "Coyote Woman, I should be honored to escort your Aunt Mokni to Taweyah's side. Then she will know of my approval of her and of her patience. Truly she must be a unique woman!"

I turned to stare at him, my eyes swelling with scalding tears. I hugged him and gave him a squeeze while my chin quivered. "Oh, Hototo, let us go to Nish't Ahote to decide when!"

They were coming. Mayan traders once again. Our scouts informed us of their progress, but the reports were different than usual. One of the traders was of high position. He traveled with his slaves and many additional soldiers. Their travel was slower than usual due to this person, who was carried on a litter. The party was large, eighteen in all. They sported feathers and royalty. This would be a new experience for me, for it might give me a chance to use my command of the Mayan language. Because their travel was so slow, it might be nearly a moon cycle before they reached us. Our scouts were to keep us informed of their progress. My curiosity was piqued, and I decided I must really spend additional time with my Mayan language teacher.

This was the topic of our conversation when first Hototo and I encountered Nish't Ahote. Taweyah listened closely, then slipped away again, giving us time to speak of Aunt Mokni. Hototo said once again that he would be delighted to escort Aunt Mokni to Taweyah's quarters. He claimed that he would hold it as a high honor to have the privilege of helping to raise Taweyah's spirits.

Hototo quietly climbed the ladder in search of Aunt Mokni. When he approached the cooking area, the music ceased while the women who ground and performed other culinary tasks stopped in awe of the presence of Hototo. This he told me after. Aunt Mokni rose from her grinding, moving toward him in rapt anticipation. It did not come as a surprise when I came to visit Aunt Mokni, but the women could not imagine the purpose of Hototo's visit.

His gentle eyes moved slowly over Aunt Mokni, taking in her grace and sweetness. Hooking his arm through hers, he wordlessly escorted her from the cooking area into the plaza and to Taweyah's quarters. Silently they climbed down the ladder to join Nish't Ahote and myself. Taweyah was still sleeping.

I took Aunt Mokni's hand after hugging her, sensing her anxiousness. Then we moved to Taweyah, and she knelt by his side. She did not move, thus forcing me to place her hand over Taweyah's cool one. For a short while time seemed suspended, as it did during my crystal meditation.

Taweyah's eyes fluttered, then opened. Loving energy radiated in the room while I held my breath in anticipation. His eyes ceased their fluttering to open wide. After finally focusing on Aunt Mokni and causing us all some apprehension, his eyes teared. "So many years have passed!" he said.

"But I did not forget!" she said. Huge tears welled into Aunt Mokni's eyes, and also into mine. I was so caught up, I failed to notice the liquid pools in Nish't Ahote's and Hototo's eyes.

"I have waited so long. I have wished many times that I might join the spirit world," he said, "but if I had, I would have missed this event, you and all my other loved ones. Mokni, is it really you?"

"Yes, Taweyah, I have been here for almost eight moon cycles. I knew you were not well."

"I am well now! Please prop me up that I may talk to this wonderful woman, the love of my life." His eyes lighted up in an energy that had not been there for a year. His eyes were big, loving, and luminous.

Nish't Ahote, Hototo, and I bowed out to allow them their privacy. I only hoped that Taweyah did not totally exhaust himself.

Chapter 16

Spring Races

Although the traders were still many sun cycles away, there was much curiosity in the complex. Rumors abounded. Some were reasonable assumptions, while many were ridiculous. Some said they were not traders at all. If they were, why would royalty be traveling among them? Why would the party be so large? One of our scouts reported that they were not laden with goods for trade, nor would they state their reason for making such a long journey. Nish't Ahote did not seem to know what or why, but he sensed ill tidings.

Once again it was time for our races in honor of the Rain God and the season of greening. Once again *pahos* were made. Cornmeal was brought to us for purification procedures. Nish't Ahote, Hototo, and myself burned sage over the cornmeal in our special ceremonial kiva, uttering prayers and offering songs. Water from the holy spring was brought to us, and we carefully stored it in a small vessel to be carried in the races.

The long winter in the complex had many of the acolytes anxious to release their pent-up energy for the day-long races. For such was the use of our smooth stone roads. They were not just used for commerce and personal travel, but for the unification of my people and for communications with the gods.

A crowd began to gather on the rooftops of all five

of our complexes even before the sun began its journey. In outlying communities, the same preparations were in the making and the same excitement was building. Our road system was long and complex and joined other communities with this, the center community. In other communities, the day-long races would be broken down into several age brackets, even including prepuberty girls. In our center, however, there would be a one day-long race. This was the first general ceremony since the snow season. For the varying ages in the families who lived within the center, there would be short races according to age-groups at the next sunrise, but none would carry the blessed corn or the sacred water.

The crowd was wrapped in blankets in the cold predawn air. The sun was only suggesting the beginning of its journey for the day. The cliffs were gray outlines against the soft light beginning to awaken Earth Mother. There was no wind, for the Wind God often awoke later in the day. The east began to brighten while Sun Father began to cast a golden glow. In the west Fahada Butte began to take on a yellow hue. The race was to begin very far away, and by the peak of the sun cycle the runners would arrive. Then they would move on until the sun began its descent. Truly it was only a run for the hardiest, but many would try, even if they had to stop to rest along the way. Many would also give up. It was a test for the strongest spirit in the complex, and much honor would be lavished on the winner.

There was a murmur among the crowd and a cheer, for the posted messengers along the route, which began in the west and moved east, had informed us that the race had begun. Fifty young men were taking part, and the excited crowd gave a cheer, "They come!" The crowd knew the wait would be lengthy, so they appeared and disappeared in small groups, usually families or friends to offer their prayers for the well-being of their favored runner.

Nish't Ahote, Hototo, and I spent time, until the sun really began its ascent, in prayer, not just for the runners but for rain and the fertilization of the crops that had been planted all over our lands.

Then a cheer rumbled through the crowd. "They come!" Everyone gathered on each side of the road. A wave of excitement rippled through the people. Sutsi, a young acolyte, who was known for his running, was in the lead. He carried a bag of sacred cornmeal in one hand and the small vessel of holy water in the other. He grinned confidently at the cheering throng, then turned to look back, for if one of the other runners caught up to him, he had to give the blessed cornmeal and water over to that runner. Such was not the problem, for the other runners were well behind him. Sutsi was spurred on by the sound of the bull roarers—sticks twirled on strings to make the sound of low thunder. The crowd got as close as they dared to cheer him on.

Suddenly a woman with a small child was hurtled into Sutsi's path, sending the holy water flying through the air. The little vessel of holy water crashed on the ground, trickling out over the smooth stone road. Sutsi managed to hold on to the sacred cornmeal, but sat on the road as in shock.

The woman with the small child pointed to a young female acolyte who stood near. "I was pushed by that young woman!" The young female acolyte, Pokiba, ran, making her guilt very obvious. Salavi, the elder who was standing nearby, shouted, "Do not let her get away!"

Sutsi erupted hysterically. "I have defiled the races!

I am worth nothing!" He tore at his eyes with his nails, mixing blood, sweat, and dirt with his tears.

Salavi bent to attempt to comfort him but could not. Sutsi continued to berate himself, scratching his arms, chest, and legs, screaming hoarsely and piteously.

Nish't Ahote, Hototo, and I by now had worked our way through the crowd, and seeing that Sutsi could not be calmed, Nish't Ahote grabbed him by the arms, pinning his arms behind his back. Sutsi seemed controlled by demons as he kicked at everyone around him, swinging his head from side to side with spittle and tears flying.

"Bind him, Salavi, Hototo. He is not in control! Coyote Woman, run to open the kiva for healing. Place the crystals in position!"

It was difficult to believe that one young man could be so strong to require three grown men to bind him. They struggled on toward the kiva. The crowd was hushed while two of the other runners arrived on the scene, looking rather bewildered as they attempted to understand what had happened.

Hototo threw Sutsi over his shoulder as he began his struggle down the ladder into the cool of the kiva. He waited for Nish't Ahote to proceed first, then began his descent with Salavi not far behind. When Sutsi writhed within his bonds, Hototo nearly lost his footing. Nish't Ahote told Hototo, Salavi, and myself to hold fast to the ladder. Climbing a couple of rungs, Nish't Ahote struck Sutsi on the back of the head at the nape of the neck to render him unconscious. At last Hototo was able to bring poor Sutsi to the healing block, on which I had placed the crystals.

Together, we gently laid the crazed runner on his back on the long slab. Nish't Ahote instructed Hototo what to do if he awoke again in an irrational state. His bonds were only slightly loosened. We also knew

that somehow we must make clear to him that it was
not he who had desecrated the importance of the race.
Moreover, his bonds must not be loosened until he
was obviously more coherent.

At that time Salavi and Nish't Ahote and I ascended
the ladder, leaving Hototo in charge.

As Nish't Ahote climbed the ladder behind Salavi, I
was unsure what to expect. The crowd was still tightly
assembled while three students brought in the young
female acolyte, Pokiba. She had medium brown skin
with long lustrous hair and dark shining eyes. Her eyes
were filled with defiance. She was probably twelve sun
cycles of age and had been in the school for four season cycles. Her body was well matured with the sweet
premature curves of womanhood. She exuded a restlessness that most of our male acolytes did not. It was
most unusual for a female to reflect this arrogance.
She held her head high when Salavi asked, "Why des-
ecrate our holy ceremonies?"

Too quickly she responded, "I did no such thing!"

"Did you not push that mother and child into our
runner who bore the holy water and sacred grain?"

"I did nothing of the sort!"

"What sort of young woman would wish to defile
our ceremonies with such an overt action?" asked Salavi as I quietly looked on to closely observe her
responses.

Her responses told me that we would get no answers from her. Nish't Ahote requested that the three
acolytes take her to the war kiva for further questioning. It was very obvious that we could get nothing
from her publicly. She seemed almost to enjoy the
attention she was receiving.

The three acolytes took her across the plaza to the
war kiva. She did not offer any resistance. She fairly

swaggered between the three young men, indicating that she might be more difficult than we thought to question.

The crowd began to disperse, and the runners as they arrived were informed of the tragic turn of events. As they knew, lack of respect for our festivals and ceremonies was the most serious offense in our culture. The only other one that was as serious was murder. In a sense the young lady had committed murder—murder of the welfare of our people—murder of the welfare of our young runner, Sutsi.

As I descended into the kiva, my heart was heavy, for I did not think that Pokiba truly understood the severity of the problem she had created. She had been one of the better students, and it seemed incredible that she could have done this deed. I wondered if we would ever really know her purpose. Two other elders joined us in the war kiva.

Pokiba was tied to a roof support beam. She glared defiantly at everyone around her. Her cotton clothing was drenched with perspiration, and she stood proudly, as though accusing us of being wrong. Tendrils of dark hair hung in loose disarray around her face.

Salavi began, "Pokiba! You are an intelligent, sensitive young woman. You have done well within the school. Your high regard for the ways of the Anasazi have always been obvious. You must surely understand the seriousness of what has happened."

There was no response—only the haughty arrogance.

Salavi continued, "The ceremony has been ruined. The welfare of all our people is at stake. Sutsi has become irrational, thinking he has been responsible. If we cannot convince him that it is not his fault, he may remain irrational, which is in the Anasazi way the same as murder. Have you nothing to say to this?"

Still the same self-righteous attitude remained, with no answer.

Now it was Nish't Ahote's turn. He walked to the young woman, pinning her with a hard, calculating look. She suddenly seemed nervous. Her eyes lost their defiance and dropped almost modestly to the dirt floor of the kiva. Her teacher was very aware of the change in her demeanor. Using this as an advantage, he lifted her chin to bring her eyes to focus on his. "Pokiba, my little promising student, please tell us your side of the story."

A tear escaped the corner of one of her eyes, but she did not speak. She was like a rock. Assuming he would hear nothing, he turned to leave the kiva. The elders and I followed. Then seeing that we were leaving, she spoke. "I am not at fault! It is my word against hers!" She shook her head defiantly while we all continued up the ladder.

The other two elders shook their heads taking their leave. Salavi, Nish't Ahote, and I stood together as they left, and Salavi cast me a despairing look. There was a solemn silence. We read each other's thoughts. The Rain Gods had not been appeased. What misfortune would befall us? Would our crops fail? What other negative events would befall our people?

Salavi spoke. "Let us see what a time of fasting may do to loosen her tongue, for this may be a new experience for her."

"But if she has had a womanly cycle, then this will not be a new experience!" Nish't Ahote declared. "But you are right. It will be the easiest method to use, both for her and for us."

Salavi grabbed his arm, saying, "We must also speak with the woman and her child. In my mind's eye, I do not think the woman speaks falsely, but we must do what is fair and honest."

We moved toward the woman and her child, who stood still, waiting in the plaza. She and her small one sat in a corner. Her face was red and swollen from the tears of agony she had been shedding. There were still huge tears that flowed down her high cheekbones while even the baby whimpered, sensing her sorrow. She looked up at us with a trembling lower lip as Nish't Ahote bent down to catch her attention.

"I ca—ca—cannot speak!" she sobbed.

"Why, woman, can you not find your tongue?" Salavi gently asked.

"I am in the presence of our, our . . ." and she broke into hysteria again.

Salavi and Nish't Ahote exchanged glances while we gave the woman more time. When finally she gained some control, the sun priest laid his hands lightly on either side of her head in the healing position, saying, "Woman, I am a person born in the same way as the wee one you hold to your bosom. We are all the same. I am the people, and you are the people. Give this some thought while you gather yourself together."

After a short period of time, she calmed. Salavi asked, "Can you tell us your side of the story?"

"I was holding my babe and watching the races, for my son was one of the runners. I—" Again she broke into a sob. We waited while Nish't Ahote continued to put light pressure on her head. "I knew he would not win, for he has told me of Sutsi's speed, but," she whimpered, "as I held my babe, I was pushed firmly into the path of Sutsi . . . I, well, there is little more I can say." She rocked back and forth, holding her child and moaning.

Nish't Ahote continued his healing for a short time, telling her to go on her way and to pray to Awonawilona. She gathered herself and her babe, retreating to a room to which she had been temporarily assigned.

* * *

Sutsi was not doing well. The early part of the next sun cycle found him no longer babbling, but he simply stared off into another world, giving no signs of recognition to anyone, including his family, who had stayed on out of love and concern for their son. He did not eat and refused drink, which added to our anxiety.

Taweyah had been told, and he foresaw it all as a very bad omen. He advised that we should not hesitate to mete out punishment, for this must never happen again. Taweyah seemed stronger with Aunt Mokni attending him. She had moved into the room next to him, giving up her kitchen duties to give him her full attention.

An uneasy tension pervaded the complex. It seemed that all my people were as concerned as Sutsi's family, the elders, and we of the priesthood. Two sun cycles passed. Sutsi's condition remained the same. The instructors and acolytes moved through their routines almost as wraiths. Everyone knew that something must be done to appease the gods. And so we waited.

Finally Nish't Ahote summoned Hototo and myself to the healing kiva. Thinking that conditions must have changed, we hastened to his bidding. Arriving at the kiva, we saw that nothing had changed, except that without food and water, Sutsi was wasting away. He was also dehydrated. Handing Hototo a large drum, Nish't Ahote bade him to play the slow, easy pattern for healing. I was to play a flute with soothing, long melodic sounds while he proceeded.

He began by burning sage to purify the room. When the room was filled with the smell, Nish't Ahote began his trance. I could see him as he sank deeper into his other world, embracing the antelope who welcomed him there. He sang a song of the antelope. It filled the room with its power. "Awonawilona, you who give the antelope the power of rejuvenation, this young man's innocence must not be defiled. May my energy, the energy of the antelope, enter and consume him that he may have that which he may need to bring him back to reality and may that which is not to your likeness be righted."

The drums and my flute continued to offer the hypnotic trance necessary for what followed. As Nish't Ahote weaved around the kiva, his body glistening with sweat, he placed his hands first on Sutsi's head. He left them for a few moments while he murmured the same prayer incantations as before. Then he went to Sutsi's mouth, sucking with his own and spitting bad energy into a bowl. I promptly took the bowl out of the kiva and returned the bowl at his side. Hototo continued the drumming. I resumed my flute. Then again with the help of his antelope spirit guide, the sun priest moved his hands to Sutsi's chest. Feeling around Sutsi's heart, he murmured the same prayers as before and bent down to suck the negative energy from the heavy heart that felt such guilt in defiling the sacred ceremonies. Nish't Ahote spat the negative energy into the same bowl, and this time Hototo took the bowl out, for flute music is love music from the heart. It must not stop, lest the pulsing of the heart be broken. Then Nish't Ahote laid his perspiring body over Sutsi's and once again we waited.

Finally we gave Sutsi our mutual blessings and left him in what we hoped would be a carefully guarded peace.

At last Pokiba called. She was hungry and thirsty. An acolyte who attended to her needs called us. I found Nish't Ahote already with her. We waited only a very short time for Hototo to arrive.

Pokiba stared weakly at the niche in the round wall

of the kiva in front of her. She looked haggard from the exhaustion of being tied in her standing position and from being deprived of food and drink for two sun cycles. Her hair hung in clumps while deep circles had set in under her eyes from lack of sleep.

Nish't Ahote was to talk while we were to serve as witnesses to what she had to say. He stepped in front of her, watching her as she simply seemed to stare through him. With a thickened tongue she said, "Water, and I will talk."

Hototo rushed to bring her water, but Nish't Ahote stayed his hand. When Pokiba realized what he was doing, she flared into arrogance, but only for a moment. She seemed to understand that time would march on and conditions would become more intolerable. Through her swollen tongue she uttered hoarsely, "Enough, I am done! What do you want to know?"

Patiently, close to her ear, Nish't Ahote inquired, "What would you like to tell us, Pokiba?"

"Nish't Ahote, I am but twelve sun cycles of age." She gasped and choked, then went on. "I, like Coyote Woman, have adored you for a long time. I could see your infatuation, or perhaps it is a deep love for Coyote Woman, and always felt I could not compete. I was not alone in my dejection, for someone else in the complex felt an infatuation for Coyote Woman. Dejection threw us together, and we became friends. To him I grew very attached, and it was for him I pushed the woman." A tear escaped the corner of her eyes while her chin quivered.

Nish't Ahote put his hand beneath her chin, pulling her face to meet his. Her eyes, however, remained downcast while he said, "Is 'he' an acolyte in our system?"

"Yes, O revered one. Rather he was." She seemed not to want to go on. Perhaps she was thinking she had said too much. "Now, may I be given food and water?"

"No, Pokiba. There is one more thing we must know. We need to know the name of the young man of whom you speak. We must somehow prevent him, if possible, from causing other disturbances to the Gods and to the welfare of our people."

Shaking her head from side to side, she cried, "But you cannot prevent him, for he is not one of us anymore!" Then breaking into a mournful wail, she lamented, "O Awonawilona! What have I done?"

That which I had suspected all along suddenly became very clear. It was Wisoko! Once again my people were plagued with his malevolence. Nish't Ahote flashed a sickened glance my way, then stated in a firm voice, "Would you prefer to become a raider as Wisoko has done? Think carefully, Pokiba, while we take our leave. Food will be brought."

Pokiba wept loudly, making strange animallike sounds. We heard her weeping until we ascended through the roof of the kiva and an acolyte covered the exit with a stone slab.

There was no need to express how heartsick the three of us felt, Nish't Ahote and I doubly so, for we were the seeds of all the unrest. A strange heavy silence hung over us until at last the spell was broken as Nish't Ahote quietly but clearly said, "We must make her atone."

A meeting was called, and Taweyah was brought in his litter. Salavi, Machakwi, and the other three elders were present, and, of course, Nish't Ahote, Hototo, and myself. Machakwi seemed his usual scowling self while Salavi and the other elders appeared as in a trance. A pipe was passed around while wisps of smoke found their way to the ventilation hole in the ceiling of the kiva.

Machakwi began with an opening statement. "We have two issues to discuss. Let us save the unpleasant one for last. First let us discuss our approaching visitors. They are still many sun cycles away, but they are not traders, or do not seem to be, and they refuse to state their business except to say that they come in peace."

Honani added, "I cannot remember ever having had one of the Mayan royalty visit our sacred homeland. I do not know if we should be fearful or honored to have such an exalted one call upon us."

Salavi shook his head, saying, "I do not think we should allow them to come any closer than the first shrine on the south road unless they will state their purpose. This will give us time to evaluate."

"It also may be," said Machakwi, "that they herald the arrival of many Mayan soldiers. I have heard of no unrest among the Hohokam and Mogollan or even at Uwitsi far to the south of us, but we cannot be too cautious."

Taweyah sat propped upon his litter while his eyes sparkled and his brow furrowed. Then raising his right hand to signal his desire to be heard, he spoke. "We are a people of peace. Since our guests will not state their purpose, we know not what to expect. Therefore, it would be my suggestion that we prepare for the worst, even though it may not prove necessary. Let us summon all our young warriors and make certain we are prepared to defend ourselves should the need arise."

A loud murmur of agreement could be heard. "So be it!" exclaimed Salavi. "Let Choviohoya be summoned to organize our forces."

Once again the pipe was passed around the kiva in

silence. It was as though no one wanted to address the next problem, but we knew we must. At long last Nish't Ahote spoke. "Our young acolyte, Pokiba, has spoken. She admits to having pushed the young mother and child into Sutsi. She also confesses that she was told to do this deed by one Wisoko, who defected from our society and our system to become one of the raiders." Having given his synopsis, Nish't Ahote retired to sit once more at Hototo's side.

One elder, Pavati, whose girth was such that he moved as does the turtle, said in his deep rumbling voice, "Does she understand the seriousness of her deed?"

Immediately Machakwi added, "Does she understand that by committing this sacrilege, she has found ill favor not just for herself, but for all of us with the Gods? Does she know what happens to someone who desecrates the New Fire Ceremony by entering and trespassing on our roads when they are closed during that holy time?"

"I do not believe she, in her immaturity, thought of those things before or during the tragic act she committed," responded Nish't Ahote. "However, her confinement for three sun cycles has given her the time to review such things."

Salavi had been sitting quietly, listening intently and evaluating everything he heard. He raised his arm midway to express his desire to be heard. "Pokiba has shown an arrogance that was broken only by more than two sun cycles of fasting. If we exile her, she may join Wisoko. In fact, this may be what she wants. In any case the people and the Gods must be appeased. We must decide what to do with her."

Machakwi joined in. "Nish't Ahote, is there nothing in the legends of our people to advise us in our dilemma?"

"The only answer I can give is that of the New Fire Ceremony. We have tradionally dismembered one who profanes our sacred roads," answered Nish't Ahote.

"I do not believe we need to be so harsh, at least not physically, to consider doing such a ghastly thing. Perhaps we could request that our three priests find a nonviolent method by which she may atone for her sacrilege, yet please the Gods and our people," suggested Salavi.

Pavati rose to add, "This is one of the most unusual events in my old life. I agree to leave the problem to our priests in whom we have much faith. It is not a problem for the elders but a problem for our holy priests. So be it!"

The other three elders agreed, and the meeting became a discussion on other issues in the complex until at last Taweyah was carried out and Nish't Ahote gave a quiet signal for us to depart.

Runners spread the news. The Purification Ceremony for the desecration of the races would be held just before the sun made its descent in the next sun cycle. This would give the people who must travel longer distances the time they would need. Sutsi had recovered but seemed now as an old man. Perhaps his trance was serving him with a vision quest. Some did not have to fast in the wilderness as I did to reach this state. Each person achieved this in their own way. The woman and her child returned home after Pokiba's confession, and Pokiba was kept in isolation with food, water, and water for cleansing. When she asked how much longer she would be held, Nish't Ahote simply told her that she would be freed after her atonement.

Nish't Ahote, Hototo, and I conferred at great length with Taweyah, who pulled from the recesses of his mind bits of a story he heard as a boy about some-one who had desecrated the Solstice Celebration and was caught in the act. He said that the guilty young man was sacrificed to the Gods in the same fashion as the Mayan sacrificial ceremonials. Now, he said, we are a people of peace who did not believe in physical violence except for purposes of defense. Of course, as Nish't Ahote had said in the New Fire Ceremony, a person who trespassed on our sacred roads was quietly dismembered and the body parts buried in four directions as far from the complex as was possible. This, however, was done in the dark of night and never before the people. It was finally decided that we would not use physical violence, but would use mental punishment instead, for the people and the Gods must at all cost be appeased.

It was nearly time for the sun to begin its ascent in the east. Preparations were complete. *Pahos* had been made. Nish't Ahote, Hototo, and myself each carried a *mongko,* whose parts represented respect, harmony, and love. The ball of earth containing water symbolized the earth and seas, while the perfect ear of corn represented man. The turkey feathers that hung from it were part of the mystery of creation. These *mongkos* empowered us with supreme spiritual authority. We all three wore our red robes. Nish't Ahote and Hototo wore four braids in their hair, each adorned with an eagle feather. I wore my hair in two traditional whorls, one over each ear with a macaw feather in each whorl and my feather earbobs. Taweyah was carried on his litter and was accompanied by Aunt Mokni to the bottom of Fahatta Butte. Salavi and two other elders flanked Taweyah on either side as the people began to gather around them. Pavati and Machakwi accompanied Pokiba and we three of the priesthood to the top of the butte. Pokiba was dressed in black, and she carried two *pahos* to plant on the shrine on top of the butte. She seemed very nervous, for her hands were not steady as she held the *pahos*. She had been assured that there would be no physical violence, but her eyes darted here and there in the gray of the morning as though she expected to see a rattler.

The gray silhouette of the cliffs across the wash began to take on a suggestion of yellow as Sun Father began to shed his light on the beauty of our fourth world. The musicians, who marched with us, consisted of four drums, one flute player, and four singers who wore copper bells at their knees. At a signal from Nish't Ahote, they began their sorrowful song. We marched ever so slowly out of the plaza and turned to the road toward Fahatta Butte. The orchestra remained behind us.

By the time we reached the base of the butte, the sky was aglow in the east, and the warm rays of the sun were beginning to be felt. We stopped at the foot of the butte to await a song of forgiveness while the people listened in rapt anticipation. Never had anyone seen a ceremony such as this, so the tension was high and all eyes were on Pokiba. I glanced in her direction to find her eyes had filled with tears and her chin was quivering.

The song ended, and we began our ascent. There were hand and foot holds in the side of the butte, and the climb was a steep one. To keep our hands free, we tied the *mongkos* and *pahos*, across our backs. The climb was slow. Pokiba led the way. She nearly lost her footing at one point and then finally took a firm hold of herself to finish the climb. I followed behind her to direct her to the shrine near the edge of the butte. Behind me was Nish't Ahote, Hototo, Machakwi, and Pavati. At last we were all assembled. The drummers below ceased, and the ceremony began.

The crowd below was hushed. Each person's face was turned upward. All eyes were on us. I was certain that Pokiba probably thought she was the only one being observed, for though she kept her eyes downcast, she was so close to the edge of the butte that I knew she could not help but see the people who observed.

Nish't Ahote stepped forward to the edge of the butte to offer a prayer to the four directions in his deep resonant voice.

Gods of the cosmos, hear us!
Hear us as we pray.
Hear us as we pray.
The life we celebrate today,
we celebrate each and every sun cycle.
The babe, the child, the essence of our people—
Protect and sanctify us in our sacred ways.
North, East, South, West, grant us new life
To purify us from the depths of the earth.
Hear us as we pray!
Hear us as we pray!

Then taking his *mongko* to the shrine, he placed it on the turkey feather down that was surrounded by a circle of rocks, then returned to his place next to me.

It was my turn. I stepped to the edge of the butte to stand next to the shrine, and raising my voice toward the upper world, I offered my plea to the Gods.

O birds on your sacred perches,
Take our message to the Gods.
May they look with love on all things.

Love and purity to people,
Love and purity to animals,
Love and purity to plants,
Love and purity to mountains.
Our spirit is one and our way is balance.
O birds on your sacred perches,
Take our message to the Gods.
May they bring us to the true path.
Truth and strength to the people,
Truth and strength to animals,
Truth and strength to plants,
Truth and strength to mountains.
Our spirit is one and our way is balance.

Then placing my *mongko* next to Nish't Ahote's, I returned to my place next to Pokiba.

Finally Hototo stepped forward. Stepping to the shrine, he offered his prayer to the Gods through the earth and trees.

O trees, whose branches reach toward the upper
   world.
O trees, whose roots sink deep into Earth
   Mother,
Take our supplications upward!
May the red of the sun be as a purification fire
   for a new sun cycle.
Set the forces of all living things in motion.
Set the forces of our ancestors in motion
That we may know purification has come.

He reverently placed the third *mongko* on the shrine, then turned to walk slowly back to his place next to Nish't Ahote.

We all three stepped forward to offer a prayer for Pokiba, for her direction in the future would depend

on the energy she received from us as well as the
Gods. In this prayer we shared the three parts. Nish't
Ahote took the first part, I took the second part, and
Hototo the third. At the end we spoke together to
repeat Hototo's last lines.

Awonawilona, hear us from this center of spiri-
tual power.
We are the Anasazi—the people of peace.
All we do, we must do in balance—
to set in motion our positive energies
To reestablish the world in balance.
In this time of confusion,
may Pokiba's guiding spirit choose the correct
path for her
A path to maintain harmony and balance for all.
May the Gods see no reason to become the
great regulator.
No floods, no eruptions, no famine, no
earthquakes!
Hear us Awonawilona!
Hear us in our implorations!
Hear us Awonawilona!
Hear us in our implorations!

Pokiba's eyes were filled with great large tears that
spilled down to leave large dark wet spots on her
black robe. Her hands trembled, showing a great effort to continue holding her *pahos*. Her punishment
was great. She alone bore the shame. I wondered how
this would affect her in years to come. Her irrational
love for Wisoko had led her down the path of the
forces of evil. Silently I prayed for her. I prayed to
the Gods to give her strength to reform her destiny
in a positive balanced direction.

Then Nish't Ahote gave the signal. The turkey must be sacrificed.

I watched the turkey, which waited quietly in its cage. Its plumage was beautiful and would not be wasted. There was a flat slab of rock behind the shrine with a long shiny black obsidian knife resting on it awaiting its prey. We of the priesthood removed our robes, handing them to Pavati and Machakwi. I was wearing only a colorful cotton apron at my loins with my medicine bag hanging from my waist. My breasts swung free in the heat of the sun. Nish't Ahote's muscular frame was covered only by a loincloth. Hototo was similarly clad.

I removed the turkey from his cage. Placing it on the sacrificial rock, Hototo would assist by holding it down. Nish's Ahote began a long, wailing chant. He reached toward the upper world, singing his high, eerie, soaring sounds, then bent down to Earth Mother in the fetal position. His chant was deep and muffled. Then rising, he took the obsidian knife in his hand, and after one quick accurate slash, he reached inside the bird's chest cavity to withdraw the palpitating heart. Handing the bloody thing to me, I held it in my hands so he could take the next step.

The fresh blood of the turkey was purifying. Walking slowly to Pokiba, Nish't Ahote drew a red line from the center of her forehead, her third eye, to the tip of her nose. He then drew a zigzag representing lightning on each of her cheeks, while chanting one of our well-known purification prayers. Our proximity to the edge of the butte would have made some very nervous, but most Anasazi were not afraid of heights.

Pokiba's tears mingled with the blood on her freshly painted face, washing out the impurities from within her soul. She trembled and turned her swimming eyes toward Hototo and myself.

What happened next, only the Gods could explain.
Eototo, the chief of all our spirit dancers, followed by
Aholi, chief spirit dancer of the corn clan, appeared
from the back of Fahatta Butte. The hand and toe-
holds in the side of the butte offered them the opportunity for a surprise appearance. Their grotesque
masks had frightened many a poor child, and Pokiba
turned with eyes brimming with tears and gasped. In
so doing, her foot caught one large stone of the shrine,
causing her to lose her balance. Her body twisted,
sending her over the edge of the butte, hurtling
through the air to the hard rocks below.

The people gasped and stepped back to observe her
poor lifeless form in all its distorted, misshapen horror. Her blood trailed over the rocks and seeped into
the earth as a small group of people began a high-
pitched keening to lament her death. My heart was
torn as I realized that the keening must be the grief
of her family, who had been watching it all from
below. The ceremony seemed to be over, but Nish't
Ahote signaled the elders below to assist in quieting
the people.

Finally when the commotion had passed leaving
only the low wail of Pokiba's mother, aunts, and sisters, Nish't Ahote's booming loud voice offered a eu-
logy for Pokiba.

> Pokiba, you are a graceful bird that
>   flies into the evening
> Where the Sun Father disappears behind
>   The Chuska mountain peaks
> To begin your travels to the land of
>   our ancestors.
> Pokiba, you brought hopes for the future.
> Remember Tawa, Sun Father,

Remember the beauty of Earth Mother,
    who gives birth to all.
Pokiba, the Gods have never faltered,
Offering love for all mankind
That brother may become father
That sister may become mother
So that you may know love.
Go with the knowledge of our love!

So began our descent down the side of the butte to join the dispersing crowd. Salavi, Taweyah, Aunt Mokni, and the other elders waited for us to join them. We quietly moved away from the pitiful scene beneath the butte. Pokiba's family would take her earthly body with them and respectfully bury it beneath one corner of their home. Her errant ways were, to the Anasazi, a reflection on the unrest in her family, who raised her. Therefore, there would be no sympathy offered her family, for the problem had always been theirs. If the Anasazi were to remain a people of peace, there must be balance and harmony in all.

Chapter 17

Discovery of the Past

A feeling of sorrow could be felt in the sun cycles that followed our sacred races and Pokiba's tragic death. We awaited our Mayan visitors, who drew nearer every day. Since they were not traders, our curiosities were piqued. By the time Tawa began his journey once again, they would have reached our soldiers, who were stationed a half a sun cycle outside our complex. We insisted that they state their business at that time or they would be permitted to come no farther.

Nish't Ahote requested my presence again that night, for there had been much tension built up in everyone as a result of the desecration of our spring races and the tragic death of Pokiba. I arrived to find our double mats awaiting us with a feather throw awaiting the chill of night. I descended the ladder to find the same strange force drawing me toward him. I thought perhaps it was even more potent than ever before. He immediately arose to enfold me in his wonderful embrace. There were no words spoken. None were necessary. The urgency between us was unbearable. We sank onto the mats to explore each other once again.

His tongue traveled languorously all over my body, making only one brief stop. It flicked lightly over my power spot for a short time, sending me from Earth Mother to the seven dimensions that hung in a cluster in the upper world. Then returning to my mouth, he descended to my throat and to my ears. His tongue tickled, then licked at my earlobes, then suddenly he bit ever so gently. Each tender bite became more intense, until at last he firmly bit my earlobes, holding on with a pain that turned to ecstasy. I felt the forces growing within me. The power gathered within me, suddenly exploding as the sun might do if it were ecstatically happy.

I was infused with passion and energy. I worshiped his lean, muscular body. I covered his body with my tongue and my nibbles, working my way to his toes and up the back of his legs. Then he turned himself onto his back to receive my praises. My imagination ran rampant as I licked and kissed and lightly bit in places usually hidden from sight from everyone. Then I encircled his engorged member with my tongue. It pulsed and sang beneath my touch. He moaned, each time louder as the tension built. Then he tightened every muscle in his body, heaving and loudly exclaiming, "I am here! I join you as one in body and in spirit!" He seized me and convulsed, moaning loudly, then gradually fading. I tasted him, and he was slightly sweet.

I looked at him inquisitively. I did not know we could fly together in this way. I thought a joining of our bodies would be necessary. Now the Gods, or was it Nish't Ahote, had shown me a new way. Even though our bodies had not joined, I felt deliciously satisfied. Such, it seemed, were the wonders of love!

After a short time, he looked at me with warm liquid brown eyes. He said nothing, but gathered me into his muscular arms as we drifted off together into the land of dreams.

He awakened me later to his kisses as we joined our bodies languorously as one. I descended into dreamland, marveling at this man who was my teacher and lover. Would he always teach me new things?

At last our visitors arrived. Our warriors stopped them a sun cycle of time outside our cultural center, allowing them to go no farther. The Mayan lord was bedecked almost ridiculously, I was told, and was indignant at being halted prior to his destination. Then he proclaimed that he would share his purpose only with one as exalted as he.

A runner was sent to our complex to give us this news, and the decision was made to send Salavi to be the ambassador. Salavi packed to leave begrudgingly, and assured us that he would return promptly to share with us the results of his conference. The time he was gone seemed as an eternity, for truly that was most unusual. No one in the complex, young or old, could remember anything so extraordinary as this. In my meditations, I felt only a great sense of evil—a black cloud that hung over me.

At long last, Salavi returned. His approach to the complex seemed slow and labored, amplifying that black cloud that had hung over me during this time. I knew in my heart all was not well. Propping his walking stick against the thick wall of our complex, he sighed in exhaustion. Then, having rested himself for a short time, he waited. He seemed hesitant to share that which he knew he must.

Nish't Ahote broke the silence, though cautiously to say, "Salavi, we have been friends for too many season cycles to mention. Your heart is heavy. What is it that you do not want to say?"

Salavi's face showed great concern as he proclaimed, "You do not want to hear that which I have to say, but I must say it, for it concerns our own Coyote Woman."

He bid us to sit down. Then looking searchingly at me, he removed my cotton attire, baring the shoulder that was covered. Then lightly touching my shoulder, he said, "It is because of this that he has come."

I looked from Nish't Ahote to Salavi and back again, for I did not know of that which he spoke. Nish't Ahote also looked perplexed. Then he asked, "Salavi, what do you need to tell us? Please tell us now."

Taking his head in his hands, he quietly stated, "Nish't Ahote, we have lost her, for she is Mayan. Our Coyote Woman is Mayan!"

My mind raced. That explained why I always knew I was different. And now there was something else to be considered, on the back of my shoulder. My mother had not satisfied me with her answers on my trip home when I questioned her of these things. What, I wondered, could it all mean? In desperation, I asked Salavi, "Who am I?"

"Coyote Woman, your father has come to take you back to reclaim your heritage. He would wed you to another. He is of royalty and so are you. My heart grieves that our own Coyote Woman should be taken from us, but thus is the mission of the Mayan lord, Al Balam. That is all I know!"

"Salavi, what is it on my shoulder that is impossible for me to see?"

"Little Coyote Woman, you carry the mark of the star that appears rarely in the sky. Nish't Ahote can elaborate, for this star has no tail, but travels slowly as do other stars and is much brighter. This is your destiny, or so that mark from birth would indicate."

Nish't Ahote's expression was crestfallen. He looked into nothingness and made no comment. Then he turned to Salavi to say, "I cannot believe what I hear. I would speak to others for confirmation." Then wrapping his robes tightly around him, he walked with a heavy step from the plaza and from our company. I stared after him, then turned back to Salavi to politely take my leave.

In my quarters, I clutched Puppy to my bosom. I could not believe what was happening. How could it possibly be? There must be a horrible mistake. Someone else must have known what the truth was, for I knew I belonged here. The Anasazi way of life was my way of life. We were the people of peace, the Mayans, the people of blood and sacrifice. The Mayans were known to go to war to gather prisoners for sacrifice. To them war and bloodshed was a way of life. True, their culture was more advanced than ours. They calculated time with great accuracy, and knew more of astrology than we did. Somehow, their astrology could tell of your fate and also of your personality. Of all of this my Mayan teacher had spoken. The Mayans built great edifices—much greater than ours. They traded more widely than we did and produced the most curious tiny bells made of what they called copper. They told us it was a part of the turquoise we mined, but refused to disclose the way of separating the copper from the turquoise. We coveted their macaw feathers for our own ceremonial use. Many of our ceremonial procedures were much like theirs, but our purpose was balance, harmony, and peace. Theirs was only the appeasement of their Gods, even if they appeased them with sacrificial human violence.

And what of this man, Al Balam, who claimed to be my father. How did he know I was his daughter? They said he was of royalty and so was I. I had no desire to be of Mayan royalty! I wished only to be me, Coyote Woman, free and happy in my road of life. Why, after fourteen season cycles, had my father finally come to reclaim me? Why not when I was a child? Of course, I thought, as a child I was not of a marriageable age, so I would have been of no benefit to him. But how could he have possibly learned of me? Who was my real mother? Why was I here with the people I had grown to love? Why had my mother, Talasiva, not answered my questions when I inquired not long ago?

To control my uneasiness, I picked up my crystals. Puppy curled up at the foot of my mat as I grasped them, one in my left hand and the large one between my legs. When they had warmed to my body, I felt a great calm gradually creep into my overextended mind. I realized there was nothing I could do until all of my questions were answered. I would have to wait. Awonawilona, I prayed, give me patience that I might make the right decision. Nish't Ahote, I knew, would advise me, once given all the facts. His loving, angular, features flashed before me, leaving me with a delicious sense of confidence. Surely he would not allow my father to ruin our love. I needed only to wait until Al Balam, as he was called, had arrived to answer all my questions. So I knew I must somehow exercise great patience.

The sun priest had not summoned me. I was alone, so alone, and wished to speak to him. He had said, however, that he would speak to others for confirmation. Perhaps he had already done so. Why, I wondered, would he not speak to me of what he had learned? Perhaps he had learned nothing. Perhaps his silence was an indication that I had nothing to fear. Then a messenger arrived to inform me of a meeting in the large kiva with our Mayan guest. I was clutched with a nervous tension that would not cease. Puppy pranced as I dressed. I carried my medicine pouch hidden under my red robe and donned my string sandals. I wore my inlaid shell and feather earbobs. My hair was coiled into two knots over my ears through which I inserted two eagle feathers.

I moved as a ghost across the plaza, hardly noticing the students and acolytes as they stared at me. At last I reached the kiva. Standing at the top of the ladder, I heard much hushed conversation below. Then I realized I could not descend the ladder, for a great dark cloud enveloped me, leaving me dizzy and disoriented. It wrapped me tightly in its fog of blackness, then dissipated as the image of the eagle stared me straight in the face. It then took wing to fly out of the plaza and out of my sight. A great calm and sense of well-being overtook me, and I was finally able to descend the ladder.

At the sight of me, all conversation ceased. I fingered my medicine pouch, then looked at all who were in attendance. My eyes fell first on Nish't Ahote, who looked up at me despairingly and lovingly. I was destroyed. What did he know? Why had he not summoned me? His eyes seemed circled and somewhat red. He had been upset. There were things I somehow felt I did not know. Our eyes seared each other's with a heat to match Tawa's—Sun Father's. My heart faltered and my insides grumbled, for I knew! Yes, I knew!

My father, as I turned my eyes to him, was robust and strong. His head was very broad and his skull was flat, not just in the back of the head, but both in the forehead and the back of the head as well. His earlobes were pierced, as ours were, for pendants, but so also was the septum of his nose. The left side of his nose was pierced with a topaz set in it. His hair was long, black, and wrapped around the head, braided like a wreath, leaving a bit to hang down in tassels. Tied to his hair was an obsidian disc. All Mayan men of royalty wore mirrors. His hair on the top of his head was singed and short. There were many permanent paintings on his body, and he was extremely cross-eyed. He wore a ponch (*pati*) over his shoulders and sandals (*keuel*) made of tapir tied to his feet by two thongs. Over his breechclout, he wore a long ankle-length skirt to which was attached the skin of a jaguar, his spirit guide and namesake. He wore a belt made of a carved row of human heads. His fingers displayed jade rings, and his toes were also ringed with jade and some turquoise. His front teeth were filed and inlaid with jade. His headpiece was carved of wood done in wickerwork. This was used as a framework for an elaborate feather ensemble topped with swirling masses of shimmering green quetzal feathers. It occurred to me that this was royalty to the Mayan. He dressed this way all the time. Somehow, though I knew of all this from my Mayan teacher, it never seemed real. My warrior was not at all like he was. It all seemed almost garish. I wondered if my father knew that I spoke Mayan. I felt I should not tell him. I would just watch and wait.

The silence seemed forever. I noted that Taweyah had been brought in on a litter and his eyes sparkled brilliantly. Then my father spoke:

"My daughter is lovely, as was her mother. She shall do justice to her new bridegroom in Tula."

Much to my surprise, Machakwi rose to speak. "If it were our decision, we the elders, and I am also certain of the priesthood, would not allow our Coyote Woman to be taken from us, for her shamanistic abilities have endeared her to us as well as to all her people. She is Anasazi raised and, I suspect, will always be one of us in the core of her spirit. We, however, will leave the decision to her, for she is the master of her fate."

My mind was shocked, for this was a kindness I never expected from Machakwi. This was the first time I had ever heard such words from him, but what had he really said? If this was to be my decision, I must be aware of all the facts. I did not know everything. This prompted me to ask, "Will someone tell me what, why, when? I cannot make a decision without knowing all that there is to know." An interpreter stepped forward who did not know I spoke Mayan.

Another silence followed. Then my father stepped forward to speak, "My daughter, hear me well! When you were a baby, my legitimate wife, Ix Can, began to disapprove of many of our Mayan ways. She left me with a small group of sympathizers, taking you and traveling north to what she heard was a land of people of peace. She died en route. Her sympathizers continued on with you to this, the land of the Anasazi. You were placed in the home of another family and raised to the magnificent womanhood you have attained. I come to reclaim you to wed you to the ruler of Tula, who presently seeks a wife."

My head spun, for now I knew my heritage. But the questions tumbled out almost without my having any control. "How did you find me? What leads you so far away from your land?" I inquired.

"My daughter, you have the mark from birth of the star that shines much brighter than others. I knew when you were born that you would be different from other children. I was proud of you, and now I am proud once again—proud to reclaim you."

"But who told you of my mark from birth?" I asked.

"When you became a woman, you chose a warrior for your puberty rites. That warrior was Mayan. He was one of my commanders in Chichén Itzá, and one day soon after arriving home from your area, he spoke of this lovely young Anasazi with the mark of a large star on her shoulder." He paused, then said, "I am here! Are you not happy to know who you are?"

He seemed so self-assured and proud. It was as if all things would surely go his way. His arrogance equaled his ridiculous appearance. We were a simple people. We dressed as he did only for sacred, ceremonial reasons. We did not hold our people in reverence for any of the reasons that the Mayans did. He seemed so certain that I would do his bidding and come willingly. Why, I thought, did not Nish't Ahote speak up?

I answered my father softly but with respect. "I do not yet know who I am. This is all so sudden. Why was I not told of my heritage before? Did no one know, or did they not want to tell me? What does it all mean? What do the Gods want me to do?"

A soft voice answered. "Coyote Woman, you have the mark of the special star on your back. It marks you as a star child—a child who will travel farther in the road of life than most of us, or perhaps all of us." I turned abruptly to look at Taweyah as he spoke. His eyes were brilliantly lit, and even his body exuded a vibrancy. "I was the sun priest when your people brought you to us. I knew of your mark from birth. I knew you were a chosen one among your people. Your mark indicated a special gift—a gift of knowledge—a gift of inner sight. I gave you to your adopted parents, who wanted you desperately. I knew they would raise you in the gentle Anasazi way. I knew that you would grow to have the qualities of a priestess and eventually to be a priestess. And my expectations were quickly filled. It is you, Coyote Woman, only you with your quick, agile mind and natural insight who fulfilled my vision. Your adopted parents know nothing of the significance of your mark of birth. They raised you with the devoted love only they could give you, asking no questions along the way. They always feared losing you, as you were a gift to them and they cherished you as they did Choviohoya, your brother. He is their natural child, but your mother feared she could have no more children and she wanted a daughter. Do not blame her, for never, ever, did I suspect that your natural father would find you. I loved you as my own. I watched you blossom into a woman. I watched many other relationships develop between you and others in the complex. I assume full responsibility and hope you will not change your feelings toward me as a result of what I tell you. Think carefully, little one, on what I have said." He then reclined again to await my reaction.

I was thrown into confusion. There was so much I did not know. With all my knowledge of a priestess, all the knowledge of my schooling, I did not know how to deal with it all. My immediate reaction was not to react. Therefore I asked, "May I have time to think on all that I have heard tonight? I am overwhelmed."

After a bit of discussion, the decision was made to give me a sun cycle to think. A meeting was scheduled for the following night, and I made my way up the ladder to think on all that I had learned.

Taweyah had known, but he had not told me. I reclined on my mat with Puppy curled up at my feet. My world had crashed into fragments all around me. The numbness was beginning to wear away, and my thoughts began to come together. I somehow had to make a decision. My life was my own. I did not have to do anything. I would just refuse to go. My life had been happy until Al Balam came. I'd just send him on his way without me. Somehow I felt I did not know all the facts. Why had Ix Can, my real mother, left him? If anyone would know, it would be Taweyah. I was certain Al Balam would not tell me the truth. Somehow I could not think of him as my father. He did not strike me as a sincere person. His vibrations were dark, and his demeanor was hateful. Why had he come to interrupt my happiness? I resolved to speak to Taweyah.

Gathering myself together, I left Puppy and climbed my ladder to cross the plaza. The night was crisp and cold. The sky was brilliantly bejeweled with friendly star constellations, and the "path of life" showed vividly in its wide streak across the sky. Few were out, for it was very late, and I realized Taweyah might be sleeping. Arriving at his quarters, I climbed down the ladder to find Aunt Mokni sitting beside him as she sewed feathers on a huge quilt. The fire she kept burning lent its light and warmed the stone walls of the room. Taweyah seemed to be asleep on his mat. His head was elevated by a pillow.

Aunt Mokni looked up and smiled. Dropping her work, she made her way in two quick steps to gather me in her ample arms. No words passed between us, but the tears flowed unbidden from my eyes. Her warm arms enveloped me until my tears began to subside. I turned to see Taweyah watching both of us with love and concern in his eyes.

Gathering myself together, I excused myself. "O revered one, forgive me my time of weakness. It is you I have come to see. I know the time is late and you must be tired, but . . ."

"Little Coyote Woman, I knew you would come. Do not apologize! There was much I could not say during the meeting. What is it you wish to know?"

"Revered one, you have known of my heritage all along. Why did you not make me aware of it?"

"Your light eyes and ocher highlights in your hair

are unusual, but not unheard of. The birthmark is your only identifying factor. Never in the far reaches of my mind did I think anyone would search you out. Never did I think that your warrior would be the link to tie you to your heritage. I knew you were royalty, and it was I who placed you with your adopted parents. I have watched you grow into the star child I knew you would become, and I have only of late loved you as my own child—the child I could never have." He moved his eyes from mine to Aunt Mokni's.

My eyes misted again, for here was another who loved me as did my beloved Nish't Ahote. "Taweyah, what does my father, Al Balam—oh, it is difficult for me to think of him as my blood relation—really want of me? What of this marriage of which he speaks?"

"Al Balam is the Mayan lord of Chichén Itzá, a large Toltec Mayan city. His power, as I understand it is waning, and he wishes to make an alliance with the Mayan lord of Tula. This he plans to do through you. He would wed you to that Mayan lord to strengthen his own position."

"Then, you are reinforcing my impression that he is a selfish man, who would do anything to further his own interests." I stated as I sat next to him with my legs crossed. "Why, then, did my mother leave him?" I asked.

"Long ago, when you were an infant, a swirl of rumors flew. But one story was consistent. Many sun cycles ago, when your father was ascending to power, Ix Can became fearful of the bloodthirsty ways of the Mayan Toltecs. You were a baby with the mark of the brightest star on your shoulder. Your mother, when she was but a child, watched her own sister sacrificed to the Mayan Gods. She watched them cut out the heart of her sister, then ... well, to eliminate the gory detail, she was afraid that you, her daughter, might also be sacrificed at some point. She escaped, leaving your father, with a band of sympathizers heading north to the land of the people of peace. The land between Chichén Itzá and here is not easy to travel. She died along the way, in the lands of the Mogollan, but her followers brought you north. Her followers were loyal. They brought you on to our center here at Chaco, and the rest you know."

A long silence followed in which I sorted out my feelings. Then a thought occurred to me. "So my mother, Ix Can, felt the mark of the star on my shoulder would be an indication that I should be a sacrificial object."

Taweyah nodded and said, "Little Coyote Woman, this is a terrible turn of events. I counted on you to be my successor that I might rest in peace, as I am not long for this fourth world." Aunt Mokni looked at him anxiously. "This is a decision you must make. You must weigh the consequences carefully, then do what you must."

"What are the consequences?" I asked, for I did not wish to leave my beloved people.

"I cannot answer that," answered Taweyah. "Your father has not given any clue of what may happen if you say no. Think carefully, little one, for we love you." He reclined to close his eyes while Aunt Mokni once again took me in her arms. Then he continued. "Your Mayan language teacher is one of the party who accompanied your mother to our lands. If you wish, you may talk with him."

Withdrawing from her loving arms, I softly made my way back to the solitude of my quarters.

My Mayan teacher's crinkled, alert eyes told me he was expecting my visit. He sat cross-legged in the corner of his room on a yucca mat. His gnarled, arthritic hands rested on his inner thighs. I had asked many questions of this man in the past. He had always been patient with me, and I prayed that he would be so today, as it might be the last time I would see him. I had never thought to ask him how he learned the Mayan language, but Taweyah's statement brought it all into focus. He knew my mother. What a brave woman she must have been!

He beckoned me to sit down on the mat next to him, as I had done so often in the past. Gathering my robes around me, I extended one hand to rest on his hand, saying, "Greetings, my teacher. You knew I would come."

"Yes, my child. It was inevitable. Your path is not easy. Perhaps I can help to ease it for you."

"I cannot thank you enough for your instruction and patience with me in the past. There are many questions racing through my mind. Have you the time to answer them for me?"

"Of course, child, but let me tell you what I know." He stretched his legs and leaned back against the wall. Closing his eyes and clearing his throat, he began. "One hundred season cycles ago, the Toltec people conquered the Mayans. The Mayans were a peaceful people who found the need for human sacrifice only an occasional thing. The Toltecs, however, are ruled not by the priests and elders, but by the military. The soldier is the all-conquering ruler. He fights to capture prisoners for sacrifice. At Chichén Itzá many are sacrificed in a moon cycle, according to the need of the Gods. Tula is the sister city to Chichén Itzá, and the same sacrifices occur there as in other cities as you know. Many Mayans still hold onto the old ways. They do not approve of the bloodshed which has gone to the extreme.

"Your father is a Toltec. Your mother was a Mayan.

When she was small, she watched her older sister be sacrificed. She heard her scream and rushed to offer help, but when she got close, she saw her sister held down by the arms and legs by four priests while a fifth priest raised a huge obsidian blade. With one stroke he plunged the blade into the chest of her sister, your aunt, and grasped her heart. Holding the bleeding, throbbing thing high, he smeared some blood on a statue nearby. Your mother fainted. She lived in fear that she would be next, but it did not happen that way. Instead it was arranged that she marry your father, Al Balam. Your mother never learned to love your proud, arrogant father. When you were born, she panicked, for you bore the mark on your shoulder of the star that only rarely shines brighter than all the others in the sky. The astrologers pronounced a bright future for you to be followed by a supreme sacrifice. Hearing this, your mother gathered a few belongings and left your father. He did not know of this for several sun cycles, due to being away on a military conquest.

"Ix Can was a remarkable woman. She said she had a vision. Her vision was of the people of peace who would welcome us with loving arms. She had shared her vision with her younger brother. He joined her on the day she left along with myself and two other friends.

"The journey was long and arduous. Occasionally people who lived along the way offered us shelter. The farther north we got, the colder it became. In the land of Mogollan, your mother died. The bitter cold was not a thing we were used to. We did our best to keep her warm, but during her sleep one night, the Gods came and took her away. She was a valiant woman who made the sacrifice for you, my child. We buried her in a small cave and pushed boulders into the mouth of the cave.

"Setting out once again, we finally arrived not long after the winter solstice, a pitiful, tattered, skinny, miserable group. Her vision was fulfilled. We were welcomed with loving arms. After a short stay in a complex nearby, Taweyah found a home for you. I stayed on to teach here at the school, and your uncle and the other two went to the large outlier to the north of us. The rest you know."

"What did my mother look like?" I asked. "Was she lighter in color as I am?"

"Your mother was the color of wild flower honey. She was tiny and delicate as you are. Childbirth did not widen her hips as most women. She too had amber eyes, filled with the wisdom of Awonawilona. You are a duplicate of your mother. I grew to not only respect her, but, child—" His eyes misted, and he paused.

"But what, my teacher?"

"I loved her! Yes, very simply, I loved her. Teaching you has been like having her with me again." He stopped, as though he wondered if he had said too much. Then, as if suddenly seized by a new thought, he said, "May I offer you some advice, my child?"

"Of course." I answered softly. Somehow I wanted to take this man in my arms to comfort him, even though I knew it was inappropriate.

"Let no one know of your knowledge of the language of the Mayans. You may find this to be to your advantage. Also, do not confront your father. He is arrogant and used to getting his own way. The blood of many is on his hands, for he is a militant Toltec through and through. Now, child, let an old man sleep, but go with the Gods. Use your wisdom. I will pray for you."

Here, it seemed, was another man who loved me, for I was the image of my mother. I prayed to Awonawilona to give me strength. To leave all these loving people was the supreme sacrifice for me.

The meeting included everyone that day. Al Balam was dressed in his usual finery. Nish't Ahote and Hototo assumed a coolness that was betrayed only by their blinking eyes. My heart was wrenched from my breast when I thought that Nish't Ahote had not made any attempt to come talk to me. I was truly alone. I could only wait to see what would happen, for I had made my decision. The Anasazi were my way of life. I would live or die for them. There was no other choice.

All eyes were on me as I walked to my usual position between Nish't Ahote and Hototo. I wondered who would begin the meeting. I also noticed that the interpretor was there. Everyone was quiet, waiting as I was in anxious anticipation. It was my father who spoke first. "So, my beauty, you have decided to go, of course." He was so self-assured.

"Al Balam"—I could not bring myself to call him Father—"with all due respect to you, I cannot just walk out, ignoring my responsibilities. I have only recently become a priestess, and I am doing my best to assume those duties. I am Anasazi raised. I believe in their gentle philosophy of equality and the balance of all things. I would be terribly unhappy being only a wife or a concubine. That is not my destiny. So after much thought, my answer is that I do not wish to go with you. I am sorry."

The feathers on my father's headdress trembled as his anger burst forth. He stood straight and tall, for it was obvious he was unused to being rebuffed. I had never seen such arrogance displayed by any of the Anasazi. His hand shook as he pointed his index finger toward me. "My daughter is a fool! You speak of balance!" he shouted. "Your world is balanced at this point in time, but will it be balanced when I bring warriors to take you by force? What of the trade relations between your people and the Mayans? By your refusal, I promise you that your 'balanced peaceful Anasazi way' will become warlike and that trade relations will suffer. What say you to that, my foolish daughter? Be ready to leave when Sun Father next begins his journey!"

If I had worn feathers at that moment, they would not have trembled but would have stood on end. My skin prickled in anger. None of the Anasazi, except perhaps Wisoko, ever displayed such conceit. Never did we call each other foolish. I detested the man as of that moment, and I could see that all the others were shocked by his manner.

Nish't Ahote, Hototo, and Taweyah all looked at me with love and pity at the same time. Perhaps that was why Nish't Ahote had not come to me. He must have felt that all would have been futile. I had much to learn, but I knew of the necessity to weigh all the consequences carefully. On the one hand, my father would destroy my happiness and that of many others. However, if I did not go with him, the Mayan warriors would see to it that thousands were left unhappy as they burned and pillaged to take me by force. Without Mayan trade we would not get our prized sacred macaw feathers, or honey or ... There seemed no other choice but to go.

Gathering my pride, I quietly said, "I always knew in my heart that I would live or die to support the Anasazi way. To maintain harmony and balance, I shall die, for if I go I am no longer a living human being. Take me, Al Balam. To all of you in this kiva, please know that I love you, and you shall be with me in the peaceful resting place in my heart. Though I want to weep, it is not the Anasazi way. You are my people, and shall ever remain my people in my mind's eye. May Awonawilona ever protect and keep you as I will in my heart." Then dropping my hands to my side, I added, "All must remain in harmony."

A tear escaped the corner of my eye as I turned to climb the ladder. I returned to the love and security one last time that my beloved Puppy and my room offered.

My heart was so heavy that it would not allow sleep. I lay awake on my mat tossing and turning. My thoughts kept me awake, but it did not matter, for where I was going I did not want to be. I packed my belongings. Puppy was uneasy, too, as he quickly sensed my turmoil. He howled a lonely wail that I had never heard from him before. He did not eat the food that I offered him. Truly he acted as a stranger.

In a short time I would leave all that was familiar to me. It would be necessary to discard all that I had been taught—all hopes and aspirations—and to adopt an entirely new set of values—values I could not accept. I would adopt a new meaning for life—one even my mother had not been able to accept. O spirit of my mother, protect me. If you are there, offer me your wisdom. Guard all my loved ones, Nish't Ahote, Taweyah, Hototo, Aunt Mokni, my teacher, and oh, yes, Salavi. May their wisdom become mine or give me inner strength. The Anasazi way is mine. There can be no other!

A messenger descended my ladder. I stirred on my mat, and Puppy jumped to my side to guard me. I was frightened, for it occurred to me that this person could be a Mayan sent to kidnap me. Perhaps my father was afraid I would not go of my own accord. Upon reaching the bottom of the ladder, he stopped and waited respectfully, setting my heart at ease.

Rising on one elbow, I waited. He also waited, then seeing no response in me, he stated his business. "O revered one, I am here to deliver a message. I cannot say who sent me, but if you will accept—"

"You are one of our acolytes!" I said.

"I have been ordered to deliver this to you," he said. Taking his hand from behind his back, he handed me a magnificent figure in turquoise. It was a carving of an antelope and was not more than the length of a finger. It was delicately carved, and its eyes were of inlaid obsidian. In its mouth was a tiny crystal. It was an exquisite amulet. I needed only to carry it with me, and, of course, I would never be able to forget. Perhaps it would offer me extra protection. I quickly dismissed the messenger.

My heart was filled with love, for he had not forgotten! My feelings were of happiness and unhappiness all at the same time. The antelope was his clan's spirit guide. He did not want me to forget all that was shared between us. I held my crystal in one hand, and his amulet in the other. In the time that it took me to warm my crystal and the amulet, I knew. I understood! I lay on my mat and felt the subtle impulses that emanated through my hands and arms. A feeling of love coursed through me, and I knew—yes, I knew! This was as it must be. I was guided, guarded, and loved. Then I fell into a deep sleep.

As the Sun Father began his journey across the heavens, I gathered my last belongings in a huge basket. This was to be carried for me, so I was told. My personal things I carried in a small basket strapped across my forehead, while my medicine bag, crystals, and Nish't Ahote's amulet were in my medicine pouch, which I carried at my waist. None of my loved ones were in the plaza to see me off. I felt truly alone as my father ordered me into a litter. I was to be carried as befitted Mayan royalty. Four of the eighteen guards who accompanied my father were making ready to lift my litter when I saw a lone figure walking despondently toward our party. I recognized the broad shoulders that seemed slumped. His dark, flashing eyes were downcast and somehow he looked older. Walking to Al Balam, he said something and then stepped around my father toward me.

My heart pounded beneath my breast. I wanted to run away with him, to escape from it all. We were meant for each other, and now? He stood next to my litter, extending his arm. As though I had no control over myself, as though he was my road of life, I walked with him to the privacy of a corner in the plaza. My eyes were as one fired piece of pottery stuck to another, for I could not take them off of his. Then, however, those eyes filled with concern as he turned to me.

"Little one," he said, "though you are being taken from me now, the stars we share are the same, for they watch over us both. We have done much to chart the stars together. Do not forget all you know. Sometime you may have the need to use all the knowledge you have acquired. Taweyah, Aunt Mokni, and Hototo send their love and guidance, and I"—He seized my shoulders and took me in his arms to offer me the last bit of love and security I was sure to feel for some time.

The tears fell unbidden. I tried to control myself, for Anasazi did not show weakness. We were a strong, proud people. To help me in my efforts, Nish't Ahote licked and kissed away my tears. Gaining some control of myself, I took his hands and removed them from me. From which Gods my strength came, I did not know. Looking into his loving eyes, I offered one last and final statement. "O revered one, you are the only one I have ever loved. Please do not forget! Your amulet will be part of me all the rest of my life."

Turning hastily from him before I could no longer control myself, I began walking across the plaza toward the waiting litter. In that short distance, which seemed like forever, I heard him murmur, "And you, my love, are the only one I have ever loved or ever will love."

The tears blinded me as I stumbled toward the strange-looking party who carried me away on the litter—away from home and all I had ever known.

Chapter 18

Rock and Mudslide

The day was hot, but I remained cool under my shaded litter. I watched the landscape as we headed south. The journey would be long, probably many moon cycles, and of course it would be hot. No one had spoken to me, for they still did not realize I knew the Mayan language. An interpreter traveled with me, but respectfully remained silent. Puppy was not happy in my arms, but rushed around yapping, then disappeared into the wilderness, returning at short intervals to jump into my lap once again. My father did not speak to me. He treated me as some alien material thing that must be cared for and pampered, but who had no brain. He spoke only to his soldiers, and I noticed one of his company seemed to be his right-hand man. Very little conversation took place that first sun cycle of travel.

Finally, when the sun completed its journey across the sky, we made camp for the night. Canopies were set up to protect us from rain. A large fire was built to offer us warmth through the night. One of the company had killed several desert rabbits and also a long-eared one, which smelled delicious as they sizzled over the fire. My small canopy was close to the fire, and I waited. My people had supplied us with corn cakes and pemmican to supplement our diet. I walked away and out of sight to relieve myself. Taking my time to return, for I knew I was being watched, I wondered if my father had seen the love in Nish't Ahote's eyes and the love in mine for him. As if having a premonition, I returned to camp to hear my father saying, "He is my age, and she looks at him with love. Then it will be no problem to pair her off with Paxal, the ruler of Tula. She seems to prefer older men."

Al Balam's aide said, "Yea, Lord, but she is beautiful. I am certain she will please him."

"She will please him if she keeps her educated mouth shut. She will have to learn her place, since there are other women before her, and she is to be one of many. She has her mother's intelligence and must learn when to remain silent."

"My Lord, if you would change your mind, I find her quite lovely and of a fiery spirit. I like that in a woman and—"

My father interrupted, "No, she is promised! She will complete the bond with the city of Tula, which will solidify my position. See that no harm comes to her unless you wish to become my slave instead of a free soldier!" He walked toward the fire, leaving his aide displaying a crestfallen expression.

I knew my fate. He was old, perhaps as old a Nish't Ahote—or older. He would look like a Mayan with the bizarre, pointed head and holes in his body for jewelry. His teeth would also be inlaid with jade, as were Al Balam's. My father did not know I understood their conversation. At that moment I knew what my Mayan teacher had meant when he had said that no one must know of my knowledge. I remained quiet, respectfully pondering my fate.

So he knew of my love for Nish't Ahote. Our last meeting must have made it obvious. He had kissed away my tears while holding me close. Instinctively I reached for my charms in the pouch at my waist. I

pulled out the turquoise antelope with the crystal in
its mouth. Holding it in my left hand, the hand that
received power, and grasping my crystal in the right,
I was once again flooded with a soothing calm. A
flashing thought told me this did not make sense. Here
I was caught in this hateful dilemma. I was at the
mercy of these arrogant, bloodthirsty people, yet a
marvelous calm settled its protective wings to enfold
me.

"The food is ready, my lord," said one of the soldiers. "Take what you wish for you and your
daughter."

My father cut the breast of the large long-eared
rabbit for himself, and a leg and thigh for me. He put
mine in a bowl, accompanied by a corn cake. Then
we silently sat down to enjoy the repast. No words
passed between us. We simply enjoyed the food and
water that marked the end of a long day of travel. At
the end of the meal, we stretched out for the night to
await the next journey of Sun Father.

The next morning dawned brightly. Sun Father,
Tawa, began his journey, and we rose to travel once
again. The day was warm. We traveled wordlessly
across the stretch of desert land. I had never traveled
more than a day or so before, and I found I enjoyed
the landscape. It had not changed much since I left
Chaco, but each rock, hill, and crevice had so much
to offer in beauty. Perhaps I was blessed—at least
at the moment, for I found beauty in the smallest
of things.

My father was interesting to watch. He was like a
male turkey. He strutted about in his gaudy attire with
his neck protruding, asserting his superiority to all of
us. I wished the Wind God would strike to leave all
his feathers in a swirl. Could he, I wondered, be the

same without all his finery? He had probably relied on his appearance all of his life. I considered what it would take to make the man appear real—to be what he truly was. His childhood was no different from mine. I was so simply raised. He was of royalty. My mother must also have been different, or she would not have thought ... but then I was told that I was like my mother. I wished I knew how to call her to me. I knew when next I got a chance I would sit quietly with my crystals and meditate.

I knew my mother was petite and lovely. She bore herself with much grace. She was Mayan, not Toltec, therefore she had different opinions. My Mayan teacher had told me of the differences. She was a magnificently strong woman. She believed in her certain way, and she lived by her convictions. What an amazing young woman. I was convinced that I should follow her example. I needed to keep my faith with the dedication that she kept hers. My situation was not as difficult. I was pampered and fed and, well, there was no comparison. Her attitude was one of hope. Mine at the moment was of despair—yet I knew I must keep her strength.

I was lifted in my decorated litter to continue the journey, and we moved on our way. The day was bright and beautiful, and as we walked, I heard my father say, "We must make better time than the last sun cycle, for we do not want the raiders or a rescuing group to descend upon us. She wields power. Her people love her. We must make haste!"

His aide scratched his crotch and exclaimed, "They are a people of peace, my lord. I do not think they will send soldiers for her."

"No, I think you are right, but our Toltecs would covet the source of their turquoise. When I return, I shall send soldiers to attack and take over their culture. Those turquoise sources will be ours!" My father glanced my way as I shuddered with what I was hearing. I hoped he was not reading my panic and my repulsion of him.

"My lord, you are a valiant leader," said his aide. "I am certain that their wealth will add to the wealth of our nation, and you shall regain the high esteem you feel you have lost. But what of me? May I not be favored with the companionship of your daughter, if only on the return trip?"

Running his hand slowly over his pointed head, Al Balam proclaimed, "You may be the guardian of my lovely daughter, but one transgression and you will be relegated to a sacrificial slave when we return! She is promised!" His aide looked solemnly at the parched cactus at his feet.

So it seemed I was only a small part of a plot. He intended to send an army anyway. Our balanced way of life was to be interrupted regardless of my going with him or not. What a terrible heartless person my father was! He enjoyed being the cause of misery of not only me, but of hundreds of my people to further his declining position. It was obvious to me why my mother could not tolerate him. His world was only within himself. He thought only of his own. No one else had a place in his life, and all probability, my mother had had no place in his life, either. I could not remember ever knowing such a person. If my father was any example of Toltec Mayan thinking, I would rather be Anasazi. Awonawilona, our God of Creation, would give me the strength I needed to face any crisis. I knew somehow there would be a way. I prayed to Awonawilona to guide me to the position of strength I so desperately needed to help my people. My people were good and peaceful. They did not deserve the punishment they were about to receive. I prayed for my mother's strength to attune my thoughts to reflect theirs, and to maintain the inner security and serenity I needed.

The evening was uneventful. After eating, we settled down for the night. Puppy was not with me. I felt certain he must be exploring the area and perhaps howling at the moon when it was not covered with clouds. The darkness was strangely peaceful while moon shadows danced lightly around.

Not long after everyone was asleep, a wraithlike figure in the camp arose and walked silently toward me. I could not see who it was, but I knew his intentions were evil. The dark outline with a pointed head hovered momentarily over me, then stuffed a large piece of fabric in my mouth. I knew even if I cried out, I would not be heard. With one of his hands, he held my hands above my head while his free hand stripped away my feather cover to completely expose me. The strange figure's free hand moved over my throat and down to my breasts. The hand circled lightly around my nipples and caressed the roundness of my breasts. I moaned, but the moan was muffled by the gag in my mouth. The camp was still sleeping.

My attacker's free hand moved down to my navel and stroked my thighs. Then using his knees he spread my legs. His fingers stroked me, and he made himself ready to enter. I felt nausea rising within me as his strength overpowered me. His hand that still held my hands above my head were bruising me, and the pain was excruciating. My attacker grunted loudly, yet no one in the camp seemed to hear.

Suddenly out of the darkness of the juniper and pinyon, I heard a coyote growl. There was a louder groan as the figure loosened his grip on my hands. Puppy had sunken his sharp teeth into the ankle of my would-be rapist. As he struggled to stop the flow of blood, Puppy launched another bite in his thigh. I heard him curse Puppy as he limped back to his sleeping space.

Hastily I pulled my feather blanket around me again while Puppy nuzzled his head against my bruised body. The camp was now fully awake. Everyone was gathered around me while the aide hobbled over to join the gathering. Puppy snarled and bared his teeth. He would have lunged at the aide, but I held him tightly.

"What is happening here?" shouted my father. Then looking at the pained expression on his aide's face and noticing his bleeding ankle and thigh, he continued. "Why were you near my daughter? You know I told you you were not to be near her!" He glared angrily at his aide as though he would kill.

"Your Excellency," he gasped as he bent to nurse his wounds, "I was but offering your daughter my protection. I heard strange noises—those of a mountain lion. Can you not see what was happening?"

"No, I do not see that you are telling the truth! Why would her bastard coyote defend her? Those are animal bites you have acquired. If you so much as come near my daughter in the future, you shall be punished. This I promise, on the ground of the holy priesthood. You shall be one of the many who are sacrificed! So I have spoken, and so it shall be!" He walked in a circle to vent his wrath as he stomped on the soil. His color was high, his hands shook as he pointed them toward his aide, and then he turned to me. Walking toward me, he said, "If you, you common whore, are any more trouble to me, you shall be showered with large stones on your head. Few survive such a punishment!" He glared at me as though I was nothing—no one. How could he be so self-centered, I could not imagine.

O Awonawilona, I prayed, if this was the way of the Mayans, spare me! I hoped I would die along the way.

We traveled through rocks and dry desert, then found ourselves surrounded by pinyon pines, juniper, and occasionally even tall pines whose branches offered a welcome shade. We had passed by a magnificent tall mountain that still had snow on its peak. Surely it must have been the home of the Gods. It looked angry as we passed it by. There were huge black rocks, such as I had never seen, strewn carelessly over the land. The land became very different from our dry desert. There were many dry creeks and some rivers flowing from the melted snow. We had traveled twelve sun cycles and were now in the land of the Mogollan.

How very different their land was from ours. The land was difficult to travel. The climbing was often obstructed by a cliff that forced us to change our direction. When finally we resumed our original course south, we found after a short while that we must double back again. The soil was rich and dark when it was not terribly rocky, a sharp contrast to the red clay of the Anasogi lands. In the shady, more moist places there were unfamiliar wildflowers growing. We passed an occasional pit house and less often a crudely built stone dwelling. I was not able to tell from afar if it was a home or only used for storage. Antelope, deer, wild turkey, and many small forms of wildlife abounded. Surely, I thought, this was a land of plenty. Why did we not trade with these people more frequently?

One evening after a long day of traveling, there seemed to be much discussion about where to camp for the night. My prayers were interrupted by Al

Balam, who said to his aide, "We will camp here. This is not a creek. It is dry and tiny. We will camp here for the night."

The aide said, "O revered one, what if it rains?"

"There are no rain clouds in the sky. This area does not look as though it has seen rain for many season cycles. No, here we will rest. There are tall pines and much protection from the mountains around us."

His aide looked doubtful, but slowly signaled the rest of the party to set up camp.

Not far away from our campsite was a beautiful creek that flowed throughout the seasons. I was elated, for it provided me the overdue opportunity to rid myself of the dust and dirt of many sun cycles of travel. Spreading my meager belongings out, I uncoiled my hair to comb it before I washed it. Just then, I noticed the aide staring lustfully at me. Picking up my medicine pouch, a large piece of cotton cloth, my yucca soap, and my comb, I began the short descent to the creek. I felt certain I must be on guard, for after what had happened, I trusted no one. Puppy and I picked our way over rocky ground scattered with prickly cactus under pinyon pines.

Reaching the creek, I noticed a refreshing herbal smell, and after rubbing my thumb and forefinger over several of the plants, I found its source. There was a profusion of a deep green spiky-looking plant that was entirely new to me. I decided to gather some to rub on my body in times when I could not bathe. I walked farther, wanting to be certain I was away from my father's party. Then finding a lovely spot with a huge rock next to a grandfather pine, I removed my clothing, laying it on the rock with my medicine pouch.

The water was very cold, but gradually I waded into it. It took a long time to work up a lather with my soaproot. The air was also chilly. I used my soaproot

only on my hair, then rinsed it and stretched out in
the shallow, cold water. My skin prickled and I shivered, but forced myself to remain there for a short
time. Somehow the water was washing away the touch
of the amorous attack of my father's aide. It purified
me. Then, leaving the water, I rose and dried myself
as Puppy yapped and played at my feet.

When I returned to camp, the party had finished
eating and my father was saying, "She was beautiful
but willful, much like her daughter. She was pure
Mayan. She did not understand that blood purifies.
My mistress understands. Even before my daughter
was born, I had a mistress. She served my every need,
and I am a man in need of the intimate act more
frequently than others." My father's voice trailed off
as he picked up a mug and drained the liquid from it.

He did not see me as I stood quietly behind a thick
pinyon tree. I was frozen as I eavesdropped. He
picked up his mug that his aide filled with liquid and
downed that, too. Then he continued, "She was untrue
to me. She was not the fiery woman I need. She ran
off with our daughter, and we—, you know." His voice
trailed off, and his words seemed somehow longer and
unsure. He sounded different than usual.

It was then that I realized that he was drinking—
probably *balch.* I had not eaten, but did not care, for
at that time I thought I might learn more by just
listening.

"Sire, you will punish her spirit by marrying her to
Paxal," said his aide.

"She was a whore! Her daughter is also a whore.
She was not a virgin when I married her, yet she
claimed there was no other man.

"She really expected me to believe ..." Again his
voice trailed off. "My daughter is a whore. I know
because her warrior from Tula told me of their night

of delights. I am certain that that old priest and she are intimate—perhaps even the younger priest. I shall get even. When I bring troops north again, we shall ravage and control her people. Ix Can's whorish spirit shall be avenged. Now, let us go for a walk, for the drink is possessing my soul!"

My father and his aide wandered off, walking directly past the tree behind which I stood. I wasted no time when they were out of sight. There was only one corn cake left and bones of the deer that they cooked. The rest of his party ignored me as I crawled between my feather blankets with the corn cake in one hand.

I nibbled on my corn cake as my thoughts tumbled over one another. My warrior had bragged of his night with me. He told him of my mark from birth. I supposed he told all the intimate details. Oh, how I hated my warrior. My father had called Nish't Ahote an old priest. Did my father think he was still only twenty and one season cycles? He had branded me a whore! Virginity must be very important in the Mayan culture, or perhaps it was important only to him.

I tossed and turned for a while, then gradually a feeling of calm overtook me. I felt a soothing energy coursing through my body. It drove most of the tumultuous thoughts from my mind's eye, leaving me with only occasional flashes of the evil of my father. At last I calmed enough for sleep to overtake me. I did not hear my father and the rest of his party as they bedded down for the night.

There was something cold and wet on my neck. I awoke out of a restless sleep to Puppy. He softly whined, making a sound that I had not heard before. I attempted to focus my thoughts, but for a moment could not. The night was brilliant. The moon was just past full, and the stars clustered around as her ser-

vants. Then Puppy whimpered again. He nuzzled me
with an urgency I could not describe. He was my
totem. Something was amiss! I dragged myself from
the warmth of my feather down, and feeling cold, I
wrapped it around myself.

The vibrations were strange. Puppy was telling me
this. Everyone was lost in sleep but Puppy! I gathered
my few belongings and followed him. In my sleepy
state I stumbled, and wondered why I was so compelled to follow my spirit guide, my beloved Puppy.
Then I heard it.

It thundered—softly at first, then increasingly
louder. It was as though all our spirit dancers were
descending on that spot at once. I was very frightened,
for at first I could not see what was causing the noise.
Puppy jumped into my arms. I clutched him and shivered. Surely the end of the fourth world had arrived.
I waited in absolute terror. The source of my terror
appeared at last.

An enormous wall of water thundered down the
creek toward the sleeping party of men. It carried
large trees and huge boulders. They tripped lightly
over the ground, transported by the spring water as
lightly as feathers. It was the rocks and boulders that
caused the thunderous noise. Too late, the men
awoke. The water and debris thundered over them.
Cries of pain mixed with horror reached my ears as I
moved farther away from the sight. The party of men
were totally engulfed. I could no longer see my father
and his aide. The entire creek that once had been so
dry was a swirling, angry mass of water and mud and
debris. Some bodies were churned in it. They were
washed away and out of sight.

I stared as if in a nightmare. It looked as though
all who were sleeping were dead. My litter was swept
away. The water continued raging as I wrapped myself

tightly in my feather down and wept. I did not know why I wept, but I was unable to control myself. Then I realized I shed tears of joy, not sorrow. I was alive! Puppy knew and had saved me. I buried my face in the warmth of his body and hugged him through my tears. I continued to watch the raging water and mud when I suddenly realized I was free. My father was gone, with all who attended him. Almost as though it had all been a bad dream, I saw no traces of any of them.

For a short time I continued to watch. The water continued its angry surge. The stars indicated it was close to the rise of Sun Father. The Gods must have sent the water out of the mountains in front of us. They intended to wash away evil and restore the precious balance in which the Anasazi so firmly believed.

Somehow I felt compelled to continue to watch. It seemed that I was mistaken when I said that all were wiped out. Three of the party dragged away from the edges of the raging creek. Their mud-covered, battered bodies were pitiful to behold. One of them, who seemed in better shape than the others, dragged himself out of the sticky muck and stared dazed into space. Then another with his arm at an odd angle rose. Both resembled our clowns who lent such an air of delight in our ceremonies. Finally a third raised himself pathetically out of the mud and to the edge of the creek. To my relief none was my father. They scraped themselves clean, as much as they could, helping the one with the broken arm to clean himself.

Then one of them noticed a figure. The figure was covered with debris and mud. Pulling the figure from the rocky mire, they acknowledged it in gesture as their superior. That had to have been my father—or his aide. After examination they covered the figure with a cloth. I could only assume the person was dead. Then collecting what little was left, they slowly headed south—out of what they probably considered godforsaken territory—toward their own Mayan lands.

Chapter 19

Badger

I was on my own—in territory I knew nothing about. The land was rocky and mountainous with much water and raging creeks. I knew I must turn about and head back to Chaco. The land was unfamiliar and would have different predators. But I was free! It was exhilarating to think I was free. I could return to my balanced way of life, and most of all to my family and Nish't Ahote.

I sat upon a rock to stare at the flash flood. The water still raged, but its level had receded. The roar was not quite so loud. I noticed a large water skin caught between two large rocks. I repressed the urge to retrieve it, for I knew the large rocks could break a foot or an anklebone as they rushed furiously along. There was little I could do but wait. Puppy stayed close at my feet as we watched the anger of the Rain Gods.

Sun Father was just breaking over the horizon. The huge grandfather pines were as spirits outlined against the gray of dawn. A family of cholla grew close by. There were no animals and no sound of birds, probably due to the flood and its dangers. Even Awonawilona's creatures had taken cover. The magnificent herbal part of creation was strangely quiet. The solitude was such that my mind took the path of my own dilemma. I knew I must think things through and not give in to

panic. The Rain God had given me a chance for life—
to retrieve the Anasazi way I loved so much. I had
spent three days before alone in the wilderness during
my womanly cycle. Why, I wondered, should this be
any different?

A rush of water fell over a nearby rock, and I filled
my water skin with it. It was imperative that I also
reach that water skin caught in the rocks. Waiting
awhile longer, I was able to pick my way from rock
to rock and grab it. Making my way to the waterfall
gushing over the rocks, I filled the second water skin,
praying it would not leak. When it seemed intact, I
once again sat upon the rock to wait and watch.

By the time Sun Father had begun to warm the
earth, the water had almost completely subsided. I
walked to the creek to see what else remained. Buried
beneath a large rock and covered with mud, I found
what looked like a down robe. Pushing the rock aside,
I pulled it from the mud. Two other light blankets
appeared farther down the creek, and I pulled them
out, hurrying to the rapidly shrinking waterfall to rinse
them. Laying them out to dry on a nearby rock formation, I once again searched the creek. Then I noticed
a knife wedged under an enormous log. Taking it from
the log, I sharpened it on a rock. Further searching
revealed some large skins, and I quickly rinsed them,
too. I cut a long strip to tie the knife around my waist.
The other pieces I saved for binding my feet. If I was
lucky enough to find some quantity of food, I knew I
must wrap it to keep out rats and mice and other
insects that might crawl in at night to ravish it.

In my own supplies I carried an awl and yucca fiber,
a yucca comb, and a mirror. I also needed to gather
something for my most personal needs. Looking
around, I spotted some mullein leaves, long and soft.
I gathered a supply and wrapped them in another

piece of leather. Then I sat back once again to think.
Somehow it seemed a good idea to spend the day
there to allow the robe, blankets, and leather pieces
to dry out. I would carry less weight if I carried dry
things.

So the time passed. Sun Father warmed the land
and dried the creek. At Sun Father's peak, I realized
Puppy was long gone. Taking my large crystal, my
small crystal, and Nish't Ahote's antelope carving, I
sat cross-legged on a large flat stone. The sun warmed
me, and I removed my clothing from the waist up.
Taking my large crystal, I placed it in my left hand,
the hand that received energy. The small crystal I held
in my right. Ordinarily I could not warm the large
crystal in one hand due to its size, but today the heat
of Sun Father would help me. The beautiful carved
antelope I placed in front of me.

Making myself comfortable with the help of my
sleeping mat, I closed my eyes and sang a soft, repeti-
tive song. My body began to relax with the penetration
of the delicious warmth of Sun Father's rays. I called
upon the spirits to help me. My head began to feel
light. I recognized that I was in a light trance. My
song wanted to go faster of its own accord, and I
trembled. I reached an almost uncontrollable shivering
and resisted an urge to lay down upon the rock, which
would throw me out of alignment and break my
trance. Gradually I began to see the hole. It opened
itself to me. I stopped my singing. I continued to visualize the opening into the earth, and then I entered
it. The cave beckoned me as the *sipapu* of the earth,
the hole from which my people climbed out to enter
this, the fourth world. I followed the cave downward.
There were crystal formations on one side of it, clear,
purple, and yellow. It opened into a series of caverns.
I was drawn to a dark, narrow tunnel on the left.

Entering it, I carefully avoided spiders and many swarming insects.

At last the tunnel opened into a beautiful landscape. Climbing out, I was surrounded by strangely colored rock and sand formations. A sparkling river ran in a crooked course amid giant trees of a kind I did not recognize. It struck me that it was most unusual not to hear any insect, bird, or animal sounds. Then the grass stirred and moved next to the river, and there appeared in my mind's eye a spirit guide, a deer. It stared at me intensely, its four-point antlers quivering as it pawed the grass. It faded, then appeared to run over me as though racing over the path of a rainbow. Then it nudged my crystal in my left hand, causing me to feel a jolt of energy surging through me. Finally, close up, I saw one of his clear dark brown liquid eyes.

Once again a power animal had offered me help. And so I decided to take him with me. Climbing to the entrance of the tunnel, we both changed into crystals and floated past the spiders and insects back into the fourth world. All that happened very quickly, and when I opened my eyes, I found myself huddled on my mat with tears in my eyes. I did not see my power animal, but I sensed its presence and which was all that mattered. Truly I was blessed. Coyote, my first power animal, was there to protect me, and I knew my second power animal, the deer, was also guarding me.

I stretched my legs and realized I must gather wood. Searching for firewood after dark was dangerous and risky. There was danger of falling over cliffs, or encountering snakes, scorpions, or even cholla and other cactus. Skunks were also night creatures. As I began to gather wood, I realized I had no one but myself to keep the fire going at night. It was important to keep a good fire not only for warmth but for a repellent for night creatures great and small. As I walked lightly over the ground, I was careful when I found dead firewood to push it aside first with a stick, for this was a likely habitat for the black widow spider. Their bite, though not usually fatal, caused much pain and nausea. There were other spiders that also caused much discomfort. Snakes also napped in the shady side of a log.

I had nearly finished my task when I stepped on something that emitted a strange little cry. I was startled at first, then caught sight of a fat little feathered body that ran hysterically through the thick, dry grass. It did not fly. Quickly I recognized it as a quail, but a different variety than I was familiar with. Suddenly I salivated. As I ran after it, it scuttled toward a juniper. Then another one jumped out. I raced after the first ground quail, and it continued to run. To my surprise I was able to catch it as I chased it between three rocks, which acted as a trap. I seized it and wrapped it in my skirt. Turning to find the other one, I saw Puppy, who had sent another ground quail toward me. I once again steered the second plump ground quail toward the rocks, where Puppy was able to seize it. Knowing Puppy would eat it immediately, I screeched a warning that caused him to stop and drop the wounded bird. I rushed in to seize it.

Wrapping it tightly with the other one in my skirt, I headed back to our campsite. Puppy leaped and jumped at my feet. His joy suddenly took hold of me, for we both had our dinner for this sun cycle.

I had never had to kill an animal or a bird before to keep from starving. Feeling pity as I wrung the necks of the poor little creatures, I asked Awonawilona his forgiveness and requested the descent of the birds into the happiness of their next level of spirituality. Puppy sat on his haunches watching me as I cut the heads of the birds and hung them upside down in a tree to bleed. I picked off the feathers and gutted the birds. Then again hanging them in a tree, I began building a fire.

At last the fire crackled around the stones I had placed in its center. With a long juniper stick I placed the two little birds on the stones and watched them sizzle. They smelled delicious, and Puppy moved closer to me to let me know I must not forget him. I had gathered some young mallow leaves, and still had corn cakes that I had been carrying. So my dinner was sumptuous! It consisted of the plump little quail, greens, and a corn cake. Puppy wasted no time with his. He licked his chops and looked at me appreciatively. I hugged him, stoked the fire, and crawled between the two feather robes for a bit of sleep.

I awakened before Sun Father began his journey to stoke the fire. In the warmth of the fire I packed all my belongings and wrapped my feet with the skins that had dried by the fire overnight. Puppy was nowhere to be seen, but then coyotes hunted more by night than by day. Taking a walk up the hill, I hoped to get a better view of the land and perhaps spot Puppy. Sun Father appeared red along the edge of the horizon. No rain appeared to be in sight, so I was certain to make good use of my travel time. Since Puppy was still nowhere in sight, I made my way down the hill again. As I rounded a huge rock formation, I froze in my tracks as I came face-to-face with a huge deer.

It was so close I could see the steam escape from its quivering nostrils. Its upperparts were dark gray with a darker stripe along each side. Its legs gradually became a pale tan. Its underparts and the middle of its tail were white. The tail was tipped with black. It had large ears and heavy antlers, proudly displaying five points on each. Its ears flickered, and its nose quivered as its huge brown eyes stared at me inquisitively. Our eyes locked, and my heart was overwhelmed by the sheer magnificence of its beauty. Never had I been so close—only in my shamanistic journey.

Pawing the ground lightly, it spoke to me. "Coyote Woman, I am one of your spirit guides. It is my responsibility to watch over you, to see that your journey is safe. Do not fear me, for all animals interact with man. We are all a part of the creation."

As I looked into the warm, liquid eyes, my heart filled with joy at the sacredness of this time. Softly I said, "I am honored, O great one. I lift up my heart to revere you."

"Coyote Woman, you could as easily have been named 'Doeskin Woman.' From me you have been blessed with beauty and grace. From me you have been given compassion and understanding. From me you can be fleet of foot, to walk away from danger. You, like me, have learned to enjoy your solitude. Visions come to those who are quiet. I also honor and revere you."

"O spirit guide, guide me and show me the way. Let me be your humble servant. May we pay homage to each other through the guidance of Awonawilona, the creator."

"May your life's journey be safe and fruitful, Coyote Woman. Grow in grace, love, and beauty." So saying, he pawed the ground and leaped uphill with a swift elegance that left me speechless.

I stared after him spellbound for quite some time before I broke the feeling of magic that overpowered me. Then falling to my knees, and placing my head on the earth I prayed.

This early sun cycle
when Sun Father
is a red bowl
who swallows up the stars
I speak to my spirit guide
who appears to me.
Sing thanks for grace, love, compassion.
Sing thanks for bone, fat, meat, sustenance.
Sing praise, my heart.
Sing praise, my song.

Pulling out my flute, I offered a wistful, dreamy
song to Sun Father, Rain God, Awonawilona, and my
spirit guides.

Having begun the time of sunlight with such joy, I
set out on my way.

The land was rugged. I could not take my eyes off
the ground for fear I would run into a cholla cactus
or stub my toe on the many large and small rocks.
The deer droppings were many. If I had had an atlatl
or the newer bow and arrow, Puppy and I could have
had a lot of meat to enjoy. It would not have been
wise for me to make a large kill, for we could not
have eaten it all and I couldn't have carried it. It
would have been a waste of a sacred animal.

I climbed up over a steep hill that offered a beautiful view of a small canyon below. The rocks jutted
out, offering mysterious overhangs, more than likely
the home of many of our animal brothers. A spring
bubbled at the top of the rocks, falling lazily and
steadily in a clear turquoise stream to form a small
pond at the bottom. Another stream of water ran
away from the pond to disappear through the rocks
and debris. The debris was from the rain that had
turned it into a raging torrent. I filled up my water

skin and offered a silent prayer to my spirit guides
that I might have no trouble finding sources for water
along my journey.

Then I noticed that I was not alone. Farther down
the stream sat a black-masked ring-tailed creature. His
face was broad with a pointed nose, and the black on
his face looked much like one of the masks of our
spirit dancers. His fur was gray-brown and his front
feet displayed long toes that looked strangely
human. He sat at the edge of the stream and stared
vacantly into space, while his fingers were busily exploring every nook and cranny for frogs and food.
This was the inhabitant of one of the small caves, I
was sure.

Resisting the urge to explore the caves to find the
rest of his family, I moved on, for I did not want to
call Puppy's attention to him. The rest of the early
part of the sun cycle passed uneventfully, and I sat
down to rest when Sun Father was directly overhead.
My experience in watching the sun, moon, and stars
with Nish't Ahote guided me faultlessly toward the
north. I had no fear of being lost. Removing the strap
that bound the backpack to me, I placed it at the base
of a grandfather pine and stretched out to take a rest.
Puppy had reappeared and sat down at my side. I
stroked him behind the ears, and we both closed our
eyes.

Awakening from dreams of Nish't Ahote and feeling refreshed, I enjoyed another corn cake and several
deep swallows of water. My dreams of Nish't Ahote
only increased my determination to return to him as
quickly as possible. I did not allow myself to think
that a replacement might have been found for me, for
though the thought flashed through my mind, in my
heart I knew it could not be so.

I knew I was being watched, for this was the land of the Mogollan. Many days' travel farther south from my location and over the high mountains was a large trade center. The Mayans sent their *pochtecas* with goods from their northernmost post many sun cycles south of the Mogollan trade center. The traders usually stopped at the Mogollan trade center before moving on to our Anasazi center. The people called mound builders east of us brought their goods to the Mogollan trade center. The people from the west coastal region also brought much skillful work, and of course, the Hohokam did the same. I passed a small house made of mud and stone. The masonry was not as fine as ours, but the design was the same. A small child wearing no cover gaped at me while sucking his thumb as he stood outside the entrance to his house. He clutched a small bow and arrow under his arm, then he timidly backed through the doorway to his house and disappeared. I was certain that I was being observed by Mogollan warriors as I passed through their lands. We Anasazi did the same.

The light of the sun cycle drew to a close, and I stopped beneath some huge cottonwoods next to a dry wash. Relieving myself of my burden, I took a bit of time to remove the skins from around my feet and then sat down to rest and to rub my sore feet. I knew I must gather wood before dark and consider my evening meal. Puppy was nowhere to be seen, but I was not concerned. Puppy was growing into an independent young adult, and I expected him to wander and eventually to leave me.

Binding my aching feet with fresh skins, I began looking for firewood. There was much debris and dead branches, and it did not take me long to do so. Suddenly I heard Puppy. He yipped and growled endlessly as though calling me to him. Following the sound, I came upon Puppy, who barked and yelped at an odd-looking creature. Its body was grayish and its long shaggy hair stuck out on both sides. Its black-striped head and its short broad flat tail were very close to the ground. The overhanging hair hid his short legs so that it appeared to be traveling on its stomach like a huge caterpillar. It gave off a highly repugnant scent—not as awful as that of a skunk but unpleasant. It did not seem to notice my presence, for its front legs were busy in a ground squirrel hole. Dirt was flying as it relentlessly dug for its prey. To my surprise Puppy did not seem to frighten it at all. In fact, it seemed not even to notice Puppy's wails and yelps. It extended its front paw down deep into the hole it had dug. Two tiny little gray-tan ground squirrels with white spots came out of the hole. One of the little creatures was caught in the claws of the badger while the second ran hastily away from the hole only to be seized by Puppy, who with a quick jerk put the little creature out of its misery.

Badger returned to his work, laying the dead ground squirrel aside. He dug even deeper and pulled out two more. Puppy took care of one and Badger the other. Taking one of his prey in his mouth, Badger ambled clumsily away to enjoy his repast. Puppy took his catch and brought one to me. Then taking the second one, he also settled down to enjoy his dinner.

And so I had my dinner. I built a fire as darkness arrived and thankfully cooked my ground squirrel over the flames while enjoying another corn cake. Allowing myself a deep drink of freshwater, I stoked the fire and settled down for the night.

Offering a prayer of thanks to Awonawilona, my eyelids became heavy and I drifted away.

*   *   *

The next sun cycle dawned brilliantly in the sky. Packing my belongings, I set out once again. This was the third sun cycle of my journey, and it would not be long before I was out of the Mogollan territory and once again in the lands of the Anasazi. I was traveling almost twice as much distance each sun cycle as my father and his pompous group were able to cover. I was enjoying the solitude and was finding my surroundings magnificent. Perhaps I should have been a member of one of the wandering tribes, for I found I loved to travel. Earth Mother was volatile. At times her beauty was soft and comforting. At times it was rugged and harsh, and at other times it was angry and heartless. I found with this experience that it was possible for me to truly understand the marriage of Sun Father to Earth Mother as our legends told.

Although Puppy still wandered, he seemed to have picked up a friend. Funny, clumsy Badger seemed to have adopted Puppy, or perhaps Puppy had adopted Badger. They were together much of the time. It was good, for they complemented each other on the hunt, and already today had routed out a pair of gophers. I had no doubts that the two of them would keep us well fed. Truly Puppy was acting as my spirit guide. I gave thanks to the four directions, then plodded on.

My water supply was dwindling, and I kept a watchful eye out for any signs of water. There were no grandfather pines now, only pinyon and juniper. As I looked down into a shallow canyon, I noticed a moist area on the surface of a sandy wash. Climbing down into the canyon, I began digging down. I dug only a short distance when water began to collect and settle in the dug-out depression. I waited for an adequate supply of water to accumulate, then took a long hollow bone from my supplies. I wrapped a thin piece of cotton cloth around one end of the bone tube and sucked the water up through the tube, spitting the filtered water into my empty water skin. In this curve along the edge of the cliff, I was preoccupied for quite some time. Nonetheless I finally had filled my two water skins, and my prospects once again looked brighter.

I decided that this was where I should rest for a short time. No sooner had I sat down when Puppy came bounding up to me with a desert rabbit he had caught. Awonawilona, truly I was blessed. I had taken care of Puppy in the beginning of his life, and now he was caring for me.

The sun cycle passed quickly. The Mogollan territory was behind me. Gone were the grandfather pines. Now the land was dotted with only pinyon and juniper. Yucca and sotol grew abundantly. Prickly pear cactus and cholla forced me to travel slower than before. At last, when Sun Father began his descent, I spotted a wash lined with cottonwood. Puppy and Badger ambled playfully ahead of me. My bones were weary, and my forehead was becoming permanently lined from the strap that supported the basket on my back, which carried all my belongings and the rabbit that Puppy brought to me. My shoulders ached. After several sun cycles of travel, my body was totally exhausted.

Removing my basket, I felt as though the world had been lifted from my shoulders. Once again I gathered juniper and pinyon for firewood. Just as I had nearly finished, I spotted Puppy and Badger. They were busily rummaging through a pile of debris, oblivious to all around them. They were as two little children busy at play, convinced that they were the universe and that there was nothing else in creation but them. Something in that pile of branches and rocks was fascinating to them. It piqued my curiosity, and I moved closer. As I slowly approached the scene, an inexplicable sense of danger gripped me.

Then I saw the reason for my feelings. Patiently, with a stealthy gracefulness, a huge mountain lion was working its way toward Puppy and Badger. It suddenly became clear to me what was happening. A mountain lion killed one or two deer a week. It usually struck those that were easier to catch—either the very old or very young and sometimes those that were sick. When the kill was made, it dragged the carcass off to a secluded spot to eat it. When it was satiated, it covered the remaining meat with leaves, soil, branches, or whatever it could find to hide it so that it might return several sun cycles later to finish it. Badger and Puppy had routed out this lion's stashed food.

The lion's color was tawny, its hair gray-tipped. Its throat, the insides of the legs, and the belly were white, while the tip of its tail was black. Its body was slender, and its legs were long and muscular. It was truly a magnificent animal. As I was held hypnotized under its spell, for I had never seen a mountain lion at such close proximity, its strength reminded me of Nish't Ahote. This was a fleeting thought, however, for I was suddenly flooded with the feelings of a mother wishing to protect her young. The full impact of Puppy's and Badger's danger hit me.

Here was a mountain lion interested only in defending his own. He would creep up on Puppy and Badger and, when close enough, make several tremendous bounds landing with its full weight to clutch its prey in its claws. Although I had this insight, there was really little I could do.

My heart pounded so loud I was sure that the mountain lion heard it. With padded feet the beautiful creature softly moved toward its prey. Eyes glittering and angry, it inched toward my beloved Puppy. I prayed to Awonawilona to intercede. Then out of a cottonwood tree between Puppy, Badger, and the mountain lion, casually dropped a snake. It was broad of head and singing a loud rattling sound. Its characteristic buzz I easily recognized. It glided its way across the area that stood between Puppy, Badger, and the mountain lion, then stopped to move its head from side to side. Looking all around it as if it commanded the universe, it moved slowly and voluptuously onward, taking its time.

Suddenly Puppy and Badger became aware of his presence. Puppy's hair raised and so did the thick hair on Badger's coat. The mountain lion stepped backward and glared at the unexpected development. He seemed unsure of what to do. I was also not certain of what I should be doing. Once again I was faced with a rattlesnake, and this time I was not intimidated. This time I knew it was a spirit guide. I could only watch and place trust in my visions, dreams, and experiences.

Puppy nudged Badger, and they immediately leaped into the air and carefully backed off from the stash of the mountain lion toward me.

I became concerned for our welfare. My campsite was close by, and at that time it might be accompanied by the mountain lion and the rattlesnake. Suddenly I was in the company of too many animals. As though in answer to my prayers, the mountain lion slowly backed off, and the snake moved slowly onward. Its rattle faded into nothingness as Puppy and Badger hastily made their way toward me.

My heart began to quiet while I embraced Puppy as Badger looked on in his own wise way. Then Badger ambled out of sight under a cholla close by. I stopped to thank Awonawilona and the rattlesnake, my ever faithful spirit guide for his interception. I prayed to the four directions, to the top of the universe, to the lower parts of the universe, and then within myself.

For the rest of the short remaining sun cycle, I cooked my dinner, stoked the fire I had built, and prayed to the seven directions for our well-being. We retired for the night.

This was the fifth sun cycle of my travels alone. There were many huge rocks that were blackened from being spewed forth from inside a grandfather mountain that raised its jagged majestic snow-covered peak to the north in front of me. The mountain loomed tall, alone, and cast its shadow as a commanding warrior over the earth. The blackened rocks were a sign of its ability to be angered.

Puppy, Badger, and I trudged on to the base of the grandfather mountain. Badger and Puppy dug out a couple of ground squirrels while I gathered wood. A sparkling creek ran close by under the tall pines that drained icy cold from the snow on top of the mountain. The evening was dark, for the moon offered no reflection. There were only stars twinkling in a special dance. They offered me assurance that although I was only a few days from home, they were the very same ones that Nish't Ahote had taught me to observe. Nish't Ahote! Soon I would be home. Soon I would be in his arms.

I slept soundly with Puppy curled up beside me. For whatever the reason, he did not wander with Badger, but stayed to offer his companionship and warmth.

The new sun cycle broke with Sun Father spreading a pink and blue glow over the horizon. After gathering my things together and filling my water skin from the creek, Puppy, Badger, and I were on our way. It took most of the sun cycle to circle grandfather mountain, but the scenery was so very different that I found it an enormously exciting experience. Puppy and Badger dug out some ground quail for our evening repast, which I washed down with water, and finished the meal with my last corn cake.

The next two sun cycles were hot and dry. Gone was the green and the grandfather pines. I was thankful to have filled both water skins before leaving the sparkling creek behind. Though my corn cakes were gone, it hardly mattered, for I was accustomed to fasting for three days each womanly cycle anyway. Puppy and Badger always seemed to be able to supply us with meat of one kind or another during each sun cycle. The remainder of the trip was uneventful.

At long last I knew I was in familiar territory, for I recalled the same landscape during the first day of travel with my father. There was little green, but as I approached our group of buildings, which seemed as dots on the horizon, I felt warm and very excited.

Surely Nish't Ahote would know I was returning, for our sentinels would have been watching. The three of us trudged on. My water supply was almost gone, and I was very hungry. It seemed very strange that I saw no signs of life.

It was then I saw him. I rounded a canyon corner to see our own Fahatta Butte as it rose magestically from the ground radiating an odd golden glow. At the top of the butte stood a figure. His robes whipped around him. His shining black hair was caught at the back of his neck. He held his hand over his eyes to offer shade as he scanned the southern horizon. For an instant we both froze. Then suddenly he moved toward the edge of the butte and began to descend using the hand and toe holds. I broke into a run as

Puppy bound at my feet and Badger waddled as he struggled to stay at our sides. My heart was leaping with joy as at long last I was swept into Nish't Ahote's arms. Home at last! My joy was complete.

Chapter 20

Death of the Old Priest

Just before Sun Father began his journey, there was a light touch on my shoulder. I awakened startled, for I was in my mind still in the wilderness. "Come to me to observe the sunrise," said a soft, caressing voice.

In my groggy state I almost thought of it as a dream, but it was Nish't Ahote's husky voice. Was I dreaming? No! He must have called me, but no one was there!

Picking up my clothes and throwing them quickly on, I cleansed myself and went toward the voice that beckoned me. I still walked as in a dream when the ladder leading to his quarters stood in front of me, and I hesitated. Then I began to realize how silly I was. Upon reaching the bottom of the ladder, he turned to look at me.

I stood as though hypnotized. He walked toward me and said, "I am glad you acknowledged my spiritual message." Looking at me through wise and tender eyes, he touched first my forehead, then my eyelids, my nose, my cheeks, my mouth, my chin, and at last he came to rest at the pulse in my neck.

"I am no longer only your teacher. I am also your mate. You have become a part of my blood. You are a part of me. The world falls out of harmony without you. Oh, yes, I could live without you, but a part of me would die. You have crept into my heart, and you will always be there. I am certain you have full knowledge of this," he said as he looked at me, then dropped his eyes as if he felt he had said enough.

My heart was so full, I felt it might burst. My happiness leaped unchecked through the universe. I was so lost in emotion after what I had been through and the happiness I felt that I was unable to speak. My doubts flew away as an eagle toward heaven. A sensation of heat began to beat in my blood, slowly, rhythmically, the eternal sound of the drum. He moved to touch me in the stillness of the beginning of Sun Father's journey.

He pulled me ever so gently down to his mat. I lay softly down, facing him, feeling the pounding urgency of his heart. He stroked my hair, pressing his full, sensuous mouth against my forehead, moving errant strands of hair away from my face. His kisses brushed my deep-set eyes and high cheekbones. The emptiness of separation was dissolved in that slow undemanding meeting.

I touched his sensitive beautiful mouth, outlining its contours with my fingers. They searched the broad lines of his face, his high forehead, high cheekbones, and over and through his thick, luxurious hair, winding it through my fingers.

There was so much to find in each other. In the great hunt, we could only know each other through our senses, but it did not matter, for we were together.

I was startled at the rings of fire dancing within my core. I felt I could ride the edges of the flame endlessly. My breathing came in deep surges as I drew him close. My body arched into him. He caressed my curving softness down to the power center of my sex, moving lightly, circling the fiery point until my warm nectar covered his searching fingers. He brought them up to taste as he looked at me with clear, honest eyes.

He moved over me with his body, molding perfectly to the curved hollow of my hips. I ran my fingers over his pulsing hardness, drawing him into me. He pressed carefully and gently into my slowly yielding folds. I clung to him as he pressed deeper, endlessly deeper. I heard my muffled cry as I quivered and felt the touch of the depths within me. Surely, I thought, this was a miracle of pleasure.

Time fell over our stillness. I never wanted him to move again, for he fit within me to perfection. Then a subtle movement of my body, pulling him yet deeper, spurred a movement against my arched body. Our increasing hunger brought us to a pitch of active seeking until our bodies gave way to a final yielding, and there was only a common rhythm. A rhythm of utter harmony enabled us to soar with complete release into the world and its mystery.

The sun shone through the corner window, throwing a shaft of light on us to further illuminate our brightness. We lay heavily together, still, while the last quick movements within me were quieted. After a time of quiet, I ran my fingers over his beloved body.

He curved around my back, resting, sculpting himself to my moist body, his arms crossed over my breasts. I ran my fingers over the hairs of his arms, so lightly, not even touching his skin. I pretended I was blind, learning through only the sense of touch to know him.

After a period of rest, he stirred and gently withdrew to relieve himself. Returning to the mat, he sat next to me saying, "My little Coyote Woman, Taweyah's health is not good. His condition worsens. Please come with me that we may attend to his needs. He will be delighted to see you."

"Come, let us go to him at once." I bounded up to don my cotton kilt and medicine pouch. Throwing my feather cape around my shoulders, I awaited my beloved, who donned his medicine pouch. Climbing the ladder ahead of him, I suddenly felt light pressure on the back of my knee. My body vibrated with delight, then we continued out into the early part of Sun Father's journey. We were alone as we made our way to Taweyah's quarters.

We climbed down his ladder, Nish't Ahote first, then myself. Aunt Mokni looked up, and her eyes lit up with love as she caught sight of me. Then she lowered her eyes and began to dutifully back out of the room to give us some privacy. Taweyah seemed asleep, but suddenly from his frail body he spoke, "Mokni, love, do not leave! This is your niece."

I ran to her, my surrogate mother. We embraced with a passion that needed no words as Taweyah looked on. Aunt Mokni was a woman who knew no hatred. She was a woman who preached patience, and with Taweyah practiced the patience of which she so often spoke. Surely she was a person of the fifth world—the world yet to come. Surely she had reached perfection.

Then turning to Taweyah, who looked wan and frail, I took his hand in mine. His fingers were nothing but bone, worse than I remembered before I left. His face was more angular and his skin was stretched tightly over his skull. His eyes were bright and alert, but the condition of his body clearly indicated that his days were limited.

He smiled with radiant love. Happily he said, "And so our Coyote Woman returns to us. The Gods have heard our plea. Welcome, little one, for now the stars realign themselves in their normal order, the moon will have no circle. Nish't Ahote will be reasonable, and our community will reestablish its harmony. Most of all, I welcome you back, for you are as a daughter to me. You are the feminine spirit, Earth Mother reincarnate. You fill the spiritual circle—Nish't Ahote, Hototo, and you. So it is foretold by the Gods and Grandfathers."

"Taweyah, our wise and revered one, I hardly know how to respond. I know only that I am here, and I have never been happier. In spite of my Mayan heritage, this is where I belong. I said that before I left. Now I return to shower you and all my people with all the love and devotion I can express."

"Little Coyote Woman, I know of your trials. My spirit, as well as Nish't Ahote's, Hototo's, and Aunt Mokni's were with you all the way. We knew you would return to us!" Then glancing at Nish't Ahote, his old eyebrows raised as though giving a signal to Nish't Ahote.

Looking at me with love in his eyes, Nish't Ahote said, "Coyote Woman! With Taweyah and Aunt Mokni as my witnesses, I declare my love for you. My world was not whole until I knew that you would return. I could not bring myself to seek a new visionary way of life until I knew!" Then he stopped. Perhaps he thought he had said too much.

My heart beat wildly as I heard his words. I had known this for a long time, but now he declared his feelings before others.

Still holding Taweyah's hand, I looked from Nish't Ahote to Taweyah to Aunt Mokni. The love I read in their eyes enveloped me. Spontaneously I lay my hands on Taweyah's shoulders and rested them there. Nish't Ahote rested his hands on Taweyah's brow. An overwhelming feeling of peace and love surrounded us all.

Suddenly our reverie was broken by Taweyah, who murmured weakly, "Now I may move into the world of our ancestors a fulfilled man, for I have all I want."

Aunt Mokni's eyes filled with tears. Seeing hers so filled with emotion, I was unable to control my own. Only Nish't Ahote's eyes remained dry, though I knew he felt the same inside, for this was his uncle. We worked silently on while Nish't Ahote chanted his healing prayer.

At last Taweyah slept. Quietly I backed away from him, as did Nish't Ahote, and squeezing Aunt Mokni's hand, we made our way silently up the ladder to the plaza. Nish't Ahote held me close. "Little one, come back when Sun Father is at his zenith, for we must give Taweyah much attention. Now go with my love to seek your own visions." Kissing me on the forehead and pressing his finger tenderly on my lips, he guided me to the ladder. We descended to the plaza, and as we parted, we turned to look at each other several times, as though fearful that the other might not be there.

Nish't Ahote, Hototo, and I spent much time with Taweyah, using our touch healing and sending messages to Awonawilona through the smoke from the sacred pipe. At one point Taweyah murmured, "My spirit is tired of this old body. It wishes to take flight." Aunt Mokni held his hand and looked despairingly at us. We all knew that if Taweyah had lost his will to live, then nothing we could do would help.

For several more sun cycles we attended to him. Then as I slept soundly on my mat, a hand tapped my shoulder. I awakened to Aunt Mokni's look of panic when she said, "Dese, wake up. Taweyah calls for you!"

Scrambling to my feet, I hastily threw on my feather robe over my kilt. After tying on my sandals and combing my hair, I grabbed my medicine pouch. Leaving Puppy behind, Aunt Mokni and I quickly climbed the ladder.

"Aunt Mokni, go to Taweyah. I shall bring Nish't Ahote and Hototo. Hurry!"

I hastened to Nish't Ahote's quarters to find him sleeping under his feather blanket. Bending over his head, I seized his shoulders and planted a light kiss on his forehead. He groaned as his eyes opened in surprise. "Ah, my love, come to me."

"Nish't Ahote, love, not now. Taweyah calls for us. Aunt Mokni came to get me. Hototo does not know. Will you awaken him, that I may hasten in answer to Taweyah's need?"

Sitting bolt upright on his mat, his long black hair sweeping his shoulders, his black eyes filled with concern, he quickly responded, "Fly, my little bird! I shall not be far behind."

I hastily made my departure and tripped lightly to Taweyah's quarters. Aunt Mokni was seated on the mat beside him, holding his hand lovingly in hers. Her eyes were full of concern and devotion. Taweyah's were closed. His body was very frail. He looked as though he might have already passed on.

I took his other hand in mine, and we remained in that position, no words spoken, for some time. During that silent time, I became aware of the presence of Nish't Ahote and Hototo. I was filled with an overwhelming feeling of completeness, of unconditional love. Here in Taweyah's quarters were all the people to whom I felt the closest, and now one of them threatened to leave me.

Taweyah's eyelids fluttered. As though it was an effort, as though he counted the seconds in our fourth world, he murmured, "The earth is created for all living things, birds, fishes, animals, plants, rocks, water, sky, air, and, of course, humankind. But you, my be-

loved, can talk and think. You can communicate with
Awonawilona without saying a word, for there is the
opening in the top of your head. I delegate my responsibilities to you. I leave this earth in your care. You
are the guardians of this our fourth world. take care
of our 'people of peace.' See that nothing is done in
excess, for this is your home. If you watch over it, it
will take care of your needs. There will be hard
times—times when you will doubt, but what I tell you
is the truth." He closed his eyes again. His pulse rate
was very slow.

We waited. His breathing was slow. Then he again
murmured, "The ancestors beckon me. They are getting closer. It is time." Once again there was a long
silence. Aunt Mokni's face was like stone. She seemed
in a trance.

His voice rasped as he said haltingly, "I die a happy
fulfilled man." Then followed another pause. "Our little Coyote Woman has been restored to us. The cycle
of three is now complete. I may rest in peace."

My eyes misted and tears fell unbidden. We, the
Anasazi, were not supposed to show any emotional
response, but for this man there was no other way. I
glanced briefly to find Aunt Mokni also weeping.
Nish't Ahote and Hototo knelt as wooden carvings.

Then at last, Taweyah's small weak voice could be
heard to whisper, "If you need me, little Coyote
Woman, I'll be there to nurture and protect you. See to
it that our people build houses, villages, complexes, and
cultivate fields of corn, beans, and squash. All must be
in moderation. Be happy! Maintain the bala ..." His
voice faded on that word, his eyes closed, and then
silence.

In that silence the ancestors reclaimed him. His face
relaxed, and a soft smile turned up the corners of his
mouth. In the repose of death, he looked truly happy.

His pain and anguish were removed. For that I was happy, but my tears flowed uncontrollably as did Aunt Mokni's. She reached for an obsidian blade laying close by and hacked off her long white-streaked hair to ear length. I reached to do the same, but Nish't Ahote stayed my hand, folding me in his arms.

"No, little Coyote Woman, you are a priestess now. A priestess does not always conform to the ways of the people." His arms offered me warm consolation. Hototo wrapped his arms in a loving embrace around Aunt Mokni. In this way we consoled each other as Taweyah's body took flight toward the land of our ancestors. My thoughts were that Taweyah was at last an eagle, free at last to keep his vigil.

Messengers were sent out to anyone who wished to pay their respects. The ceremony that followed the death of an Anasazi was a simple and short one. We handled the death of a loved one with great reverence, for our reverence for life led logically to reverence for the dead.

Aunt Mokni washed Taweyah's gray hair in yucca suds, thus purifying the body and soul, while Nish't Ahote, Hototo, and myself dressed him in his feathered priestly garb and placed his favorite turquoise necklace around his neck. We rubbed his body with sacred cornmeal and blackened his chin. Then lifting him carefully, we took him to a burial room. His body was so light. He weighed no more than a young doe.

We laid him on his mat in a reclined position on his back, then wrapped his body with a blanket. We placed a string of *pahos* around his head, flanking a mask of white cotton. The cloud mask made the body light enough to float among the clouds, since now Taweyah would live in the land of the cloud people and our ancestors. Aunt Mokni moved as in a trance as

we placed piki bread and little pieces of meat next to
his body so he would not be hungry during the trip.
At last a planting stick was laid next to him, so he
might use it to climb to the land of the underworld
and the land of the ancestors. A clay mortar was
made, which we lovingly pressed over his body. As I
patted the mortar into place over his medicine pouch,
and over his pipe, I cried once again as did Aunt
Mokni.

Acolytes and students began to pay their respects,
and I dried my eyes, for a priestess must be strong.
We all offered our silent prayers for Taweyah's journey. The elders appeared each in his own time to put
a *paho* around the body of Taweyah. All who knew
him offered their prayers for his journey. Nish't
Ahote, Hototo, Aunt Mokni, and myself kept our vigil
for four sun cycles. Then, when they were complete,
we broke our vigil with a pipe. The smoke purified us
from any evil spirits that might have somehow entered
the room. Each person who paid their respects to Taweyah did the same. Then placing the remaining mortar over him, we took our leave.

Returning to Taweyah's quarters, we began to light
a pipe, again to purify all spirits that might reside in
his room. The room was clean, for Aunt Mokni had
given it immaculate care. She, however, seemed restless. Nish't Ahote walked to her and took her in his
arms. She said nothing. Stroking her grayed cropped
hair while he held her, he said, "Mokni, revered older
one, you have made his last lunar cycles happy. I'm
sure he told you, and so we also tell you. I am sorry
we did not know of the love you had for each other
sooner, for he would have had many more happy days
and so would you. Know that you are a very special
person to us. It was not only Taweyah who knew your

value, but also all in the complex and many outside of it who know the gift you brought to him. Do not forget this, for it is so."

For a brief time she remained in his embrace, then seemed to grow restless once again. It was as though she wished to say something and yet was not quite ready.

Sensing her discomfort, Nish't Ahote stood aside saying, "Mokni, Taweyah's quarters have been yours for the past two moon cycles. If it is your desire, you would honor us by remaining here to guard his spirit."

Turning away from us both, Aunt Mokni responded quietly, "You do me great honor with your request. However, it is my desire to return to my former quarters and to assume my former duties. I do not feel Taweyah has need for a guardian for his spirit. His spirit is with me now, and will visit me often in times to come. It has been a great honor and a joy to serve him, for it was done out of love." She did not turn to look at us, but stood firmly as a tree rooted to the ground.

Remaining where I was in respect for her privacy, I offered, "Aunt Mokni, we hold your decision in esteem, for we love you. I am glad you have not decided to leave the complex to join our family. Who then would I have to confide in as I would my mother?"

She turned and, taking a step toward me, folded me in her ample arms, holding me to her bosom. We spoke no words. After a short time she broke away, saying, "I go now to make ready my own room, for there is much to be done. May Awonawilona shower his blessings on you both with many years of fulfillment and love."

So saying, she climbed the ladder to resume her old duties with the other older women in the cooking area.

Nish't Ahote turned to me with the light of love

shining in his obsidian eyes. Placing his hands on my shoulders, he said, "Little one, will you come to me when Sun Father finishes his journey? Time is precious. Let us enjoy each other while yet we live and breathe."

My heart leaped with anticipation of his touch. "Of course! There is little I can think of to keep me from you."

Planting a kiss on my lips, he led me to the ladder to ascend to the rooftop. We parted once again until the moon began its journey.

I returned to my cave for my womanly cycle. The nights were warmer now, and I enjoyed the chance to again be close to Earth Mother. We had had several penetrating rains that late planting season which had filled the edges of the Chaco wash with lush vegetation. Cottonwoods and willows offered periodic shade to marsh grasses, rushes, canes, and reeds. That was sharply contrasted to the floor of the canyon, which supported only black greasewood, saltbrush, rabbitbrush, a little sage, and some tumbleweed. In the side canyons the rains and winter snows had produced stands of golden currant, squaw bush, some chokeberry, and an undercover of grasses and herbs. My cave was hidden in one of those side canyons. It seemed something of a wonder that nothing occupied it now, so I cleaned it out and gathered firewood for the night.

Puppy was only with me occasionally, for he would far rather be out in the open lands that were his birthright. He and Badger were busy working together to rout out food. The moon rose early, and though it was only a thumbnail, it brought the familiar howl of the coyotes as they beckoned to Puppy while he howled in return.

By the third day of my cycle I felt a bit giddy. That, however, was not unusual, for three sun cycles without food did strange things to my mind. It was soon time that Tawa, Sun Father, dipped below the horizon. The colors in the sky were a magnificent azure contrasted with pinks, oranges, purples, and yellows. My fire was ready, blazing with steady warmth inside my cave. I slipped out into the cool of the coming darkness to marvel, for the sight in the west was breathtaking. The colors made the rock formations and ground cover seem a more vivid contrast than usual. A stubby juniper to my right seemed to give off an unearthly beauty. The color of the trunk was so dark and vivid that while observing that miracle I did not turn to look, although I sensed a presence of someone. That presence finally drew my attention away from the beauty of Earth Mother, and I turned. A hazy form stood behind me at the entrance of my cave. I could not tell who it was even as I turned to see. The form stood unthreateningly in front of me. I struggled to bring it into focus. Then slowly the details of the figure materialized, and I gasped as I recognized Taweyah.

He seemed years younger, perhaps the age he had been when I had come to the school nine season cycles before. There were no folds in his skin. He seemed plump and robust, not fat but healthy. His color was good, and he did not show any signs of the degeneration before his death. I was overcome with humility. I knew not what to do or say, and so my mouth hung open.

His eyes twinkled and shone with love. He attempted to speak, then stopped. "Taweyah?" I said timidly.

"Yes, little Coyote Woman, it is I. I am very happy in the land of the Grandfathers. You must not touch me, for I am not made as are earthly people. I come not to frighten you, but to bring you love and caring from the land in which I dwell." He paused, and I continued to stare. I was afraid to take my eyes off him for fear he might disappear. I could not believe it was really happening to me.

"Little Coyote Woman, I appear to you for a purpose. You are as a daughter to me. Nish't Ahote is as a son. The two of you are loved not just by me but by the people. You have no blemish on your life as others have." Taweyah continued, "You are a woman loved by the people. Your decisions draw from the four directions, north-wisdom, south-innocence, east-illumination, and west-introspection. Few know how to draw on these four powers. You will always be loved by the people if you draw on all four. Little one, your way is difficult! Keep nothing from Nish't Ahote. Allow him to unfold the bud into full flower."

He began to fade from my vision, then suddenly grew strong once again. "There is much dissension within the authority in the complex. Speak out, little one, for without you, there will be no control. Guard our resources, for there will come a day . . ."

His voice faded, and I moved toward him to try to hear what more he had to say. His voice was gone, and his presence was also nothing more than a memory. I said aloud, "No, Taweyah, you cannot go, for I do not hear what will happen on that day! Please come back! Taweyah!!!"

A dark silence followed. I stood in awe, for how could I ever explain? I vowed I would return to the complex in the morning to speak of that to Nish't Ahote. Then the feeling of being a woman blessed consumed me. Taweyah had blessed me with the privilege of seeing him and speaking to him. In my mind's eye he was not dead. He lived to be a guide to me, and once again I had acquired a new spirit guide—

the deer, the coyote, the snake, the eagle, and now Taweyah. Truly I was a woman exalted!

As I turned those thoughts over in my mind with all that Taweyah had said, I moved silently into my cave and to the warmth of the fire. I gazed into the fire for some time before my eyelids grew heavy, and I allowed my body to slowly relax. The sleep that overcame me was not a sound one, for I was much too full of thought.

Chapter 21

Summer Solstice Ceremony

I returned at sunrise to the complex. Upon entering the plaza, my eye traveled to the eagles, whose feet were tethered to eagle platforms built on the rooftop of the the complex. There they awaited sacrifice at the conclusion of our Solstice Ceremony. Early in the spring the acolytes set out. Nests were spotted on the sides of cliffs. Each acolyte planted *pahos* to express their desire in prayers that the eagles would come willingly to our complex and live happily until their spirits were released at the end of the ceremony. The acolytes than lowered themselves on ropes from the tops of the cliffs or climbed precarious ledges to reach the nests, where they removed from the nests the birds too young to fly. The eaglets were brought back, where they were fed daily and treated with much respect until they matured.

Gazing at them for a time, I briefly felt sorry for them. Then I quickly put aside such thoughts, for I knew of their value as messengers to the spirit world. The eagle was one of Nish't Ahote's spirit guides. How wonderful it would be, I thought, to be able to fly as did the eagle—to explore the world above. Perhaps someday, if the Gods willed it be so, I would learn of that separate reality.

I moved on across the plaza to my quarters, to the security and familiarity of my room. Puppy was not with me, for he seemed to prefer the company of Badger during the sunshine hours to my company. It was not long before an acolyte descended my ladder with a bowl of steaming corn gruel sweetened with a little honey. I broke my fast savoring the delicious sweetness. After washing this down with some water, I cleansed myself and refreshed myself. Running my hands over my breasts and hips as I rubbed my body with sage, I gave thanks to Awonawilona that I was woman. Putting on my skirt and top tied at one shoulder, I added my sandals. Using my pyrite mirror, I touched my cheeks with red ocher, and put on my feather earbobs and inlay shell necklace. Feeling complete, I ascended my ladder to report to Nish't Ahote.

I found him working with one of the cooks whose hands were gnarled and stiff with pain that often comes with age. He treated her hands with an herbal pack and sang a soft prayer all the while. I sat down to watch and wait. At last after removing the pack from her hand, he patiently escorted her up the ladder and out into the plaza.

As he returned down the ladder, he continued softly humming. Turning toward me, he sat down on the hard earth floor next to me. He took my hand and touched it to his lips, sending a little ripple of energy through my arm straight to my nipples and power spot. I looked into his eyes with joy and a smile. He flashed one of his rare sparkling smiles in return, saying, "Your eyes speak of new knowledge, little one. Do you wish to speak of this?" He continued to hold my hand as he offered me that wonderful sense of security that only comes when you are with the one you love.

A short period of time lapsed until at last I said, "He told me to keep nothing from you." I paused again, hesitating to go on.

Nish't Ahote urged, "Who told you this, little one? Was it Taweyah?"

My eyes flashed to open in wide amazement. "Is there anything you do not know, my teacher?" I asked.

"I too have spoken with Taweyah. He told me of his intention to speak with you." He did not prod me, but waited with loving patience for me to respond.

At last I spoke. "He says my decisions must draw from the four directions. I must learn to make my decisions accordingly. He says it will not be easy."

"Is there more?" he asked in a very soft gentle voice.

"Yes, my teacher. He speaks of much dissension within those who are in authority in our community. He says to guard your resources, for there will come a day . . ." I stopped and stared away from him.

"There will come a day when what?" Nish't Ahote's voice took on an air of concern that I normally did not hear in his voice.

"I do not know, for he faded from my view and from my hearing at that time."

"Little Coyote Woman, it may interest you to know that my conversations with him have always ended in the same manner. He never wishes to discuss what will come that day."

Suddenly I felt as a seer. "Do you think perhaps there will come a day when we have none of these resources to rely on? I have noticed the widening of many arroyos where trees have been felled. It is as though the roots of the trees were important. Taking the life from them is taking the life of our soil—that which sustains us."

"Sweet one, I believe this is so. Much of our good soil is washed away. The land has changed even since I was a boy. Thanks be to Awonawilona for providing us with an abundance of rain, but that rain is washing away soil—rich soil, where once proud trees stood."

"I also wonder if our buildings and our road systems keep the bison and antelope from wandering our way." Once again my mind spun through its logic.

"All this I believe is true. Taweyah and I have had many such discussions. We must care for Earth Mother and put back that which we take, for it takes time for Earth Mother to regenerate."

I took his hand firmly in both of mine. My concern was great, for truly we were on a path of self-destruction if all that were true. "Then we are in agreement," I said. "The impulsive building must be slowed. We must find a way to slow it down."

"Yes, little rabbit. Something must be done." His hand touched my lips, then my chin, and all cares were swept away as my body jumped at his touch.

His hands traveled from my chin to my throat and then to my bare shoulder. With a touch as light as that of an eagle feather, he traced a line from my shoulders to my breasts, where he slowly caressed my nipples. He placed his free hand behind my neck to pull me toward him in a kiss—a kiss that sent my blood racing to quicken the desire within me. Then softly he said, "There is much to be done, for several of my acolytes need me for counseling, and two female acolytes have asked to see you. There are several who need healing. We can attend them together. Hototo may also join us. When Sun Father has made his descent, come to me."

I sat quietly on my mat. Picking up my large crystal, I cradled it lovingly in my hands and waited for it to warm. Closing my eyes, I took several deep breaths to relax my mind and body.

When at last my crystal was warmed, I looked into

it. It was like holding a piece of warm ice, if that were possible. The gold color of my fingers shown through it. I inhaled deeply and exhaled onto my crystal, giving it the vital force of my body to blend with its forces. I visualized the union of these forces. Once again I rubbed it with both of my hands. Focusing on the inside of my crystal, I felt it begin to pulsate. My vision became diffused. Nothing was coherent. I slowly forced myself to concentrate on one spot, and I forced my mind to relax. I opened myself to any impressions. I tried to remain open, relaxed, and focused. My crystal seemed to become larger. I then lost myself entirely within it. My eyes remained open, and I felt there was only the crystal and what I was seeing. My body wished to assume different positions, and I found myself making different strange sounds.

Impressions flitted in and out of my mind—and then! His image appeared! Wisoko! The memory of his smell, the memory of his harshness—of his hatred caused me to shiver. Would I never be free of his twisted evil person?

As though hypnotized, I continued my vision. It seemed that his features were distorted. He pulsated as he turned to look at me. It seemed that his features changed as he drew closer, and my breathing became ragged. At times his eyes were larger than his other features, and at times his mouth or his nose became the dominant feature in his face. As all these changes were taking place, he walked shakily toward me. He came closer and closer until his hateful face totally filled the crystal. The face continued to move closer until all I saw was one of his eyes with millions of blood veins that seemed to pop out at me. At long last the eye receded, then the face, the body, and at last Wisoko faded gradually away.

I remained within my crystal for a time in an effort

to release the tension in my body. After being in that space for a while, I slowly began to back out. I became aware of the mat on which I sat, and heard my own breathing. I let go of my diffused vision to bring it back to normal. I stretched and shook myself until I was back into this reality. I breathed deeply for a time to ground myself, then went in search of Nish't Ahote to speak of my vision.

"So you have seen him," said my teacher and lover. "Truly you are both a seer and a healer. You need only to have command of placing yourself in a separate reality to complete your requirements of a shaman."

"But did I not go into a separate reality within my crystal?" I asked, for I did not understand his meaning.

"Yes, my sweet, you entered into a separate reality, but you did not become something or someone else. That is the difference."

"But, then, how must I achieve this end?" I asked, for truly I was concerned.

"I cannot answer." He paused to place his energy-filled hand on mine. "This is a journey you must take by yourself."

"Why must this be 'by myself'? All else you have taught me, or so my other teachers have taught me. Why is this so different?"

"There are certain learning experiences in life that can only be learned alone, little one. This is one of those experiences."

"But if I already know how to go into a 'separate reality,' as you call it, then discovering this can be only one step away!" I exclaimed excitedly.

"This is true," he said. Then he added, "But it may take sun cycles, moons, or even season cycles."

"If I think on this in my meditation time, will it come sooner?"

"I cannot say, my love, for each person is different. That is one of the most baffling mysteries the Gods have bestowed upon us. You are you! There is no one else like you in the universe. This you know from your previous studies. I cannot begin to predict your actions. Perhaps that is one of the reasons I love you."

"Then, it seems I must sit back and wait. It may be that other experiences may help me along the way," I said as I pulled on my medicine pouch.

"Speaking of other experiences, little Coyote Woman, there is a meeting tomorrow night that we must attend. It seems there is talk of a new, very large kiva almost directly across from us. It could be that your insight may be needed." His forefinger lifted my chin, forcing me to look directly into his magnetic eyes.

"I shall be in attendance, my teacher." Then, forcefully dragging my eyes away from his, I begged my leave.

He placed his lips on mine very briefly saying, "We are but the instruments of Awonawilona. Let us use our best judgment."

I left his quarters to return to my room and my studies.

The meeting had been called to order. Salavi began by clearing his throat and rose to speak. A hush enveloped the smokiness of the kiva as the pipe was passed around. All the elders were present. The chiefs of trade and building were also present. After the pipe had been passed to everyone and prayers had been offered, Salavi commenced. "We gather here for a progress report on the new kiva, the grain storage bins, the storage rooms, and irrigation canals."

Wikwavi, in charge of building, rose from the bench. "Most of our work is centered on the new kiva and irrigation canals. The need for these is greater at this time. The kiva is about half complete, and the new irrigation canals are nearly complete. The canals must be finished quickly, as the warm seasonal rains begin soon. Following this, we shall turn our workforces to the storage bins and storage rooms in the trade center." Having completed his report, he resumed his former seat on the stone bench built into the circumference of the wall of the kiva.

It seemed strange that Taweyah was not in attendance. My eyes traveled from one elder to another, to Hototo at my right and finally to Nish't Ahote on my left. Both Hototo and Nish't Ahote stood as solemn statues with feet planted firmly on the ground and arms folded across their broad chests. It was not unusual for the priests to remain standing, for seldom did they speak and usually only when called upon.

Machakwi rose from the bench to speak. "I have noticed that it has become necessary to transport logs from greater distance than in the past. The large pines that once stood nearby are gone. Perhaps the logs could be floated down the creeks during the rainy seasons to ease the burden over the greater distance."

"That is the thought that is now being considered," answered the building director.

Pavati stood. "It has been suggested that due to the growth both in our communities and in our outliers that we consider building yet another kiva directly across from this center. This would offer further unity and appeasement to the Gods. Perhaps in doing this, the Gods would offer us additional protection from the raiders."

A nagging feeling of discontent overtook me. Taweyah's spirit surrounded me as I heard his words once again. "Guard our resources." I had thought all along that the erosion and the cutting of new arroyos was due to the felling of our trees, for the roots were no longer there to hold Earth Mother in her place. And now they spoke of still another kiva when the other was only half complete. Surely someone must see things clearly, I thought. I waited anxiously, wondering if I should speak. Should I tell them of Taweyah's advice from the Grandfathers? I supposed when in doubt, one should wait.

Salavi rose. "It is my opinion that we have much time to consider yet another new kiva. Let us finish the business at hand before we consider new business. Perhaps an evaluation of this need for another kiva should be done. If it is your desire, I volunteer my services in the evaluation."

My mind rested easier with Salavi's words. I might be able to pass on my concerns to him and not have to speak of Taweyah's visit to anyone. My special relationship with Taweyah's spirit was something that somehow I did not wish to share with anyone except Nish't Ahote. In giving up all secrets, one loses the power.

Machakwi, Wikwavi, Noona, the manger of trade, and the elders all nodded in approval, and the subject seemed to be laid to rest. Each of us gradually went our separate way.

At that moment life was in full flower for us in the upper world. In the lower world, however, the people were having their season of cold solstice. To the lower world our spirit dancers had to appear. So it was with our warm season Solstice Ceremony that those spirit dancers would make their departure. The real meaning of that ceremony was acknowledgment of four powerful forces in life: the power of germination, of heat, of moisture, and the magnetic forces of air. To those four powers we owed the harvest and, of course, our sustenance.

The ceremony was darkened, however, by a terrible report. The runners gave us news of the raiders once again. Nish't Ahote stayed behind, for there were people in need of his counseling and healing. Hototo and I were requested to go to give the prayers that the dead might pass untroubled into the world of our ancestors. Hototo and I readied ourselves as quickly as possible and set out upon the road to the west. The attack had taken place not more than a short walk away. I feared for Kunya and Yamka, who also lived not far off but farther down the west road.

As we neared the scene of tragedy, my head spun. Perhaps it was from the heat, but then suddenly I saw Wisoko's image before me. His hideous, hateful mouth twisted as if to say, "I shall make you pay!" Hototo grabbed me to keep me from falling to the ground while I whimpered in his arms. Then quickly the vision passed, and I disengaged from his caring arms to approach the horror of crime.

The road was littered with the dead. Seven of our workers who had been hauling large logs from the mountains in the west lay dead, each in a different grotesque position. Five more were seriously wounded, and most of them showed little sign of life. The logs had been very carefully piled up and burned. The smoke was still thick, for the huge logs would burn for at least a sun cycle.

Hototo held my arm as we surveyed the carnage. I was very distressed, for that was the very same road I traveled to visit Choviohoya, Kunya, and Yamka. What if it had been them? Pushing these thoughts aside, I rushed to the first of the five wounded men. Hototo went to another. My patient was not at all coherent. He had an arrow in his side that had missed his heart, but he was not doing well. I offered my prayers to Awonawilona, then firmly grasped the arrow and pulled it out. Fortunately, it did not break off. The entire arrow came out leaving a gaping wound. The young worker moaned. I quickly pulled out some leaves from my medicine bag to stanch the flow of blood.

Hototo worked with a younger man with a nasty gash in his shoulder. After doing much the same as I, we both moved on to another patient. Mine had an ugly head wound, and Hototo's had a leg and arm wound. It was then that we realized the fifth wounded worker had passed on. Frantically I cleansed the head wound of my patient, then applied a compress of herbs. He, too, was delirious. Hototo did the same, cleansing first, then using compresses. We prayed as we worked.

Litters were brought for both the dead and the wounded. As each dead worker was placed on his litter, Hototo and I prayed for their safe journey to the land of the Grandfathers. We flexed their bodies into the fetal position and closed their eyes. Runners were dispatched to the family of each of the deceased, who would come to claim them to bury them beneath a corner of the house in which they lived. The wounded would be kept in our complex until they were well if that was the will of Awonawilona.

Our solemn procession returned to the complex, where we were silently assisted by Nish't Ahote, Salavi, Machakwi, and another of the elders. As the details of the grisly scene were made clear to them, Salavi said to the third elder, "Perhaps we need to call an emergency meeting as a result of this misfortune. It must not happen again."

The elder nodded in agreement while Machakwi spoke. "You are right, Salavi. We must waste no time.

Let us call an emergency meeting for the next descent of Sun Father."

"Once again we meet—this time in regard to the tragic incident that has just occurred," said Machakwi as he solemnly lit the pipe. Tendrils of smoke encircled his head while he passed the pipe to Salavi. A heavy silence settled over us all—a silence that pervaded the entire community.

"This terrible event has brought us together to make some long-needed decisions," stated Salavi.

Pangwu, who seemed to have recovered from his illness at the last meeting, rose to say, "A terrible loss has been inflicted upon us by the raiders. It is yet early in the season and already we experience a great loss—a loss in human life, but also in our precious resources. Precautions must be considered."

Pavati rose laboriously, for his girth was great. At last, arranging his robes and clearing his throat, he added, "If we are going to finish the projects at hand and begin still another kiva directly across from this complex, we must take some precautions. The season of raiding has just begun. We doubled our guards at the grain storage bins many moons ago with the hope of preventing future tragedy. Let us also consider doubling the guard around our workers. The loss of human life we cannot afford."

Pangwu interceded once again. "It seems clear to me that we must double or even triple our guard around our workers. The guard must be instructed to be on the alert at all times to prevent further misfortunes. This must not be allowed to happen again." His voice carried a highly emotional pitch.

The elders all nodded in unanimous confirmation followed by soft murmurs throughout. Nish't Ahote raised his right hand forward and above his head to signal his right to speak. When all was finally hushed, he began, "My brothers gather to prevent future tragedy. In light of this effort there is one here who would speak." He turned to look at me and nodded.

I stepped forward to address my concerns. I extended my right hand toward all in the kiva. "I speak from the heart as well as my mind. I want to express an uneasy feeling that haunts me. I see the stumps of the trees we have cut. I also see that where these trees have been cut, the ground around them is gradually being washed away by arroyos. Somehow I know that the trees had some command over the soil, and now that they are gone, the soil erodes. We are forced at this time to go far away into the western mountains to obtain the logs necessary for our construction. We must be respectful of the trees we bring back, for they give of their life to provide us shelter. We must use them wisely or we shall destroy that resource that is so precious to us." I paused for a short time, then continued. "But I have still another concern. As you know, our war chief, Choviohoya, and his wife and child live not far down the same road on which this accident happened. Kunya feels insecure since Choviohoya is away much of the time. She confided in me these feelings by asking me to become the mother-by-the-gods to little Yamka, their daughter. She fears she may be kidnaped by the raiders or worse yet slaughtered, which would leave Yamka with no one. I am aware that my acceptance of the laws of the priesthood forbid me the privilege of being mother-by-the-Gods, but for the sake of securing safety for human lives, our most precious commodity, I would request that we address these problems." I stepped back in line with Nish't Ahote and Hototo to await any reactions.

"First let us deal with the simple problem," said

another elder. "It is true that the duties of our war chief call him away from his family much of the time. It is also true that his appointment to this position is very recent and has resulted in even more time that he must be without his family. We must show honor and appreciation for our chieftain. We must post guards in the nearby vicinity—perhaps double the number of guards, for our Coyote Woman is right!" He resumed his place on the bench.

Machakwi stood to speak. "When the raiders learn of our new war chief, he will be the one they want the most. I say we do as my elder friend suggests. Let us post a double guard in that area, but let us also consider that we move into the most important of our religious ceremonies, that of the summer solstice. Certainly we do not want that ceremony blasphemed with violence, or the Gods who leave us now will not wish to return. If we are all in agreement, let us post double guards not only in that area but also at all our outposts and at all our shrines."

A murmur of affirmation rippled through the small group. At that time I felt a light touch as Nish't Ahote's fingers touched mine. He was thinking as I was—that the battle was half won.

Silence once again resumed. At last Salavi rose. "I have had little to say so far in this meeting, but I feel it necessary to address the problem expressed by Coyote Woman. Though this one is more complex, it cannot be ignored. The raiders are smart. They know that our two most precious commodities are humanity and, of course, wood for our buildings. These buildings are for our safety and protection. They should be constructed for those reasons and only those reasons. Kivas are for protection of the Gods, but we must first protect and secure ourselves. Many of our buildings in my complex are in need of repair and fortification.

This should be a priority after all the construction that goes on now is completed. After all this is accomplished, we can consider a new, even larger kiva, but the time now is not appropriate."

It was as though he had spoken blasphemy to several of those in attendance. The elder whose girth was great rose in a huff to say hotly, "Let us pray that the Gods were not listening, for you speak disrespectfully. The protection of the Gods must come first, for without them we are nothing. How can you speak in such a manner?"

"I speak not out of disrespect, but because all things should be done in moderation. This the Gods tell us all. We must first protect our people or the Gods will desert us anyway, for there shall be none of our people left to worship them. This I say in good faith!" Salavi once again resumed his seat.

The tension was thick. I had the intense desire to speak, but refrained from doing so.

At last Machakwi rose. "My friends, we are missing something as our tempers rise. We throw logic out the window with our emotion. We forget that we have just agreed to double guards in all the usual locations and add many new ones in new locations. In doing this we will not be left with enough people to accomplish such high ambitions. Come, my friends. Is it not obvious that we must postpone any new projects until the raiding quiets? It is not only our natural resources that become limited, but also our human resources!"

A hush descended on all in the kiva as Machakwi's words were evaluated. The tension dissipated to some extent. I waited anxiously glancing briefly at Nish't Ahote. He looked straight ahead. His eyes were half shut, as though deep in thought. Hototo also stared straight with a deep furrow between his brows.

At long last Honani rose to say, "My friends, Machakwi's logic rings true. Let us put away our hot tempers, and postpone additional building efforts. This is the most beautiful season of any of the four. We are preparing for the most important ceremony of the warm season, the Going Home Ceremony. Let us send the Gods to their home on the other side with love and logic in our heart, or it may be as Salavi says, 'The Gods will not wish to return.' "

With his speech all seemed to quiet. No one stood to dispute his words, so after a short time each elder took his leave. Nish't Ahote, Hototo, and I were left to think over all that had been said. No words were spoken between us for a time.

Nish't Ahote turned toward the ladder. Placing his foot on the first rung, he said, "Now we may give our undivided attention to the beauty of the Going Home Ceremony. Let us depart in the love that will assure us that our people remain 'the people of peace.' "

Chapter 22

The Dream

The sun shone brilliantly over the lush green mountains. A gigantic rock formation jutted out over an obscure path, inviting protection and cool shade. Behind us on the inside wall were some figures carved by someone before us, who had found that place cool and inviting.

Removing the strap that held the supplies on my back drew a sigh of relief from my poor exhausted body. After spreading my mat on the cool, damp ground, I reclined to enjoy the peace and solitude that special place had to offer. A river raged by not far from that spot, seemingly in a hurry to reach its destination as it leaped around and over huge rocks, allowing nothing to stand in its way.

I reached out to touch my companion, tracing light circles on his back. He had spread his mat next to mine and sat close to me, staring at the river. As he turned toward me, his smoldering eyes held mine. Then drawing me to him, he led me into a sexual trance that bound me to him. He was a part of me. My fatigue disappeared, long forgotten in my state of bliss. I could not keep my hands off him. It was as though I was possessed. Even after we both were satisfied, it was not long before I reached for him again.

At last we fell into a sound sleep, but upon waking, I found my fingers traveling once again to his center of

pleasure. An ecstatic moan escaped his wide, sensuous
mouth. In sleep he looked like a little boy, for his eyes
were the source of his power. They were so fiercely
compelling and sensuous that I was hypnotized. I did
not know the young man, and yet it seemed I had
always known him. He also seemed possessed, for he
seemed ready to make love at any and all times.
Surely we were intended for each other. The fact that
his seed could impregnate me did not worry me in the
least, for I had cast aside all my responsibilities as
a priestess.

After we once again attained fulfillment, he took
my hand, guiding me to the river. He took his lance
in hand to stab a huge fish as it rushed by us. Laying
it on a rock, he removed my sandals and then his own.
Naked as the day we were born, we plunged into the
river, whose depth was waist-high. He pushed me beneath the water. I came up sputtering and laughing. I
pushed him under the water, and soon we were wres-
tling and playing like two children. Then suddenly he
pulled me toward him, and we coupled once more
with the cool, clear water washing over us.

Taking my hand, he led me back to our mats. He
built a fire, cleaned the fish, and roasted the fish for
our dinner.

The moon rose full, promising a brilliant starlit
night. Truly the world was beautiful. We enjoyed our
repast and then settled in for the night. The stars
began to make their appearance, entering the upper
world as dancers. The night creatures took over, filling
the world with the cry of the coyote and the hooting
of the owls. He took me once again, and then we fell
into a blissful sleep, for truly this had been a sun cycle
of great beauty.

Several times during the night I woke to touch
him—to love him again. Surely I was a woman pos-

sessed. But if that was so, so be it. I had never been
happier. The Gods had shown me sensuality, and it
was good. Our night was spent in bliss.

We made love once more as Sun Father began his
journey. Then we packed our supplies to resume our
journey. Somehow I did not know where we were
going. We traveled east beyond the mountains and
past a small village. Then as we came out of the rocky,
rugged country, we reached some lush grass on either
side of the river where we stopped. A figure approached us. He seemed somewhat older than my
lover. His nose was pointed but softly rounded. His
eyes were thin slits of fire, and his mouth was strong
and full. He wore a piece of fabric as a headband and
wore one earring. His hair hung in two thick braids
with an eagle feather attached to one. He wore nothing but a loincloth and sandals. His broad, muscular
chest was decorated with chunks of turquoise in an
exquisite double-strand necklace. He looked long and
steadily at me until I was mesmerized.

All at once I did not even know who I was. I could
see no one but him. The commanding new figure had
replaced the one I was with, and I was drawn shame-
fully away from my former lover to this one. His sinewy body beckoned. His fiery, narrow eyes did the
same, and I was drawn away.

I did not even look back. I had no care for my
former lover's feelings, and I felt ashamed. The new
man was mature. He aroused the same sexual feeling
as did my former lover, but in an even more compelling way. We moved on, leaving my former lover
behind.

His gait was knowing and sensuous. He stopped at
one point to touch me. He touched me in all the
important points until he had me begging. I desper-

ately needed satisfaction, but he did not offer it to me in the normal way of man and woman. He waited.

We moved farther on, and once again he brought me to a point of no return and backed away. I was beginning to regret having left my former lover, for at least with him I knew ecstasy. I began to berate myself. Why was I doing this? I, Coyote Woman. I had no needs. I had no wants. I was not listening to the Gods, for if I had been, none of this would have been happening. But I was irrationally driven by this man.

We beheld an area where the hills were brown and a stream ran through. He led me to a small housing complex. The smell of hot water was close at hand as a hot spring welled up beside us, forming a pool. We stepped into the pool after removing our clothes. The water temperature was almost to hot, but by gradually working our way into it, we enjoyed the refreshment. My weary muscles relaxed very gradually, leaving me with an afterglow of wholeness and pleasure. My eyes closed as I neared a feeling of bliss. His hands touched me, caressing me until I felt I might pass on into the land of our Grandfathers.

His caresses stopped, and I opened my eyes to two women, one young and one old, who looked at me with longing in their eyes. My lover rose from the hot water to pull me toward them. I could not imagine what might happen, but I had heard! Yes, I had heard that some women preferred the attentions of other women. Then I remembered Aryl, my female instructor. The attentions of women were perhaps not so bad.

Then the two of them lead me inside the housing complex, where they placed me on a mat. My lover was close by observing all this. My hands were free as were my legs and body. I waited in anticipation of I knew not what. The room was dark but for a small fire in one corner. There seemed to be nothing in the room but my lover and the two women.

My lover bent over me to once again hypnotize me with his eyes and kisses. He then moved to my breast, lightly suckling them. I had moved into a state of ecstasy when I felt a quill inserted into my upper arm. Somehow it did not hurt. He moved his tongue to the inside of my thighs. A yucca whip whistled across my breast. It too did not hurt. He stopped to gaze into my eyes, and once again the whip sang while another quill was inserted. That went on for some time, and at last the women stopped, for I had reached a plateau of no pain. They backed off quietly while my lover and I packed up again to begin our travels. We bedded not far away for the night.

Before dawn we were up. We moved back toward the area with the same mountainous green place from which we had come. We walked this time up and over the mountains and down and through many creeks. We passed many spots of rocky, sheer beauty, and at one point we paused long enough to take advantage of the sparkling beauty of a waterfall as it rushed over some rocks. We bared our bodies, and together we stepped into it. When we had overcome the shock of the extremely cool water, he took me into his arms. His long heavy black hair clung tightly to the contours of his neck and shoulders, causing his eyes to dominate his face even more than before. They gazed at me with a piercing, dark sensuousness as he pressed my wet body urgently to his. Once again I was lost as we coupled beneath the waterfall as the sun shone brilliantly upon us. A rainbow could be seen shining through the water even before it hit the ground.

We rested next to a lush patch of wild mint that filled our nostrils with its sweet fresh odor. Sun Father's rays warmed our nakedness. We fell into a delightful sleep. We awakened shortly, and once again rinsed our bodies beneath the waterfall. He rubbed my body all over with crushed mint leaves and then I did the same to his wonderful mature lean muscles. There were no parts of our bodies that we missed. At last we dressed and went on our way.

As we traveled, I experienced an overwhelming feeling of guilt. I had been living as a wanton. I had had no thoughts for my expected monogamous way of life. I had thrown aside the responsibilities of being a priestess. I had reveled in passion, not caring at all for anyone's feelings but my own. I had walked away from my former lover with no thought at all for his feelings. I was not even sure who the mature handsome warrior I was with at that moment could have been. I truly felt uneasy.

Then as quickly as those guilt feelings assailed me, they left. We moved deeper into the lush mountains. The terrain was steep, then leveled out. A beautiful lake emerged among the grandfather pines, juniper, and pinyon. All at once we both heard a soft sound of thunder. . . . But no! It was not thunder. It was very gradually getting louder. We waited a bit longer, then saw.

An enormous herd of pronghorn antelope thundered their way over the rocky mountainous terrain heading straight for us. Their hooves kicked up the earth and stone as they approached us. My lover pulled me toward him quickly as we made our way toward a wall of rock with a line of trees protecting the front of it. We hovered behind the trees up next to the rock—waiting.

The herd seemed to be a thousand. They pounded the earth sending vibrations through the ground and rock. They were all so close I could feel their breath upon me. They were smaller than a deer. Their general color was a dark tan with white underparts. There were black stripes on their faces and necks with a prominent white rump patch. The horns were the length of a man's foot with a single flat prong extending toward the front. They were not much longer than our women were tall. Their black cloven hooves supported their sturdy bodies on thin legs that were surprisingly agile. They were known for their speed and could outrun a great many of their predators.

The herd thundered past until one of them lagged back. I could tell it was deliberately slowing, but I could not imagine why. The rest of the herd moved on leaving the one who had separated himself from the rest. He swung his majestic head from side to side and moved toward the line of trees that offered us our protection. He seemed to be seeking me out.

I huddled back and against the rocks, for I knew not what to think. The magnificent animal moved toward me to stand imperiously over me. He licked my neck, then my ears. Then he backed away to look at me.

"Rise, my love!" he seemed to say as I stared in astonishment.

At that moment my former lover was forgotten, and the only living creatures that existed in the universe were that beautiful animal and me. I rose to stare into his beautiful brown liquid eyes fringed by long lashes. He nuzzled my neck once more, then beckoned me to come and play as he tossed his proud neck and kicked up his black hooves.

I entered his world. We played—rolling and kicking. He nuzzled my neck and breasts. I ran my hands all over the lovely buff hair on his back and then through the softer white of his underbelly. I could only think how wonderful it would be to be as beautiful, strong, and fleet of foot as that animal. My love for running had been great as a child. I always imagined that I was a deer or an antelope, for then no one would have surpassed me. At that moment I felt as a child once again.

Quite suddenly he lay still on his side. He did not move but beckoned me to his face. As I looked into his dark, misty eyes, he said, "I cannot rise. You must help me."

"But what can I do? I have not the strength to lift you."

"Then, I shall lay here and die," he said while he rested his head in a resigned manner on the soft grassy earth.

My heart was torn. Somehow our play had now turned serious, and I knew I must help him. I stroked his long black nose, saying soothing, "What then would you have me do?"

He lifted his massive horned head just slightly to speak. "You must put your hands under my back and lift. Think only positively. If you can lift me, the universe will know."

I was filled with compassion and love for him. He was so beautiful. I could not let him die. I closed my eyes to breathe deeply of the scent of him. The air, sweetly scented from the trampled grass, filled me to expand my consciousness. Placing my arms under his back and assuming squatting position, I uttered words of praise to Awonawilona.

As if in answer to my worship, my beautiful partner somehow became light as a feather. Surprisingly, with very little effort, I was able to move him into a sitting position. Then placing my arms under his belly, he effortlessly rose to his feet.

He nudged me, and I nudged him as he turned to say, "We are one. You are a part of me. Follow me, my love."

Turning so that his white rump that framed his buff tail was toward me, he moved away. His scent was overwhelmingly attractive to me. Then looking down at myself, I saw why that was so. I walked on all fours as he did. My coat was buff, and my belly was white. My head felt sleek and my feet were cloven and black.

He turned once more to beckon me, then began to slowly trot away from me. I had no other thoughts but to follow him. We trotted together briefly. He stayed at my side. Then he picked up speed. I moved much faster. He began to run, and to my surprise I was able to run and stay with him. The wind whistled over our sleek bodies as we continued to run. A feeling of freedom and total abandonment engulfed me. I became a part of the wind. Never had I been happier.

Then there were walls. There was no wind. There was no grass beneath my cloven feet. There was no one else. He had gone. I opened my eyes to realize that it all was a dream—a dream more vivid than life. I felt terribly alone and confused, for I knew not what the meaning of it was.

My nose picked up an odor. There was nothing in my room with that scent. It was the scent of my antelope lover. He left his scent on my neck and breasts. It was myself that I smelled. Had it really been just a dream? I would speak of it to Nish't Ahote, for perhaps he could interpret it.

Sun Father was only barely beginning his journey. I found Nish't Ahote, as usual, plotting the path of Sun Father in his observation room. He did not seem surprised to see me, even though I did not visit him at that hour unless invited. He smiled while saying, "I have been expecting you."

I was at once inflamed with curiosity. How could it be that he knew my every whim? His mind must have connected with my anxiety and confusion. What an incredibly sensitive man he was. I wondered if I would have such depth of perception when I was his age. A short period of silence followed as I pondered.

At last I began. "Nish't Ahote, my revered teacher . . ."

"And lover!" he added.

"Nish't Ahote, I would speak of a dream—a dream that has me confused and upset, for I cannot decipher its entire meaning. Parts of it I believe I understand, but other parts I do not." Once again I stopped to look at him with renewed curiosity and love.

"Speak to me of this dream, little one. Begin at the beginning."

I then related the dream sequence to him, for it remained vivid in my memory. When at last I completed my recital, he said, "What is your interpretation, sweet one?"

"Nish't Ahote, never have I experienced such ecstasy in a dream. Never have I so totally abandoned my own self-control—been so immoral. Yet through this abandonment I produced an ecstasy so strong that I felt no pain when the women inserted quills into my body."

"I must agree with that much of your interpretation," he swiftly declared.

"Then, it must follow that only ecstasy can overcome pain. If I could learn to put myself in that frame of mind, could I do the same in this physical world?" I inquired.

"The mind can be trained to do incredible things. Your dream has shown that you may shift into a separate reality if you choose to do so. It is a skill to be cultivated and nurtured. Only you can do this."

"But, honored teacher, can you not help me?" I asked.

He placed his hands on my shoulders then pulled me close. "Coyote Woman, I can only help you to achieve that state of ecstasy."

It was at that point in time when a familiar odor assailed me once again, that of my antelope lover. The same musky smell remained on the skin and clothing of Nish't Ahote, yet I knew he had not touched me until now. My mind experienced once again a disruption of my thought process. I backed away to stare at him, for I was at a loss for words. He seemed to sense my bewilderment, and his warm eyes caressed mine as he waited.

Intuitively I knew, but I could not believe. Should I be so bold as to ask? I wondered. Then in an agitated state, I inquired, "Nish't Ahote, were you my antelope lover? Can this be so?"

"What makes you ask? Do you not already know?" he responded as though he was surprised that I asked.

Pulling my emotions together, I closed my eyes in shame, for I knew not what to say. What more should I already have known? Then looking up at him through perplexed eyes, I told him, "I must leave now, for my shame is great. I shall think through this dream on my own time."

"No, my love, you must not leave, for I must know why you feel ashamed."

"Nish't Ahote, I know you were my antelope lover, for the scent of musk is still heavy on us both, but I behaved as a wanton. I ran from one lover to another, which is not a part of my nature. Why might I dream of such total immorality? I feel embarrassed, and I need time to sort out my feelings." I looked away from him, for my love for him engulfed me and I could not imagine what he might be thinking of me at that moment.

"My lovely Coyote Woman, I would speak only the

truth to you. Your shame is unfounded, for I was not only your antelope lover, but also your other two lovers as well. Have you forgotten the shaman's power to take on whatever physical reality he so desires? Now stay and tell me what else you have learned from your dream."

Though I was surprised, I realized I should not be, for the reality of the present was not that of dream reality. I was, however, at a loss for words. As my mind began to clear, the dual meaning of the dream began to become clear. I moved into another spiritual level in my dream. I had become a female antelope. Looking at Nish't Ahote, amazement filled my heart as I inquired, "Did I truly become a female antelope? Can I do so whenever I wish?"

"Let us sit down and speak of this, sweet one." He sat cross-legged on the mat. His lustrous waist-length hair hung loosely over his shoulders and chest. His sultry black eyes held me lovingly, making it difficult for me to think. For that reason I lowered my eyes. "If you think of love and concentrate on only that which you wish to be, not allowing anything else to enter even so much as a tiny corner of your mind, you will achieve the state of ecstasy. In this state of mind, all things are possible," he said with gentle assertiveness.

"Then, each day I must put aside time for meditation to try to achieve that end. Is that not so, my teacher?"

"It is so," he said.

"Will you come into my state of ecstasy if I think hard on this?"

"My love, I would have no choice, unless I am counseling, healing, or unless I am deeply involved in other of my priestly duties."

After taking time to ponder what he had said, I

timidly asked, "Nish't Ahote, why did you choose to come into my dream?"

Again there was time he took for consideration. I wondered if I had asked the wrong question. Then he carefully chose his words saying, "Within each of us lies an enormous collection of sensual longings which ever demands the fulfillment of our desires. We would be selfish in what we do if we committed ourselves solely to pleasure. In our role in the priesthood, we cannot run away from our responsibilities—at least not in this, our fourth world. Therefore, we must enjoy abandonment in the next world."

His words left me with a profound recognition of his wisdom. He was saying that together we wander in the resplendent beauty of our love. I responded to him with these words, "Sometimes when I look at you, the gentle animal rising within you causes me to forget my morality."

"And so we gently slip within each other's lives. It may be done in this, the fourth world, or any other reality. I drank of your love and filled myself with your emotion. Such was my need." His finger traced a line from my forehead to my mouth as he spoke those words.

My mouth quivered with delight. My heart burned with love. I lightly placed my fingers on his mouth, saying, "I would walk with you in gentle rays of sunlight. I become fulfilled in your company. My logic half floats from the beauty of you within me."

A long loving silence followed. Then as though we both suddenly awakened, we remembered our responsibilities. I slowly rose to depart. Was being in love an illusion from which I would surely awake?

Chapter 23

Supernova and Eagle Sacrifice

The pilgrimage for spruce was complete. The spruce is always alive no matter what the season, as are the Gods. The acolytes and teachers had returned bringing with them a small male spruce tree and a small female spruce. We could tell the difference from their needles. The spruce tree had a magnetic power on which the clouds rested. Its branches were a throne to the clouds, for its branches swung upward and outward reaching for the Gods. It was the spirits of the spruce, the clouds and rain who had given life to us. So we offered our prayers to the male and female branches. That same procedure went on in all the buildings in our area. Large bundles of spruce branches were also brought and taken into the kiva designated for that ceremony. They were placed to the north of the fire pit, sprinkled with cornmeal, then blessed with smoke, which Salavi, who was the purification chief and Nish't Ahote who was the father of the spirit dancers, blew upon them. That welcomed the spirits into our community.

Two sun cycles before the dance, all the masks of the spirit dancers were painted, feathers were tied on them, and the masks and costumes were placed on the

bench that ran the circumference of the kiva. They
awaited the service for the planting of the spruce trees
at the designated time during the night.

At the midpoint of the hours of darkness, the teachers and oldest acolytes dressed in their elaborate costumes, but without masks. The ritual was conducted
by Salavi, Nish't Ahote, and myself. I had been chosen
to assist because of my position within the community.
It must be remembered that a young woman took part
in the Purification Ceremony in the cold season who
sat on the seeds to germinate them. Now it was myself
who assisted in the ceremony, for I represented the
children who had come to bless us, who helped us to
grow and be fruitful.

The male spruce tree was planted on the west side
of the plaza. The female spruce was planted on the
east side to represent birth and hope. We planted
pahos at the base of both trees, and a line of cornmeal
was drawn from west to east. Prayer feathers were left
along the cornmeal trail to welcome Tawa, Sun Father, as he rose to bless the ceremony and our village.

From that point until the final dance, we fasted,
taking neither food nor drink. By fasting, we humbled
ourselves to the spirit of the Rain God.

I wandered slowly toward the kiva, where the masks
were lined on the bench. Some unexplainable force
was drawing me. I wished to see them once more before they were taken at dawn to the shrine outside
our community, where the men would smoke, pray,
and dress in their costumes. Perhaps it was the magical
sacredness of the kiva, which was the most sacred spot
in our complex at that time. Certain places contained
power at certain times. I descended the ladder knowing that I would probably be alone.

I placed my knees on the earth of the kiva while
sitting on my heels. My hands rested quietly on my

thighs, palms down. I did not usually assume that position for meditation, but somehow it seemed right. After maintaining that position for a short time, suddenly I felt a tremendous surge of energy coming from the earth and passing through my body. My body began to change shape. It became miniscule, then disappeared. I stared at the mask across from me. My neck seemed to prickle and scratch, and then I realized I was wearing a collar of spruce. My skin felt drawn, as though painted, while my head felt weighted, as though wearing a headdress. I had no arms to touch, but I knew I had become one of the masks. I was yellow on the left side and blue on the right. On my head rose an ornate tiara tufted with wild wheat and eagle feathers topped by two eagle tails and two parrot feathers, symbolizing the power of warmth from the south. Above my face arched a red rainbow over a field of white on which was painted a frog. I was looking at my reflection in the mask on the bench. The other masks were bright orange with hair whorls as worn by our maidens.

The air was tense until I gradually began to relax to accept my new form. Then the mouth on one of the masks moved very slightly. Could that be happening or was it my imagination? As I continued staring, I noticed a light purple glow around it. The mouth opened once again to say only two words—"Coyote Woman!" There followed a period of silence. The purple aura became more intense, and finally the mask resumed speaking.

"Coyote Woman, I bring a message. The Gods have declared a celestial event. You as a star child must use this event to the advantage of all your people. The experience you are now having has proven completion of your shamanic training and abilities. You may will yourself to become anything that the Gods have cre-

ated. Use your power wisely." The purple color faded
again as the mask grew silent.

I pondered the words I had just heard. I realized
that some major change would soon be taking place
in my life. Then once again the mask took on life as
the purple color deepened. "This celestial event will
mark the rise of your power. It is your destiny to
moderate the people. Our natural resources are all we
have. They must be carefully guarded for the sake of
the welfare of the people."

The purple aura faded and then disappeared altogether. The silence in the kiva was almost like death.
I felt my body begin to form and grow once again.
The scratchy spruce collar disappeared. The skin of
my face felt soft and pliant once more. I looked down
at my hands on my knees. Very slowly I came out of
my meditation. I felt magically alive and blessed.

Over the years that I had seen our Solstice Ceremony, it was never more beautiful. Many had come
from far away to witness the Going Home of the
Gods. Nothing broke the silence except the proud eagles tethered by one leg on their platforms nearby. No
living beings ever soared as high as those magnificent
birds. Pride did not permit them to pick at the leash
that tethered them. They simply flapped their great
wings to soar aloft, only to be jerked down again and
again. We all knew that those proud eagles would die.

Then as shafts of sunlight began to beam on the
horizon, the dance began. The spirit dancers came single file through the entrance to the plaza. Salavi led
the way displaying his mature muscular body. He was
unmasked and wore a single eagle feather in his dark
lustrous single braid and an embroidered kilt around
his loins. He led Nish't Ahote, the spirit dancer, and
myself, who was his assistant. We wore plain kilts and

were followed by all the other spirit dancers. The spirit dancers were painted black with the symbols of brotherhood painted on their breast. Spruce branches encircled their waist and around their arms.

Each of the female spirit dancers wore a black manta, a red and white blanket and sandals laced around their ankles. Each contributed to the music with a pumpkin shell, notched stick, and a scapula bone of a deer.

As they entered the plaza, Salavi sprinkled each of them with cornmeal. Nish't Ahote talked to each of them, encouraging them to come in. Suddenly the leader of the spirit dancers shook his rattle. His legs rose and fell in a powerful stamp. The dancers voices broke into a low song. The song would last all day. If one really listened to its nuances and infinite variations, one would hear the compelling beauty and its deepest meanings.

They danced in a line that slowly curved north then west, but it was broken before a circle could be completed. That represented the incompletion of the first world, which was broken and destroyed. Then the dancers moved west to south and again broke to represent the second world. They then moved to the south curving east, representing the third world. There was no fourth position, for all was still in progress in the present fourth world. We did not yet know if that pattern would be broken.

The dancers appeared at sunrise, midway before the high point, and after the high point of the sun. When they returned for the fourth time, they danced until sunset. When they filed in at sunrise they brought gifts, which they heaped in a huge pile in the plaza. Those were to be distributed later as Sun Father began his descent.

The spirit dancers searched out the acolytes despite

the blazing sun and the acrid dust whipping across the plaza. Sweat dripped as each dancer said a prayer of blessing to each child. "When you were a child, you thought that these were spirits who came from far away. Today you will feel that wonderful things will come to you both now and in the future. Care for them as you would your children."

Salavi and Nish't Ahote carried a small bowl of water and a pipe. They sprinkled water and blew a cloud of smoke on each spirit dancer. Each dancer turned over an ear of corn to be blessed and taken by Salavi to the solstice kiva. Throughout the rest of the day until Sun Father descended to the horizon, we retired to pray and concentrate.

And then, just before Tawa had made his descent, the dancers came out again to do a farewell dance. The complex was packed with people. My parents and my brother and his small family were present. Each stared to take in the magic and majesty of it all.

I, as leader of the female spirit dancers, knelt, and began to make noises with my notched stick on the pumpkin shell. My instrument resonated, and those with rattles shook. The dancing began with renewed vigor. Again the spirit dancers were sprinkled with water and cornmeal. Then I slowly passed along the line of spirit dancers, and raised my arm before each of them. Very few even realized what happened, for I was blessing them with purification as they moved on in the road of life.

As Nish't Ahote delivered his farewell blessing to the spirit dancers, he glanced at the heavens. Even through his costume, I saw him falter. He paused to stare at the sky, then recovered to deliver his farewell speech to the spirit dancers.

"Now is the time for departure. Take with you our humble prayer. Take this prayer not just from our humble people, but from people everywhere. Take with you the prayers from the animals, the plants, and the living singing rocks. Hear the prayers from the insects, the birds, and all the growing things that make the earth a mat of green. Take this message to the four corners of the world that we may receive moisture and renewal." He looked up again into the star-filled sky, losing his continuity for only a second. Then he resumed his prayer. "Spirit dancers, I am honored to have done my small part in caring for you on this most honorable event. May you go on your way with grateful hearts and happy thoughts." He then shook his rattle, and the leader of the spirit dancers shook his rattle to acknowledge that they had received the message. That also assured that the message would be delivered.

Now it was done. People came to the spirit dancers to pluck a piece of spruce to carry to their own homes and plant in their fields. During that time, I took the time to stare at the sky.

I lifted my eyes to allow them to rest on a star. It was a new star. It blazed majestically, as though trying to compete with the moon that shone so full on that mysterious night. It was then that a feeling of evil overtook me. It was an intuition that danger hovered very near. Although there were dancers in front of me and behind me as we filed toward the butte, I had a clear perception that my life was in danger.

The crowd parted as we danced. Someone stepped out of the crowd toward me. I recognized Wisoko. He held a knife in his hand. He knew that no one would offer me protection, for that would have ruined the sacredness of that ceremonial event, thus displeasing the Gods. His body was completely concealed in clothing. His head was also covered, but his odor was, as usual, increasingly offensive as he stepped closer toward me.

I realized that I must do something that I had done once in a dream and once in the kiva with masks. I stepped out of the line of dancers away from Wisoko. He continued to move toward me, interrupting the line of dancers. I closed my eyes. I was standing at the bottom of the butte.

I knew I must rise into one of the many other dimensions above this physical earth. In another astral plane it would be possible to escape Wisoko. I was vaguely aware of my people gathering around my crumpled body and of Wisoko's dark figure moving away. I could feel the new star offering me energy, an energy that first transformed me into the green leaves of a globe mallow. My roots soaked up nutrients from the soil.

I gladly gave up my nectar to a bee, who gathered my pollen to share with other flowers. As a bee I enjoyed sucking up the nectar, and I knew without thinking that I would share the pollen with other flowers. I also knew that I would take plenty of pollen back to the hive to the extensions of myself who lived there.

Then I felt a trembling in my throat as I sang my mating song and tipped my feathered tail to balance myself on a rock nearby. Hands reached for me at the moment that I flapped my wings, rising into the air. I felt as one with the universe as I rose above the dancers and the crowd. My great wings allowed me to soar over the crowds and up toward that magical star. My flight was brief. At the top of the butte I folded my wings to stare at the dancers. No man followed them now. The moon and stars reflected their unearthly shapes as shadows as they moved to the other side of the butte and on to the house of the spirit dancers.

In her trance Coyote Woman had a dream. Her parents were beautiful. Their feathers around their neck were the color of gold. Their wingspread was enormous when they left the nest in search of food. Her brother sat close beside her in the nest. When she peered out of the nest, the world seemed terribly large and very intimidating. Would she ever have control over the sky as her loving parents did? There were only the two of them.

Their nest was in a medium-size pinyon pine that grew out of the side of a cliff. Because of their location, there were few animals to threaten their welfare. Life was peaceful, quiet, and good.

Sun Father had just begun his journey. The air was crisp and cold without the warmth of their mother's feathers. Both Father and Mother left in search of food. No sooner were they out of sight when she experienced a terrible sense of foreboding. Something was not right. Once again she peered over the edge of the nest. There was nothing to be seen except the bottom of the canyon with a trickle of water in the creek below. Seeing nothing below her or around her, she tilted her head up. Something long and thick was being lowered alongside of the nest—something that was not there before. Her brother looked up and gave out a frightened screech.

They both stared as though in a trance as an enormous creature wound itself along the suspended length and worked its way down to hang next to the nest. A snakelike appendage with hooks on the end reached for her brother to remove him from the nest. He was covered with something strange and dropped into a deep container that was carried on the body of the creature.

Then it was her turn. The snake with hooks on the end seized her and covered her in the nest, shutting out the world and then causing it to spin. She, too, was dropped into the deep container. Her little heart

beat loudly as the world remained without light and
bumped and thumped around. That went on for a very
long time until at last, all was still. The world remained dark and still for quite some time. Then the
bumping and thumping began again. She was very
very hungry, and wondered why her parents had not
tried to help. Why was this happening?

As her mind turned those questions over and over,
suddenly everything was still. The hooks wrapped
around her while gently removing the cover at the
same time. She was tucked against the body of the
creature as it gently wrapped something around one
of her legs. She was placed upon the open ground,
looking down on many of the creatures as they stared
up at her. She attempted to move away only to find
that she could only go so far with the tether on her
foot.

She knew she was theirs. Her brother was tethered
beside her, and they were captives. She thought,
"When will they bring food? I feel weak from the sun,
for there is no shade."

Then one of the creatures approached. In his hooks
he carried a baby prairie dog. Dropping the bleeding
thing in front of them, they both made short work of
it. Its tender little body became one with their flesh
and the few feathers they had.

Now she was almost fully feathered. The weather
was hot during the light and very chilly during the
darkness. Almost fully matured, it was even more frus-
trating being tethered. In the time she had been captive, she had been fed well. There were no real
dangers on top of the flat thing on which she lived.
She was also used to the creatures who cared for her.
She was aware that they would not hurt her. At least
they had not hurt her yet.

One of them climbed onto the flat surface where they were tethered. He offered to her brother a live prairie dog to feast upon. To her he offered a wounded young rabbit. Its back leg was bent at an angle, and she wasted no time putting her untethered claw at its throat. Oddly enough it did not look frightened. Its small black eyes stared up at her. Because it did not seem afraid as all normal animals would, she removed her claw from its neck. Its expression seemed to be one of love and concern, an expression she could dimly remember in the eyes of her parents. Indeed, this seemed very strange.

The rabbit did not move. Its small body remained as though paralyzed. Then its mouth began to move, and it spoke. "Coyote Woman, my love, though your form is that of an eagle, I know it is you, for I have entered your reality and found you."

She moved her feathered body back a step to weigh what it was that she had heard, and to evaluate what unbelievable things the creator was doing to her. Her feathers ruffled, and she became angered. Once again she placed her claw around the rabbit's neck intending to tear at its throat and put it out of its misery.

"If you kill me, you will anger the Creator, for he has sent me into your reality to bring you back," gasped the rabbit.

Once again she loosened her grip and backed off. Spontaneously she asked, "Bring me back? But where? Why?"

"To your people, Coyote Woman. Your people need you in your human form, not in the form of one of your spirit guides. I have come to ask you to return."

Surely, she thought, the rabbit must be special. "How do I know this is not some kind of trick?" she inquired.

"It is no trick. You are Shawanadese, Coyote Woman, priestess of your people. I am Nish't Ahote. I have entered your eaglet world as a rabbit in order that I might reach you to communicate with you. Though I know this journey to be filled with many dangers, I chose to come to take you back." The young rabbit pulled himself into a more upright position. Looking at her intently with his little ears twitching, he asked, "Why are you so angry, little one?"

Her feathers ruffled once more. "How dare you say that? I am four times your size!"

"Size is only based on the reality in which you exist, and the reality in which you are trapped right now makes you smaller than you know."

"But my reality is that of the eagle. I am all powerful! I can soar above the highest mountaintops, and I can see the smallest creature for miles away so that I may pounce on him." She stood straight and tall, her feathers sleek around her slender body. "My power knows no bounds!"

"Then, fly with me to the highest mountain now," exclaimed the furry one, "or do your tethers chain you to this roof? Let me see you pounce on a lively rabbit miles away, or do your powers now limit you only to play with this illusion of a poor wounded rabbit who lies helplessly at your feet. That is what you have been reduced to in this reality."

The rabbit's calm unruffled appeal had worked some magic on her. His words were wise and yet . . . "But it is I who choose to stay tethered to this roof. It is comfortable for me now, and it is you who has been brought to me as sacrifice by my redskin creatures."

"No little one," continued the rabbit. "That is the illusion in this reality, for when next the sun rises, it is you who will be sacrificed, and I will have been neither a conquest or even a memory. As you can see, I have no fear of you, though I do not deny the danger of my position. You, however, do not recognize your own precarious existence, and this is your only chance to escape from the reality of this time into the reality of your own true greatness. You took on this reality to escape from a previous danger, but now you must return.

"Now, listen to me carefully! Once you had a powerful love. That love was me, Nish't Ahote. Physically and mentally we were one. I need you, Coyote Woman, but more importantly the people need you. Before I confessed my love for you, your Mayan warrior returned to take you away, but you chose to stay for the good of your people, and I would hope, for my love as well. Then your rattlesnake spirit guide tried to take you from this, the fourth world. As though that were not enough, your haughty Mayan father tried to take you back to Chichén Itzá, but my love and the love your people have for you brought you safely back to us. Now you yourself are trying to leave this world by deluding yourself and choosing to remain in this reality. Please come back with me, Coyote Woman, for if you do not, you will leave this world when next Sun Father rises."

Her small black eyes dilated as a shadow of doubt seemed to flit in and out of her thoughts. As in a dream, she murmured softly, "I do vaguely remember. Were these conversations I heard while soaring over a complex of a house?"

"No, little one. You have soared over this complex only in thought. These are the thoughts that are stored in your memory, for you know them to be true," the rabbit said.

"You must give me time to consider all that you

have said. This is not a decision to be made in haste."
She ruffled her feathers and closed her eyes to think
on all that had transpired.

The rabbit rose still taller, saying, "There is little
time, but hear me well. You must not eat me. You
must not eat anything. You must fast. I will stay with
you, but I go now to gather herbs." Although he
limped a little, he moved quite well on his three good
legs. He limped away on the flat surface and then
disappeared.

Time marched on. Sun Father was at its zenith when
rabbit returned. His fur was dotted with dirt. It
seemed he had been digging. He spit upon the surface
on which she sat. Out of his mouth came a profusion
of small pieces of white. "Eat!" he said, "for this is
your herb."

She pecked the white root pieces swallowing them,
then settled herself for a period of thought. Her
thoughts were interrupted by one of her captors standing over her with a concerned look in his eye. He
reached for her, and she quickly moved, pulling at her
tethers in an attempt to stay away from him. Once
again she settled her feathers and body to rest. Rabbit
sat quietly beside her. She was in a state halfway between sleep and being awake. Images were dreamlike.

Then she heard rabbit faintly speaking, "You must
look at me, Coyote Woman," he said. This he repeated four times. She found her attention focusing
now on his left eye. In it she detected something re-
sembling explosions of sparks. The sparks flew toward
her and then retreated.

She felt somehow that rabbit must have turned his
head around, for she was suddenly looking at a field
that her captors had worked.

Then rabbit spoke to her again. "Do you see one

of your captor creatures in the field?" It took her a moment to understand him. "Watch very closely," he said. "Your life will depend on it." He repeated that over and over.

Gradually the form of a captor creature emerged in her vision. She had no fear as she experienced a detached feeling. She watched the captor stop walking in the field. He seemed to scan the area. He turned slowly to the right so she could see his profile. Then at last he turned his entire body toward her until he was looking at her. The way he jerked his head, she knew he saw her. He extended his right arm in front of him, pointing toward the ground, and held his arm in that position as he walked toward her.

"He comes!" she screamed involuntarily.

Rabbit turned her head around. He told her to gaze at him until she saw his glow.

As she looked at him, his face was glowing. She devoted her attention to his face. His face seemed crisscrossed with beams of light. She focused on rabbit's left eye. She perceived it as a clear pool of liquid light. The pool had extraordinary depth and created exquisite reflections. The glow touched her, soothed her, and gave her exquisite sensations.

Rabbit turned her head once more, for once again she saw her captor in the field. She completely lost her focus as her captor vanished and so did the entire scene.

She did not know how she returned, or how rabbit brought her back. She only knew she awoke in her usual spot with rabbit by her side. Then she closed her eyes to fall into a deep restful sleep.

Rabbit dozed not very far from her. Her brother also had closed his eyes. She thought over the events that followed her taking rabbit's herb. For the first time since her capture, she saw her captor as the enemy. Rabbit had said her life would depend on what she saw. Her captors had cared for her and her brother in a most loving manner. Why, then, did she see her captor as an enemy and a threat? Why did rabbit cause such exquisite feelings deep inside her?

Her reverie was interrupted by a captor, who brought them their second meal. This time her meal was a wounded prairie dog. Rabbit had told her she must not eat, and so the frightened little prairie dog sat in front of her shivering in anticipation.

It was then that it happened. Her captor took note that she was not eating. He noticed rabbit, who sat quietly nearby. He pushed the prairie dog closer to her talons, then picked up rabbit and placed him beside the prairie dog. Looking at her closely, he said, "Eat, young eaglet, for if you do not, I shall be forced to give your portion to your brother. Why do you not eat this rabbit?" He watched her for a time, and seeing that she was still not eating, he gave the poor prairie dog to her brother.

Her captor then seized rabbit, saying, "Eaglet, if you do not eat, this rabbit will be given to your brother!" He slammed poor rabbit down and seated himself close by to watch her.

She realized that rabbit had been right. They were to be sacrificed! Their kindness was superficial. She ruffled her feathers and stood proud and tall. She let out a long screeching wail, then said, "Wait! Do not hurt my friend rabbit! Bring him back to me!"

Her captor turned toward her, staring at her as though he could not believe what he had heard. Still clutching rabbit in one of his appendages, he stood over her, asking, "Can this really be happening? What manner of eaglet is this? Did I really hear the eaglet speak?"

"Yes, you hear me speak!" she declared. "I speak

on behalf of my friend the rabbit, for he has shown you to me as the true enemy you really are. You must not hurt rabbit, for his are the powers for seeing. He is not a true rabbit. He is Nish't Ahote. He is my teacher, mentor, and lover. Put him down or he may work his magic on you!"

Her captor was so surprised, he dropped rabbit at her side. The world spun. She took rabbit by the fur of the neck with her beak, then spreading her young wings, she broke her tethers and flew from the flat surface where she had been held captive. Rabbit and she soured into the unknown. At long last she was free!

My eyes fluttered open, taking in the plastered painted walls of the healing kiva. Nish't Ahote's head rested by my side. I felt very weak but exhilarated at the same time. I reached over to stroke his magnificent head of lustrous black hair. He stirred and lifted his head. His liquid black eyes bore into my own as a tear softly escaped. "Little one, you have returned." He looked very tired.

"How long have I been here, Nish't Ahote?" I inquired.

"You have slept for several sun cycles, little eaglet. Your people will be glad that you are one with us once more. I, too, am happy, for once again I thought I had lost you. Awonawilona be praised!" He stood beside me, taking my hand in his. He bent to plant a soft kiss on it, then moved toward the ladder. Turning to look at me once again, he added, "When your strength returns, we must talk, my little love. I shall have food brought to you." He climbed the ladder, leaving me with my thoughts.

He had called me "eaglet." How strange and yet appropriate.

Chapter 24

Lust Unleashed

I was much improved. It was only a sun cycle since my return to the fourth world. I was once again in my quarters. The star still shone brilliantly in the sky by darkness and could even be seen by day. In perhaps another sun cycle I should have regained my strength to assume my regular responsibilities once more. I was anxious to discuss my journey with Nish't Ahote, but he did not seem to be available since he and Hototo had walked me to my room. It occurred to me that I might have done something wrong. Even Puppy was not there to offer me company and solace, for I was told Aunt Mokni was watching over him. Perhaps if I meditated, I thought, the answers would come. I was at a loss as to how to handle my sudden ability to assume a different reality.

A short period of time passed. In my meditative state, I was suddenly interrupted by Nish't Ahote's presence. It had been a long time since last we moved into another world with our lovemaking. I felt his magnetic power. He moved to sit beside me never saying a word, then placed his bronze hand on my crossed leg. A feeling of fire worked through my soul.

A period of silence followed as I patiently waited to hear what Nish't Ahote would say. At long last he passed the palm of his right hand over my face lightly and very tenderly. His fingers brushed the side of my neck, my shoulder, and ultimately my hip, returning to my upper leg, where it came to rest. Very softly he said, "I am thankful to have you back." He seemed to want to say no more.

My desire to speak of my journey was unleashed, for Nish't Ahote was a man from whom I kept nothing. There were no secrets between us, for secretiveness bred negativity and unhappiness. "Nish't Ahote, I was in the reality of the eaglet—the eaglet that we sacrifice. I could not help myself. I became one of those eaglets."

"I know of this, Coyote Woman, for I was there," he said.

"What do you mean, you were there, revered one?" I asked as I immediately thought over my flight. Who had he been? Was he one of my parents, my brother, one of my captives? Then I added, "Yes, you must have been rabbit."

Nish't Ahote's demeanor darkened, and his brows furrowed as he gathered his thoughts. He confirmed my statement by adding, "I am glad you chose not to eat me."

I placed my hand on his cheek, moving my fingers lingeringly from his face to his neck, then from his shoulder to his nipples. I watched them grow hard in response to my touch. "I could not eat you, for your wisdom penetrated my being. Somehow I must have known it was you." My hands rested in my lap as I looked down at them. "You placed yourself in great danger, for if it were not I who might destroy you, it may have been my eaglet brother or any of my captors. My love, once again I am overwhelmed by how much you care."

There was a period of deep silence between us. My one niggling thought was one of concern as I added,

"I must not allow you to pursue these great dangers again. How can this be done?"

"This, our present reality, is filled with dangers. Each sun cycle we face them. We deal with them as best as we know how. However, the other realities are also fraught with similar perils. A journey to another reality need not be filled with the hazards in this one. One must choose his or her times for journeying carefully. There are appropriate times and inappropriate times for using shamanic powers." He stopped to bow his head, as though waiting for me to think on what had been said.

After a bit of thought I commented, "So you are saying that until I can become proficient in my shamanic abilities, I must have a care."

"Yes, sweet Coyote Woman, for without this knowledge you may become trapped."

"Nish't Ahote, you made my captor suddenly seem frightening to me. Should I be frightened of other human beings? What is the lesson I must learn?"

"Your captor was not as your eaglet brother, my love. He was typically human, for all humans have a dark side—a side that cannot be trusted. You see, humans are their own worst enemy. They plot for control, they cheat, they lie. Animals do not do this. To trust an animal is pure, but to trust a human is foolish."

"But, Nish't Ahote, I love you. Surely you can trust me!" I cried.

"I can trust you in all ways but one!" he said almost under his breath. I waited patiently for his further comment. "My sweet child, you possess the best in shamanic abilities, however, you must learn when to use them."

A dark feeling of uncertainty overcame me. I pondered his words. Here was a man who had placed himself in great danger to prove his love and concern for me. He could easily have been killed by my eaglet brother or my captors. A dark shudder engulfed me, and I cringed as I visualized my eaglet brother tearing at him with sharp claws. "It is obvious that I must become more proficient in my shamanic abilities, or I may cause myself and others to become trapped."

"Indeed, that is so, little one!" he added. Then he moved his lips close to mine to brush them ever so lightly, causing me to quiver with delight. Moving his lips to my earlobe, he nipped firmly, causing me to scream in the strange ecstasy that pain has to offer. Once again we entered the world of sexual bliss, to become one with the universe. His hands were everywhere, and my peaks of ecstasy were many as we rode on into eternity. At the moment I was sure I was spent, he reached down to stroke my power spot, sending me into a shimmering euphoric journey that ended in an explosion of pleasure. Then turning me over as I continued to pulsate, he took his pleasure, which culminated in an urgent moan and the words, "Ah, my love, I am here!"

Wrapped in each other's arms, little was said for quite some time. I had no desire to speak, for my guilt was great over having put the person who meant the most to me through so much danger. Although I was certain he read my mind, he offered no comment, for he surely knew that this was something I must work out.

He rose on one of his elbows. Looking at me through the misty, hooded eyes of love, he softly said, "I swore an oath to myself that I would never make love to you in your quarters, for there are too many possible interruptions. Though everyone knows of my love for you, no one is certain that our love is both mental and physical. We should be sure to place the privacy *paho* at the entrance of our rooms, especially if we are to maintain discretion."

"Yes, my love, for I know we must be available if any of our people have need of our services. As for me, I am delighted that you took this time to spontaneously welcome me back to your world of bliss. It is here I wish to stay." My fingers traced little tender circles around his nipples.

After another short silence Nish't Ahote sat up. Taking my hand in his, he said softly. "There is another problem we must discuss, sweet one. Aunt Mokni wants you to know that she loves you and sends her regards, but she is having a rather difficult time with Puppy. He picks fights with the other dogs and howls relentlessly at the moon every night, all night. She does not know what to do with him. She awaits your suggestion."

Rolling into a sitting position, I assured him that I would speak to her at once. Then slowly he rose to climb the ladder and return to his quarters.

I wasted no time speaking to Aunt Mokni. She enveloped me with a huge bear hug, murmuring a prayer to thank Awonawilona that I was well. I suspected she was also relieved that I had come for Puppy.

He leaped all over me, lapping my face to let me know he had missed me. As I looked at him, he somehow seemed more mature than last I remembered—or had I not really been seeing him for what he was? His fur was thick and luxurious in shades that blended with the desert fauna for protection. His ears sat up proudly. His face was somehow more pointed than I remembered. His wet nose resembled a piece of obsidian, while his eyes were warm and tender. I took him in my arms, and he seemed happy but restless.

Aunt Mokni finally insisted that we both sit down

on a nearby mat. Taking my face in her hands, she declared, "It is enough, child. You have tried to escape us too often lately. Will you not stay in this fourth world for a while? It really does have a lot to offer."

"Yes, Aunt Mokni. I realize now that this world is where I must be—where I am needed. How have you been?"

"Oh, this old body is all right—always aches and pains."

"What do you mean when you say I was needed?" I asked.

"Little Coyote Woman, not only has your coyote missed you, but your people have also been concerned about your absence. There is a star in the sky, and there is a star on your shoulder. This has meaning, for you are a chosen one much as was Taweyah."

"What of Taweyah? Was he also a chosen one? Of this I am ignorant."

She shuffled her weight on the mat and smoothed a few hairs into place. Then very quietly she said, "Two generations ago there was also a star. This star was more brilliant than the one that shines now. Taweyah, so it was rumored, had a star at birth imprinted on his inner thigh. Few knew of this, but it is so, for I attended him before his death. It was his talents and intelligence that led us out of the pit house era and into the era of the complex buildings of which you are so familiar. He was a true leader in his time."

All that information was new to me, and I sat silently to absorb it all. Was I born to be a leader? Somehow I did not feel that way. What were the people thinking? Those who remembered the first star— what did they expect of me? My mind was in a confusion of thoughts. I sat alone and absorbed in my own world.

At last Aunt Mokni said, "Has all this really come as a surprise to you, child?"

"Yes, my loving aunt. There is much I must think on. There is a responsibility here of which I was unaware."

"Indeed, my sweet, you must decide what to do with it, for it is a great responsibility. Nish't Ahote, Hototo, the elders, your parents, Taweyah, and myself have known of your star birthmark for many years. We thought of it as an omen, but we did not know when or even if it would come to pass. You know the rest, for it has come to pass."

I was very quiet for a period of time. Why had Nish't Ahote not spoke of that? Then suddenly remembering why I was there, I asked, "Aunt Mokni, I am here to reclaim Puppy. What has he been doing? Nish't Ahote speaks of your anxiety with Puppy."

"Puppy's male urgency has surfaced. In my opinion he needs a mate if he does not already have one. He does not want to be in captivity. He howls and prowls all night long. He obviously is not happy. Much of his dilemma may be due to being here with me. I did not let him out, for I did not know if he would return, but my honest feeling is that he must be set free. I know you are fond of him, but he reaches out for his freedom, and this we must give to him."

"Aunt Mokni, you are wise. I will take Puppy, and I thank you for watching over him during my journey."

The day, as usual, was very hot. The canyon was magically green as a result of the warm summer rains for which we so earnestly prayed. There was water running in the wash, and our crops were doing well. The cottonwoods had left their cloud-like deposits in subsidiaries of the wash. There were places where it seemed as though clouds of cotton had been blown in huge piles, indicating their ability to take a message to Awonawilona the creator.

We moved through the canyon and its jagged out-croppings, stopping to rest in a shaded spot. Intuitively I moved toward my cave that I used for my womanly cycle. At one point we moved through a deep trench, and suddenly the small, plump body of Badger emerged. Puppy bounded warmly up toward him. They converged with familiarity and worked their way through the cracks and crevices in the ground and canyon walls, methodically searching out all that there was to know. Together, one could only imagine what they would dig up. Badger was very methodical, flipping and throwing out clumps of dirt until, at one point, a small nest of baby rabbits became their prey.

At a point not too far from my cave, the land was green and flat with much undergrowth. Puppy and Badger became suddenly vigilant. Puppy's hair rose straight up, his body became rigid, and his fluffy tail grew still and suddenly alert. He moved pointedly toward a rock indentation not far from me. Blended almost into the rock was another coyote, smaller, not as full in hair, and more delicate. Though the beautiful creature blended in with the surroundings, I saw that she was a young female. He moved toward her, nudging and smelling her. She returned the nudging and smelling while each made it obvious of their attraction for each other. She rolled over on her back as if to play, but only after she had urinated on the spot to mark her territory.

Somehow it did not upset me, for to me it was beautiful and symbolic. Much the same happened to humans. The same happened to Nish't Ahote and myself. Puppy had met his mate close to my cave. I also had met Nish't Ahote close to home. The parallel was much for my heart to take. I realized how we were all alike—how all creatures were so similar. It seemed impossible, but it was so. I worked my way through my feelings, for they suddenly became mixed. I was happy for Puppy, but at the same time, I felt I had lost him to another female. I had known it had to come, but I was not ready for it. I was a mother losing her child, and suddenly my heart was filled with an emptiness.

They tussled and rolled for a short time until Puppy seemed to awaken from his infatuation and pranced toward me, leaving her sitting on her haunches to eye us critically. Puppy sat down in front of me. His beautiful face looked up at me as though to seek my approval. I bent down to stroke him while tears of both happiness and misery fell unbidden. Of course I knew it must come. Nothing was forever! I had raised a child, and it was time for him to leave the nest.

Suddenly my heart leaped with joy, for Puppy was my baby I had raised. I could not have children, for it was tradition that a priest or priestess must not, but Puppy's mate was beautiful and he would have children. Taking Puppy in my arms, I buried my face in his fur, leaving it wet with glad tears. Then after an extra tight hug, he moved first to Badger, then back to the female who attracted him so strongly. He moved only a short way, then sat down to watch me. After a short time he rose and went a bit farther, then again sat down as though beckoning me. I was not sure what to do, and I patiently awaited his next move. Once again he rose to move on, the again sat down to look at me. I was baffled.

When he rose once more to move on, I followed. Moving over the ordinary harsh grasses somewhat softened by the summer rains, I found a small dugout cave. Puppy and his mate had been preparing a shelter for some time. She did not seem at all concerned that

I was there. I could see that they were prepared for the time of snow and cold. He had grown and so had I. We had grown together. Though I was losing him physically, I knew I would never lose him mentally, for he was one of my spirit guides. His clever ways would always be part of me, and what was more important, I had become a mother. Now the cycle was complete.

Slowly, with a heavy heart that was somehow mysteriously fulfilled, I walked away from his cave. My steps were heavy, as though my sandals were filled with stone. I turned once more to glance at him. He sat regally guarding what was now his as he watched me tenderly from his small slanted eyes. His pointed nose with its dark-set point twitched gently as he caught the various scents in the air. His pale-colored fur blended in well with the desert surroundings.

I walked on not daring to look back.

Thinking on this and allowing my mind's eye to wander, I heard a slight rustle not far away. Thinking it must be Puppy and his mate, I listened briefly, then took no heed. My mind wandered to the complex— to Nish't Ahote, Aunt Mokni, Hototo, Salavi, and all the rest of my family.

Suddenly a hand clasped over my mouth. I smelled a body. It reeked of uncleanliness. I could not breathe! I was being lifted—where I could not say. Though I was unable to see who was pinning my arms and holding my mouth, the smell was familiar. My mind at first could not place the odor, then quickly I realized I knew who it was. The hair on the back of my neck bristled, and a horrid chill ran down my spine, for I knew that it was Wisoko. "O Awonawilona." I prayed, for once again I was in his hands.

At first I struggled, then I quite suddenly realized

it was of no use. If I struggled, I would only be hurt. This was a young man not much more than my own age who killed, pillaged, and probably raped. He, in all probability, thrived on anger, therefore I knew I could not show my own fear and anger. His arms tightened around mine, causing pain. My mind struggled to rise above what was happening.

He dragged me away into a small canyon where four other raiders awaited his company. They were all very shabby and filthy, seeming not to have a care for their physical well-being. One of them hastened to build a fire. They then set up camp, putting down skins for rest near the fire. Wisoko dragged me to a tall pine and tied me to it. My hands were bound behind the tree, and although it was dark enough that I could not see him clearly, I could smell him. His odor was foul. What he planned for me, I was afraid to imagine.

He approached me with a glittering strangeness in his eyes. His was a look I could not fathom. It was one to which I was not accustomed. His eyes seared into mine, and he said gruffly in our own Anasazi tongue, "At last I have you, and my desires shall be appeased!"

Then turning away, he began to walk back to his fellow raiders. He turned back to stare at me briefly while his right hand stroked his most private parts, offering a suggestion of my destiny. He silently returned to the campfire not very far away, to enjoy a repast of desert rabbit roasted over the fire.

My hands were bound so tightly that they tingled. I wanted to shout of my discomfort, for the night air was growing colder and no one offered me a blanket or a skin or anything for warmth. I twisted and turned in an effort to keep warm. A chill overcame me as my body shivered and went into shock. My teeth chattered, and my body tried to adjust to the cooler temperature. I thought perhaps it was all in my mind, yet I was unable to control my shivering. It was apprehension. I was very frightened. I did not have any idea what to expect. I only knew that he was evil—the dark spirits controlled his soul. I needed to summon all of my inner powers to deal with this onslaught against my senses. The pain became excruciating in my wrists, and in agony, I commanded the forces of nature to surround me with a cloak of protection to shield me from the blows of Wisoko.

He approached me slowly, glancing nervously into my eyes. It was as though he knew he was wrong, but could do nothing to correct his deep inner problem. He approached me casually. Then my nightmare began. His steps were heavy. His body odor was foul. He untied my hands only long enough to drag me to his blanket that was spread under a low juniper. Pushing me onto his blanket on my back, he tied my hands over my head to the trunk of the tree. I wanted to fight him, but I realized the futility of it. If I fought, he would very possibly turn me over to his friends and allow them to have their way with me. Somehow I knew I must be strong. I prayed to Awonawilona to give me the strength I needed.

His friends seemed not to be aware of my dilemma. He stripped away his loincloth to reveal his engorged member. The day I secretly watched him relieve himself I observed his size, but now he seemed larger than I remembered. Bending over me, he tore away my cover and skirt. Taking one of my nipples between his thumb and forefinger, he twisted and pinched bringing a mist of pain to my eyes. His eyes glittered in the dark shadows, reflecting the dancing lights from the fire. His fetid breath was more than anyone would

ever have had to bear as he bent over me to claim
what I must say began as a kiss, but ended in a bite
as his teeth sank into my lower lip. I tasted my own
blood. I wanted to cry out, but intuitively I knew that
was what he would want me to do. So I kept my pain
within me.

It was obvious that this was a man who was
crazed—a man who was irrational. If I wanted to remain alive through this ordeal, I knew I must become
someone else. I needed to be someone who simply
observed. My spirit guide had confirmed my welfare.
Therefore I forced myself to disappear from reality
and into my large crystal. Perhaps if I thought positively enough, Nish't Ahote would join me there. I
closed my eyes and concentrated.

Wisoko was a man who was in another world—an
evil world. He picked up a yucca whip and laid it
violently across my body. My breasts welled up with
a livid purple-red stripe. He bent over me again to
suck one of my nipples and then bit it. The pain was
searing, like a hot coal placed directly upon it. I
gasped, but somehow did not cry out.

Once again he stood over me, his dark malodorous
shadow covering my body. The sky was blocked out.
The only thing left of the real world was his hideous
form. I retreated once again into my world. Very
briefly I wondered where Puppy and Badger might
have been. Surely the world around me was gathering
gloom. If it ended for me, I knew I must accept it
and be unashamed. Once again I realized I must not
cry out.

He spread my legs and lunged with the full force of
his manhood in my unmoistened private parts. He
rode for a brief time, then in a disturbed voice he
yelled, "Make some sign! I must know that you
enjoy!" He slapped my face as he yelled again his

orders for me to enjoy. I clamped my mouth closed and forced my brain elsewhere. I was in the serenity of my cave. The air and surroundings were quiet as I chiseled more of my picture into the wall of the cave.

He rode on—mercilessly. I had moistened out of self-defense. Therefore he did not hurt me internally, only mentally. His yucca whip beat me once again, and suddenly he turned me over. The sting of the whip on my backsides once again brought tears to my eyes. I winced briefly, then without flinching, I accepted the pain of the moment with a steady strength that defied explanation. After he had beaten me, he penetrated me once again to ride with a furious harshness, perhaps in anger, that was out of control. Though he may have been out of control, I felt no pain and no emotion. I was where I wanted to be. I had risen above all that was happening.

Suddenly, without warning, or perhaps I was no longer a part of my body and was not aware, he yelled a hoarse, loud cry and collapsed on top of me. For a moment time was suspended, for there was no motion and nothing happened. Then violently pushing me from him, he backed away for a short time to stare at my battered form. Hauling me to my feet, he dragged my aching body back to the tree to which I had been formerly bound, and once again tied my arms so tightly that they hurt.

I dared not cry out. My body ached all over, and I shivered once again. My body was not cold. It only seemed cold, for my balance was broken. Somehow I knew I must regain the harmony within me. As Wisoko backed away from me, I thought hard on Puppy, on the deer, and on the rattlesnake, my spirit guides. I prayed that they had not deserted me . . . that they would remember my need and protect me. Then, when all was finally quiet, the tears came silently and unbidden. Then suddenly there was a nibble at my wrists, then a tugging. It was Puppy who chewed at my bonds. I praised the Gods, for they had not forgotten me.

Wisoko rose once again to add some juniper to the fire. He paused to watch the flames licking brilliantly around the burning logs when, suddenly, an arm snaked around him and another was clasped over his mouth. He bolted in an attempt to see who his captor was. The knife held in the one hand that held him scraped him as he wrenched free, drawing a line of blood across his chest. Turning angrily, he saw his raider friends lying in pools of blood. There were Anasazi everywhere. He faced an enraged warrior who glared at him with glittering hate in his eyes. They circled each other looking and waiting for a moment to attack. Wisoko's thoughts were that this warrior would be no problem, but he knew he could not fight them all. He must try to escape.

As though reading his mind, the dark warrior said, "You are surrounded. You cannot escape. Surrender now, for Coyote Woman is the one for whom we came. We do not seek to take your life, too. Return with us to your Anasazi heritage. Give up your raider ways!"

Flashing him a wicked smile, Wisoko answered with one simple word. "Never!"

"Then, look! Coyote Woman has risen above you, for she stands untied looking piteously at you!"

He turned to look in astonishment, then realized his mistake. The warrior closed in quickly to toss him onto the ground. They rolled and struggled, looking for an opening. Wisoko's knife slashed the warrior's arm, and he winced momentarily. Then angered, the warrior pinned him to the ground, his knife coming precariously close to his throat. Giving a heave of strength, they rolled again and again. Instantaneously it was over. There was a gurgling sound coming from Wisoko. He felt no pain, but his hand went to his side. The warrior stood over him. He appeared in Wisoko's vision as only a shadow. Darkness descended as a veil. It was over.

I rubbed my badly chafed wrist. Then seeing that Choviohoya was all right, I knelt down to give thanks to praise to Awonawilona and my spirit guides. Strong arms enveloped me.

"Little sister, are you all right?"

Looking up into the loving eyes of my brother, I said, "My beloved brother, I only sing praises to Awonawilona for bringing you to deliver me. Yes, I am all right!"

Then throwing my arms around him, I crushed my body against his, feasting in the love of my brother and of my people. The nightmare was over, and I would return to Nish't Ahote, Hototo, Aunt Mokni, and the rest of my adopted family. Most of all I was overjoyed to be able to return to my people, for there was where I belonged.

We held firmly onto each other for quite a while, then I pulled away and he said, "Little sister, I saw what went on between you and your adversary. I want you to know that it was despicable. He wanted to treat you as a piece of property—"

"My brother, do not be troubled by what has happened. What has happened is in the past, and now we are in the present. What is happening now is what is important. Let us live in balance and know that whatever events transpire are intended to expand our consciousness. We must only use good judgment and weigh the answers well."

He grasped me in a firm hug once again. "Little

sister, you are the source of my love. I would console you, but it seems you are already in command. What can I do? I would protect you, but you do not need it."

"My fine, worthy brother, I am protected by the Gods and my spirit guides. All of this was preordained. There is nothing that has happened that I have not known of. All is directed by the Gods."

Choviohoya continued to hug me to him. Then he said, "You may tidy yourself up with the help of our mirrors and cosmetics."

"No," I answered. "I have in my pack what I need. I shall do very well with what I have."

So we traveled on. The huge complex came into view. The moon rose at the edge of the sky, while the only sound was that of an occasional coyote echoing through the canyon. Stars twinkled brilliantly in a milky haze across the sky.

I saw Machakwi coming toward me. The huge warm smile on his face was surprising. He was usually very serious, even surly and gruff. He extended his arm to me while flashing a smile to Choviohoya and his warriors. Next to him stood my beloved Nish't Ahote and Hototo. Machakwi led me to stand between Nish't Ahote and Hototo. During that time I stole a glance at Nish't Ahote, whose stern expression betrayed none of his feelings. Though I desperately wished he would show some feelings, I knew better than to expect it. Still his handsome face with the lines of laughter were a treat for me to behold. I truly thought I might never see that wonderful face again.

"Choviohoya has returned our Coyote Woman to us. For that he shall be honored. His warriors must also be honored. Our universal harmony has been restored. Choviohoya shall become war chief of the entire Chaco region. His warriors shall be duly

honored," said Machakwi. He bent down and picked
up several *pahos*. Handing one to each of the warriors,
he ordered, "Now go. Take your *paho* and plant it
outside the entrance to your dwelling. It shall bring
peace and prosperity to you and yours."

He summoned Choviohoya to stand next to him.
Taking two beautiful eagle feathers from Nish't
Ahote's hands, he presented then to my brother. "For
you, Choviohoya, our war chief, I bestow two sacred
eagle feathers. Tie them to your braids, and allow
them to protect you and your family."

Choviohoya's eyes shone with surprise and gratitude
as he accepted the feathers. He then stepped away to
join his warriors once more. My heart went out to him
as I wished that Kunya and Yamka were present to
share that moment.

Machakwi turned to me. Raising his hand and mine
high into the air, he proclaimed, "Harmony is restored!" So saying, he handed to me a sacred *mongko*.

My hands trembled as I accepted this rare gift. Then
turning to them, I assured them. "I will do the best I
can to deserve this honor you bestow upon me. My
heart is Anasazi and always shall be!" My voice wa-
vered, and a tear escaped the corner of my eye.

I was given food, and accepting that and my *mongko,* I went to my room. Someone had kindly brought
my belongings to my quarters and built a fire to warm
me. Puppy was nowhere to be seen, nor did I expect
him. At long last, I was securely settled with my
people.

Looking around my quarters at all my belongings,
it somehow seemed I had been away for a lifetime.
Everything was in its place as I had left it. Then as I
pulled my mat close to the fire, I noticed a large chunk
of turquoise and an eagle feather. Feelings of love and
warmth washed over me, for I knew it had been Nish't

Ahote who had built the fire and put my belongings away. Those feelings of love changed to uncertainty. How, I wondered, would Nish't Ahote feel toward me now? Would his feelings remain as they had been before Wisoko soiled me, or would he feel that I was unclean?

As if in answer to my thoughts, Nish't Ahote descended the ladder to my quarters. I rose anxiously to receive him. He gathered me in his arms and held me for quite some time. He held me so tightly that I could hear his heartbeat. My love for him was never more precious as it was at that moment. Tears gathered in my eyes as at last I looked up and into his warm ebony eyes.

Pulling me down to my mat, he took both of my hands in his. "So, little one, we are together again. Awonawilona, be praised!"

Tears of release flooded me. "Nish't Ahote, I . . ."

"Sh! Don't try to talk. Just know that I am here and always shall be."

Struggling to compose myself, I inquired, "Then, you have not changed your feelings toward me? You do not think of me as a soiled woman?"

"Little foolish one. My feelings have not changed. I am only concerned for you. Are you all right?"

"I don't know. I think I am all right, but at times I feel dirty. I can still smell Wisoko's foul odor, and feel the hate he directed toward me. I can only hope that in time those memories will fade."

"Time is a great healer, but the most important thing is you. You must not let your mind dwell on negative events. Your people love and respect you, and so do I. I praise the Gods that you are alive and were not killed by Wisoko. Surely you must realize that Taweyah, your guardian, must have been watching over you. He gave directions to Choviohoya. Now dry those eyes, and come to me."

As we lay on the mat wrapped in each other's arms, I murmured, "I am so happy that you and I are still unchanged in our love. With your help and your love I am whole again."

"Little Coyote Woman, we must dedicate ourselves to our duties and our love for each other, but now enough said. Let me just hold you."

My heart sang with the healing music of Awonawilona that would forever echo in my soul.

Epilogue

The evening of the previous sun cycle, I was informed of a meeting. That meeting was about to begin. The pipe was passed around to all who were present. The pipe, a symbol of unity, balance, and cooperation, served to establish the proper mood and prospective for the meeting.

Machakwi broke the silence by saying quietly, "We have need of the ceremony of the animal spirits. Many of our students and a few of our acolytes are of the age to establish an animal spirit guide. The need is strong. I suggest that the preparation for the ceremony being." It was not in character with Machakwi's personality to speak with such a gentle, softened, controlled tone. I stared at him with unabashed surprise. He was always so hard and gruff.

Honani responded almost immediately. "I am in complete agreement. It has been two season cycles since we have had this ritual. Many of our young who have not been intent in their meditation need this ceremony. It will lend strength to them and thus to our people." He paused to adjust a feather at the end of his single braid. Then, clearing his throat, he added, "Our Coyote Woman has more than established an animal spirit guide. She has become one with it. She has demonstrated now all the abilities of the true shaman. I suggest that we use this ceremony to initiate her into the role of high priestess, so she may truly stand in the position she deserves."

I was taken completely by surprise. It was hard to believe I had heard correctly what he had said.

Salavi stepped in again to say, "I am in agreement. Our Coyote Woman is blessed with all the powers of a true shaman. We can do no more than to acknowledge these powers. May we hear your thoughts, Nish't Ahote, our revered sun priest?"

Nish't Ahote rose and stretched to his full height, which was a bit taller than most of the other men. He seemed as though in deep thought, then suddenly became alert. He moved toward the heat of the fire. Quietly crossing his bronzed arms over his chest, he spoke. "Our little Coyote Woman has the star on her shoulder. That star continues to shine in our sky. Our Coyote Woman has escaped Wisoko. She has shown valor, wisdom, and a sense of balance in many instances. I am in agreement with you that now is the time for that ritual. Let us involve Coyote Woman and our acolytes, and with her success in that ceremony make her high priestess." He moved back toward the bench.

There was a murmur of verbal consent. All in the kiva gave me a vote of confidence. Each in turn walked to me to touch the star on my shoulder while offering me words of praise and respect. I was overwhelmed with humility. I knew I must preserve the confidence that my people were showing me.

Preparations were being made for the magic fire ceremony. The ceremony would culminate with many acolytes walking barefoot across hot coals, while others would jump naked into the fire pit, roll around, and come out without a burn. This, of course, depended on their frame of mind. The ceremony would take place in the plaza and was open to any who wished to watch it. My parents arrived to view the occasion. Choviohoya, Kunya, and Yamka were also in attendance. The plaza was crowded with the people and excitement was high. Choviohoya had ordered many in the village to bring firewood. The elders dug a shallow pit in the center of the plaza. Lines of ashes were drawn around the pit. No one was permitted to cross those lines. If someone did and was caught, he or she might be forced to join in the fire-walking activity during the ceremony along with other unusual initiation procedures. Those procedures were assumed to be most unpleasant, so there was little danger that anyone would deliberately cross over the lines.

Four huge pots were brought by the cooks, and were lined up against the low wall of the kiva. Aunt Mokni solemnly bore one of the pots. The pots were then partly filled with water. All was ready while we awaited the peak of Sun Father's journey.

I felt a soft tap on my shoulder. I turned to look into the warm almost black eyes of my brother. Beside him was Kunya who carried Yamka in the wooden cradle on her back. Pochti and Talasiva were behind them. After a warm embrace from them all, my father spoke. "We bring our love and greetings, Dese. We are delighted to know that the decision has been made to initiate you into the high priesthood. We would not miss being in attendance, for we are proud of you." He turned to flash a warm look of affection toward my mother.

"And how goes the road of life for you, Mother and Father? And you, my brother, sister, and niece?" I inquired.

"All is well. My trade keeps my occasionally achy bones happy and busy, and your mother's love fills my mind," responded my father.

"I am also well, my sweet daughter. My duties as a wife occupy me well while your father's love keeps my heart singing," my mother answered. "You look radiant and happy. That also gladdens my heart."

"I am content." Turning to Choviohoya, I added, "I hope all is well with you, Kunya and Yamka."

"It is so. My duties now as war chief keep me away from home more than I desire. Except for that we are well," he said.

"And is my sister well guarded in the times you are away?" I inquired.

Kunya responded brightly. "Yes, my sister, Choviohoya has seen to it that four guards be posted one in each of the four directions."

"It is good. Yamka also seems well. I see no mucus, and she smiles happily." I gently allowed the little fingers of one of her tiny hands to wrap around my own.

"Her health has been good, I am glad to say. Since you last visited and treated her, she has done well," Kunya responded.

At that my mother said, "Dearest daughter, we know you must make ready. We look forward to the conclusion of the ceremony."

The conclusion of the ceremony was a worry I could not explain.

I readied myself for the ceremony. I had been told to give my egret feather cape to Nish't Ahote and to wear my crystal headband to the ceremony. I returned to my quarters to make the necessary preparations.

I covered my face with a thin coating of sunflower oil. I applied a bit of kohl to outline my eyes and some red ocher on my cheeks, chin, and neck. I rubbed my body with sage. I used yucca string to cleanse my teeth. After arranging my hair into a coil at the nape of my neck, I wrapped a cotton multicolored skirt around my hips, attached black stone pieces to my ears, and placed my crystal in my pouch. In it I also placed my eagle feather and fetish that Nish't Ahote had given me. After a prayer, I joined the acolytes, who awaited the ceremony.

I was nervous and ill at ease, for I knew what was ahead of me. I knew I must remain calm and grounded, for if I was not, I would be as many of the acolytes . . . unnerved and in pain. I must focus my energy to attain my goals.

The ceremony began. When Sun Father was at his peak a fire was built in the pit. A considerable quantity of wood had been gathered for that purpose. The women built a fire under the pots. Then all of them went inside except for a couple (Aunt Mokni was one) who kept watch on the roof. The acolytes and myself were naked except for a breechcloth for them and the short skirt for me. Of course, I also wore the crystal headband. We were all led out into the plaza. All of us were barefoot and painted with ashes. The acolytes' hair was tied up on the top of their heads.

All the elders and priests went to the pit. The ashes and live coals danced and sparked with a life all their own. The elders and priests danced from right to left in a circle around the pit while singing four songs. Then they lay their rattles aside and removed their eagle plumes. The fifth song began. Nish't Ahote stooped down by the pit to stir the glowing live coals with his bare hands. He then jumped into the hot bed of coals, seemingly oblivious to pain. He jumped from east to west, and was followed by Hototo and all the elders. None seemed to be bothered by the heat.

At last Aunt Mokni threw a basket of shelled corn into the pit. An acolyte was then seized and thrown to the pit on top of the shelled corn. He alighted on his back. Nish't Ahote, Hototo, and the elders all quickly stooped over him to stir everything together, the ashes, coals, corn, and of course the screaming acolyte. They took him out and made him stand. All the other male candidates were thrown in similarly. Two of the acolytes, I noticed, slunk away hoping to be unnoticed in the crowd.

Now it was my turn along with one other young girl, who seemed terribly intimidated. I touched her on the shoulder and quietly told her she would not be thrown in—that she must walk. She declined and walked away.

I tried to visualize and feel that I had already walked those coals and achieved my goal. I knew that I must truly believe that this experience would not be painful. I could not allow myself to waste time feeling any negative thoughts. I removed my skirt. I kept on my medicine pouch and black stone pieces in my ears. I was now naked as the day the creator brought me into the fourth world. I was anxious, yet I knew I must do this thing. The people—always the people! My heart pounded, for I knew I would not be thrown in. This was my choice. The decision was mine alone. I wondered why they did not just throw me in and be done with it. My mind was in a turmoil.

Suddenly a hand rested on my shoulder—the shoulder with the star that marked my way. I was soothed immediately. Confidence surged through me as I raised my head and began my first step. My mind was so at peace that I did not notice the hush that descended over the crowd. I took my first step. The hand was still on my shoulder. The coals were hot, very very hot, yet somehow a buoyant happiness overtook me. My body began to tingle with delight, and I knew that I would not be burned. My exuberance was such that I smiled—almost laughed. At that moment a part of me died, and another part of me was born. I was so confident now that I turned around to walk the length of the coals again. The hand was no longer on my shoulder. I walked alone straight to Nish't Ahote, who held me in his arms, then wrapped me with my egret feather cape.

It was at that point in time when I turned my head to recognize the reason all the people had been hushed. He stood at the end of the fire pit straight and tall, as I knew him as a child. I realized now that it was his hand on my shoulder. It was his hand that helped to give me the confidence that I needed. I was struck dumb. I could only stare at Taweyah as he stood exercising his old jurisdiction over the people. No one spoke. The magic was felt by everyone.

He stood with authority. Then, as though he wished to speak and could not, he began to grow and expand. When he had grown several times larger than all of us and loomed over the plaza filling it with his presence, he spoke.

"As a new spirit dancer it is my last duty to be the messenger. I am the link and the bridge between the land of the spirit and the land of the living. I am not dead but simply fulfilling another way to be Anasazi.

"Give love to all that is created, people, animals, plants, mountains, for all is one spirit. With your new high priestess, Hototo and Nish't Ahote continue to sing the 'Song of Creation.' Prayer and meditation are the only way to stay on the true path. Let Earth Mother guide you. Use her gifts wisely and in moderation or she will retaliate with earthquakes, floods, hailstorms, drought, and famine. You are the caretakers of life. Walk in balance and beauty."

His huge form slowly faded, leaving a feeling of unity and love with us all. I noticed a coyote sitting ietly at the threshold of the plaza, and also the look of love and peace in the eyes of my people. I now realized my responsibilities as a high priestess were to use my wisdom as a means to lead my people in the direction of love, peace and understanding. The ceremony was concluded, but my work had only begun.

Author's Note

No one can visit the Southwest without somehow being changed. The Four Corners area is filled with thousands of ruins. Probably the most impressive in Chaco Canyon. My visit to Chaco Canyon began with a tour of the largest of the buildings, which today is called Pueblo Bonito. Upon entering the plaza with the tour guide, I had the feeling that somehow I had come home. The experience was so intense that I felt compelled to write. With legal pad and pencil *Coyote Woman's* story came forth.

While writing, I spent three summers in the Southwest exploring ruins, interviewing archaeologists, and taking part in Native American ceremonies. Though there are many questions unanswered about the Anasazi peoples, I have attempted to write archaeologically and anthropologically as accurately as possible. I have also tried to point out that the problems that plagued the Anasazi were not any different from our own. We also have to deal with problems in saving the environment and living in balance and moderation. Perhaps we can learn from them and try not to make the same mistakes.